Anna's Journal

Anna's Journal

a novel by
Harry Pollock

mosaic press

Library and Archives Canada Cataloguing in Publication

Pollock, Harry J., 1920-
    Anna's Journal / Harry Pollock

ISBN: 0-88962-871-8 (pbk.)

    1. Title.

PS8581.O33A55 2006   C813'.54   C2006-905441-X

Publishing by Mosaic Press, offices and warehouse at 1252 Speers Rd., units 1 & 2, Oakville, On L6L 5N9, Canada and Mosaic Press, PMB 145, 4500 Witmer Industrial Estates, Niagara Falls, NY, 14305-1386, U.S.A.

info@mosaic-press.com

Copyright © Harry Pollock, 2007
ISBN 0-88962-871-8

Mosaic Press in Canada:
1252 Speers Road, Units 1 & 2,
Oakville, Ontario
L6L 5N9
Phone/Fax: 905-825-2130
info@mosaic-press.com

Mosaic Press in U.S.A.:
4500 Witmer Industrial Estates
PMB 145, Niagara Falls, NY
14305-1386
Phone/Fax: 1-800-387-8992
info@mosaic-press.com

www.mosaic-press.com

For Vera
who never doubted,
In Memoriam

Also by Harry Pollock

Gabriel

The He and the She of It

Max

My thanks to:

John H. Pollock, Q.C.
for his tireless support

Ronald Gauthier

Humani nihil a me alienum puto.

Terence, 190-159 B.C.

Friday June 22, 1973.

After the funeral I retire to the study amidst the books and records that crowd the shelves. Volumes of Shakespeare, Greek and Roman Mythology, Comparative Religion. Dictionaries and Encyclopedias. Symphonies, Masses and Chamber Music. The accumulation of thirty years during which time I have been Gabriel's lover and devoted companion.

I put on the old 78 RPM recording of Brahms Fourth Symphony with Serge Koussevitsky and the Boston Symphony Orchestra. The opening statement followed by thirty-one variations then the theme, low then high, then hidden in the middle and above it all, the trombone repetition.

The music releases a flood of memories.

1

Montreal. Saturday October 9, 1943. My married cousin Shirley Bieler wants to introduce me to a young man she met at the Jewish Community Centre. He is from Toronto. Attractive. And unattached, she enthuses but I would rather listen to the broadcast of the New York Philharmonic. As usual she wears down my resistance and that is how I meet Gabriel. We sit in the living room and chat for a while then Shirley has to leave to attend to her ailing mother. Silence now, except for the closing bars of the Brahma Fourth Symphony on the radio. When it is finished, Gabriel says he enjoys classical music. A kindred spirit! There is a touch of the poet about him. Lean, long-haired, intense.

It is such a lovely autumn afternoon so we leave the apartment and stroll up Queen Mary Road past the Wireless Station of the Royal Canadian Air Force to St. Joseph's Oratory. On the stone stairs reserved for women ascending on their knees the faithful are fingering their rosaries. Dewy virgins, pregnant matrons, withered crones praying to St. Joseph and seeking favours from Brother Andre whose heart is preserved in a chalice. Castoff crutches and braces attest to the miracles performed by the Brother. In the empty vastness of the unfinished basilica Gabriel imagines how Bach's Toccata and Fugue played on the organ would sound.

We visit the souvenir shop with its display of embossed pens and pencils, crucifixes, note paper and miniature cathedrals under glass.

Out again through the formal gardens and into the street. Beyond the Wax Museum we take the trail parallel to the Catholic Cemetery up the slope of Mount Royal to Beaver Lake where children are sailing toy boats. At the chalet we purchase ice cream and stand at the lookout admiring the Montreal panorama with its old world charm.

Toward evening we return to the apartment and I select my best dress, a wine taffeta with full skirt, comb my hair and tie it with a blue ribbon. Gabriel has invited me to Moishe's on Main Street where we enjoy broiled rib steaks with kosher dills and dance to a string orchestra. After dinner we walk along neon-lighted, lamp-lighted, moon-lighted Ste. Catherine Street. The cross atop Mount Royal glows over the city. At Guy we board the number 65 tram that winds past the Hermitage and the mansions of Westmount down Côte des Neiges to Queen Mary Road. It is after midnight when I unlock the door and precede Gabriel through the dark hall past the bedrooms with the sleeping sisters.

Recumbent on the couch we kiss. From the radio issue the shimmering notes of the Moonlight Sonata and I am afloat on a boat under the stars on Lake Lucerne. Gabriel caresses my breasts, his tongue snaking the nipples erect, and I feel the stirring of desire. His hands are between my thighs and I give myself to him.

The sun is lighting up the vacant lot across the road when the first trolley of the day clatters by. We part reluctantly.

Gabriel returns for supper. Frank Sinatra is crooning *Won't you tell me when we shall meet again?* and my sisters Louise and Claudia exchange knowing glances. He responds politely to their questions about Toronto and talks about his interest in music and theatre. At ten o'clock I accompany him to Central Station where we chat until departure time. As he strides down the corridor I wipe away the tears.

He is back during the Christmas holidays. We go to the movies to see Blanches Neiges et les Sept Nains. We dance in a tiny hall in the east end to the music of Charley et son band. At the American Cafe on Ste. Catherine Street East we drink beer out of quart bottles as the chorus girls kick their heels to the Poet and Peasant Overture. We celebrate my nineteenth birthday at Moishe's, and Gabriel presents me with an album of Brahms' Fourth with Serge Koussevitsky and the Boston Symphony. Then he is gone again.

We write daily. He woos with poetry. 'How shall I write a sonnet in thy praise?' On weekends he telephones with avowals of love.

In July I take the night train to Toronto, arriving on a Sunday morning. Gabriel has reserved a room in the Metropole Hotel near Union Station. He is eager to make love although I have my period and we do it in the shower for fear of staining the sheets. We sleep until noon.

The only restaurant open on the Lord's Day is Bowles across from the Victorian City Hall. We have greasy bacon, cold toast and tepid coffee.

Gabriel has arranged for me to stay the week with a woman friend since his mother will not hear of my sleeping in the same house as her son. She knows that sex is the only thing on the minds of young people.

Gabriel introduces me to the writers, artists and actors who gather in the Rainbow Tea Room for interminable discussions on life and art.

We take the street car to Sunnyside and dance at the Palais Royale. We attend an open air concert. We visit the Museum and

Art Gallery. And we make love back stage at the closed-for-the-summer Toronto Little Theatre on the sofa used in the production of Noel Coward's *Blithe Spirit*.

Montreal. Wednesday October 18, 1944. The wedding ceremony is scheduled for half past four in the afternoon in Rabbi Hershenhorn's study on Park Avenue. I am dressed in a grey linen suit and plumed hat with veil. Gabriel is wearing a business suit.

-Behold thou art consecrated unto me by this ring according to the law of Moses and Israel. Standing under the chuppah with my aunt and uncle and Gabriel's parents we recite the ancient marriage vows. The rabbi delivers a homily about sharing. Our possessions. Our joys. Our sorrows. We drink from a silver wine goblet. Then Gabriel shatters the glass with his shoe in remembrance of the destruction of the Temple in Jerusalem and everyone shouts Mazel Tov. I am twenty-one, just graduated from the nursing school of the Montreal Jewish General Hospital. Gabriel is twenty-four.

When we get to Moishe's Restaurant the guests are already gathered in the reception hall for cocktails. Gabriel's mother is impressed with the doctors and business men in my family. Everybody is so well-mannered. Mike Brenner, my brother-in-law, fortified with Chivas Regal is especially attentive to her. During the dinner my uncle rises to offer congratulations but regrets that my mother and father did not live to enjoy this day.

Then it is over and everybody disperses. Mike insists on driving us to the Mount Royal Hotel despite Vivian's objections that he has had too much to drink but he has his way and we arrive intact. Alone at last we prepare for bed. Kissing and stroking I cleave to my beloved who has no trouble achieving orgasm. I enjoy the sexual intimacy but am unable to reach a climax.

Dawn brings the promise of a lifetime of shared experiences. We fill the day in a leisurely exploration of downtown Montreal. We browse through Eaton's and Birks. At Morgan's we sample the cheeses. We admire the stained glass windows of Christ Church Cathedral. The pigeons on Phillips Square swoop about the statue of Edward V11 that was commissioned by the Anglo Saxons of the city and sculpted by Phillipe Hèbert, a son of New France. The public lavatories called Camiliens after the mayor Camilien Houde who has been interned by the federal government for opposing conscription. Nearby, the building owned by St. James United Church houses the garment industry revitalized by orders for thousands of military uniforms.

Farther east the Gayety Theatre features Lili St. Cyr, ecdysiast extraordinaire. This section of St. Laurent Boulevard is a jumble of pinball parlors and stomach-churning eateries, junk shops and bars with its human flotsam of derelicts and prostitutes. The facade of the American Cafe appears shabby in the daylight.

We board an east bound tram for an excursion into the other solitude. The stores that flash by are not so grandiose, the signs are in French. Tourists seldom come to these neighborhoods where tavern and church vie for hegemony.

At Viau the street car turns around and lurches back to Centre Ville where Ste. Catherine Street West displays its opulence. Frank de Rice, Italian Restaurant, capitalizes on the popularity of the American President, the initials F.D.R. boldly painted on the plate glass window behind which are displayed mounds of spaghetti.

-Basta pasta! We shall dine in style tonight. Broiled lobster at Desjardins.

October 19, 1944. In the second class coach the portly conductor punches our tickets and admires my corsage of white baby roses. Newly weds, huh? Honeymoon in New York, huh? He took his bride to Niagara Falls many years ago. He booms his felicitations as he waddles away.

Across the Quebec border into Vermont the midnight Empire State Express devours the miles. The lights have been dimmed, the porter has been through with broom and dustpan and I am nestled beside Gabriel. Outside our window the blurred shapes of trees and farm houses rush past, the darkness lit up occasionally by the neon sign of a restaurant or automobile dealership. The train whizzes past lonely whistle stops.

The hours pass with dozing and waking. Seated in the toilet as the train hurtles through the dark I listen to the pounding of the wheels on the tracks. The insistent clackety-clack harmonizes with the notice posted above the wash basin. Passengers will please refrain from flushing toilet while the train is standing in the station...I love you. *Humoresque*.

Dawn breaking. The city is rushing to meet us. Rows of tenements. Sky scrapers coming into view. Manhattan.

As we pull into Pennsylvania Station the fatigue of the long night gives way to anticipation. The concourse is astir with commuters. Loud speakers announce departures and arrivals. The Travellers Aid kiosk is open.

On Seventh Avenue the surge of cars and buses, the smell of diesel exhaust, the blare of horns. The clang-clang of a fire engine. We carry the suitcases to thirty-third street stopping at a restaurant for bagels and eggs.

America at war. Red, white and blue bunting drapes the buildings. Posters urge the purchase of War Bonds. Air Raid Shelters are designated by red-striped triangles. 'Volunteer to be an Air Raid Warden. Receive lessons in First Aid, treatment of gas victims, rescue work and fire fighting.' Newspaper headlines boast advances against the enemy. And everywhere the fresh-faced young men in olive green uniforms.

At the Claridge Hotel we join the queue waiting to register. When we finally face the desk clerk he can find no reservation in our name. No vacancies. Gabriel remonstrates with him but he waves us aside.

The search for accommodations in midtown Manhattan proves unsuccessful. All the hotels are fully booked. In desperation Gabriel consults the telephone directory. After several phone calls he connects. A two room apartment on the West Side, not far from Times Square, only twenty-five dollars for the week. But we better come right away.

The taxi stops before a brownstone building, the area littered with garbage. We exchange doubting glances but decide to have a look. The bell summons an unshaven individual in undershirt and trousers.

-You the guy that phoned? Come in. Follow me, he wheezes, grasping the bannister, pulling his skinny frame up the stairs to the fourth floor. I've had a dozen calls already. Okay here we are. He pulls a cigaret from a crumpled packet and lights it, puffing in shallow gasps.

The kitchen is furnished with a table on rickety legs, a couple of chairs, a two burner gas stove. The sink is in the toilet down the hall. Peeling wallpaper in the bedroom, the curtainless window fly-specked. A centipede scurries across the linoleum to safety under a dresser. A brass bed is unmade, the sheet stained with night crawlers.

-You gonna take it? I got others waiting.

-No thanks, Gabriel says. This isn't what we had in mind.

-O.K. No problem. He clumps down the stairs ahead of us. At the door he erupts into a brittle cough.

-Listen, you kids want a real nice place? Friend of mine runs a hotel. I'll phone him. He re-appears after a while. All fixed up. Here, I wrote out the address, off Central Park, cab'll get you there in no time.

Twenty minutes later we arrive at the Park West Hotel, a decaying five -storey building. A pudgy fellow with an acne-ridden face, a cigar hanging from his lips, rises wearily from his chair. Seven dollars a night, pay in advance for the week. He pockets the money and pulls a key from a pigeon hole behind the desk. Satch! he hollers. A young black man takes our bags to the elevator, slides the door shut and the cage jerks uncertainly upward.

Room 405 has a double bed, night table, dresser and mirror. A faded print of Sorrento hangs on the stucco wall. The bathroom contains a chipped sink and four-legged tub. Satch deposits the luggage on the frayed carpet and waits until Gabriel gives him a dollar to surrender the key.

-This place is better than the flop house, grimaces Gabriel.

-It will do just fine, I say cheerfully. We're lucky to get it.

-Yeah, real fine location. I never figured on spending our

honeymoon in Harlem.

-It doesn't matter where we stay as long as we're together, n'est-ce pas, chèrie? Let's unpack.

The toiletries go in the rusting medicine cabinet. Tooth brushes, soap, deodorant, shaving lotion, razor. Perfume, hair brush, bracelets and pendants in the dresser. The condoms are sequestered in the night table.

-Now for a bath.

We wash each other, laughing away the morning's irritations, and hasten to the bed. After a brief foreplay we make love but I still can't reach orgasm. Gabriel is disappointed. It's all right, I soothe him. It will be better next time.

Satch is hunched over the counter reading the Daily News. Goin' out, huh? Don't know if you catch a cab in this rain. What time you expec' to be back? We lock up after midnight but you just ring the bell 'n I let you in. Really comin' down now.

The rain blown by gusts of wind scours the sidewalk clean of debris. Taxis splash by, unheeding of Gabriel's signals. At last one pulls up and a black woman with orange hair gets out. We hurry to take her place.

-Where to? The figure behind the wheel wears a cap and jacket.

-Cafe Royale on Second Avenue. Do you know the place?

-Yeah, I know, he mutters as he logs the run on his pad and accelerates, the windshield wipers sloshing back and forth, the rain a steady tattoo on the roof. The hack license displays a photograph of the pug-battered face of Jacob Galinsky. The taxi rattles through Central Park, past leafless trees, the tires sounding a steady sibilance.

At Fifth Avenue we continue cross-town, the meter ticking away the fare. On Second Avenue the traffic is stop and go, pedestrians hurrying beneath umbrellas. Forty-second street. Twenty-third. Fourteenth. Twelfth.

-Here y'are, Cafe Royale. When Gabriel adds ten per cent to the fare Galinsky explodes. Jesus, I shlep you all this distance in the rain from 96th street when I could of had a hunnerd short

Anna's Journal · 9

hauls and for what, for a lousy tip. A couple more bucks won't break ya. I got a wife to support and four kids at the Yeshiva. Thanks. By the way, where ya from?

-Toronto, Canada.

-Freezing cold up there, huh? The land of the Royal Canadian Mounted Police. Well, have a good stay.

Dodging the puddles we dash down the stairs and push open the fogged glass door. The warmth is mixed with the savory smell of yiddish cooking, the atmosphere a high level hubbub. Waiters are scurrying about. One leads us to a table, takes our coats and promises to return in half a minute.

Hearty appetites here. Family groups attacking soup, fish, chicken, flanken. The bartender mixes drinks with a flourish. A busboy dodges between tables, his tray laden with dishes and glassware balanced on one shoulder.

-Hymie, you forgot the ketchup bottle, shouts one of the customers.

-I'll put it in my ear, he retorts.

-He's some character, that Hymie, with all that hair sticking out from his head. The Cafe Royale wouldn't be the same without him. Somebody should put him in a play, include all his smart aleck remarks.

-So, now I'm ready to take your orders. The waiter stands before us, pencil poised. First you will want a drink, yes? For a night like this, something to warm the cockles. What will it be?

-Two martinis, Gabriel replies.

-Nosiree, he disagrees. I recommend for the young lady, for her cold which I see she is suffering from on account of the coughing, for her I recommend a schnapps with honey and hot water and a slice of lemon. It is an old remedy from my mother, alluva sholem, works better than the best medicine. As for you my friend, a double egg nog to keep up your strength, if you get my meaning. Without waiting for approval he instructs the bartender and flatfoots away to welcome a new arrival, a distinguished- looking gentleman in a black cape.

-Here you are. Putting down the drinks he whisks some bread crumbs from the table cloth and waits for our response. Good? You betcha. Already the young lady isn't coughing. You see that person with whom I was talking? That's Jacob Adler the famous Yiddish actor who takes the same medicine for his cold that I prepared for you. I prescribe the treatment for all the actors from the Yiddish Art Theatre next door. Last year they were sold out every night for the Family Carnovsky. The customers came from downtown, uptown and out of town. And the reviews! Magnificent! But this season they're closed. Ah, all the wonderful plays I have seen. Yoshe Kalb, The Dybbuk, The Cherry Orchard. It is a great pity that Maurice Schwartz isn't producing anything. Now, what would you like for dinner?

-We have decided on the schmaltz herring to start, then pea soup, the broiled sirloin and...

-Yesterday, maybe. Not today. Take my advice, today you should have the chopped liver which is very appetizing. After that matzoh balls in chicken broth garnished with dill. A *meichel in beichel*. To be followed by rib steak grilled medium.

-No, I demur, make it rare, please.

-All right, medium rare, he compromises. It will melt in your mouth. With the steak you also get pickles and a baked Idaho. For dessert I will bring you our home made strudel and a glaysele tay. With lemon of course. You agree? You will thank me later.

He scoops up the menus leaving us to our drinks while the musical trio scratches out a yiddish melody.

The liver arrives with a flourish, the waiter eager for our response.

Delicious? Of course. Enjoy.

The soup is equally deserving of praise. The steak exactly as promised. The strudel fresh and flaky.

We linger over brandy, enjoying the familiar music. Beltz, mein shtetele Beltz, the waiter hums as he itemizes the food and drinks we have consumed. Presenting the bill on a plate he urges us to stay a while, there's no hurry. Gabriel and I agree that he deserves a royal tip. He helps us into our coats and at the door bestows his blessing.

-May you both have a long life full of health, happiness and prosperity and lots of nachez from your children. So seit gesund and come again. As we leave he hollers for Hymie to clear table number three.

The rain has eased to a drizzle. We walk up Second Avenue past the dark Yiddish Art Theatre and the luggage shops with their ubiquitous umbrellas. At Fourteenth Street we descend into the subway and take the shuttle, transferring to the Broadway line. Passengers slumped in their seats or faces buried in the tabloids. A girl holding out her tin cup is leading a blind man. Above the clatter of the train I can make out the words of her song...'the white cliffs of Dover, to-morrow when the world is free.'

When we emerge at Times Square the electric spectaculars are twinkling and flashing, their messages mirrored in the wet road. Pepsi Cola. Bond Street Clothes. Felix the Cat, animated by hundreds of light bulbs. Smoke rings issue from the mouth of a young man who declares, *I'd Walk a Mile for a Camel.* Another bulletin boasts that Lucky Strike Green has Gone to War. The Mexican Hayride poster shows Bobby Clark leering behind painted spectacles at a scantily dressed June Havoc. Baghdad on the Hudson.

The dancing feet have forsaken Forty Second Street and the theatres have become sex cinemas. Amusement arcades offer Pokerino and Fascination. Shooting galleries. Hamburger and hot dog stands. Orange juice stalls. Pizza Parlors. The shop windows display provocative merchandise. Nutcrackers in the shape of women's legs. I like pussy T shirts. Black lace brassieres, garter belts and open-crotch panties. Leather vests and skirts. Comic books and sex magazines and James Joyce's Ulysses advertised as the most intensive exploration of a woman's erotic desires. A barking plush puppy hops about on the sidewalk. Toy soldiers march to the beat of drums.

The hustlers are everywhere. A black man with a seeing-eye dog, the sign around his neck says Thank the Lord You are not Blind. A woman swaddled in sweaters singing *Rock of Ages.* A fiddler's squeaky rendering of *My Yiddishe Momma.*

The clock on the Times Tower shows half past ten. Soon the theatre curtains will be ringing down on Mary Martin in One Touch of Venus. On the all black cast in Carmen Jones.

At 48th street where Seventh Avenue intersects Broadway,

a uniformed doorman coaxes the customers.

-This is the place, folks, Lou Walters Latin Quarter where you will be entertained by a lavish, dazzling, breath-taking review in the style of the Folies Bergeres. Twelve scenes, twenty-two numbers including the spectacular Can Can like you've never seen it done before. Next show starts immediately.

We've never been in a night club and caught up in the promise of an evening to remember we join the queue at the foot of the stairs behind a contingent of United States Marines. We chart our sluggish upward advance in the wall mirror and by midnight reach the lobby where the air is blue with cigarette smoke and it is standing room only. Some time later we have progressed to the cordoned area where a major-domo stands guard. Consulting the reservation list he calls out the names, his patrician features relaxing when he recognizes a middle-aged gent in formal attire with a red-haired companion, evening dress scooped low about the bosom. Thank you sir, the steward palms the banknote.

Another couple is admitted, then a master sergeant and his sweater-girl companion. We have been waiting two hours.

The lights in the night club have been dimmed and the show is about to begin. As Gabriel reaches into his wallet pocket the attendant recognizes our presence. Smiling he bids us advance and as we walk quickly past without rendering the cash tribute he stiffens in surprise. By now we are following the maitre d' through the closely packed room. Employees are clearing dishes and positioning additional tables into tight spaces. Through the pall of smoke I can discern the quilted pink ceiling and the red velvet walls. Lighting seeps through the ostrich feather decorations.

The orchestra is tuning up. Waiters are hurrying with magnums of champagne in ice buckets. A fanfare. A raspy voice booms over the loudspeakers. Welcome to Lou Walters Latin Quarter Review produced by Madame Natalie Kamerova of the Folies Bergères de Paris featuring the gorgeous, breath-taking Latin Quarter Girls.

As the stage curtains part we are delivered to a distant corner behind a pillar and seated at a small table decorated with a yellow rose in a bud vase. The floor show has begun but all we can catch is a glimpse of high-kicking legs.

-Are you ready to order? The waiter stands before us. The carte de menu lists steak, chicken, roast beef, lobster and lamb, each item priced astronomically. As the waiter waits impatiently Gabriel seeks my assistance. Anything will do, I asssure him, mindful of our limited resources. When Gabriel explains that we are not very hungry the waiter smirks. Doesn't matter, even if we order a sandwich there's a minimum charge so what'll it be? We settle for lobster salad and a bottle of California sauterne.

Acrobats are bouncing about on the stage to the accompaniment of brassy circus music. They are followed by jugglers. We crane around the column to get a better view. The music is seductive now and into the spotlight sweeps the bisexually-attired Lela Moore, the female persona caressing the male in an erotic performance that delights the patrons. Our salads arrive just as Frank Mazzone and partners explode on stage in the simulated mayhem of the Apache Dance. Mazzone pummels his tight-skirted girl and is roughed up by another Parisian thug. Much breaking of furniture. Much feigned pain. Much applause.

The finale is a patriotic extravaganza of rotating coloured spotlights with a corps of baton-twirling majorettes high stepping to the roll of drums and the blare of bugles in a melange of *America the Beautiful, To the shores of Tripoli* and *Three cheers for the red, white and blue*. The audience rises in a prolonged applauding, cheering and whistling. The master of ceremonies wraps up the evening with a prayer for the safety of America's troops overseas.

The bus boys clear the tables, the customers depart and we are presented with the cheque. Gabriel places the exact amount on the plate and adds a token gratuity which increases the waiter's surliness. Gluckstern's customers, he sneers as we hasten out to the packed lobby and down the stairs.

When we arrive at the hotel it is three o'clock in the morning. Satch unlocks the door, yawns in greeting. Guess you folks had a good time, huh?

In our room we prepare for bed. On the mirror above the

sink a message has been scrawled in lipstick: Everybody loves nooky.

Morning sunlight. Voices drifting up from the street. Man, you shoulda seed it, da fucking rat wuz leas' a foot long. I grab dat motha fucker by the tail 'n smashed him against da wall. Sounded like a goddam 'splosion. All blood 'n guts. I gonna send it to da fuckin' landlord by special delivery, all wrapped up in fancy paper.

Ejaculations of delight. You do dat man, you do dat. Real nice present for Mister Charlie.

Whistles of admiration. Man looka da ass on dat chick. Laughter, hoots, catcalls. Gabriel joins me at the window.

The gang in windbreakers with Ebony Dukes splashed across the backs has gathered outside the hotel. I've read about the gang wars in Harlem, the stabbings and clubbings, the killings with home-made guns. Imperial Huns and Pals of Satan on the prowl. The Chancellors and the Copians in a rumble that stemmed from a dispute over a stolen cap leaving one dead fifteen-year-old, two with shattered jaws and a cop with a bullet in his belly.

After breakfast we take the subway to East Broadway and walk the short distance to the subsidized apartment building where the Kirschmeyers live. The halls and elevators are littered with refuse. Gabriel's aunt, a wrinkled replica of his mother, welcomes us in Yiddish. The uncle moves slowly and says little. The older daughter, heavy with bleached hair, puts on the kettle and resuscitates the tea bag that has been drying on a saucer. She whispers to her skinny younger sister that Gabriel's bride is so sweet, with that little nose she looks like a shikse.

-How is your mother, the aunt queries.

-Fine, answers Gabriel.

-How is your father?

-Fine.

-And your brothers? the older sister asks.

-Fine.

-You hear that, pa? Everybody's just fine up in Canada. A smile hovers about the uncle's face.

-And how is everybody in New York? Everybody is fine too but Cousin Rachel is worried about her boyfriend who is serving in the South Pacific. They hope to get married on his next furlough and she has remained steadfastly true to him, obeying the musical imperative, Don't Sit Under the Apple Tree with Anyone Else But Me. She attends Victory Bond Rallies and block parties in aid of the Soldiers Welfare Fund until the day When Johnny Comes Marching Home. Rachel knows nothing about Canada's participation in the War, about our government's proclamation on September 5, 1939 to stand by Great Britain and the immediate mobilization of Canadian troops.

After an hour Gabriel seeks an excuse to leave, citing another appointment. Upon our departure the aunt hands me an envelope, a wedding present. May we have a happy, healthy life together until 120 years. We embrace and kiss goodbye, their felicitations echoing down the hall.

We spend the afternoon walking about the lower east side, fascinated by the neighborhoods of Cherry Street and Canal Street, the Polish shtetl transferred to the New World. The fish market. The bakery. The stalls of fruits and vegetables. Hebrew signs on the store windows. Men in long gabardines and yarmulkes.

-There go the trucks of the Jewish *Forward* with today's edition, says Gabriel. All the news, international and domestic. And the sagas of Yenta Telebenda and Moishe Kapoyr.

On Delancey Street the Hebrew Publishing Company displays Yiddish translations of Chekhov and Charles Dickens as well as prayer books. Gabriel says that instructional manuals like *Preparing to Become an American Citizen* were much in demand during previous waves of Jewish immigration. Also popular was The Yiddish-English Letter Writer on how to conduct romances by mail, which included phrases that could not but help touch the heart of the female recipient: The burning love consuming my heart must find some expression.

Supper at the Automat on Times Square. The compartments open with the insertion of nickels to provide sandwiches, soup, desserts and beverages. We choose baked beans, apple pie and coffee.

For entertainment we visit Radio City Music Hall. The movie is *Mrs. Parkington*, with Greer Garson as a hotel maid and Walter Pidgeon as an oil man in Nevada during the frontier period, a teary family saga developed through flashbacks. Not nearly as good as *Mrs. Miniver*, about British courage during the war where everyone sings *Land of Hope and Glory* amidst the ruins of a bombed-out church.

The stage show is American Rhapsody produced by Leon Leonidoff with the Glee Club, Rockettes, Corps de Ballet and Symphony Orchestra. Later we take the tour.

-Radio City Music Hall is the jewel of Rockefeller Centre, declares the elegantly uniformed guide. The Grand Foyer is sixty feet high with floor to ceiling mirrors and murals. Observe the immense crystal chandelier, the sweeping staircase, the patterned broadloom. The smoking lounge is finished in glistening black, the rest room walls adorned with paintings.

-On opening night, December 27, 1932, the program consisted of sixteen acts, put together by S.L. Rothafel, the great showman known as Roxy. The performers included Martha Graham, Ray Bolger, the Flying Wallendas, the Tuskegee Choir and of course Russell Markert's Rockettes, the 36 line dancers who delighted the audience with their machine-like precision in soft-shoe and tap routines, arms behind each other's waists, the straight line broken into geometric patterns, circles and diagonals. Every one of the 6200 seats was occupied when the Symphony Orchestra rose from the pit. The stage show lasted until two in the morning so they trimmed it to under an hour and added a film, *The Bitter Tea of General Yen*, with Barbara Stanwyck and Nils Asther. The format of four shows a day has continued to this time.

The guide informs us that the Rockettes have been costumed as cowgirls, poodles, scarecrows, bunnies, daffodils, robins, cadets and wooden soldiers retaining their perfect symmetry even when the stage is revolving. The Corps de Ballet has triumphed in excerpts from Swan Lake and Giselle especially choreographed for them.

-Since the stage is so huge, 60 feet high by 144 feet

wide and framed by a series of golden arches, one outside of the other, spectacular pageants have been presented like the Roman extravaganza with chariots pulled by live horses and a reproduction of Westminster Abbey for the Coronation of King George the Sixth. During the 1933 Easter Show finale a tableau of the Last Supper rose from the basement. Of course the Nativity is always shown before Christmas.

During our last three days we view the city from the 102nd storey observation tower of the Empire State Building. Visits to the Museum of Modern Art and the Metropolitan Museum. A boat ride on the lake in Central Park.

The final evening we have supper at Paddy's on 34th Street. Clam chowder, broiled lobster, cherry cheesecake and coffee. Supplied with the New York Times and Life Magazine we are ready for the journey.

The Grand Central Express wails its midnight threnody as it speeds north toward Albany past rural outposts, then westward to Syracuse and the Finger Lakes, arriving in Buffalo where we transfer to the Toronto-bound train.

A crisp dawn greets our arrival in the Queen City.

2

We are having Sabbath dinner with Gabriel's family. As one of the twins gazes indifferently at his bowl the other jostles him and the soup sloshes onto the table cloth. The mother screams at them to behave.

-When do you move into your flat? enquires the father.

-Monday, says Gabriel. We kiss and I call him my little shmucky, a term reserved for the privacy of the bed. The twins laugh and the grandparents pretend not to have heard.

After the roast chicekn and compote of apples and pears, an argument develops about attendance at synagogue. The twins reluctantly accompany their father and grandfather to the Kiever Shul but just wait, after their bar mitzvah they'll stop going, just like Gabriel.

-Are you sure that the bedroom furniture will be delivered on Monday?

-It'll be there Ma, don't worry.

-You should have chosen the other design, the one I liked. So beautiful.

-I guess Anna and I don't share your tastes.

-Sure, what does a mother know?

-You've been very good to us mother, Gabriel tries to placate her. Anna and I appreciate your generosity, the dishes and cutlery and the drapes. And the General Electric Highboy Radio.

-Phone the relatives, maybe they'll invite you to dinner. But they're such cheapskates. Let me know which of your father's sisters and brothers don't give you a wedding present.

Mrs. Feldman and her two cherubs are sitting on the verandah of the three-storey house when we arrive. The older one fixes us with an unrelenting 'you are not welcome' stare. The other is probing his nose.

-My husband is upstairs already. The landlady rises wearily and pads inside to switch on a bulb in the hall, the two kids scampering up the stairs ahead of us. The master of the house stands in the middle of the empty room, his belly ballooning over stained trousers.

-I started with the washing of the walls, see? Spic and Span makes them look real clean. You can do the rest.

-I understood you were going to paint, Gabriel counters. When you asked for the first month's rent in advance you agreed to decorate the flat.

-It doesn't really need painting. Look how nice it is where I already washed. A couple of hours and we will be finished. Then we can do the kitchen. So, let's go to work.

We begin our assault on the wall under Feldman's direction, smudging one area at a time and rinsing until the chalky white appears.

-You're doing fine, Feldman nods approvingly, just fine. Now you will excuse me, a call of nature. He waddles away leaving a burst of farts in his wake. Outside in the maple tree birds are chirping. Spangles of sunlight dance into the room as we wash, rinse and dry. Feldman appears after a lengthy interlude, standing at the door breathing heavily, appraising our progress.

-Good. Good. That's the way. I can see you won't need my help, you are doing so well. You'll excuse me, it's almost time for the evening service. He calls down the stairs, Hushie, Shimmie, get dressed, we're going to Shul.

By the time Feldman returns Gabriel and I have scrubbed the walls down to their pristine plaster pallor.

-You didn't do the kitchen yet? Another hour and you'll be finished.

The moving van arrives in the morning. Two men unload the oak dresser, wardrobe, vanity, night table and bed. The kitchen is already furnished with a table, chairs, stove and ice box purchased from the previous tenant, a widow who has retired to Miami. The Canadian Pacific Express delivers a shipment from Montreal. A couch, floor lamp and coffee table.

The electric fixture in the bed-sitting room has three sockets but only one sixty watt bulb. Similar low wattage incandescence in the hall and kitchen. The electric company is plenty rich already, asserts the landlord.

The gas-fired heater in the basement produces enough tepid water for our Saturday night bath. While Gabriel and I are in the tub one of the kids bangs on the door.

-Pishy, wanna make pishy.

-Shimmie, come down, the mother whines. Mendel, make him come down.

-Come down, right away, Feldman bellows and returns to his perusal of the Jewish Journal. Silence, then Shimmie's voice.

-I come down. I already made pee pee in the hall.

The snow descends during the night, first in eddies then a white downpour. The bedroom is cold with only a sluggish current radiating from the warm air register but it is cosy in bed under the blankets. We kiss in open-mouthed abandon discovering responsive zones hitherto untried. Arm pits, neck and breasts. Gabriel's fingers glide down to the moistness between my thighs in deft foreplay, and as he enters my receptive body, thrusting deeply, I feel intense pulsations. Fire is racing through my blood and a rainbow of colours flashes across my eyelids and the contractions become more intense and I convulse in a climax just as Gabriel explodes inside me. After our first simultaneous orgasm we repose in a state of delicious lassitude. And the snow continues to fall.

The morning news gives the war secondary importance. The weatherman reports that December 17, 1944 will go down in the records as the worst blizzard in Toronto's 110 year history. Power breaks everywhere. Traffic halted. The city is paralysed.

At eight o'clock, swaddled in coat, muffler, tuque, gloves and boots Gabriel leaves the house. From the window I can see him sinking into the snow drifts as he struggles ahead.

The telephone rings at eleven. One of the Feldman kids shrieks that it is for me and I race downstairs to take the call. It is Gabriel who has just arrived at the office and he might as well have stayed home for the Royal Canadian Air Force will not be operational this day. He describes his three hour labourious journey through the snow-drifted roads, the street signs and buildings erased by the white-out. Vehicles stranded. Nothing moving except a few figures bent into the wind. He intends to return after lunch.

Mrs. Feldman is sweeping the verandah as Gabriel arrives. She instructs him to shake off the snow and remove his boots before going into the house. Newspapers wet with slush cover the floor.

-The little monsters have been running up and down the stairs all day, I greet him. Hucky shit himself. You should have heard Mrs. Feldman cursing.

-And where's himself?

-Sleeping. He shovelled the walk so he has to rest. Oh my, your trousers are wet, off with them. Might as well remove everything and get into some dry clothes. Tell me about your morning.

-Well, when I got to Number One Training Command the elevators weren't working so I had to hike up to the sixth floor. I was only the third person to sign in. Sergeant Cashman, puffing on his pipe, was perusing the current issue of the Readers' Digest and was eager to tell me about the unhappiest women in the world (condensed from the Saturday Evening Post) and how parents change children into mental misfits (from Your Life). He beguiled me with this item from the Picturesque Speech section of the magazine: She was all sugar and spice with a dill pickle for a tongue.

-Ha. Ha. It's fun to put down women. So how did you help to advance the Allied cause to-day?

-I read the weekend edition of PM, particularly the columns by I.F. Stone and Max Lerner. And of course Barnaby the comic strip for adults.

-Did you have lunch?

-Hamburger and coffee in the restaurant. I was the only customer. Sat at a table watching the snowblown figures struggling past the Strathcona Hotel. When I checked into the office again the place was deserted.

-Have much trouble getting home?

-I plodded up York Street to the Prince George Hotel and headed west. Past intersections with nonfunctioning traffic signals, past a slow moving snow plough. A rider on horseback appeared, no sound of hoof beats as in a silent movie. Two men on skis. Kids making snow forts.

-Are you ready for a drink?

-Love one. I'll have Scotch and water.

-And Vodka on the rocks for me.

-What's for dinner?

-Soup and a salmon sandwich. Lemon meringue pie. Coffee.

-Perfect. I have a present for you, the butterfly earrings you admired in the jewelry store on Bloor street. I have been saving them for our second anniversary, two months since we were married.

-Embrasse-moi, chérie. Mmm.

-Do you feel what is happening inside my robe? I am stiff with desire. Quickly madame, off with your culottes.

-What, here in the kitchen?

-Love brooks no delay. Sacre bleu, you are not wearing them.

-When I saw you from the bedroom window I felt the grand passion. I wanted to be ready.

-Then let us do it. Here on the chair.

-Mmmm. I love you.

Love in the afternoon. At bedtime, in the middle of the night, before breakfast. Love on the sofa, on the floor, in the bathtub. Against the wall.

Tonight's concert at Massey Hall is taking place as scheduled despite the twenty and a half inch precipitation. Nor snow, nor wind, nor sleet can keep the music lovers away.

The Shuter Street music hall was presented to the city in June of 1894 by one of its most generous citizens, Hart Almerrin Massey as a memorial to his eldest son Charles. A wall plaque details the family's history.

Born in a log cabin east of Toronto the pater familias founded the farm implement company that was to become an international corporation. A Methodist, he left most of his fortune to educational, religious, social and cultural causes. He built the Fred Victor Mission in memory of his youngest son who died at the age of twenty-two. The Massey family endowed a College and a Household Science Department for the University of Toronto and a student centre named Hart House. The first native-born Governor General of Canada was Vincent Massey. His brother Raymond, an acclaimed actor, was the incarnation of Abraham Lincoln on stage and film.

Massey Hall was inaugurated with a performance of Handel's Messiah. Since that time the world's great musicians have praised this acoustically perfect auditorium.

We deposit our skis in the lobby and climb to the second balcony. An air of informality prevails among the sweatered patrons. The members of the orchestra come on stage and the warm-up of brass instruments, winds and strings begins. Sir Ernest MacMillan appears to hearty applause and apologizes for the informal dress of the musicians due to the inclement weather. Facing the orchestra he raises his baton and everyone rises for God Save the King.

We drift away on waves of melody beginning with the *Academic Festival Overture* of Johannes Brahms followed by Haydn's *Symphony No. 92 in G Major*, the so-called Oxford. During intermission we have time to read the program notes of Ettore Mazzeleni. The second half of the concert is highlighted by Nathan Milstein's rendering of the Goldmark *Violin Concerto*. In conclusion we are treated to Debussy's *Iberia*, number two of *Images pour Orchestre*. A well-rounded evening of Classical, Baroque, Romantic and Impressionist pieces. Then out into the star-lit, snow-bright night, homeward bound.

Gabriel and I are immersed in music. Concerts at Eaton Auditorium, the Royal Conservatory of Music and Hart House. Performances by Rudolf Serkin, Myra Hess, Jascha Heifetz, Yehudi Menhin, Dennis Brain and Alfred Deller. The NBC Radio Symphony Orchestra conducted by Arturo Toscannini. Recordings of Marian Anderson singing Bach Cantatas. Wanda Landowska's interpretation of the *Goldberg Variations* for harpsichord. Beniamino Gigli and Jussi Bjoerling. The Texaco broadcasts from the Metropolitan Opera every Saturday afternoon.

Mrs. Feldman is worried about being pregnant. Maybe she is just late, I suggest. Oh no. It has been seven weeks since her last period and she feels sick in the morning. Since I am a nurse can I help her? Maybe my husband knows somebody.

On his next visit to the drug store Gabriel obtains a quantity of pills from Benny Kirsch. Guaranteed to induce uterine contractions. Mrs. Feldman swallows them without success, not even the slightest cramp. A neighbor in whom she has confided advises her to jump. Jump? Yeah. Jump down the stairs. So Mrs. Feldman jumps. Two stairs at a time. No change. She tries three and lands in pain as the carpet slides from under her. She is taken by ambulance to the hospital where her broken arm is set.

The fetus is undamaged. Mrs. Feldman is resigned to giving birth to a third little angel, it should please God.

Thursday April 12, 1945. Franklin Delano Roosevelt, President of the United States of America, dies suddenly at 3.35 pm in Warm Springs, Georgia. He was sixty-three years old. Vice President Harry S. Truman has been sworn in to become the 32nd President. The newspapers carry banner headlines and front page stories about the life of Roosevelt, whose ancestors came over on the Mayflower and who could trace his genealogy back to William the Conqueror.

Monday May 8, 1945. VE Day. There is dancing in the streets and crowds converge on City Hall. The lamp standards on Bay Street are draped with the banners of the Royal Canadian Air Force, the Royal Canadian Navy and the Toronto army regiments. The Union Jack, the Stars and Stripes, the Hammer and Sickle, the Tricolour and the Canadian Ensign flutter everywhere. Gabriel and I celebrate in Chinatown with egg rolls, chow mein, chicken balls and spare ribs. The fortune cookies prophesy an Allied Victory.

Monday August 6, 1945. A B29 Superfortress of the 20th U.S. Air Force, the Enola Gay, explodes the Little Boy bomb from a height of 112,000 feet over south western Honshu. The detonation levels four square miles of Hiroshima and kills over 100,000 of its inhabitants as well as the entire second Japanese Army.

Thursday August 9, 1945. A second atomic bomb explodes over Nagasaki killing 36,000 people.

Tuesday August 14, 1945. At seven o'clock in the morning President Truman announces the Japanese surrender.

Monday September 3, 1945. Gabriel resigns from his civilian position with the Royal Canadian Air Force.

-Gottesman, when you gonna move? Hucky whines.

-Soon, Gabriel assures him. You will be the first to know. We'll have a going away party. You like barbecued pork? Hucky backs away in disgust. We are weary of the Feldman menage. The feces smeared on the walls, the urine on the floor, the chlorine fumes from the Sunday laundry, all the unventilated odors. One day Gabriel wearing a gas mask arrives at the house and rings the bell. When Mrs. Feldman opens the door she screams.

-I guess you didn't recognize me, he laughs.

-A fine joke, you almost scared me to death.

-It's for protection against foul smells including the passing of wind.

-If you don't like it here you can find another place. There are lots of couples who would like the flat. And for more money too. I am giving you a month's notice.

I scout the neighborhood and find two rooms, newly decorated, on Bathurst street near Bloor. Gabriel accompanies me for the second inspection.

-Come in. The landlady, the widow Vinograd, is plump and jolly. White hairs sprout from her chin. She breathes heavily as we mount the stairs.

-My favorite creamy colour, so bright and airy, I think we should take it. Gabriel agrees and we give Mrs. Vinograd a ten dollar deposit. As we stand talking in the hall a woman in a peignoire slinks by.

-That's Miss Pendergast from the middle room, a model. Well, go in peace and return in peace.

Moving day. The Feldman kids are running up and down the stairs, peering into cartons, making faces at Miller's Moving men. Himself is at the printing shop having left instructions for his wife to stand on guard lest we damage the walls. Recently returned from the Mount Sinai Hospital where she was delivered of an eight pound girl, Mrs. Feldman supervises from the verandah, rocking the baby carriage. As the loaded van pulls away from Feldmania the kids shout goodbye Gottesman. We wave in farewell. Goodbye kucky, goodbye pishy.

We are sitting in Mrs. Vinograd's kitchen around a circular wooden table where she has set out bread, cheese and hard-boiled eggs. We must be hungry having worked so hard arranging the furniture. She pours tea from a brass samovar and while she sips from her glass tells us stories about her childhood in Vilna, her arrival in Toronto after the first world war and the death of her husband at age thirty-four during the great influenza epidemic. She takes issue with the Lord for leaving her alone with three children. It is better to dwell in grief than in widowhood. Clasping my hand she prays that I may never have to know any sorrow.

We become acquainted with the Vinograd sisters. Jessica, the youngest, a silent 27-year-old, sits beside the radio most of the time. Imperious Miriam, three years older, works for a firm of chartered accountants. Katy the eldest, heavy like her mother and with a similarly happy disposition, is a cashier in the corner grocery store. After the evening meal she washes the dishes, Jessica dries them and Miriam retires to her room.

As the summer wanes and the days grow shorter Miriam's hand-lettered signs appear. Make sure the front door is locked. Switch off the bath room light after use. Then the notes slipped under our bedroom door. Yesterday the hot water tap was left dripping all night. At three o'clock Friday morning the light in the kitchen was burning.

The Saturday bath schedule is posted and we are allotted the four to five afternoon segment. The Vinograd family washes irregularly. Occasionally while Gabriel and I are having supper we hear the swish of taffeta into the bathroom and then a trickle of water. Miriam at her ablutions.

Winter brings snow and cold. The widow attends to the furnace, sifting the ashes, adding fresh coals, lighting the bed of paper and sticks and blowing to coax the flame ablaze. But it is never warm enough in our rooms.

Sunday evening we entertain Pandora Beveridge, the gentile secretary of the controversial Reform Rabbi Isaiah Morgenstern. After dinner, swathed in blankets, we relax on the sofa in the bedroom. Pandora tells us about the Rabbi's protestations against the singing of Christmas carols in the public schools. She has sent out press releases guaranteed to gain maximum publicity in the media.

-God it's cold, Pandora breaks off. Can you crank up the heat?

-The landlady promised to pile on more coal but that doesn't seem to have helped.

-I think I have the solution. I should have thought of it before. Unscrewing the grill of the hot air register Gabriel discovers that warm air from below is rising to the third floor. He inserts a flattened tomato juice can into the duct, deflecting the flow into our room. Half an hour later as we are enjoying the warmth, Mr. Boardman from the floor above races down the stairs to the Vinograd kitchen.

-But I tell you it's ice cold in my room, Boardman is shouting. Put some coal in the damn furnace.

-I'll have you know the furnace is blazing, Miriam counters.

-But I'm still freezing. Come and see.

They pass by our door, up to the attic. A shuffling of feet above our heads, the clanging of metal then Boardman's voice. You can't feel a damn bit of heat coming out.

-I'll see what I can do, Miriam hopes to mollify him. On the way down she requests permission to check our situation. Hmmm. Not much warm air coming out of here either. I can't understand what the problem is.

After she leaves Gabriel replaces the metal diversion.

Mrs. Vinograd has adopted me. No sooner have I washed the breakfast dishes than she calls in her cracked voice, Anna, tea is ready, come down. She always has a pile of clothes for mending. Better an ugly patch than a beautiful hole, she declares. Her speech is stocked with aphorisms.

-Poverty runs after the poor and riches after the rich. If Jessica could only bring herself to go out and get a job and if Miriam could find a husband and if Katy...there is a saying, a mother must have a big apron to cover the faults of her children. Ah well, the tired eyes brighten, it never gets any lighter until it is first quite dark.

We sit in silence, sipping tea, while popular ballads from Jessica's radio float out beyond her closed door.

-But I am happy for you, my beautiful tochterel who is soon to be a mother. I like Gabriel too, so educated, you have to be educated to be a writer, no?

I don't tell her that Gabriel is a copy writer at an Advertising Agencies downtown.

When I start to stain Mrs. Vinograd insists I remain in bed. When the cramps begin she stays by my side until the ambulance arrives. After the miscarriage she visits me at the hospital.

Upon my return home, Mrs. Vinograd fusses over me with chicken soup to build up my strength. When the phone rings she hobbles down to answer it.

-That was Gabriel asking how you were feeling. I told him fine, thank God.

The phone again.

-Your mother-in-law. How is Anna? I said you were coming along nicely. You're not fooling me, she asked? Should I come to see her? That would be very nice I told her. But you say she is all right? Yes, she is fine. Well, your mother-in-law said, in that case I'll come next week to visit but you are sure she's all right? Mrs. Vinograd shakes her head. It is a good thing you are not living with her. A mother-in-law and a daughter-in-law in one house are like two cats in a bag.

The widow consoles me over the loss of the baby. She is sure that next time I will have a successful pregnancy.

It is a sunny Saturday afternoon and I am able to move about again. Mrs. Vinograd has been making allusions to my youthful appearance.

-I'll show you a different Anna, says Gabriel. From his theatrical make-up kit he selects a wad of crepe hair that he fastens to my chin with spirit gum, a little trim with the scissors and voila! Direct from Ringling Brothers Circus...Annushka...the bearded lady.

Seated on the porch in a blouse and skirt I puff on a cigarette. The Cohen youngster skips by, stops to gape and runs screaming, mommy, come and see. Strollers glance in my direction. A passing police cruiser brakes suddenly then moves on. Minutes later it returns, the driver pausing to gape at the bearded woman who is blowing smoke rings into the air. Mrs. Vinograd is laughing, her belly quivering.

Weary of the charade I remove the fuzz with rubbing alcohol and dab cold cream on my face.

-She looks like my beautiful Anna again, the widow marvels.

New milestones are set at the Nuremburg Trials. Blind

obedience to superiors is declared to be ño defense. Entire organizations such as the SS are found guilty.

No news about the fate of Gabriel's grandparents, uncles and aunts in Poland. The thriving Jewish community in the town of Opatow where Gabriel was born has been eliminated.

Saturday October 19, 1946. We celebrate our anniversary at the Embassy Ballroom. Gene Rosenblatt, eyes watering behind thick eye glasses, arrives with Jacqueline, a handsome woman whose grandfather was an Ibo chief.

The band is playing *April in Paris*. One of these days we'll take off for Europe, vows Gabriel. Leave his job at Beaver Publishing. Travel all over. Gene produces a flask of whisky and conceals it again in a paper bag as the waiter appears with bottles of beer.

Sometimes I wonder why I spend the lonely night...the band opens its second set with *Stardust* and I coax Gabriel onto the dance floor...*the melody haunts my reverie...when our love was new.* Two years have passed. I press closer to him as we glide around the room.

Gene is holding forth on religion as the opiate of the masses and capitalism as the worst of all tyrannies since it demeans the human spirit in the pursuit of unbridled profits. He recounts how he has joined strikers on the picket lines and suffered abuse and physical violence. He has also protested against restrictive covenants that keep black people out of city neighborhoods and summer resorts. What about discrimination against Jews, I inquire. What about the exploitation of workers in the garment industry by Jewish bosses, counters Gene.

Gabriel steers the conversation to recollections of the group that used to frequent the Rainbow Tea Room. The ones who enlisted and never returned like Flying Officer Ted Hoffman, shot down over Normandy. Like Captain Sandy Lewis killed at Dieppe. Sergeant Freddy Shoshinsky mortally wounded at Anzio. And those who left Toronto after the war. Danny Halpern enjoying la vie bohème in Paris and working on the great Canadian novel. Lenny Jacobs playing American characters in British films. Raphael Beckerman painting in a Greenwich Village studio. Nobody knows what happened to Max Rubinstein.

Sophisticated Lady. Jacqueline entreats Gene to dance with her. The people at the next table are whispering about them. All evening we have seen their furtive glances.

At half past ten the waiter arrives with a cake purchased earlier by Gabriel from Woman's Bakery. The band plays Happy Anniversary with everybody in the ballroom joining in the singing and then Gabriel and I blow out the candles. Gene pours beer into his glass, adds a sizeable measure of whisky and downs the drink.

-Can I make anyone else a boilermaker? Gabriel? Here you are.

-Down the hatch.

-Cake everyone? And coffee.

-At half past eleven beer service ceases. The band is playing *Blues in the Night.* Gene pours another boilermaker. Then one for Gabriel. At midnight the band segues into *God Save the King* signalling the onset of the Sunday Sabbath and the shutting down of dance halls, cinemas, theatres and beverage rooms. But Chinatown is just coming alive.

By the time we get to the Kwong Chow restaurant Gabriel is feeling woozy and has to be helped up the stairs. We order chicken chow mein, sweet and sour spare ribs and fried rice, but Gabriel, head slumped on the table, sleeps through the Cantonese dishes. He awakes as we are about to leave, surprised that we have already eaten. He doesn't feel well.

-Let's get you out into the fresh air, I urge.

On the street Gabriel takes several tentative steps and vomits onto a parked Cadillac.

-Boilermakers can be deadly if you're not used to them, Gene says.

March 22, 1947. President Truman signs Executive Order 9835 calling for a loyalty investigation of all Federal Employees. The House Committee on Un-American activities has collected a file with over one million names of known or suspected

Communists, Fellow Travellers, Dupes and Bleeding Heart Liberals.

April 2, 1947. Cocktail lounges open in Toronto. The doors of the Silver Rail open at noon to thirsty patrons. Bar rye is 40 cents a one ounce shot. Crown Royal costs 65 cents. Canadian beer is 25 cents a bottle. At closing time customers are still clamouring to be admitted.

May 1947. Forty-eight Naxi officers and guards are hanged by the U.S. Army at Landsberg Germany for mass murders at Mauthhausen Concentration Camp.

June 9, l947. The guardians of morality swoop down on Beaver Publications and impound magazines and printing plates on charges of obscenity. In the weeks that follow while lawyers prepare to argue freedom of the press, morale among the employees ebbs. The publisher threatens to liquidate the business rather than be subjected to repeated police harassment.

Gabriel peruses the Help Wanted advertisements in the newspapers and mails resumes with a tip-on attention getter, a penny that I have polished to mint-like brightness. A few replies arrive. What a clever idea. Sorry we have no vacancies but try us again in the Spring.

June 16, 1947. A positive response from the International Electric Company inviting Gabriel for an interview. At two in the afternoon he arrives at the luxuriously appointed reception area and is offered coffee and a copy of Fortune Magazine. After a short wait the secretary informs him that Mr. Abercrombie is available and leads the way to the office of the Personnel Manager.

-Ah, good of you to come, he booms, rising from behind a massive desk and extending a manicured hand. What is so rare as a day in June? Beautiful weather, perfect for sailing, wouldn't you say? I am a member of the Royal Canadian Yacht Club but I suppose you indulge in other recreational activities. Do you enjoy baseball? I know it is too early to speculate but which teams do you think will make it to the World Series? I am rooting for the Yankees. Boston may have Ted Williams but New

York has Joe Di Maggio. I won't discount the Dodgers although I wonder if the Brooklyn team is doing the right thing signing a Negro, that fellow Jackie Robinson, the rookie first base man. I wonder how he'll get along with the other players?

Abercrombie is a mine of baseball information. The leading pitchers, the most valuable players, batting averages and major league pennant winners of past seasons. His heroes in the National Baseball Hall of Fame are Ty Cobb and Whitey Ford.

-Well now, as to the purpose of your visit. That was an ingenious letter you sent and it came at a most opportune time because we do have a vacancy, that of editor of the company House Organ. If you will fill in the Application for Employment--you may use the desk in the adjoining office--I shall process it as expeditiously as possible.

The questions are designed to provide a comprehensive profile of the applicant. Age. Country of birth. Birthplace of parents. Education. Marital Status. Hobbies and Interests. Nationality. Religion.

Ah, there's the rub. Religion. Should he confess to Hebrew? Maybe Agnostic. But that would be considered the same as Atheist which would brand him as a Communist. Should he claim affiliation with the Timothy Eaton Memorial Church? Would they check? In the end Gabriel enters Hebrew.

More questions requiring specific answers. Clubs or societies to which you belong. Have you ever been arrested? Have you been treated for: Epilepsy, Diabetes, Alcoholism, Tuberculosis, Venereal Disease. List record of employment.

The questionnaire completed, Gabriel gives it to Mr. Abercrombie who smiles encouragingly. Part way through his perusal the Personnel Manager's sunny disposition grows cloudy, the brow furrows.

-Well, now, I believe we have everything we need for our records, he announces crisply.

-When may I start?

-I can't rightly say at this time. I shall have to review your application and assess your suitability.

-You led me to believe that I qualified for the position.

-Oh, yes, you do, eminently so. Your education, your experience, your service with the Royal Canadian Air Force. The fact is, however, that you are over-qualified. I am not certain that you would be content with a position that is below your exceptional ability.

-I would work very hard to succeed.

-I'm afraid you don't understand. Our environment would not suit you. It is a matter of compatibility. All our employees have the same background which enables them to function as members of the team. I'm sure you won't have any trouble finding employment elsewhere. You will be happier working with...your own people. Good luck.

Mr. Abercrombie summons his secretary to escort the gentleman to the elevator. She is gracious. She is compatible. She is Gentile.

During the summer of his discontent while I am at work as nurse in Dr. Leo Wettstein's offrice Gabriel fills the time between job-hunting by seeking escape from reality, reading fiction. He is beguiled by Erich Maria Remarque's Arch of Triumph, sympathizing with the war-weary lovers and intrigued by the quantity of Calvados they consume.

The summer slips by. Then autumn and winter. Gabriel, still out of work, has turned to books on Advertising and Public Relations.

3

Friday May 14, 1948. Israel Independence is proclaimed with David Ben Gurion as Prime Minister and Haim Weizmann President.

Sunday May 16. The children of the religious school are in the sanctuary and the organ plays *How Lovely Are Thy Dwellings Lord*. When Rabbi Morgenstern robed in white appears on the chancel all sound ceases and all heads bow as he calls upon the Eternal to watch over the fledgling State for from Zion shall go forth the Law and the word of the Lord from Jerusalem. His words emanate from the loudspeakers in magnified eloquence caroming about the concrete walls and vaulted roof of the Temple. Now he asks the junior congregation to join him in reciting: Blessed art Thou O Lord who has sustained us and brought us to this day. The sermon follows, a detailed history of God's redemption of Israel. The children are dismissed with the injunction that they bring their parents to the rally at Maple Leaf Garden.

Throngs are massed on College Street along the route of the parade. The blue and white flag of hope, the Star of David in its centre hangs in windows. It flutters on storefronts, posts, cars and bicycles.

When the General Wingate Branch of the Canadian Legion swings out from the school yard on Bathurst Street, drums and bugles shattering Toronto's Sunday somnolence, a mighty shout goes up and applause greets the Jewish war veterans, medals gleaming on blazers, heads held high. Behind them follow the Jewish Boy Scouts, Girl Guides and Air Cadets. Then come the Zionist Youth singing in Hebrew and English the songs of the pioneers. The onlookers cheer the labour leaders and members of Parliament. The Star of David mingles with the Red Ensign, the Union Jack and the Stars and Stripes. Banners urge Canada to permit arms to Israel.

Today we are not afraid to proclaim our Jewishness. Today we are all Lions of Judah. No longer the stooped, fearful, stereotyped yids. At this hour Jewish heroes are contending against the combined Arab Armies. A Jewish Prime Minister is meeting with his Jewish cabinet.

A quarter after seven the doors of Maple Leaf Garden open and the crowds surge in. From the top row down to the floor every seat is occupied. High-spirited voices fill the air. Shouts of Next year in Jerusalem. Songs of praise from the Hazamir choir.

As the dignitaries file onto the rostrum the applause ricochets throughout the hockey arena until Marvin Gelber the chairman brings the meeting to order.

-Let me begin by extolling the courage and wisdom of our

greatest statesman, Dr. Haim Weizmann whose many diplomatic battles have been crowned with the American recognition of Medinath Israel. We know that peace in Palestine rests on the will of the great powers and more particularly in London and Washington. Let us pray they will be found worthy of their trust.

Now the assembly rises to sing Hatikvah, the anthem of hope for generations of diaspora Jews. Before the final cadence has ended the cheering breaks out anew.

Rabbi Maurice Perlzweig demands that the Security Council of the United Nations take appropriate measures to hold aggression at bay. Egypt's invasion of Palestine is an affront to the world. He asks His Majesty's Government to direct the Arab Legion trained by British officers and paid for by British taxpayers to evacuate Palestine.

Sir Ellsworth Flavelle, Chairman of the Canadian-Palestine Committee, warns that Israel must rid itself of terrorists. The survival of the Jewish State depends upon the success of its government in eliminating the activities of the Irgun and the Stern Gang whose operations as gunmen and assassins have been condemned by all civilized people.

Senator Arthur W. Roebuck rejoices in the establishment of the State of Israel and calls upon Canada to follow the lead of the United States in recognizing the government headed by David Ben Gurion.

Lieut. Col. David Croll, M.P. declares that as a Canadian and a Jew he is proud to hail the birth of Israel and lauds the role that Canada has played in making possible the United Nations decision, citing the efforts of Canadian statesmen like Pearson, St. Laurent and especially the Prime Minister, Wm. Lyon McKenzie King.

-But let us remember that declarations don't make a nation. Every Jew in the world must rededicate himself to build and protect an abiding State of Israel. Jewish troops during the war proved themselves in the Middle East as an efficient, unified fighting force. Our duty is to stand behind them to the limit. I know that it has become fashionable to criticize British policy in Palestine but let us not forget the positive contributions by His

Majesty's Government. Israel cannot live in isolation. The past is dead. Let the bitterness and disappointment die with it.

Rabbi Isaiah Morgenstern in a ringing peroration warns that the romantic glamour of an epochal moment must not be allowed to obscure the practical considerations. The big powers must protect Israel against Arab aggression in violation of the U.N. charter. The first step is to lift the embargo on arms to Haganah. The second is to enable Jews everywhere to come to Israel's defence. The third is to extend long term loans to its government.

-And the fourth is addressed to all who are present tonight. I ask for your financial commitment during the present emergency in Israel. For the rebirth of a Jewish state is not something we observe and witness from a distance. It constitutes a rebirth of ourselves.

July 8, 1948. I suffer a miscarriage in the 13th week of my pregnancy. After ten days in hospital I return, weak and dispirited, to the new flat on Shannon Street and meet my care giver Laurie Marchmount, twenty-three with an easy smile and a frank disposition. An only child, she grew up in an Elizabethan house on the Kingsway and attended Branksome Hall private school for girls. Her father is on the board of the National Bank of Canada. Her mother heads the Women's Committee of the Toronto Symphony Orchestra.

On flower-scented afternoons we relax in the garden. The tennis players in the court beyond the fence are whacking racquet against ball against clay. Laurie is drowsing, saffron hair tumbled about the serene face, breasts gently rising and falling within the sleeveless blouse. I feel a tinge of jealousy. Am I still attractive?

An autumn weekend in New York at the Astor Hotel on Times Square, the cross-roads of the world. John Jacob's hostelry opened in 1904 occupies the block between 44th and 45th street with Shubert Alley at the rear. Meet me at the Astor. She had to go and lose it at the Astor. Everybody knows the Astor's pink and black flecked Georgian marble exterior and revolving doors with the florist's shop in between. Our room looks out upon the Pepsi Cola spectacular that lights up the night sky.

Marlon Brando is electrifying Broadway with his performance in *A Street Car Named Desire.* Ticket sales are brisk for *Born Yesterday.*

Patricia Drylie, late of the Boris Volkoff School of Ballet in Toronto is dancing at Radio City Music Hall, whipping off numerous fouetées and turning en pointe during the four shows each day. Milly Herman the other Volkoff graduate has left Radio City for George Balanchine's Ballet Theatre.

Saturday night after the curtain has descended on Cleopatra's lingering demise, Gabriel and I find ourselves outside Sardi's Restaurant when a taxi pulls up.

-Cab mister? Gabriel shakes his head. Hey Gabriel! It's me, the driver shouts. Max!

Max Rubinstein informs us that he moved to New York two years ago. He and Judy Lane, the hostess he met at the Stage Door Canteen during the war, are living together in the Village. She has a bit part in an Off Broadway production. He would like us to spend Sunday with them but we have to take the flight back to Toronto. Gabriel suggests that we have a bite to eat. Max wouldn't mind but he'd better get back to work since this is the best time for short hauls. As for eating, he recommends Hector's Cafeteria. We should try the buffet. And the seltzer is free, comes right out of the tap.

-And you want to see Broadway characters? Hector's is full of them. Well, enjoy your visit. And listen, next time you are in town get in touch.

January 2, 1950. Toronto City Council approves Sunday Sports. The Star headlines the decision: The Thin Edge of the Wedge. Will movies be next?

Senator Joseph McCarthy speaking before the Women's Republican Club in Wheeling, W. Virginia: I have here in my hand a list of 205 names known to the Secretary of State as being members of the Communist Party but who are still shaping the policy of the State Department.

Fear that a motion picture dealing with the life and

exploits of Hiawatha the Mohawk Indian chief might be regarded as Communist propaganda has caused Monogram Studios to shelve the project. It was Hiawatha's efforts as a peacemaker among the warring Indian tribes of his day which brought about the Confederation of the Five Nations (the Iroquois League) that gave Monogram particular concern, according to a studio spokesman. The movie might be regarded as a message for peace and therefore helpful to Communist designs.

A short circuit in the New York City subway causes over 1,000 passengers to stampede in the belief that World War Three has begun. Many shriek: The Russians! War! The Russians!

Julius and Ethel Rosenberg are sentenced to die in the electric chair for stealing atomic bomb secrets and passing them on to the Russians.

General Grow, U.S. Military attache in Moscow, confides to his diary: War! As Soon as possible! Now! Communism must be destroyed!

W.E.B. Du Bois is handcuffed, fingerprinted, searched for concealed weapons and brought to trial for not registering as a subversive.

June 7, 1950. Gabriel has been appointed by Toronto Fashion Industries to publicize the Showing of Fall Fashions. I help him prepare the press kits with human interest stories and 8x10 glossy photographs.

Retailers from across Canada mingle in the Crystal Ballroom of the King Edward Hotel for cocktails and hors d'oeuvres. They will dine on rib-eye steak, Caesar salad and baked Alaska.

During dessert a fanfare introduces Cindy Ellen Farquharson the noted fashion commentator, stunning in a summer white gown, who promises an exciting evening of Fashions in Toronto with Horace Lapp's orchestra providing the music.

Down the ramp that bisects the ballroom glide the Penelope Ayres models in originals copied from New York and Los Angeles. Cindy Ellen coos over dresses and gowns, that just beg to be worn to the theatre, symphony and opera. Lingerie frail as a whisper. Brassieres that lift buoyantly. Waist nippers so essential to the New Look. Sheer witchery in full-fashioned nylon hosiery. The female foot will look utterly sensuous in shoes with pointy toes, low cut throats and peek-a-boo sides, the ankles wrapped round by slender straps. Cindy Ellen does not mention the report in the Canadian Medical Journal warning that stiletto heels alter the adjustment of the female figure, pushing out the derriere behind and the bosom in front with every mincing move, each shift of position creating a tremor of the body in an effort to maintain the vertical while balancing on the half-inch balls of the feet.

The Betty Oliphant School of Ballet presents a segment from Sleeping Beauty while the guests get up from the tables to replenish their drinks.

After the interlude Cindy Ellen, looking younger than her forty-one years thanks to Matt Traynor's Dis-Guise, the cosmetic cream that helps conceal lines and blemishes, announces in a voice tremulous with expectation that this is the moment we have all been waiting for. The orchestra introduces the familiar music by Felix Mendelssohn as the wedding party fills the runway.

-Our bride is Countess Annaliese von Furstenberg, radiant in a majestic gown of ice blue satin. A scarf of heirloom lace falls across her shoulders and sweeps over the full court train. Her veil flows from a matching lace crown. She carries a cascade of mauve orchids. Her six attendants wear ballet-length gowns of midnight blue satin. And aren't the flower girls adorable?

Applause fills the hall as the models pose amidst the popping of flash bulbs, and the orchestra swings into the theme that signals the conclusion of Fashions in Toronto.

October 18, 1953. Gabriel and I celebrate our ninth wedding anniversary at a preview showing of the new Charlie Chaplin film, Limelight, with Milly Herman dancing under the nom de ballet of Melissa Hayden. The critics rave about her lithe strength, her control and dramatic ability.

Gabriel remembers Milly at the Boris Volkoff Studio with its dirty windows and large mirrors. An upright piano in one corner and a box of resin in another. The odour of sweat and wet wool. A few students in tights, limbering up at the barre, half an hour of stretching, sliding and jumping. Volkoff, spare and agile, walks in with his crooked grin. Margie, the pianist, knows intuitively what tempo he wants. Pliés in the five positions, turns, ronde de jambe a terre, ronde de jambe en l'aire, petit battement developé, battement frappé, grand battement. Volkoff beats time with his black briar cane, hitting out at a student, muttering God damn t'ing. He lectures them: Classical Ballet is to dance what poetry is to literature. So says Diaghilev. Milly Herman just turned sixteen, practises pirouettes and arabesques.

Milly at Hart House in 1940 dancing in Volkoff's Suite Sur Les Pointes to the music of Frederic Chopin. Milly at the Royal Alexandra Theatre in the Polovetsian Dances. At Massey Hall in Chopiniana.

Boris Volkoff danced with the Imperial Russian Ballet in Moscow and toured with the Bolshoi across Russia to Siberia and down to Harbin in Manchuria. He joined a new company that performed in Shanghai, India, Burma, Malaya. On the return to China he formed his own ballet troupe and set out on a grand tour of Japan, Hawaii and across to California, arriving in Toronto in 1931 as an illegal immigrant.

He designed the first ice ballet for the Toronto Skating Club carnival. He was chosen to take a group of students to pre-war Berlin to interpret the dances of the Canadian aborigines. For the Promenade Symphony Concerts he staged the Red Ear of Corn, based on an Indian legend set to the music of John Weinzweig. He represented Canada at the X1 Olympiad. He created ballet sequences for the Toronto Opera Company. The Volkoff Canadian Ballet with Milly Herman, Patricia Drylie, Barbara Ann Scott and Linda Keogh performed at army camps.

The melancholy Slav was courted by the Anglo Saxon ladies of the Granite Club. He married Janet Baldwin.

Friday October 15, 1954. Gabriel opens his own company, Advertising Services, next to the Evening Telegram on Bay Street. Open House is scheduled for three o'clock but the downpour that began early in the morning shows no sign of abating. Since he is located in the business and publishing core of the city he hopes for a good turnout with the resulting publicity.

The media people arrive on schedule and fortified by wine and canapes exchange the latest gossip about Account changes and Agency personnel moves. They talk about the recent meeting of the Magazine Publishers convention in New York and the forthcoming Newspaper Advertising Executives winter sales conference in Palm Beach. They press Gabriel for details about advertising appropriations and he promises to reveal the figures in a forthcoming news release hinting at sizeable budgets for Alluring Hosiery, Scharfman Brassieres and Heavenly Scents.

The reception ends early because of the increasingly foul weather. The window panes are rattling and the gusting wind is chasing garbage cans along the street.

Saturday October 16. The cyclone that originated over Haiti on the 12th of October and swept up the eastern United States veered west into our region with gale force winds and record precipitation causing flooding and destruction. Of the 147 deaths attributed to Hurrican Hazel 38 occurred on one street alone, Raymond Drive in the suburb of Weston when the swollen waters of the usually tame Humber River carried away a row of low-lying houses.

We escape with a demolished car and a flooded basement in our newly purchased house on Wilson Heights.

4

October 1957. Rabbi Jules Auerbach is pleased with the fundraising brochure prepared by Advertising Services..

-We are nearing the fulfilment of the dream, he sighs contentedly after sabbath dinner in our home. During my three years as a rabbinical student when I commuted from New York as your weekend guest, holding services in public schools I waited for this moment. Now the day is at hand..

-Just imagine what it will be like to worship in our very own Temple, he expands. The eternal light flickering above the ark. The chancel with throne chairs and pulpit. Our sanctuary will reflect the warmth of religious fellowship. That is why our fund-raising dinner must be a success. We value your expertise in the field of Public Relations.

-All the facilities of Advertising Services are at your disposal, assures Gabriel.

-We should exploit the ecumenical aspects of the evening, the presence of the Christian clergy with whom we have established a growing interfaith relationship.

- And the appearance of the star attraction Sammy Arnold should guarantee good press coverage. How about a photograph of Arnold and Alex Davis?

-Good idea. Well-known industrialist and world-famous show business personality. Alex is prepared to contribute a sizable amount to the building fund. Don't forget to include Mrs. Davis.

-We'll pose Beverley in a separate shot with Arnold. She'll likely be wearing one of her haute couture gowns. We'll send copies to the Jewish Review and the society departments of the dailies.

In the ballroom of the Surfside Hotel on the shore of Lake Ontario the members of Temple Beth Torah greet each other effusively, the men in tuxedos and dress shirts, their wives extravagantly-plumaged birds of passage.

The head table personalities are directed to the President's suite on the penthouse floor where they are welcomed by Sheila Brownstone.

-Can I get you something, Rabbi Auerbach?

-I'll settle for a glass of Canada Dry. Nothing stronger, doctor's orders, an old gastric problem.

-You're too young to have a duodenal. If you were in the legal profession like Meyer I could understand. Would you believe he is only thirty-seven? There he is, talking with Rabbi Morgenstern.

-You can be certain, Meyer, that we'll do everything possible to help, declares the rabbi of the senior temple. Our Board is eager to see your group develop into a beacon of spiritual life in the northern reaches of this city but bear in mind that we of the Tree of Life Congregation have pressing needs as well. A new wing for the religious school, a second auditorium, a study for the assistant rabbi as well as enlarged administrative facilities. We'll be embarking on a building campaign of our own and I don't want you to solicit funds from our members. I'm sure you'll do well among your own. How many do you have?

-As of yesterday, 121 families.

-Rabbi Auerbach tells me that some of them are quite well-to-do. They have chosen to affiliate with your Temple instead of ours because of the challenge, I suppose. Well, no matter. We shall enjoy a close relationship.

-I think yours is Dubonnet, right? Sheila Brownstone hands Morgenstern the glass.

-To your good health my dear and to your continuing labours in the vineyard of the Lord. The Jewish life becomes you. I remember the day Meyer brought you to my study to discuss your conversion and how quickly you learned our customs and ceremonies and the role of a Jewish wife. I recall that you received the names Sarah and Rachel after the mothers of Israel. Excuse me my dear but I see the Reverend Walker Stevens has just arrived.

-Ah, there you are, Isaiah. My apologies for being late. I was detained at a counselling session. You understand how it is.

-You are in good time, Walker.

-I trust you are well in body and spirit, rabbi.

-My dear friend, I am beset with the usual intra-mural problems.

-I know what you mean.

-How can a United Church minister possibly appreciate the aggravation faced by a rabbi of a 2,000 family Reform congregation?

-I admire your convictions.

-That's what Judaism is all about. Not just atonement once a year. But to thunder against injustice like my namesake the prophet Isaiah.

-Like inveighing against Christmas carols in the public schools.

-I've had to defend my position before my own Board.

They protest that I am stirring up the animosity of decent Christians.

-Stop fighting so hard. You have left your mark on the community in many ways. Begin to think about your retirement. Ease off. Write your memoirs.

-Can I get you some refreshment, Reverend Stevens? Sheila flashes a beguiling smile.

-I wouldn't mind a small orange juice.

-Certainly. I'll be right back.

-Say Jules, what's the delay? Isn't it time we got started? The senior rabbi is not used to waiting.

-Isn't this a splendid gathering? Fr. Preston Taylor, highball glass in hand, joins the company of the servants of the Lord. By the way I don't recognize anyone from the other Hebrew denominations.

-You can expand ecumenism so far,Rabbi Morgenstern responds. Our form of progressive liberal Judaism is considered heretical by the Orthodox rabbis and we're barely tolerated by the Conservative movement.

Alex Davis arrives with Sammy Arnold, star of stage, screen, radio and television who commands the highest fee of all the entertainers listed in Fund Raising for Religious Institutions.

-Where is my broad, Arnold growls as he removes his suede and alligator oxfords in the V.I.P. suite. He slips off his gold watch, dangling it before the committee members to show them where his name is spelled out on the face in place of the numbers. S A M M Y * A R N O L D. Hey, have you ever seen cuff links like these? Miniature Torahs. They were presented to me in Jerusalem last year by David Ben Gurion. Okay, now get the masseur in here. As the comedian removes his shirt the telephone buzzes. The call is for him, from Hollywood.

-Hello sweetie, how are ya? You're lonely? I'll be back next week. What's that? Sure I miss you. I love you too. Bye sweetie, have to go now. He hangs up, removes the hair piece and wipes his glistening pate. Those broads, they never leave you alone.

The celebrity is draped in a towel when the masseur

arrives. Arnold greets him affectionately, asks about his family, is he making a living?

-My good friend, Wilson Mizner used to say: Be nice to people on your way up because sure as hell you'll meet them on the way down. Okay, I'm ready for my workover.

-Will you look at that physique, Russell Miller the social convenor marvels.

-Pretty good for a guy my age, huh? Would you believe I'll be sixty-eight next month? Be with you after the workout. The committee withdraws to the adjoining room. Twenty minutes later he is finished.

-Hey, fellas, pay the man will ya? Arnold pours himself a tumbler of Chivas Regal. The one-time hoofer who played four a day with the Marx Brothers, with Jolson and Cantor, disappears into the bathroom. His bass rumbles over the splashing of the shower. Tseyna, tseyna, tseyna, tseyna.

Shaved and talcumed and elegantly outfitted, the vaudevillian is escorted to the Presidential Suite.

-Peace be unto the house of Israel, he proclaims. I crave pardon for my tardiness. As it is written in the good book, to be late is human, to forgive divine. It is an honour to be part of such a distinguished gathering.

Sammy Arnold's hooded eyes dart about the room appraising the women. Zelda Posen, willowy in a satin dinner gown, minces over to him.

-Here you are, Mr. Arnold, a double scotch. I know that's your favorite drink. I saw you sipping it on the Late Night Show.

-Oh no, my dear. Theatre people always jest about their alcoholic consumption. Take Dean Martin for example. Pure put on. Do you know what I was imbibing the night you saw me on television? Iced tea. I kid you not as Jack Paar would say. However, I will accept a glass of Carmel Sauvignon Blanc.

-This is a very worthy enterprise you are embarked upon, the building of a House of God. I myself have been involved in such causes all over America for many years. I have spoken at Bond Rallies on behalf of the State of Israel. Synagogues have conferred honourary memberships on me. Your church, Fr. Taylor, has been no less generous in its appreciation of my modest efforts. I reveal with pride that I am the recipient of a medallion from the Society of the Sacred Heart of Jesus. After all, have we not one Father, has not one God created us all? I go wherever needed, offering my humble talent, doing good works in the name of the ineffable Playwright of this ever-beginning, never-ending human drama.

The mummer maunders on, upstaging the clerics until Gabriel manages to draw him aside.

-Here is a list of the important members of the congregation, the ones who are going to set the pace for pledging. I've indicated their occupations, and honours with flattering tid-bits about their families.

-Good thinking. What about pictures?

-My photographer will cover the dinner and the reporters will have their own people. Anna has put together press kits with your bio and background material on the formation of the Temple.

-Get some group shots of me with the clergy. Also a couple of the priest and myself. I want to send them to the Mother Superior of the Ursuline Sisters, the nuns I'm taking on a tour of the Holy Land next summer.

-No problem. We've taken photographs from the moment you arrived.

-Marvellous. I figured as soon as we met, there's a Public Relations pro. If you're ever in Hollywood call me on my private phone number. I know dozens of starlets, the most beautiful shikses who owe me for what I've done for their careers. By the way, who is that red-haired woman, the one talking to the bald gent?

-Ruby Mason and her husband.

- What does hubby do?

-Freddy is a gynaecologist. We've had trouble getting him to pledge as much as we think he should. Says he's still building his practice.

-Leave it to me. I'll compliment him on his position in the community. I've raised a few million for Cedar Sinai and other hospitals.

The congregation is in an alcohol-induced state of euphoria by the time we descend to the ballroom. Russell Miller shouts into the microphone for everyone to be seated. He signals with the lights. It takes a drum roll that ends in a crash of cymbals to produce silence. As the head table personalities enter, the assemblage rises, applauding. Another drum roll and the orchestra plays *O Canada* and then *Hatikvah*.

After Rabbi Morgenstern has blessed the bread the waiters appear bearing trays of tossed salad.

During dinner the orchestra plays songs of the shtetl. The vocalist, sinuous in a silver metallic gown slit to the thigh croons *Vetaheyr Leebeynu* encouraging the diners to sing along with her. Between the courses of vegetable soup and roast beef the congregants dance to the music of Cole Porter.

With the lights turned down the flaming Baked Alaska is brought in and applauded. During coffee the Master of Ceremonies calls for silence.

-Ladies and gentlemen, may I have your attention. We have come to the part of the program that gives meaning to this evening. It is my great honour to present the distinguished head table. Beginning at my extreme right, Father Taylor of Holy Name Church--please hold your applause until I have introduced everybody--George Lewis, Chairman of the Temple Mortgage and Financing Committee and his charming wife, Alex Davis our Building Fund Chairman and Mrs. Davis, Our own Rabbi Auerbach. The next gentleman needs no introduction. On his left, Sheila Brownstone President of the Sisterhood, our good friend and mentor Rabbi Morgenstern of the Tree of Life Congregation, Meyer Brownstone, President of the Temple Beth Torah, the Reverend Stevens, minister of Cambridge United Church, my lovely wife and myself Chick Martin, President of the Brotherhood. Now it is my pleasure to call upon Rabbi Auerbach to say a few words.

-Rabbi Morgenstern, Reverend Walker, Fr. Taylor, members of Temple Beth Torah. Our sages tell the story of the man who came to the rabbi and implored, help me. I am old and a sinner and I want very much to die like a good, upright Jew. To which the rabbi replied: Why do you worry about dying like an upright Jew? Better live like one and you'll surely die like one. And that my friends is the reason we are assembled here. Tonight each of us is re-affirming an act of faith. Not the *Auto da Fe* that forced our brethren during the Spanish Inquisition to confess their Jewish heresy or perish on the Quemadoro or to worship secretly in underground places while purporting to accept conversion but a proud, voluntary commitment to the God of our fathers.

-In our reaching and wandering age we need a spiritual home, a place to pause. In our Temple we and our children shall grow in strength and security by knowing the sources of our faith. We shall share with friends and families the passing of the days of our years. If we but will it--it will be no dream.

The Auerbach delivery is smooth, the articulation precise with a hint of Boston back bay. His appeal receives a warm response. Meyer Brownstone is called next.

-We are committing ourselves tonight to the building of a House of Worship for ourselves, for our children and for future generations. The phenomenal growth of the congregation is outstripping our capacity to provide service through temporary facilities and voluntary help. We have been meeting in a church basement and we shall require a hall for the High Holy Days. The erection of the Temple therefore is a matter of sheer necessity. Here then is an opportunity that can be expected to present itself only once in a lifetime. Let us meet this challenge with zeal, with dedication and with faith in our ultimate success.

As the traffic to the bar resumes, Chick Martin begs for order and introduces the next speaker, the spiritual leader of the Tree of Life Congregation.

Isaiah Morgenstern rising slowly looks out upon the membership, willing it to silence. He speaks at last, saluting his fellow clergymen and the esteemed guest from the entertainment capital of the United States. While tonight is a momentous occasion charged with the promise of achievement he knows all too well the difficulties of attaining goals, for he himself has encountered delays and frustrations in the seventeen years of service to his congregation. He has no doubt however that Temple Beth Torah will be built and that future generations will tell the story of how this came to pass.

Morgenstern embarks upon the history of Reform Judaism in Germany in response to the Enlightenment. He cites the contribution of Moses Mendelssohn, the Orthodox Jew and towering intellect (the grandfather of Felix) who translated the Bible into German.

The rabbi now chronicles the dedication in 1818 of the Hamburg Temple, the West London Synagogueue 24 years later and at the start of the twentieth century the establishment of the Union Israelite Liberals in Paris.

-The Reform Movement in the U.S. had its beginnings in Charleston, South Carolina, where as far back as 1824 members of the Beth Elohim Congregation petitioned the trustees to have the important prayers read in English and an English sermon delivered each week. Reform Temples sprang up in Baltimore, New York, Chicago and Philadelphia by the middle of the nineteenth century. In 1856 the first synagogueue was established in Toronto and became the forerunner of the Tree of Life Temple which introduced the use of the organ, the seating of men and women together, the introduction of shorter services.

When the coughing in the hall begins Rabbi Morgentstern terminates the history lesson but his oratory flows in other channels. The censure of Senator Joseph McCarthy, the dispatch of a thousand paratroopers to Little Rock Arkansas to permit nine black students to attend the all-white High School and the launching by the Soviet Union this very day, Saturday October 5, 1957 of Sputnik the artificial space satellite. He expatiates on the presence of God in the arrangement of the stars and planets and the wonders of the universe. But he is no longer capable of holding his audience who drift away to the bar. Sammy Arnold whispers to Sheila that in the theatrical profession there was always the hook to remove a tiresome performer.

-And so I greet you with heartfelt felicitations. We of the Tree of Life Congregation are filled with joy and pride like a mother when her child realizes a dream that both have shared. May God grant you courage and wisdom that you may go from strength to strength. And finally...

As Morgenstern reaches for the water glass a sporadic handclapping starts that is taken up on all sides. Those on the rostrum are applauding as well. The rabbi retires.

The mood in the ballroom of the Surfside Hotel shifts from boredom to expectancy but there are Memorials to be endowed in enduring bronze or glass or stone, a perpetual blessing to a cherished one. Some have already been spoken for: the Eternal Light, Candelabra, Kiddush Cup and Sabbath Candle Sticks but others like the Ark, the Rabbi's study and the Bridal Room are still available.

-And now the moment we've all been waiting for, announces Chick Martin. I have the privilege of presenting one of the great personalities of our time, a member of the Lambs Club and Variety Club, a gentleman who has met with Presidents of the United States and the President of Israel, a true son of Zion who also finds time to speak on behalf of religious institutions of other faiths and for worthy secular causes as well. Mr. Showbusiness himself, the one and only Sammy Arnold.

The audience rises in tribute. Arnold adjusts the microphone, takes a sip of water, clears his throat and looks out at the adoring faces.

-Thank you Mr. Martin, the gravelly voice fills the hall. Reverend sirs, Mr. President, Committee Chairmen, Ladies and Gentlemen. The compliments about my unworthy self reminds me of the minister who was called to deliver the eulogy over a stranger. His comments were so flattering that at last the widow couldn't control herself any longer. She got up from her seat and approached the casket to see if the figure reposing in it was actually her husband.

-I wish to say how pleased I am to be here tonight although I must confess that this is my two thousandth kosher dinner and that reminds me of the customer in the Jewish restaurant in the lower east side of New York who ordered roast duck. I'm sorry, the waiter replied, we have no roast duck today, only roast goose. Tell the boss I want roast duck, the customer repeated. The waiter told the owner, Mr. Goldberg wants roast duck. Tell him we have no roast duck, only roast goose. I told him but he insisted on having roast duck. The owner sighed, All right, tell the cook to cut a portion of duck from the roast goose.

-This evening I had the distinct pleasure of meeting the officers of your Temple and I was indeed impressed with their qualities of leadership. I said to myself, the God of Israel who neither slumbereth nor sleepeth could take a little nap tonight because the work of the Lord is in very good hands. It is further enhanced by the presence of the representatives of the Christian denominations and I am reminded of the following story. At a gathering not unlike this one, four clergymen challenged each other to reveal their vices. The United Church minister confided that he consumed a bottle of Scotch every day. I'm crazy about pork spare ribs, admitted the rabbi. The priest confessed that he had a girl friend. It was the turn of the Presbyterian who when pressed for his secret sin shrugged. I like to gossip.

-I remember the time my good friend Bishop Fulton J. Sheen was honoured at the film awards dinner. Each recipient in accepting the award thanked somebody. When the Bishop received his citation he stepped up to the microphone and said humbly, I want to pay tribute to my writers, Matthew, Mark, Luke and John.

Sammy Arnold's anecdotes, his jokes and asides elicit bursts of laughter. Now he segues into the role of super salesman. His friend David Ben Gurion the Prime Minister of Israel told him that the Jewish State's survival depends in large measure on the strength of the Jewish communities in the diaspora and that every time a new house of worship is dedicated Jews everywhere in the world feel more secure.

Arnold praises the women of Beth Torah. As for the men, he has never met so many professionals in one gathering. Show him a Jewish boy who doesn't go to medical school and he'll show you a lawyer or a dentist or accountant. The comedian reaches for the water glass, waiting for the laughter to diminish before continuing. He has met Alex Davis and other members of the Temple who have made their marks in the construction of shopping centres and office buildings, apartment complexes and stately homes. Their experience will be indispensable in raising up a new House of Worship. Those present tonight are being asked to contribute. Each person shall give as he is able to give and he shall be blessed in the giving, says the Torah. Arnold himself pledges a portion of his fee. During the applause that follows he whispers to Davis, I'll have my agent send you a cheque.

As arranged, the wealthier members rise to announce their financial commitment followed by others less endowed by fortune. Beverley Davis pledges regular amounts from her chequing account. The other women are ready to make offerings in honour of bar mitzvahs and baby namings.

Chick Martin presents a cheque for $3,550, proceeds from the Brotherhood Cadillac Draw. Sheila Brownstone contributes $476 realized at the Sisterhood Rummage Sale. Rabbi Auerbach divulges that he is contributing ten per cent of his salary and Fr. Taylor quips that this is known as the tithe that binds.

As the campaign begins to flag Sammy Arnold is on his feet again with the story about Joe Frisco the stuttering comic.

-So, Joe buys this painting of The Last Supper at an actors' charity function. After a few bad days at the track he takes the work of art to a pawnshop. The pawnbroker looks it over and says he doesn't know much about paintings depicting Jesus and His disciples at The Last Supper. What do you think it's worth, he asks Frisco. Well, says Joe after some consideration, at least t-t-t-ten dollars a p-p-p-late.

The committee has been tallying the pledges and announces that the evening's objective has been oversubscribed. This revelation merits resounding applause. Chick Martin calls on the Reverend Walker Stevens for the benediction and a hush descends among the bowed heads as the minister requests the blessings of the Lord upon the congregation. The dancing and drinking resume. Gabriel rescues Sammy Arnold from his admirers explaining that members of the press are anxious to interview him.

The Arnold suite is crowded with journalists and photographers. Drink in hand he is ready to answer their questions. Who is his current female companion? How much alimony does he owe? What about the paternity suit he is facing? The Canadian Broadcasting Corporation would like half an hour with him for the Arts Tonight radio program.

-Sure thing, sweetie. You'll excuse me, gentlemen, while I talk with this lovely young lady. But first I need to take something for my indigestion. And that reminds me. A Jew and a Christian were arguing about their heritage. The Christian spieled off all the accomplishments of his people in music, art and literature. To which the Jew replied indignantly, that's nothing, when your ancestors were picking up acorns in the forest mine already had diabetes.

It is after midnight when the reception committee and the media people have departed. Mr. Show Business is in the bathroom. As Gabriel and I are about to leave there is a knock on the door. The visitor is a young woman with an overnight case.

5

Gabriel's Advertising Agency has relocated to the seventh floor of a new building on Eglinton Avenue. To service the growing client list he has hired artists, copy writers and a television producer.

Caryl Chessman, convicted in 17 counts of robbery, kidnapping and attempted rape in 1948, is executed at San Quentin despite appeals for his life by Albert Schweitzer, Pablo Casals, Aldous Huxley and thousands of others. In the past 12 years during which he received 8 stays of execution Chessman taught himself law and wrote four books, including *Cell 2455 Death Row*, which sold half a million copies.

1961
April 12. The USSR puts the first man into space. Yuri Gagarin completes one orbit of the earth in 108 minutes.

April 17. The 1500 Cubans who landed at the Bay of Pigs are killed or captured within 3 days. They were trained and armed in Guatemala by the CIA.

May 4. Thirteen Freedom Riders leave Washington DC

for New Orleans to test the desegregation of public facilities. En route their ranks swell to twenty-seven. The two buses are attacked and fire bombed in Birmingham and Montgomery, Alabama and in Jackson, Mississippi.

August 13. East Germany builds the Berlin Wall, closing access from East to West Berlin and blocking the flight of refugees to the West.

December 11. Two US military companies arrive in South Vietnam. They include 12 helicopters and 4,000 men assigned to Vietnam units but under US orders to fire only if fired upon.

1962
January 26. Orson Welles' 1941 film Citizen Kane is voted the best movie ever made in a poll of 70 film critics from 11 countries. It had failed to win any of the major Academy Awards including best picture, best director and best actor categories.

February 20. John Glenn orbits the earth 3 times in space capsule Friendship Seven and is seen on television by 135 million viewers.

August 5. Marilyn Monroe is found dead of a barbiturate overdose in her Los Angeles home. The death of the sex goddess is declared a suicide.

October 23. The US blockades Cuba after announcing that reconnaissance photographs show the existence of Cuban-Russian missiles capable of sending nuclear bombs one thousand miles into America. The US threatens to invade Cuba if the bases are not dismantled. Russia threatens nuclear war.

October 28. Russia agrees to withdraw the missiles and dismantle the bases.

January 1,1963
The guests begin to arrive at noon for our New Year's Day Levee. We have invited advertising people, journalists, actors, writers, artists and old friends. By evening the house rings with bonhomie.

-How's the wife, Rory?
-We're not living together.

-Sorry to hear that.

-It was bound to happen. She hated the advertising business. But I was making good money as an Account Executive and we were living in great style.

-Why did you split?

-Mainly because of the booze. I was hung over most of the time. And often I had to stay late at the hotel entertaining clients. Julie didn't like that. So after several ultimatums she checked out.

John Kandell, theatre director, arrives in the hearse that he uses to transport the family and the St. Bernard. Says he gets a lot of respect from the other drivers. The kids enjoy riding in it and wave from the windows. Sure startles people.

-I know my love by his way of walking and I know my love by his way of talking. Colleen's reedy soprano. *Well I know my love in his jersey blue and if my love leaves me what shall I do?*

Judd Flack removes the paintings from his portfolio. The series of 37 signed prints depicting the legends of the human race in a limited edition of 150 will sell for a thousand dollars. Many libraries and museums have already subscribed. They'll be worth twice as much a year from now, he insists. Wisps of white hair protrude from the beret that covers the cadaverous head.

Amidst the dishes and cutlery, the cups and saucers and flickering candles I set out the roast turkey and the French bread aromatic with garlic butter. The guests surge toward the table.

-Gabriel me lad, do you have a gargle?

-How about the mulled wine?

-Ah, to be sure, there's the wine, Patrick O'Rourke admits. But is there not any usquebaugh on the premises?

-Not a bottle.

-I'm not believin ye. What kind of Israelite house is it without a drop of the craythur?

-Who might ye be? O'Rourke squints up at the bow tie.

-Dr. Stephen Rosza.

-Would ye have the kindness to inform me what is the cause of the ache in me back? 'Tis sometimes accompanied by dazzling lights in the head.

-I'm not a general practitioner. I counsel patients with sexual dysfunction.

-Is there a treatment for such a problem? I might be interested.

-Come to my clinic. We have group sessions.

-Is it all gab, then?

-We have a social hour afterwards with refreshments.

-Do you mean drink?

-Coffee, tea, biscuits. No alcoholic beverages.

-Ah well, I 'm afraid I wouldn't have the time. I'm after working on a literary project, do ye see?

Sniffling, he shuffles away.

-He's up to his arse in cadging. A remittance man stuffing his gob and blathering away, never doing a day's work. I've seen the likes of him in many a Dublin pub. These professional Irishmen make me sick.

-May I enquire what vocation you follow? asks Dr. Rosza.

-I'm an electrical engineer. Hugh Riordan is my name. My wife and I are from Dublin. We have been over here for three years.

-I suppose she is occupied with the children.

-Ah no, she's a forensic sociologist. She spends two days a week up in Penetanguishene at the Hospital for the Criminally Insane. She is completing her dissertation on Social Dysfunction as a Determinant of Sexual Interaction.

-I don't suppose you have problems with sexual interaction?

-Not at all. We just enjoy it.

-The missionary position I take it. The Christian clergy exalts the face to face connection. The Shulchan Aruch, the Jewish code of laws rejects any other technique for achieving orgasm.

But sophisticated, I should say emancipated, people will agree that getting there is half the fun. There are more byways than highways. Take cunnilingus for example.

-I am not keen on that.

-The lure of the female loins, the most compelling scent in all creation, the reason animals are always smelling and licking each other. Do you know that a million varieties of male insects are aroused to frenzied sexual activity by the aromatic outpourings from the female sex organs?

-Potent perfume indeed.

-The female moth or the ordinary housefly can atomize from the tip of her abdomen a millionth of a gram of sex hormone that will tantalize a male several miles away. Do you know what would happen if humans had that power? The same minute amount of vaginal emission from one woman living in Winnipeg would cause a stampede of all the men on the east coast. Have you ever watched the chimpanzees at the zoo enjoying cunnilingus? Horses, cows, cats, alligators, bears, even elephants do it.

-Is that a fact!

-Among some primitive African tribes the woman inserts a small fish into her vagina and the man arouses her by sucking it out. Then he eats it.

-Thirty-nine. I have thirty-nine lines in the play. It opens next week at the Waverley Theatre.

-My book should be out in the spring. I call it *Love's Drolleries*. Twenty-seven poems. A total of two hundred and one lines.

-I should like to sing a lament written by the blind poet Anthony Raftery from County Mayo about the drowning of 18 people near Galway in the early nineteenth century. Maureen's fingers caress the strings of the Irish harp. Her keening soprano flutters like a wounded sparrow.

-Goodnight my dear hostess. It has been a splendid evening.

-I'm so glad you could come, Dr. Rosza.

-Watch out for him, Anna. He is descended from a line of vampires.

-Only when is full moon.

-Have another glass before you leave.

-I do not drink...wine.

Four o'clock in the morning. The weariness is setting in as our guests bid their parting salute to the new year. Alone at last I survey the debris. Wine stains and candle drippings on the table cloth. Cigaret butts in the coffee cups. The carcass of the turkey. Fr. Desmond Fitzgerald, S.J. is staying over so he can celebrate mass at St. Margaret's around the corner. Put out the lights. Clean up to-morrow.

Moonlight bathes the bedroom. In the den the priest is chanting Tantum Ergo Sacramentum. Gabriel cannot sleep. Besieged by intimations of mortality he stands at the window looking out at the dark-blue sky as he murmurs the familiar litany. Time driveth onward and in a little while our lips are dumb. How futile the storing up of possessions. The grand house, two cars, country cottage. The alcoholic dependency. The sexual exacerbations. Vanity of vanities. All things ripen toward the grave. Ripen and fall and cease.

Gabriel infused every activity with an intense energy in an effort to arrest the moment, convinced that death was waiting for him in the small hours of the night although the men in his family aged well into their nineties. I cited those hoary participants at life's feast: Bertrand Russell, Buckminster Fuller, Count Basie and Colonel Harlan Saunders.

The civil rights demonstrations in the United States concerned him. The segregation protests in Birmingham, Jackson, Nashville and Atlanta. The march on Washington headed by Martin Luther King. The murder of Mississippi civil rights leader Medgar Evers.

Friday November 22, 1963

President John Fitzgerald Kennedy, riding in the Dallas motorcade, is shot while waving to the crowds at Dealey Plaza.

We watch on-the-spot television coverage of the assassination followed by documentaries detailing the shootings of Presidents Lincoln and McKinley as well as the attempted murders of Andrew Jackson, Theodore Roosevelt, Franklin D. Roosevelt and Harry Truman. The conspiracy theories to prove that Lee Harvery Oswald had not acted alone. The solemn procession with muffled drums, the clop, clop of horses' hooves, the iron ring of the caisson wheels, the honour guard and Hail to the Chief repeated along the funeral route.

As it was in the beginning. After God created the heavens and the earth. And after God created Man in his own image. Cain slew Abel. And Jael hammered a spike through the head of Sisera while he slept. And Medea did away with Pelias in a vat of poison and Clytemnestra axed Agamemnon in his bath. And Brutus pierced Caesar and Mark Antony dispatched Cicero. And Thomas à Becket was murdered in Canterbury Cathedral and Czars Paul 1, Alexander 11 and Nicholas 11 were silenced and so was Rasputin. The assassination of Archduke Ferdinand of Austria precipitated the grand orgy that had *God On Our Side* and *Gott Mit Uns* on the other. And Leon Trotsky was felled with an ice pick in Mexico. And Mohandas Karamchand Gandhi. And Che Guevara. And Patrice Lumumba. And...

Gabriel's Public Relations business prospers and we continue to give dinner parties and attend social functions.

And the carousel of time whirls on ever more swiftly.

6

Wed. May 19, 1965. Our first trip to London with the Toronto Men's Press Club. We look forward to a week of discovery before continuing to Dublin.

A visit to St. Paul's. Christopher Wren designed the Cathedral to replace the old one that was almost destroyed in 1666 during the Great Fire of London. His fee was 200 pounds, the cost of construction 736,762 pounds, 2 shillings, 3 pence, 1 farthing. It was completed in 1708 but repairs began almost immediately and have continued to meet the exigencies of time and fortune. In September 1940 a delayed-action bomb buried itself 27 feet in the ground near the clock tower and was removed by the disposal squad. The following month a missile penetrated the outer roof of the choir and destroyed the altar. In April 1941 a bomb destroyed the portico inside the north door and most of the stained glass. Restoration was completed seventeen years later. The new high altar was unveiled as a memorial to the men and women of the Commonwealth who died during World War Two. The American Memorial Chapel commemorates the sacrifices of the British and American peoples and in particular the US Servicemen whose names are recorded on the roll of honour.

The Cathedral is again under repair, laced with scaffolding. Help Save St. Paul's, urges the fund-raising brochure.

The Tate Gallery given to the nation in 1892 by Sir Henry Tate occupies the site of the old Millbank Prison. Extensions effected through the generosity of Sir Joseph Duveen house the Turner seascapes and a sculpture court. The collection contains paintings by Blake, Hogarth and the Pre-Raphaelites as well as works by the Impressionists, Futurists, Dadaists, Surrealists, American Abstract Expressionism and Pop Art.

Alberto Giacometti's bronze sculptures including Head of Diego are on display. We admire Henry Moore's Recumbent Figure and Barbara Hepworth's hollowed, wooden shapes.

Standing on the embankment watching the marine activity on the Thames I imagine London during the war, blacked out with barrage balloons riding over the city and Tower Bridge, the anti-aircraft gun emplacements in the parks. Sandbags piled outside buildings, store windows taped against the bomb blasts, the Home Guard on duty near Whitehall, the civilians going about their chores, carrying the government-issued gas masks. The children evacuated to the country. Troops at Victoria Station, motor convoys on Waterloo Bridge. In the face of the terror of the air raids, the breaking down of social barriers, the pubs resounding with Roll Out the Barrels and Knees Up Mother Brown. The undertrained crews of the Royal Air Force in patched up Spitfires and Hurricanes during the Battle of Britain forcing thousands of German bombers and fighters to retreat across the

English Channel. Churchill's ringing declaration that 'Never in the field of human conflict was so much owed by so many to so few'.

Saturday May 22, 1965. Through the rain-spattered window of our room in the Rubens Hotel we can see the guard in his hooded waterproof astride a caped horse emerging from the Royal Mews of Buckingham Palace. By the time we have finished our breakfast of gammon and eggs, tea and toast in the dining room the sun has appeared and a rainbow arcs away toward Kensington Gardens.

The Underground takes us to Notting Hill Gate and we walk the rest of the way to Portobello Road. The tintinnabulation of cymbals and the beat of hand drums signal the arrival of the Hare Krishna procession, saffron robed apostles with shaven heads chanting Hare, Hare, Hare Rama. Stalls display pewter mugs, silver napkin rings, brass hunting horns. Baubles and bangles. A parrot on a perch selects cards of fortune from a tray. A street musician tootles on a recorder.

After a ploughman's lunch at the local pub we rummage among the book stalls where Gabriel discovers two volumes in grey paper covers: *Ulysses* by James Joyce. Published by the Odyssey Press in Hamburg in December 1932. Not to be introduced into the British Empire or the USA. This edition revised by Stuart Gilbert at the request of Joyce is considered the most accurate text of *Ulysses*. The plates were reportedly destroyed in the bombing of Hamburg during the war. Gabriel pays the bookseller 17 shillings and six pence.

Tonight at Sadlers Wells we enjoy a performance of *Orpheus in the Underworld* by Jacques Offenbach, a delightful satire on the Orpheus myth. A late supper of Tandoori chicken at an Indian Restaurant. A leisurely stroll about Picadilly. And so to bed.

Monday May 24, 1965. The express train from London arrives at Holyhead on the northwest tip of Wales about three in the morning and we board the Sealink ferry, separated from the tourist passengers who are huddled together in the dark.

In the brightly lighted first class lounge children are bedded down beside their parents. Old folk sit unseeing, eyes veiled in memories. A collegium of priests occupies the comfortable easy chairs. Well-fed representatives of the Holy See, their soutanes freshly-laundered, their boots well-heeled. The lay travellers acknowledge the presence of the clergy with practised deference and the Fathers return the greetings with blessings and the assurance that the Lord will set their feet firmly on land again. As the S.S. Hibernia holds to its course in the choppy waters of the Irish Sea the men collect at the bar for Guinness and Irish Whisky. The priests, breviaries resting on skirted laps, sip brandy. The steady thrum of the engines indicates that all is well.

Seven o'clock. We arrive at Dun Laoghaire to the squawking welcome of gulls. Drizzly morning. On the landing the Gardai stand politely observing. At Irish Customs and Immigration the questions are perfunctory, the concern is with Hoof and Mouth disease; have we been in contact with cattle during our stay in Britain. Since we have nothing to declare, the official marks the luggage with chalk and directs us to the siding. Squeezed into a compartment with a family of five we have a forty minute wait until the train chugs away from King Leary's fort and the seven and a half mile panorama of sea and strand unreels. Cockle pickers are already poking in the mud flats. The Pigeon House power station flashes by. Sandymount strand. Dublin.

In Westland Row station the loungers regard us idly. Gabriel observes that the paralysis of the city is as manifest this grey morning as it must have appeared to the bespectacled young man who fled to Paris at the beginning of the century. At the taxi rank an emaciated driver stows our bags into the trunk of his car.

-Jury's Hotel on Dame Street.

-Indeed I know it, sir. Haven't I been taking fine people like yourselves there a thousand times. It is but a short distance. By the by, have you heard about Dr. Martin Luther King leading all those marchers in Chicago? Over five hundred of them have been arrested. And aren't you glad to be getting away from

America for a while?

-We're Canadians. Although we share a four thousand mile undefended border we have our own government and our own attitudes which sometimes differ from those of our neighbour.

-Well now, Canada is a grand country to be sure and wouldn't I be the first to admit that the Canadians are darlin' people. I've said it many a time, d-a-a-r-lin' people.

-A Joxer by God. Our first few minutes in Dublin and we encounter a Joxer, marvels Gabriel.

-And why shouldn't you? the cabbie responds. The land is full of them. Did you think O'Casey invented Joxer Boyle out of his imagination. You'll see Joxers all about. And high-spirited women as well.

-I'd like to meet Molly Bloom.

-Who is she when she's at home?

-Do you mean you aren't familiar with James Joyce's bountifully bestowed earth mother, the raven-haired Molly with the Spanish eyes?

-Ah to be sure, the one in *Ulaysses*. The priests got very worked up over that book but sure you can find copies of it any day in Hodges Figgis. But I'm more keen on O'Casey. That was a boyo who wrote about the working man. And he didn't have much good to say about the church either. O'Casey is very popular with the tourists. They're always flocking to see *Juno and the Paycock* at the Abbey Theatre. John Synge is very popular too. *The Playboy of the Western World*, you know. Well, here we are and it's a grand stay I'm wishing you both.

After we have registered in Jury's modernized 18th century hotel Gabriel and I explore Dublin's fair city. O'Connell Street. Parnell Square. Dorset Street. On Eccles Street, number 7 stands desolate, the windows shattered, the roof partially torn away. The door is open and we pick our way through the gutted interior of the fictional Bloom domicile. I notice the wallpaper in Molly's bedroom. Faded roses.

Maeve O'Neill from Bord Failte greets us at the Martello Tower where Joyce's brief residence is to become a Museum. The stone walls have already been whitewashed. Soon they will be installing the display cases and hanging pictures and posters. The dampness is chilling.

-Mammy knows a lot about James Joyce, would you like to meet her? She can take you all over and show you places and things. I'll phone her.

We have coffee with Maeve's mother in a Grafton Street cafe. Maureen O'Neill is a silver-haired widow with a wan smile and soft words. She will be pleased to take us on a tour of the eleven Joyce residences, starting with 41 Brighton Square where Jimmy was born on February 2, 1882. We get into Maureen's four passenger Morris and as the hours pass we visit Rathmines, Blackwood, Mountjoy Square, Drumcondra, North Richmond Street and the three locations in Fairview as John Stanislaus Joyce moved his family from one address to another in a descending spiral of economic debilitation. At No. 8 Royal Terrace the unshaven occupant in trousers and undershirt sings out a cheery greeting.

-Cead mille failte. Are you over here on a pilgrimage or what? The Joyce family lived in this very house in May of 1900. Come in and I will show you something of interest.

We follow him into the hall where he brings forth a cardboard box from the closet.

-Ye see these bits of coloured glass, they're from the original fanlight. I've been thinking I might let some American university have them. Will you accept one of these pieces? I take it you are admirers of Mr. Joyce?

Gabriel offers him payment, which he refuses at first; then he accepts the one pound note.

-Wasn't that kind of the old codger? Gabriel inspects the glass as Maureen starts the car.

-A piece of the true cross, Maeve retorts.

-You've been codded, agrees Maureen. A popular Irish pastime, fooling the tourists. I dare say you are the hundred and seventy-seventh recipient of a shard from the original fanlight of No. 8 Royal Terrace.

At Sandymount Strand we stop beside the Star of the Sea Church and walk along Leahy Terrace down to the rock where Leopold Bloom spied on Gertie. 'Oh sweetie, all your little girlwhite up I saw', quotes Gabriel as mother and daughter continue ahead.

-You've offended them, I chide.

-I'm sure they're familiar with the Gertie MacDowell chapter in *Ulysses*. I doubt they're observing Catholics.

-Didn't you notice they dipped their fingers in the holy water as we left the church? Come on, let's catch up with them.

Merrion Square is our next stop. This bit of Georgian Dublin is still a fashionable district, says Maureen. Oscar Wilde resided here with his father Sir William, the famous eye surgeon and his mother the poet who wrote under the name of Speranza. W.B. Yeats lived here as well. Maeve says the square belongs to the Archbishop of Dublin. It was bought as the site of a Cathedral but the Irish have a way of putting things off.

-Stephen's Green. Stephen Dedalus calls it 'my green' in A Portrait of the Artist as a Young Man. It was laid out by Sir Arthur Guinness at his expense in 1880 for the public enjoyment.

-You can see the memorial to Wolfe Tone and next to it the construction of an Irish family depicting the disaster of '98.

-Very moving.

-The Mansion House. Maeve points to the official residence of the Lord Mayor of Dublin. On January 21, 1919, the first Dail Eireann, our Irish Parliament, met there.

We drive past the National Museum and The National Gallery. Switzer's and Brown Thomas on Grafton Street. Trinity College, founded in 1591 by the first Elizabeth and rebuilt in the 18th and 19th centuries with figures of Burke and Goldsmith by the main gate. Facing Trinity is the statue of Henry Grattan, who resisted the Act of Union. Across the road the sooty bulk of the Bank of Ireland, formerly the Irish House of Commons. On to Dame Street formerly known as Dame's Gate after St. Mary.

-Here we are at last, Maureen pulls up before Jury's.

-Thank you for showing us around.

-Not at all. It was a pleasant outing for me, a welcome change from being indoors at my memoirs. Tell me, what is your agenda for this evening? I was hoping you could join us at The Pearl on Fleet Street. About eight o'clock. You can? Splendid.

They are already seated in the upstairs lounge. Mother and daughter, son Patrick and his girl friend. After the drinks have been ordered Patrick announces that the discussion this evening will be about Irish culture.

-Let us begin with a consideration of Irish poetry which is rooted in ancient mists and nourished by rural speech with a reputation for eloquence.

The talk ranges across the first centuries of the Christian era, the influence of the Bible, the lives of the Irish saints Patrick, Brigid and Columba and the oral tradition of the Shanachies.

The discourse turns to an examination of Irish art beginning with the Lion of St. Mark in the Book of Durrow and its magical healing powers. The Tara Brooch. The Cross of Muiredach at Monasterboice dating from the 9th century with the detailed carvings of scriptural scenes. The eight inch high shrine enclosed in patterned plates of silver and gold created in the 8th century. The Ardagh Chalice studded with rock crystal and enriched with silver and gold tracery. The illuminated figure of St. John the Evangelist in the Book of Kells.

Gabriel brings up the subject of Irish Catholicism and we are launched into a disquisition on the uncompromising attitude of the clergy in matters of contraception, pre and extra-marital sex and control by the church of diverse aspects of the temporal life which in other countries are considered matters for the secular authorities. Gabriel urges our companions around the table to embrace the concept of rationalism but debate is averted by the call of 'Time, gentlemen, please'. We part, vowing to meet again.

Our walk back to the hotel brings us to Fishamble Street. At the site of Kennan's Iron Works a plaque memorializes the Music Hall where on April 13, 1742 George Frederick Handel conducted the first performance of *Messiah* as a benefit for three of Dublin's charitable organizations. The event took place at noon with an orchestra of thirty-five and a chorus of twelve. Ladies were requested not to wear hoop skirts (circumference nine yards) in order to get as many as possible into the hall and 700 were accommodated. Among the soloists was the mezzo-soprano Mrs. Cibber, sister of the composer Thomas Arne and wife of Theophilus Cibber, son of the Poet Laureate Colley Cibber.

In 1859 at the Crystal Palace Sir Michael Costa conducted *Messiah* with an orchestra of 460 and 2765 in the chorus, and the entire audience (as had become the custom since the time of George 1) rose for the Hallelujah chorus.

Our last night in Dublin we dine on saddle of lamb in Jury's Copper Grill. The stone fireplace, mahogany panelling, copper murals and sage green furnishings provide a pleasant atmosphere. Music from Jury's Irish Cabaret trickles in from the dining room. *When I play my fiddle in Dooney.* The baritone rendering of *Father O'Flynn*. Tap dancers. Accordion and Pipes.

The waiter arrives with Irish coffee and as he sets the steaming glasses on the table reveals the secret recipe: Cream rich as an Irish brogue, coffee strong as a friendly hand, sugar sweet as the tongue of a rogue and whisky smooth as the wit of the land.

June 1, 1965. Home again. A letter from Fleur Darlington grants Gabriel permission to stage the Canadian premiere of *Ulysses in Nighttown*, her adaptation from the novel of James Joyce.

Gabriel's fascination with the theatre started at an early age. On stage at the age of twelve in *A Midsummer Night's Dream* at St. Christopher House. Gilbert and Sullivan in High School.

Every Friday night, seated in the back row of the Standard Theatre, adrift on a sea of enchantment enjoying the plays of Avrom Goldfadn the Father of Yiddish Theatre: A song, a jig, a quarrel, a kiss. Delighting in the antics of Molly Picon and Leo Fuchs. All the stars of the Yiddish stage appeared at the Standard including Jacob Adler, Maurice Schwartz and Boris Thomashefsky. Jacob Ben Ami striving for a truly Yiddish Art Theatre patterned after the Russian experiments of Constantin Stanislavsky created a cohesive company with no star system, dedicated to literary excellence, aesthetic distance and suspension of disbelief.

Gabriel appeared in the Dramsec Theatre's presentation of *Spinoza the Maker of Lenses*, presented in celebration of the tercentenary of the birth of the 17th century Jewish philosopher of Amsterdam. In white beard and wig the fifteen year old actor was transformed into an aged member of the congregation demanding of the Chief Rabbi that Spinoza be cast out for his heresies.

Gabriel joined the Theatre Project troupe for Sidney Kingsley's *The World We Make* with rehearsals held in a loft downtown. Cast as the foreman of a laundry and searching for truth in character he worked for a week at the Home Laundry on Harbord Street, and by the time the play opened he had achieved the Inner Creative State demanded by the director. The play ran three weeks to good notices. The cast party was interrupted by police who confiscated the beer and laid charges under the Liquor Control Act. Theatre Project disintegrated..

Gabriel drifted to Peter Burley's Masquers, who performed in the basement of a factory opposite the Toronto Hospital. Goatee'd Peter Burley directed the plays, constructed the sets, sold the tickets and drew the curtain. To open the season he chose Andreyev's *He Who Gets Slapped* with Gabriel as Papa Briquet, the manager of a provincial circus.

Gabriel's passion for the circus had begun at age thirteen. As a member of the Circus Fans Association of America he was permitted to carry water for the elephants when Ringling Brothers came to town. He could sit with the troupers listening to their stories about the notch houses that were off limits. The joeys talked about the great clowns of the past like Grimaldi and Grock. Claus Narr the natural fool. Pagliaccio the Italian clown whose name meant chopped straw.

Gabriel was there when they put up the Big Top helping the guying-out crew work their way around the tent, taking up the slack in the canvas to the chanting of the rope caller: Take it, shake it, make it, break it, walk along. The command of the big boss: Speak your Latin. The rope caller's response: Ah, heebie, hebby, hobby, hole, golong.

Gabriel performed the role of Papa Briquet in *He Who Gets Slapped* with undeniable authority.

He is ready for the production of *Ulysses in Nighttown* with himself in the role of Leopold Bloom.

February 1966

Rehearsals are held in an empty warehouse. Gradually the actors learn to make sense of their lines in all the Joycean prose-fusion.

The advance publicity begins to appear in the media. Scene Magazine: The director of *Ulysses in NIghttown* advises us that he needs a mongrel dog who can play dead, roll over and obey other commands. Should be used to playing opposite women in various stages of undress. Show Business: Those four letter words won't be deleted despite threats of visits from the police. Globe: Fleur Darlington arrived yesterday for the Canadian premiere of *Ulysses in Nighttown*. Seated in the lobby of the theatre in the Lotus position the 74-year-old grandmother admitted there is a lot of erotic material in her play.

The day of the dress rehearsal we move the set into the theatre and cue visual and sound effects. The run-through doesn't begin until after midnight. It goes badly with missed cues and delayed entrances but everybody believes in the superstition of bad dress rehearsal, good opening.

The advertising and publicity have generated a lot of interest and advance ticket sales are encouraging. On opening night every seat is occupied.

Curtain up. Act One. Stephen Dae dalus broods on the death of his mother. Leopold Bloom mourns his dead son. His hallucinations are sparked by the appearance of the massive whore mistress Bella Cohen and end with Bloom's immolation in flames to the accompaniment of the Alleluia chorus. Act Two. Stephen and the ghost of his mother. Stephen and Bloom. A son in search of a father. A father in search of a son. The end. Numerous curtain calls.

In a speech from the stage, Fleur Darlington praises the production. During the reception in the lobby the cast poses for the photographers, and the first-nighters gush with compliments. Father Desmond Fitzgerald S.J. interviewed for one of the literary magazines expatiates on the catholicity of *Ulysses in Nighttown*.

He postulates that Molly Bloom is both the Blessed Virgin Mary and Mary Magdalene and Leopold Bloom the crucified Christ and the merciful father.

The reviews appear in the Saturday newspapers: A play that grips and fascinates and leaves the audience struggling for meaning. Bloom's face and gestures border on the marvellous... In many respects this is a remarkable production. At times it sings with something close to James Joyce's lyric intoxication. It captures the bawling, coarse and merry vitality of the Dublin brothels...A fervent portrait of Leopold Bloom as all the world's stand-in complete with Chaplin derby and baggy pants... The personification of the eternal shmuck being led by the nose through the full gamut of his psyche, now exalted, now degraded, but always Leopold Bloom, the Jew in Dublin, the outsider everywhere.

Word of mouth is enthusiastic with patrons paying return visits. Many because of the exuberance of the language, some for scholarly reasons. A number of citizens having read in the press about the use of four letter words urge the police to close the show.

The police do not lay charges. The theatre is sold out for every performance of the four week run.

Autumn 1966. Gabriel is experiencing the male mid-life crisis. He is depressed by his involvement in business. Regretting all the wasted years. Obsessed with the imminence of death.

How do others cope?

Walter Branson departs for Spain anxious to reconnect with old war buddies of the MacKenzie-Papineau battalion who fought against Francisco Franco. Charles Davidoff, respected community leader, is found in bed with the wife of his business associate. Brackett Anderson, corporate lawyer, commits suicide in the basement of his Rosedale home.

Dr. Mosshammer advises Gabriel to consider another vocation. Many of the great achievements in the arts and sciences have been accomplished by those between the ages of forty and seventy.

Perhaps Gabriel should turn to religion. Find the heart's

ease in the bosom of the Lord.

In the shtetls of east Europe our forefathers prayed in the humble Bet Hamidrash. As immigrants in the new world they built modest houses of worship. They did not anticipate the rearing up of edifices like cathedrals with loudspeakers and closed circuit television..

Gabriel is beset with doubts about the existence of God. Bertrand Russell avers that the concept of God is derived from ancient oriental despotisms. William Blake refers to God as Old Nobodaddy. James Joyce writes of the God who remains beyond or above his handiwork, invisible, indifferent.

But what of God and His chosen people? Where is the dialogue between the individual and God in the concrete situations of daily life? Martin Buber the Jewish existentialist philosopher saw none in the sanctuary. Formal observance can hide from us as nothing else can the face of God, he declared. What of those Jews who freed themselves from the tradition but maintained their Jewish affinities? Sigmund Freud wouldn't go to the synagogue. Albert Einstein believed in Spinoza's God who reveals himself in the orderly harmony of what exists, not in a God who concerns himself with the fates and actions of human beings.

Tuesday December 13, 1966. From the New York Times
May Monaghan A Sister of James Joyce
She aided Efforts to Honour Writer

Mrs. Mary Kathleen (May) Joyce Monaghan, a younger sister of the writer James Joyce, died Thursday in a Dublin Hospital after a short illness. She lived with her son Kenneth in Terenure, a Dublin suburb. Mrs. Monaghan, one of ten children in the Joyce family, was 18 years younger than James, who died in 1941. There were four boys and six girls in the family although James Joyce sometimes referred to 'My 23 sisters'. Known to her friends as May, her mother's name, Mrs. Monaghan closely followed efforts to commemorate her brother and helped to establish a Joyce Society in Toronto during a visit to her daughter there. Mrs. Monaghan was a widow.

Letter from Maeve O'Neill
Dublin. December 14, 1966.

Dear Gabriel . I hate to be the sender of bad tidings at this time of year and it is with deep regret that I impart to you the news that dear little May is dead. The day was grey for her funeral and as I was walking up the pathway to her grave side I thought of 'the Last Journey' and about Jim when he was buried in Zurich. It was a sad moment when May was lowered into the cold earth. The sun shone out momentarily as if to bid her a last farewell before the start of her Fabulous Voyage. The pale winter sun softly lit the wreathes of goldbrown rust and vermilion-coloured chrysanthemums which were nodding their sad little heads in the breeze. Ah well, we know not the day or the hour. Yours. Maeve O'Neill.

Gabriel had called a press conference when May Monaghan came up from New York and she posed for pictures with her grandson. The reporters asked if she had read all her brother's works. Did she find them difficult to understand? Was she shocked by the four letter words? She responded graciously. That evening, February 14, 1964, the first meeting of the James Joyce Society of Canada, Gabriel read *Gas From A Burner* and *Ecce Puer* and then the Hades episode from *Ulysses*. Actors presented the hell-fire sermon from *A Portrait of the Artist as a Young Man* and the end of Molly Bloom's monologue. Fr. Desmond Fitzgerald, S.J. commented on the catholicity in Joyce's works. Jack Hishon, a jovial Irishman, informed the gathering that he had been a school mate of Jimmy Joyce at Clongowes. The meeting ended with a recorded excerpt of Joyce reading the Anna Livia Plurabelle segment from *Finnegans Wake*.

May Monaghan wrote from Dublin to thank Gabriel for honouring her brother.

7

Heathrow. June 14, 1967. After a holiday in London we take our seats aboard the Boeing 737 christened Cormac after the most illustrious of the Irish Kings. The travellers feel secure in the knowledge that this plane was blessed two weeks ago at the annual invocation of the Irish air fleet in Dublin. Gabriel vows that the church will bless any undertaking. On the high seas, in the mines, on the farms, at seed time and harvest time, imploring divine favour for the cows and horses, dogs and cats and the busy bees. As Cormac drones across the Irish Sea the attendants offer refreshments. Brigid O'Hearne will be at the airport. Her letter was effusive:

-Wonderful news about your coming to Dublin. You are quite welcome to stay with us. I expected to have moved but we just couldn't get anything to suit and so we are stuck in this sardine can for another year. It's not such a grand life I can tell you.

-The four boys have been poured into the main bedroom as the house is so small. I managed to get it in less than a week after our arrival from Canada. The place had to be taken furnished so of course now we have furniture behind the furniture (ours and the landlord's) and every bed is raised off the floor because of the extra mattresses under them.

-You should see the drivers over here. They're quite unbelievable. People tell you how Micky Pat who never drove a car in his life went in the day of the driving test and got himself a license. The bloody country is lousy with Mickey Pats. And they had the neck to fail me! I was so cautious with the damn inspector.

-We have the house until the middle of May next. We are going to put an advert in the papers for somewhere bigger about January. I know a place way up in the Dublin mountains where I would just adore to build our dream house but of course we've no lolly.

-Having been devoid of relatives and their problems for so long I now find much of my time taken up visiting them in the hospital. At the moment Cornelius has a sister in the Rotunda. A first cousin, once-removed, aged 16, is in the Mater Misericordiae after a bad smash-up on his motor bike. And there is a second cousin of mine on a frame out in Wicklow. My great aunt in Clane isn't so hot either. And I've had to drive another cousin out to Naas as her mother has become seriously ill. They're all doing bad if you ask me. Oh, and to crown it all, me dog's in heat.

-Mary Kate my precious five year old has become so rough that she has licked every child in the neighborhood and none of them will play with her! Eithne, the precocious adolescent thinks Irish men are the most but I keep telling her to get a nice Jewish boy who won't get drunk all the time and leave her. Sean fell for some little trollop down in Monasterevan. He was helping in my uncle's shop and she came in to buy potatoes and that's how he met her. I tried to explain that no nice girl would let herself be picked up like that. Peter and Liam have made five television commercials between them for one agent and so far haven't received a penny. Some Equity actors tell me that they made movies over twelve months ago for reputable English companies and haven't gotten any money either. I haven't worked since we arrived. My 91 year old mother-in-law stayed with us for a few days before taking off by air for Lourdes. Great suffering Jesus!

-Would you ever bring me over from Eaton's a very, very magnifying mirror, a shaving mirror would do fine, for applying make up? I'm so blind. I'm trying to scrape up funds to buy a quantity of liners and eye shadow. God's curse on the bastard who stole my make up kit from the car when we were doing *Ulysses in Nighttown* in Toronto. Be jaysus there was $200 worth of grease paint and powder in that box. I had hoped to bring it back to Ireland with me, maybe that's why I haven't been getting any work. I'm a little tired of praying to St. Anthony so I've switched my allegiance to Padre Pio. He's very big over here. I paid the taxes on the car yesterday but I didn't get the door which was pushed in by an old dear right outside the house fixed yet and the front tyres need replacing. Do you have a place to rehearse? If you are stuck we could put the kids out on the grass and get down to it in the parlor, small as it is. Yrs. Brigid.

Coming down now out of the blue sky into roiling thunder clouds (hands clutch rosaries, lips whisper in prayer), Cormac alights on the rain-soaked tarmac. It is a short walk to the terminal building where Brigid is waving frantically.

-And isn't it about time you got here? We've been waiting on your arrival for over an hour with Mary Kate making a holy show of herself, not able to sit still for a minute.

-Want to go home, the child tugs at her mother's skirt.

-Okay, okay, we're headin' for the ranch, Brigid responds. Whenever the little urchin embarrasses me in public I pretend we're from Cheyenne. Wouldn't want the natives to think I'm Irish and not knowing how to bring up me own child. Like, you know how it is, man. Come along, the old jalopy is outside.

The dented door on the driver's side is stuck. Brigid yanks open the other, shoos Mary Kate into the back seat with Gabriel and motions for me to sit beside her.

-Prepare for take-off. She accelerates and the Citroen catapults out of the parking space; she brakes to a stop at the exit, and then we're off again.

-It has stopped raining, I observe.

-Just as well, since the windscreen wipers don't work. Nothing wrong with the gas pedal however.

-Still driving without a license?

-Ain't it the truth. The Gardai stopped me yesterday for speeding and Mary Kate set up such a wailing when she saw him you'd have thought there was a banshee got into her and the nice polis man asked was there anything troubling the little darling and I said it was her tummy and we were on the way to the Rotunda so himself said he would proceed ahead and clear the traffic and we were going so fast that by the time we got to the hospital Mary Kate was in such a state that I was glad to have her examined wondering was she perhaps really sick but it was only a case of the hysterics. I tell you there is a great future for that one in the theatre. Will you observe her now, so drim and drew?

On Drumcondra Road, Brigid swerves to overtake a slow-moving lorry, expressing her opinion about the driver's limited mental capacity. Traffic is heavier now as we pass All Hallows College, St. Patrick's Training School, the Archbishop's house, and cross over the weed-choked Royal Canal into Dorset Street. Brigid slows at a red light then continues across the intersection. Parnell Square. O'Connell Street.

-Here we are, the Gresham Hotel but you are still welcome to share our digs. No? I guess you'll want your privacy. I'll call for you later.

The desk clerk receives us courteously and rings for the bell man to carry the luggage. The bed-sitting room is decorated in Wedgwood green and white. The window looks out on the widest street in Europe, the centre boulevard verdant with trees. It is good to be back in Dublin's fair city where the girls in miniskirts are so pretty and there is an abundance of Guinness on tap.

Outside the Gresham an old man pushes a perambulator stacked with newspapers. *Irish Times*, he whines. *Irish Press. Independent.* He holds a copy whose front page carries a photograph of Jackie Kennedy on her arrival at Shannon Airport. Seated in rocking chairs on the porch of the hotel we read about the fortitude of the sweetly smiling widow.

The claxon's blare announces Brigid's arrival. 'Tis a grand day for a drive if we don't mind going in her jaunting car. The shock absorbers need replacing but it's still better than public transportation.

At O'Connell Bridge she turns onto the quays where the Liffey flows, old and tired with patches of peat on its surface. Beyond Bachelor's Walk she indicates the Four Courts.

-That's where his honour Judge McNamara presides. Just last week I had the misfortune to appear before him on a traffic charge and he fined me five pounds.

-He is to deliver a paper at the James Joyce Symposium, says Gabriel.

-Bully for him and his two shirts a week.

-No doubt he'll be attending the performance as well.

-Wonder will he recognize me in my negligee as Molly Bloom?

-I'll bring him to your dressing room.

-Sure and he'll be enraptured.

-The O'Hearne poitrine is a thing of beauty.

-You may think so but Irish men are lousy lovers and it's the drink they prefer. Now the Toronto fellows, those are the boyos can make a woman feel desirable.

-Are you getting any satisfaction from Cornelius?

-Ah no. He's either at work or chancing his arm or suffering from a dose of the Dundalks. It's just as well I suppose. First thing you know I'd be pregnant.

-There are ways to frustrate the designs of nature.

-The Bishop of Dublin is opposed to contraception.

-That leaves the rhythm method or coitus interruptus.

-Coitus Interruptus Eternus. C.I.E. That's what the wags call the Dublin Transportation System. Look, there on the bus! Coras Iompair Eireann. Well here we are, Phoenix Park. Seventeen hundred acres of pasture land, one of the biggest grazing grounds in the world. See, the cows and sheep munching away? They leave their flaps in thanks. There's the Wellington Monument. The zoo. The peoples garden. And that is the house of the President, Eamon de Valera, Ireland's grand old man who founded the Fianna Fail party.

-Your gas gauge is showing empty, I observe.

-Jaysus, I asked Mary Kate to remind me to get some petrol. Should be a pump at Chapelizod. Hang on and cross your fingers.

We make it to the Caltex station where the aged attendant greets us with a comment on the salubriousness of the weather. Brigid requests six litres of regular petrol.

-Chapelizod. Chapelle d'Iseult, explains Gabriel. This is *Finnegans Wake* country. The Bristol Hotel should be nearby. I wish I had known James Joyce when he was taking those long walks.

-He was nothin' to look at, the old fellow declares. I used to see him before he ever left the country. He was writing a book down in Sandycove in the Tower you know and he used to ramble around Dublin. Ah, he was a plain, simple-minded man, you know.

-Simple-minded?

-I mean to say he was a bit of a...he wanted to be always recognized for his writing ability. Of course he had some difference with the clergy because they educated him and then anything he wrote it was always...in some way he was condemning them. Many a priest he used to serve mass with and all that sort of thing and his sister was very upset about his writing.

-Which sister was that?

-She was a nun. I didn't know her, you see. But Joyce, he wasn't a great scholar, not at all, the very opposite.

-Have you read any of his books?

-Oh yes. I read *Dubliners* for one. Any boy could have wrote that, you know. It's a bit childish in the way that he exposed all the little weaknesses and all that sort of thing around him.

-Have you read *Ulysses*?

-I have.

-Do you consider it obscene?

-Well it is, oh yes. But I wouldn't condemn him for that. He was...ah...a bit of a genius in his own way, you see, but only in his own narrow way.

-Do you remember him at all?

-The last time I seen him was down in Talbot Street talkin' to two men. But he was nothin' to look at. Of all men in the world Joyce was a very insignificant figure, I mean in appearance. But you see, he went to the Jesuit College and he learned French and German and Italian. Then he left Ireland. He was teaching for a while on the continent.

-How do you know all this about James Joyce? I ask.

-Well, I took an interest in all men of letters. I used to hear people talkin' about *Ulaysses* and I was curious, you know. But Joyce never struck me as a real genius. I knew far greater men than Joyce.

-Who in your opinion is Ireland's greatest writer?

-Oh well, I have no hesitation in saying that Dr. Dillon was the greatest writer that Ireland ever produced. He wrote *The Valley of the Squintin' Windows*. He was superior to Shaw and all.

-How about Sean O'Casey?

-Yes I knew him too of course.

-Have you met Paddy Kavanagh?

-Oh I've often had a drink with him at the Bailey. He's a sort of handy man for it. He has a lot of gifts mind you but he chances his arm a lot. They made a show of him here, in the law courts. People call him a bum and all that sort of thing. But he is very amusing. He published a paper here, you know, *Kavanagh's Weekly* which was very interesting. I used to buy it.

-Who are you? What do your friends call you?

-Well it wouldn't do for my name to be known because you see I run into trouble before over Joyce and all those other writers, you see I made a study of them and a fellow got jealous of me in London and he brought over the English polis and created an awful scene. Anyway, James Joyce was never very popular in Ireland.

-Not even today?

-The Americans have made him a bit popular. They come over here and they ask, Where is Joyce-land? Well, that makes me sick. Joyce-land. They go around the slums and the streets of Dublin looking for Joyce-land. He used to like to expose, to tell little stories about boarding houses and things like that. *Dubliners* he called them. Well now, I read the stories carefully and I said to myself, that's just nothing, nothing at all and you'll agree with me if you read them. You'll agree with me.

-I have read *Dubliners*, admits Gabriel.

-Well, it was nothing was it?

-I wouldn't say that.

-Well you see, I know Dublin. I know Dublin for fifty-six years. I married a Dublin girl. But I'm from Meath. And I'm 76 years on St. Stephen's Day. And I tell you *Dubliners* is nothing. I could have wrote it if I had a mind to.

-Mother of God, interrupts Brigid. We had better get back to Ballsbridge. I have a roast in the oven that will be a pile of cinders.

The wheels scrape against the curb and Brigid rushes into the cottage, past the O'Hearne brood clustered about the television. After an interlude of banging and cursing she appears wiping her hands on a towel.

-Rescued the roast just in time. Which one of you immigrants was supposed to have kept an eye on it?

-I did mummy, Eithne admits. I was about to take it out.

-And where's your father?

-He phoned to say he'll be delayed.

-Jaysus, wouldn't you think he'd get home on time oncet in awhile. Did he say where he was calling from?

-No mummy, he didn't.

-Probably from Davy Byrne's, suggests Sean.

-He could be at any one of the 655 licensed premises in Dublin. Your da is democratic, he patronizes them all. Well, let's set the table.

-Aw, it's time for Star Trek.

-Bill Shatner can wait. Come on, jump to it.

The kids go about their allotted tasks, putting on the table cloth, arranging the cutlery and dishes.

-Well, that's that. Now we wait for his eminence. If his shadow doesn't fall inside the doorway in the next half hour we'll start without him.

Cornelius O'Hearne shows up as Star Trek is ending. Apologizing for his lateness he goes to the kitchen, returning with bottles of Guinness. Slainte. We have time for a brief chat before Brigid leaves to slice the meat.

-Come and get it, she calls. Cornelius, seated at the head of the table, offers a short grace and the roast is passed around. Eithne cuts the meat into small pieces for Mary Kate. Sean tells him about the television commercial he has just completed for the Milk Marketing Board and asks Gabriel if there is any work for a thirteen-year-old in Canadian Television.

-Holy Saint Ginesius and aren't you getting enough work here? Brigid rebukes him. You're doing more than any of us. It's me should be complaining without even a walk-on since we got back and these little people appearing in all kinds of adverts. Even Mary Kate grins at you from the billboards.

Mary Kate knocks over her milk glass and starts to cry. Eithne takes her from the room since dinner is just about finished. Cornelius settles into his chair in the parlour with the *Irish Independent*.

-I'm leaving the lot of you to wash up so I can drive Gabriel and Anna to the reception, Brigid announces.

-I'll be here all evening, Cornelius assures her.

-That's decent of you. I'm relieved to know that our happy home will be blessed with your presence for a change. Will you see that the young one gets to bed on time. I don't want to be finding her still up when I return.

The scholars from Europe and America have gathered in the Silver Swan on Burgh Quay. Amid the noise and smoke and the clinking of glasses the language of James Joyce floats about the room in a variety of accents and cadences.

-He married his markets cheap by fowl like any Etrurian Catholic Heathen, don't you know? The Oxford don.

-Consider the grace development in *Ulysses*. The professor from Cracow.

-It was Joyce's search for an Anglo-European language that was at the root of the word play in *Finnegans Wake*. The Zurich specialist.

-My lecture with music is called: Storiella as she is syung. The academic from Indiana.

-The theory of cyclic history, Giambattista Vico's Nuova Scienza, is much evident throughout the Wake. The editor from Milan.

-Who sleeps at the *Wake*? An inquisitive young person from Belfast.

-Much of what I am hearing I really do not understand. The woman from Stockholm.

-No matter, the older gentleman with the Cornwall accent reassures her. Joyce was incomprehensible in many respects, to me as well.

-Ah, but your contribution to Joyce scholarship is indispensable, Mr. Budgen. I have read your book , *James Joyce and the Making of Ulysses*.

-I just happened to be present at the time. Anyone else could have done the same thing. I don't know half as much as these people here tonight. They are all Joyce theologians. I'm just a little synoptic. I knew James Joyce very well but I don't understand the intricacies of his work. The vast interest in Joyce is phenomenal. As far as I am aware it has never occurred with any other writer. They all had to go down in limbo to be resurrected on the third day or third century. Not Joyce. I suppose *Ulysses* was part succes d'estime and part succes de scandale. As for

Finnegans Wake, why it has all the charm of a crossword puzzle that nobody can solve.

-I shall prove that *Finnegans Wake* is constructed like a gigantic phallic tree.

-Dream talks are wake talks of centuries ago. In the *Wake* the writer was giving expression to his dream of a world in which men had grown up and had become capable of discovering the unity which underlay their kaleidoscopic pluralities.

-Ireland   illuminates Joyce and the converse is triumphantly true.

Thursday June 15,1967. The proceedings of the First International James Joyce Symposium are about to begin and a buzz of expectation hovers among the participants in the banquet hall of the Gresham Hotel as the official from Bord Failte advances to the microphone. Greeting the visitors to Ireland's hospitable shores he assssures them that he is indeed cognizant of the scholarship devoted to the works of James Joyce, especially in America. He is delighted to welcome Giorgio Joyce and his wife Dr. Asta Jahnke-Osterwalder whose home is in Munich. Now he wishes to present a man who needs no introduction, a writer with an international reputation, an Irishman, friend of Mr. Joyce and of all who are assembled here this morning. Mr. Padraig Colum, President of the James Joyce Society of New York and President of the Irish Academy of Letters. As the hand clapping begins the aged poet approaches the rostrum, a smile lighting up the fey features.

-This to me is a very solemn occasion. (The dry voice enunciating measured phrases gathers strength.) I remember many years ago walking down the street in Dublin and meeting Joyce who had been away some time. He had a little boy with him and this little boy was Giorgio. Joyce had been to see his publishers Maunsel and Company and they weren't going to publish *Dubliners*. George Roberts of Maunsels told me afterwards it was the one thing in his life he regretted deeply, this rejection. It seemed so tragic, Joyce standing there, the man who was to make his name synonymous with that of the city, was in a desperate state not knowing where to turn. He went on to

London afterward and I didn't see him again for some time and the remembrance of that day brings a solemnity to our gathering here today.

Colum reads his Elegy to James Joyce then asks Giorgio Joyce to come forward. The gaunt figure approaches with the aid of a walking stick.

-It is my honour to present to you the bronze copy of the death mask of James Joyce.

-I thank you very much for this precious gift which you and the Irish people have given me. (Giorgio puts together the words in halting, Italian-accented English.) As you know the original mask was taken from me in Zurich after my father's death. Nobody is going to take this one away.

After the applause and the jockeying to be photographed with the son of the famous father the scholars adjourn to the bar.

-I remember, recalls Arthur Power, that Joyce was always reserved. Quite different from what people supposed he was from reading his books. He looked on everything with detachment but when he was writing he was emotionally engaged. Take the hospital scene in *Ulysses*. Joyce told me when he was immersed in it he was terribly upset. He felt he was mixed up with unborn children, swabs and sterilizers. People assume he lived the rowdy life he wrote about. That's not so. He wasn't much of a bohemian even in Paris. Nora used to joke about her husband's appearance. She wondered if she could trust herself to that disreputable-looking man but she did.

-Joyce's attitude toward Dublin and Ireland generally was a love-hate one. Do you regret being Irish? I once asked him as we walked down the Champs Elysees. Yes, he said, I regret the temperament it gave me. He had a deep love of Ireland but was annoyed by some of the characteristics of its citizens. He had no interest in the Free State or Sinn Fein. He told me about a man who went into one of the Dublin boostores and asked, Do you have a copy of *Ulysses*? The clerk said yes and the man replied, the author better not come back here alive.

The celebrants move on to University College leaving Gabriel to rehearse the play in the Gresham ballroom. During the initial run through, Judge McNamara arrives with his twelve year old daughter Sorcha who is to provide guitar interludes.

-I hope she won't be offended by the explicit dialogue, Gabriel apologizes in advance.

-Indeed she will not. We Irish know the value of words. We may proscribe certain literary works but our constitution makes it mandatory that any censored book be released in due course. As for *Ulysses* I can tell you that it has never been placed on the Index Librorum Prohibitorum.

The after-dinner speaker is Milton Hebald, the Rome-based American painter and sculptor whose statue of Joyce was dedicated last year in Zurich at ceremonies in the Fluntern Cemetery.

Hebald recounts how he first came across *Ulysses* in High School where he persuaded a woman teacher to borrow it for him from the library for a two-week period and how the time stretched into a month because he broke out into a severe case of chicken pox and was quarantined with the book. In those days everyone knew about the eroticism in *Ulysses* but few attempted to read it. This month, largely because of the Joseph Strick film, a new edition with photographs of the semi-nude Barbara Jefford as Molly Bloom is number eight on the *London Times* book list, enjoying sales of a thousand copies a day. The movie is banned in Australia but not in New Zealand and charter flights are ferrying plane loads of men from Sydney to Auckland. Sweet are the sweets of sin.

Tonight after dinner the symposiasts are treated to the erotic meanderings of Molly Bloom fragmented into three personae.

As the lights in the dining room dim the spotlight picks out voluptuous Olwen O'Sullivan in black night gown. Running seductive fingers through her long red hair she yawns. She speaks, spilling a cascade of words familiar to everyone in the audience. 'Yes, because he never did a thing like that before'. Blonde Brigid O'Hearne in frothy negligee enters as Molly number two. Auburn-haired Aileen Mulcahy provocatively underdressed passes among the spectators, exuding perfume of embraces. She joins the other two Mollys in a recitation of boredom and desire culled from the last forty pages of *Ulysses*.

After the final fervent declaration of Yes I Will Yes, the performance is over and the curtain calls attest to the success of the presentation. Giorgio Joyce is persuaded to pose back stage with the three Mollys, the photographs to appear in the *Evening Press*.

In the Gresham lounge Giorgio and his wife hold court. It is his first visit to Dublin in 45 years. He is content to reminisce about his parents and sister Lucia until the enquiries become too intimate and the attention shifts to his wife, who practises Ophthalmology in Munich. Things are going well for them at present but those were bad times during the war when Germany was bombed by the Allies. Her first husband, a pilot in the Luftwaffe, was killed in an air battle while defending the Fatherland. In the silence that follows she and her husband plead exhaustion and leave.

The academics turn to the consideration of the occult by Wm. Butler Yeats and other members of the Order of the Golden Dawn like Aleister Crowley and Bram Stoker. Everybody is familiar with Count Dracula written in 1897 by the Dublin-born Stoker, but what of his supernatural stories, 'The Lady of the White Worm' and 'The Lady of the Shroud'? As for Crowley, whose followers considered him the Messiah, how many have read his *Book of the Trigrams of the permutations of the Tao with the Yin and the Yang* otherwise known as the *Yi Qing*?

Brigid yawns. Two o'clock in the morning. Time for us to leave. The night porter unlocks the gate and we walk to the car. Her farewells from the sputtering Citroen fade away down dark, silent O'Connell Street.

Lying in bed, I recall the episode in Joyce's short story *The Dead*. Was it in this room that Gabriel Conroy, full of desire for his wife Gretta, learned about her affair with Michael Furey? She turned away from her husband that night. I do not leave my Gabriel unrequited.

Fri. June 16, 1967. After the Bloomsday tour of Dublin the Joyceans gather at the Bailey for the dedication of Bloom's door, rescued from the wreckers and set into the brick wall of John Ryan's public house. At half past five, himself raps for silence and calls on Patrick Kavanagh. Ireland's peasant-poet, balancing Bloom's bowler on his head, declares:

-The proper inscription on this door should be what the dead hand wrote: Bloom is a cod. This door is as famous in the mythology of Dublin as 221B Baker Street is to London. The first and last time a valid piece of native propaganda for the Joyce thing happened was on the 50th anniversary of Bloomsday in 1954 when a few of us led by Myles na cGopaleen, John Ryan and myself and a cousin of Joyce hired four unrehabilitated cabs and pilgrimaged to the Tower. Not only were there no press cameras to record the event but we were indeed the subject of some jeering in the pubs we visited. And that's the way it was before the Americans, the symposeurs as Seamus Kelley of the *Irish Times* calls them bit the dog till he laid a golden egg.

Milo O'Shea, who plays Bloom in the film version of *Ulysses*, is urged to say a few words. A voice from the assemblage intones: Aleph, beth, gimel, daleth, meshuggah, yom kippur. O'Shea offers: Free money, free love and a free lay church in a free lay state. He informs the listeners that it was the door of No. 5 Eccles Street that had been used in the filming inasmuch as No.7 had already been removed when the crew arrived.

Ulick O'Connor, barrister, writer and television personality delivers an appreciation of the Bailey as the model for the Burton in *Ulysses* and it is thus fitting that Bloom's door should find its final niche in this place.

In the upstairs lounge the air turns hazy with cigarette smoke and the Joyceans are babbling like gossipaceous Anna Livia. Patrick Kavanagh, with only one lung functioning, fractures the bonhomie by intercepting Gabriel.

-Are you a Jew or what are you, he snarls, and voices his displeasure of all Jews, especially those in the Holy Land who are using blitzkrieg tactics against the Arabs. Kavanagh lunges at Gabriel and, missing, topples to the floor. Sympathetic hands help him to a seat.

-Here you are Paddy. Drink up.

-Did you hear what happened last week, Paddy? A group

of citizens trooped down to the Chief Rabbi of Ireland and volunteered to fight alongside his people.

John Ryan calls for drinks on the house and the excitement over the altercation subsides. Judge McNamara apologizes to Gabriel, assuring him that Ireland has never persecuted the Jews. Any individual outburst like tonight's is to be deplored.

Sunday June 18, 1967. The symposiasts disperse giving the city back to its inhabitants. Brigid arrives complaining about the Mickey Pat motorist who ran into the Citroen on Eden Quay. The Gardai agreed it wasn't her fault but invited her to appear in court for driving without a permit.

-Do you feel up to making the trip? We can take a taxi, I suggest.

-Don't be daft, get in, I'm wearing my St. Christopher medallion. You'll be safe, no fear.

-He's not so big with the Holy Father these days.

-It doesn't matter what the Vatican decrees, St. Christopher will always be the patron saint of travellers. Throw your stuff in the back and let's go. Brigid maneuvers the car into the flow of traffic on O'Connell Street. Despite its age the Citroen rides easily, the smoothness of its hydraulic function interrupted by the driver's sudden stops and spurts.

At the airport a quick embrace and a hurried check-in. We are the last passengers to board the Aer Lingus SAC lll christened St. Malachy, the flight attendant informs us, her Irish eyes smiling. The other Malachy comes to mind. Malachi Mulligan the blasphemer, the Joking Jesus balladeer.

What's bred in the bone cannot fail me to fly
And Olivet's breezy...Goodbye now, goodbye.

8

June 20, 1967. Paris the glory of France has been described by one of its poets as the centre of the accumulated stratification of wit, reasoning and good taste, the planet's freest, most elegant and least hypocritical crossroads. The bus ride from Le Bourget

Airport reveals a few of the splendours of the city. Le Bois de Boulogne, Avenue Foch, L'Arc de Triomphe and La Place de la Concorde.

The Air Terminal des Invalides is in a chaotic state after the labour unions called a one day general strike and all services have been suspended. No taxis except for entrepreneurs charging inflated prices.

Hotel Lenox at No.9 rue de l'Université is a modest establishment. James Joyce stayed here in 1920 on his arrival from Trieste. A balding fellow in a grey shirt is sorting mail behind the counter. Oui Monsieur? he questions. Chambre a deux, Gabriel replies. Having confirmed our reservations he asks for the passports which must be taken to the prefecture. Madame appears, a trace of a smile hovering about her sallow countenance, and takes her husband's place. She enumerates the rules of the house: No eating in the room. No washing of clothes in the sink. No visitors. The bath is at our disposal for ninety centimes. Breakfast is from seven to nine. The front door is locked at midnight so please to inform monsieur if we expect to be out after that time. She provides the room key which is attached to a heavy metal disc.

-L'ascenseur est a votre service.. Monsieur holds the elevator door open until we have crowded inside with the luggage. The grille slides closed and the cage rises, stopping with a spasm at the third floor.

The hall is faintly illuminated by a wire filament bulb. The door of number 17 opens into a high-ceilinged chamber furnished with a double bed and armoire. Anxious to explore the neighborhood we throw our bags on the floor and leave but the passageway is dark and the elevator isn't working so we feel our way in the dark down the stairs to the lobby where le patron is shouting into the telephone.

-Toutes les chambres sont occupées. Oui, occupées. Demain? Oui. Quel nom? Bien Stock. Comment? Ah, Benstock. D'accord M. Benstock. A demain.

-Monsieur, I inform him, la lumiere dans la toilette...

-Oui, je sais, et l'ascenseur ne marche pas. Le fusible, je suppose. Madame s'en charge.

The street vibrates with energy. Automobiles and motor cycles rumble along the cobble stones, screeching to a stop at the traffic lights. Women carry string bags filled with fruit and vegetables and the ubiquitous baguette. Students congregate outside the medical building of the University of Paris, their vehicles parked on the sidewalk. Wall posters announce political meetings and cultural events. We pass the tobacconist, the patisserie, the antique shop, the outdoor cafe.

Our guide book informs us that the Abbey of Saint-Germain-des-Prés was named after St. Germanus the bishop of Paris who is buried in the church. Founded in the 6th century, most of the building was destroyed by fire during the French Revolution, but its collection of manuscripts was saved and passed to the Bibliothèque Nationale. The green meadows where clerks in holy orders used to stroll have ceded to asphalt and the roar of traffic. Propped against the church railings, paintings of Notre Dame and Sacre Coeur are for sale as well as imitations of Toulouse Lautrec and van Gogh.

Boulevard St. Michel is a carnival of music and laughter, of ice cream bars and hot dog stands, record shops and book stores, ladies fashions and cocktail bars. Le Départ Café, Gilbert Jeune, La Vie Bohème. Gabriel sees himself in these young people. Sharing a room in a garret with a midinette who works while he writes the immortal novel. Evenings spent in a bistro with other bohemians discussing literature, art, music, and la condition humaine.

We have supper in a tiny restaurant where the customers sit on benches, eating in silence their prix fixe meal of pea soup and biftek, drinking vin ordinaire diluted with water.

Returning to Saint-Germain we stop at Les Deux Magots for Perrier Menthe and observe the stream of strollers and lovers. It has been a long day and the Lenox Hotel beckons.

Moonlight and lamplight outside our window. Snatches of song drift up from the street. Shouts and responses. The mating cries of felines. Gabriel sleeps through them all. I doze fitfully as the hours advance and the night noises dissolve with the dawn into the familiar daylight dissonances.

After breakfast of croissants and coffee we are out into the bustling rue de l'Université. The shopkeepers are sweeping their sidewalks. Somebody has painted Avec Israel on the wall of the medical building. In the Odèon, Metro posters extoll the merits of Dubonnet and Vichy Water. Gouda and Edam cheeses. The joy of shopping at the Galeries Lafayette.

The train eases into the station on rubber tires and we crowd into the Second Class coach with its press of open-bloused women, freshly-shaved businessmen and schoolchildren with satchels on their backs. An amputee occupies a seat reserved for disabled war veterans, his grey sweater spit stained, trousers secured by a cord around the waist. The smell of garlic is omnipresent. It is a short ride to Montparnasse.

From the Sevres-Babylon Metro Station we walk to Number 27, rue Casimir-Perier, where the door opens into a courtyard. In response to our ringing, a window blind goes up, a face looks out and the concierge, having certified that we are expected, directs us to Madame Leon's apartment. When we emerge from the elevator a shaft of light in the hall reveals a stooped figure beckoning us. A woman appears and coaxes the old man back into the apartment.

-Ah, there you are, she greets us. That was my father. He hasn't been well but he is curious to see visitors. I told him you are friends who have come to enquire after Mr. Joyce. Father has retired to the bedroom where he will read his Russian newspaper.

-Do come into the parlor. Here is where we entertained Mr. Joyce. My husband Leon worked with him at this table. Everything remains as it was when Mr. Joyce used to call. The chairs, the photographs, the knick knacks. Please be seated. You will have coffee?

Lucie Leon is dressed in a black frock. Her movements are graceful, her diction precise, the English inflection superimposed on the French and Russian.

-So you have come to interview me. I see that you have brought a tape recorder. Very well. As you know I am the widow of Paul Leon who was James Joyce's friend, associate in his work and his alter ego. Mr. Joyce used to come to this house regularly, usually twice a day or he would ring and my husband would take the phone and say, 'Good morning sir. How did you sleep? Will you be coming here today? I'll tell the secretary that you will need her.' Or they would meet at the corner bistro for an aperitif.

-Was Paul Leon a lawyer? asks Gabriel.

-He sometimes advised friends but he never practised. He obtained his doctorate in France (we left Russia in 1918 for London and in 1921 came to Paris) but Paul was un homme de lettres. His main interests were Benjamin Constant and Jean Jacques Rousseau yet when he was a student at the University in Moscow his thesis was Irish Home Rule. That was about thirty years before he ever heard of Mr. Joyce.

-Where did you stay during the war?

-When France fell we left for the Free Zone, the village of Saint-Gerand-le-Puy where Maria Jolas had moved her school, the Ecole Bilingue. We went down there to get away from the Germans but since they overran the whole country anyway we decided to return to the occupied zone and Mr. Joyce made plans to get out to Switzerland. When we arrived in Paris in 1940 my husband was concerned about the great mass of papers and books in the Joyce library and decided to save them, especially those textbooks that had been used during their work together. If it hadn't been for Paul there would have been no *Finnegans Wake*. For twelve years, twice a day they worked on the book here in Paris and even when we were exiled in Mrs. Jolas' village, as we called it, they used to go over the only existing edition of the Wake and try to find errata. They sometimes walked down the main road, which led to Moulin, not too far from Lyons where the line of demarcation went through, and they would sit on a felled log along the high road and make corrections. Or he would come to the little farm where we lived. Paul thought of all the books Mr. Joyce worked with and those that had been dedicated to him with inscriptions from famous authors and friends and so he tried to salvage what he could. He went with a push cart and a man to help him. He knew he risked being caught by a German patrol or by somebody who might denounce him.

-The apartment had not yet been sealed and Paul gave

the concierge 200 francs. He made two trips and tried to save everything of interest. Books by Ibsen and others that Mr. Joyce particularly valued, that Paul used to read aloud to him. Some he brought here, papers and contracts that I hid and found again when I returned. You see, I was obliged to get out of Paris because the Germans were picking up dependents of arrested men. The bulk of his haul including the family portraits he took to the lawyer Maitre Gervais. They are now in the collection of the Lockwood Library at the University of Buffalo. After the war Mrs. Jolas and I made a list of all the items that were saved and had them catalogued by two Russian ladies who were librarians and quite knowledgeable. It took them a month and it was this work that made possible a few years later the wonderful Joyce Exhibition at the Librairie La Hune. All the first hand personal stuff, the portraits, Joyce's own books and masses of papers, clippings and photographs. The showing was an international event.

-How did you come to meet James Joyce?

-Through Peggy Guggenheim whom we knew very well. Peggy introduced us to Helen Fleischmann whose husband was a reader for Boni and Liveright and Helen met my brother who had come down from Cambridge and was giving English lessons and one day she said to him, 'Alex I want you to meet a writer by the name of James Joyce who is interested in taking Russian lessons'. It was the summer I was in England and when I got back I found the entire pattern of our lives had changed. Everything was orbiting around Mr.Joyce. It was quite extraordinary. He was very conscious of the demands he made on Paul because he would say to me again and again, 'Mrs. Leon, I'm wasting your husband's time. Why don't you throw me out?' It was very touching.

-Some people refer to Paul as Mr. Joyce's secretary. That's not true. A secretary does a specific job and is paid for it. Paul was a man of manifold interests and chose to spend the hours with Mr. Joyce because he was fascinated by the process of creation. The relationship was a close one because Mr. Joyce was always in some kind of trouble or anxiety. He seemed to be dogged by tragedy. I think his daughter's illness was worst of all. Mrs. Jolas did what she could for Lucia, seeking a cure and finding people who would take care of her. Different doctors, new sanitoriums. Lucia has come out of it as well as she ever can. We get letters from her.

-How did you hear about Joyce's death?

-Have you noticed downstairs there's a little shop with two young women sitting by the window? No? Well, maybe they're not visible; that's because they do invisible mending, Paul used to say. Over the years they got to know Mr. Joyce very well what with my husband leading him out and putting him in a taxi or bringing him into the house because Mr. Joyce's eyesight was in such a terrible state. Well, that day, January 13, 1941 the two women had been listening to Radio Lausanne, a clandestine station forbidden by the Germans but people were always listening to it behind closed shutters just as we listened to the BBC. The women heard the news, and when my son returned from school they called, 'Alexei go and tell your father we heard that Mr. Joyce died.' That evening we saw it in the papers. Simply three lines that the well-known writer James Joyce had died in Zurich. My husband was shattered.

-Under what circumstances did your husband die?

-Paul was arrested and sent to the Drancy concentration camp outside Paris. I joined the Red Cross and managed to visit him several times. Just before the liberation of Paris the camp was being evacuated but Paul could not move quickly enough to suit his guards. They shot him.

-How do you spend your time these days?

-I'm a fashion writer, known professionally as Lucie Noel, the name I use in the *Herald Tribune* columns that are syndicated in America. I'm quite friendly with the Paris designers. I've been at it so long that I feel like one of the family. The other day I put on a Fashion Show for the American Students and Artists Centre and they raised a lot of money. Now, I'm afraid I must terminate our little chat. I have a deadline to meet but we shall see each other again.

The clochards at the Seine are warming themselves in the sun. A bateau mouche full of tourists chugs by. On the embankment spray-painted in black letters are the words: Avec Israel. We cross Pont St. Michel to the Isle de la Cité where Notre Dame de Paris rises into the azure sky. The guide book describes the Cathedral as the finest example of early French Gothic with its ribbed vault, flying buttresses, statues sculpted into the fluted stone columns, griffins and gargoyles and bas-reliefs of Adam and Eve. Here, Henry VI of England was crowned King of France and Mary Queen of Scots was married to the future Francois 11. On this site the Druids worshiped and the Romans built a Temple. Notre Dame, desecrated during the French Revolution was the first national cathedral. Within the immense interior are the painted visions of Paradise and the Inferno, the statues of the Holy Family and the great altar. Notre Dame is said to be the repository of 'the most beautiful and holy relics in the world including the foreskin of our Lord which is of his own flesh and of which there is no other part in all the world.' The distance from Paris to the borders of France is still measured from the portico of Notre Dame, the nation's Omphalos. Children are playing in the gardens. Infants in perambulators. A vagrant asleep on a bench, a copy of Le Figaro over his face. Young people in denims. Our lunch on the grass includes a baguette, half a kilo of Camembert and a bottle of Nuit St. George purchased at a Prisunic.

The bells of Notre Dame ring out and ripple away. At the river's edge a sign indicates Musée, the arrow pointing to the Mémorial des Martyrs de la Déportation. A narrow staircase ends in a space at the water's edge where stone walls containing 200,000 facettes reflect a flickering flame. Chiselled into the marble floor: Ici repose un déporté inconnu. Deux cent mille Français sombres exterminés dans les camps Nazis. Ils allerent a l'autre bout de la terre et ils ne sont pas revenus. Pardonne... N'oublie pas! Maidanek * Auschwitz-Birkenau * Dora-Ellrich * Oranienburg-Sachsenhausen * Buchenwald * Bergen-Belsen * Dachau * Neuengamme * Mauthausen * Stutthof * Aurigny * Flossenburg * Gross-Rosen.

-You wish to take the bath now? I 'ave reserve the time for you. Come, I shall unlock la chambre de bain. Monsieur announces the tidings in a manner befitting the grand occasion.

He cautions us to use only the allotted quantity of water. If we draw more we shall be charged extra. Entendu? He clumps away.

-Do you think James Joyce washed himself in this tub?

-I doubt it, says Gabriel as we undress. Buck Mulligan declares that the bard bathes once a year. Stephen confesses to Bloom that he (Stephen) is hydrophobic, his last bath having taken place in the month of October of the preceding year. Lie back and I shall soap you. Breasts, belly and thighs. And your golden pubic hair. This is the trysting time in Paris, the *cinq a sept* when Frenchmen make love to their mistresses before going home to dinner with their families.

-What are we waiting for?

Buoyed up by the soapy water I present myself to his eager penetration.

-If I were to expire during such exertions, what would you do, asks Gabriel.

I shudder at the thought.

-It has been known to happen. Pope Leo V11 succumbed of a stroke while committing adultery. Not far from here, at the Quai D'Orsay, a President of France was untimely cut off during his devotion to Priapus. Felix Faure, a lusty votary of the late afternoon romantic interlude, was being fellated by the wife of his official portraitist when he suffered a heart attack and died with her face in his crotch and his fingers about her head. The servants had to pry him loose. The doctor told Faure's wife her husband had been the victim of a cerebral hemorrhage.

-*Tombé sur le champs d'amour*, I quip.

The Restaurant des Beaux Arts on the rue Bonaparte opens for dinner at eight o'clock. The customers exchange greetings with M. Poussineau the patron before making for their accustomed tables. Salutations circulate about the room. Waitresses bustle about balancing plates and bottles of wine.

The savory aromas have sharpened our appetites and we order escargots en aile, veal cutlets, crudités and a carafe of vin rouge. Assuming that our table companion, a weather-beaten fellow who is sopping up gravy with his bread, is an artist Gabriel asks him about the Ecole des Beaux Arts on the other side of the street. Alas, he shrugs, the state-supported institution has declined in influence and funds, having fallen victim to the modernists. We can see by the paintings on the walls of this restaurant. For 20 years L'Ecole was the centre of the French Architectural establishment and famous for its school of painting and sculpture. Beaux Arts inspired the designs of the Paris Opera and Grand Central Station in New York as well as the Jefferson Memorial and National Gallery in Washington.

-But I am a poet, not an artist. Allow me to introduce myself, Pierrre Longchamps. And you, monsieur? So, you amuse yourself with the Irish writers. You are no doubt familiar with the works of Oscar Wilde?

-Oscar Fingal O'Flahertie Wills Wilde? Of course.

-He came to this restaurant all the time. He lived not far from here, in the Alsace Hotel. Now he lies in Père Lachaise cemetery with Proust, with Moliére and Balzac, with Chopin and Bizet.

-Cigarette? I offer Longchamps an American king size filter tip. The poet inhales slowly. Pas mauvaise. But he prefers the stronger Gauloises.

Contented with the dinner and a second bottle of wine shared with the garrulous poet we get up to provide places for those waiting. Pierre limps along with us.

-You will find many good restaurants in Paris. Do you know Le Polidor? It is on rue Monsieur le Prince. James Joyce ate there many times. Also, you must try Le Procope near the old Comédie Francaise. It is the oldest cafe, open since 1684, popular with Voltaire.

-Maybe we can go there tomorrow.

-It was the meeting place of Georges Sands and her admirers. Also of Zola and de Maupassant.

-Je dois faire pi-pi. Gabriel hurries to the nearby pissoir, Longchamps following. When they return, the poet is explaining that this convenience, called a vespasienne after the Roman Emperor, is a new one, bringing the total to five hundred and sixty-seven.

-Y a que Paris pour ca. Let us rendezvous tomorrow for an apéritif at Vagenande not far from here. As we part from him at the Metro his high-pitched voice trails after us. À demain. Je vous attends.

We get off at Étoile to a view of L'Arc de Triomphe. The stone colossus decreed by Napoleon after the battle of Austerlitz in 1806 is circled with spotlights. In a marble tomb encompassed with flowers and memorial wreaths rests the unknown soldier. The flame of remembrance is kindled every night in this grandiose Altar of the Fatherland dedicated to the glory of the French Army. Citroens and Peugeots swirl about the Arch and spin off to the twelve Avenues that form the Star.

At Avenue George V, Fouquet's 'chic prize ring' frequented by James Joyce still attracts loquacious patrons. On the Champs Élyséés the shops display haute couture with internationally recognized labels. We stop at a cafe for double espressos.

Eleven o'clock. The director of the Lido welcomes the journalist from Toronto and his companion and summons the maitre d' to guide us through the sumptuous night club. Crimson walls, midnight blue ceiling, cream moorish fretwork. A pool in the centre. We are seated next to a party of tourists, the women in evening gowns, diamonds sparkling on ample flesh. Celebrating with champagne-induced jocularity. Prosit!

The grand Carté de Menu lists a multitude of hors d'oeuvres, entrées, desserts and wines. What will Monsieur and Madame drink, inquires the waiter. Le Moet et Chandon? Le Mumm? Le Piper Heidsieck? And for dinner? He is distressed to learn that we are here only to witness the evening's spectacle. The German group is gorging on lobster thermidor served out of silver casseroles. The orchestra has just finished *sous les toits de Paris* when our server returns with two small stem glasses and a split of Lanson Black Label. As he pours the Brut he mutters with disdain what a pleasure it is to be of service but we will not be intimidated. We have quaffed champagne--Dom Perignon, the monk who discovered the bubbly wine, called it stars in a bottle--out of wide-mouthed coupes and tulip-shaped glasses.

Divine Apollo, who appointed Paris to mould the first cup from the breast of Helen and to fashion it of precious metals so the gods on Olympus could drink from a chalice of the most sensual shape, cause this churlish fellow to stumble and the crystal on his tray to crash about his feet.

The musicians warm up for the evening's extravaganza. Blasts from the brasses. Pizzicatto on the strings. Percussive beats. Bursts of dissonance. In the silence that follows, the curtains part and the stage rises from below to reveal a glittering salon. Soft music now as background for the announcement: Welcome to the world-famous Lido Cabaret starring the 60 Bluebell Girls and 100 additional artistes.

Elegantly gowned, exquisite breasts bared and buoyant, the statuesque Blue Bell Girls (most of them imports from England) fill the stage and undulate onto the ramp, posing to acknowledge the applause, then exit all too soon. The program is a two hour, fast-paced melange of dancers, aerialists, acrobats, jugglers and magicians. A reprise appearance by the Bluebell Girls. The finale is Tchaikowsky's 1812 Overture ending in a cascade of exploding rockets and streams of fire simulating the burning of Moscow.

It is three in the morning when we get back to the Hotel Lenox where we ring to summon Monsieur. He appears, weary, complaining that there has been much activity in the quarter and he hasn't had any sleep. It is the fault of the chauffe-culs and their clients in the house at the corner. All the drinking. All the shouting. Emmerdeurs!

The card in the window reads: Shakespeare & Company, 37 rue de la Bucherie, Paris 5. A Private Library Open By Invitation To The Public. Writers' Guest House. Poetry Readings and Other Events. George Whitman, billy-goat bearded, age indeterminate gets up from the desk to greet us.

-Welcome to the Free University of Paris. There are 25,000 books on three floor. I am reading my way through them, a book each night. Psychologists estimate that the average person achieves two per cent of his potential. I figure my own is probably one per cent which should make me an American. I take pride in being the bastard great-grandson of Walt Whitman. In the years when France was the sick man of Europe I was to all appearances a Frenchman. Now when England stands out as the muddle-head I ask myself if perhaps I am an Englishman. But on consideration I feel the only country which is said to have gone from barbarism to decadence without an intervening period of civilization has the most claim on me. Since I am one of those individuals who go from prolonged adolescence to premature old age without anything remarkable happening in between I am reconciled to being an American.

-Your book store is unusual, both library and hostel, Gabriel marvels.

-Sylvia Beach of the original Shakespeare & Company on the rue de l'Odeon said this was the kind of book store she liked. Maria Jolas has lectured here. Stuart Gilbert drops in. You are at liberty to hold forth on James Joyce or if you prefer to write I shall find a place where you can have privacy. Do you see the young woman in the back room? That is Hèléne Joseph. She is writing an article about the reactions of Parisians to the Six Day War. She has been to the Israel recruitment office on the rue de la Paix to enlist.

-Do you sell many books?

-I am forbidden by the authorities to engage in commerce because I don't have the foreign businessman's card. I am appealing to the Minister of Culture, Andre Malraux, informing him of my background, my studies at the Sorbonne where I was a member of the French communist party, my desire to live for humanity. Andre Malraux in his youth was a Marxist activist and fought in the Spanish Civil War on the side of the Loyalists and in the French resistance during the war against the Germans. I hope the author of Man's Fate will sympathize with my situation.

-Allow me to show you proofs of the first issue of the Paris Magazine which will feature letters of Lawrence Durrell, a protest against the war in Vietnam by Jean Paul Sartre and a poem by Allen Ginsburg. It will also carry my reply to a comment by a certain correspondent in one of the newspapers who alluded to beards as the 'existentialist fuzz on the fringe of the art world.' In taking exception to this perverse view I point out that historically the beard developed in the Left Bank as a reaction on the part of those who saluted the stars with their own bright shield of innocence only to find that the stars were the lidless eyes of a mindless universe. The beard became the insignia by which they were known to each other when they crossed the river into the alien soil of the Tuileries and the Embassy teas.

-Ah, but it is time for my visit to the Armée de Salut to select my summer wardrobe. Would you care to drop a couple of coins into the wishing well? Your hopes may not materialize but they will assist me in maintaining the place for I am beholden to the kindness of friends. I shall be gone about an hour. Perhaps you would like to browse among the books or would you prefer to talk with Hélène Joseph.

After the introduction, Whitman leaves the shop in charge of a co-ed from Wisconsin. Gabriel asks Mlle. Joseph how her work is progressing.

-Merde, she retorts, flicking ashes from her caftan, running fingers through her Cleopatra-styled coiffure. I have no patience to continue. Perhaps you would like to take a walk. What aspects of Paris have you not yet investigated?

-We should like to visit the Marais. We have met no Jews except a shop keeper off the Champs Élysées who offers discounts up to 35% on perfume to members of B'nai B'rith and says how much he detests General de Gaulle.

-Le grand Charles is not a friend of the Jewish people, that is certain. It was he who referred in a speech to 'those who are among us but not of us.' There is a sense of mission about de Gaulle. As head of the French government in exile during the war he symbolized the supreme patriot. Francois Mauriac wrote about him that only one time in the history of the world has a man said he was the Messiah without being locked up.

-We have always suffered from those with a sense of mission. Did you know that the First Crusade was inspired by the French Pope Urban II, organized by Peter the Hermit, a French preacher and carried out by French knights who raped and plundered Jerusalem while shouting Dieu le veut! That was France's first colonial empire, the Kingdom of Jerusalem.

De Gaulle has described the Crusader Castles in Lebanon as an expression of French rayonnement. He remains obsessed with the old Jacobin notion that France consists of patriots or traitors and the patriots are naturally Christians. He ignores the contributions of those who have brightened the rayonnement in man's soul, the Jews who brought radiance to medieval France. I refer to Rashi of Troyes, the Prince of Bible commentators. There was also Levi ben Gerson the religious philosopher of Perpignan and Avignan who was influenced by Maimonides.

-French Jews have made many contributions especially since the year 1791 when they were declared to be free citizens of the Republic. Statesmen like Adolph Crémieux and Léon Blum. The composers Offenbach, Bizet, Saint-Saens, Dukas and Milhaud. The harpsichordist Wanda Landowska. The conductor Pierre Monteux. The actresses Rachel and Bernhardt. Camille Pissaro the painter. The writer Jules Romain.

-But Andre Malraux your Minister of Culture is one of us so maybe de Gaulle has some redeeming qualities, counters Gabriel.

-So, you want to visit the Marais? Come along. Capacious handbag slung over her shoulder, she precedes us out of Shakespeare & Company.

At the Pont de l'Archevèche she asks if we have seen the Memorial des Martyrs de la Deportation. I reply yes, it was very moving.

-Nowhere does it mention that most of those deported were Jewish citizens of France, betrayed by their neighbors. Do you know that the French Police Commissioner during the Nazi occupation a M. Jean Leguay authorized the French police to carry out the arrests of Jews for deportation? In July of 1942 they rounded up over 12,000 men, women and children and by 1944 the Vichy regime deported 76,000 Jews. The government has not yet destroyed the Jewish file of the Gestapo.

-But what about the French resistance movement, the Maquis?

-Oh yes, here and there, a bit of scattered heroism. But it is a fact that the most active collabourators were the Parisians. The black market operators and the German officers drank together at the Moulin Rouge. The Parisians filled the Palais des Sports for Nazi rallies and chanted 'England is the enemy'. They put on German uniforms and fought on the Eastern front against the Bolsheviks and the Jews who they said had conspired to defeat la patrie. They learned the Heil Hitler salute and Nazi songs. Some even adopted German family names. When the Jews were required to wear the yellow Star of David the French Christians produced 400,000 of them. The showings of haute couture continued as usual. And the women spread their legs willingly to accommodate les schleux des allemands.

-But there were Frenchmen who fell in battle fighting with the allies.

-Tombé sur le champs d'honneur. Always it is on the field of honour, ever since the death in 1800 of Latour d'Auvergne in Bavaria. In every city and village you will see the Monument aux Morts. The statues of helmeted poilus waving their comrades forward or falling with the tricolour draped over them. The Winged Victories, the weeping Mariannes and the Rolls of Honour. It is said that the man who dies young for his country will have known only life's roses and leave no orphans.

From the square of the Ile de France we cross over to the Ile St. Louis with its massed apartment buildings as Hèléne Joseph continues her discourse. Pont Louis Philippe. Hotel de Ville. Rue de Rivoli. Rue Vieille du Temple.

-Rue des Rosiers, the heart of the Marais where I was born twenty years ago. You see, after my mother was liberated from Majdanek she returned to Warsaw but not one member of her family had survived. Her parents had been gassed. Her sister had been sent to Auschwitz where she worked in a munitions factory but she was caught smuggling gunpowder out of the plant and was hanged. So my mother searched out an uncle in Paris. He arranged for her to meet a Jewish lawyer, Andre Joseph who was a survivor of Drancy, the camp just outside Paris and they married and produced me. Last year my father became ill and he is now in the Hôpital de Ville Evrard, the Pyschiatric institution that is just a short distance from the Gare de l'Est. I add to my mother's unhappines because I am still without a husband and I do not go to synagogue, not even on the High

Holy Days. Look, here is a small one, the Temple de Beth Yaacob. It used to be a shop and now a few people hold services in it. Can you make out the Hebrew on the window?

-Ki Bethi Tefillah Yikrah lechol Ha-amim. Something about the house of prayer summoning all the people, Gabriel translates.

-My parents attend the Grand Temple but I cannot pray to this Jehovah who requires six million martyrs to sanctify his name. If he does exist he is no doubt thinking about some new way to plague his chosen people. I prefer the pantheism of the ancient Greeks. I should not mind being Leda to the swan of Zeus. It is one of my fantasies. Have your read the *Psychopathology of Sex* by Krafft-Ebing? But enough of that. Let us move along.

The Jewish Centre is closed because of the approaching Sabbath but visible within the courtyard beyond the iron gates is an enormous grey urn, the symbolic repository of the ashes of the Six Million. Bronze letters encircling the monument spell out the familiar names: Auschwitz--Dachau--Bergen-Belsen. A wreath of withered flowers lies at its base.

As we continue our walk Hèléne comments on the number and diversity of Jewish activities in Paris. The medical and pharmaceutical associations. The charitable institutions headed by Elie and Guy de Rothschild. The World Jewish Congress. The Alliance Israelite. The Aliyah Movement.

We have arrived at the most popular Jewish restaurant in the Marais. The proprietor is behind the counter slicing brisket of beef. At a table a patriarch is savouring a bowl of chicken soup and kreplach. The bill of fare offers roast chicken, kishque and carp a la Juive. We must come here for Sabbath dinner.

Hèléne has become our Baedeker. En route to the Louvre she provides a history lesson about the 600-year-old Museum with its thousands of treasures. It used to be a prison where the inmates were hanged from the beams of the Salle des Cariatides. Men used to fight bears and lions in the courtyard. Ballet performances were presented before audiences of four thousand. Louis X1V is said to have been conceived in one of its rooms.

-The Louvre is so immense that one can return for many years without having visited every section. But first you would like to see La Giocande, yes? Come, we shall have to push through the crowds.

Leonardo da Vinci's masterpiece hangs against a velvet curtain in a roped off area behind a shatter-proof glass shield. I am disappointed. The face in the small square of wood is drab, the colours muted. An English-speaking guide is explaining that our expectations have been spoiled by the countless glossy reproductions. What we are looking at is the original portrait of Lisa Gherardini who was born into a large, impoverished family in 15th century Naples and married a wealthy Florentine merchant, Francesco del Giocondo. Da Vinci worked at the painting for four years and did not finish it.

-Consider the smile, the guide continues. Enigmatic, yes? Was Lisa a pregnant Madonna? Was she perhaps remembering the illicit pleasures of the bed with Leonardo between sessions of posing? One theory holds that she was, in fact, Isabella of Aragon, Duchess of Milan. La Giocande was stolen in 1911 by an employee of the Louvre who took it back to Italy but it was later recovered. There have been other attempts. A madman slashed at it with a knife. So we are protecting her as you can see.

We move on to Titian and Delacroix. In the Apollo Room it is impossible to get close enough to inspect the Crown Jewels.

The Greek and Roman sculptures are on the lower level. At the far end beyond the statues of emperors and heroes, stands the magnificent Nike Samothrake, the Winged Victory, daughter of Pallas Athene, radiant in the rays of afternoon sunlight.

In the gardens of the Palais du Louvre before the Arc de Triomphe du Carrousel a stranger pulls Gabriel aside. Does Monsieur wish to buy any French postal cards?

We continue toward the Jardin des Tuileries which was laid out in the classical style four hundred years ago. The Royal Palace of the Tuileries stood on this site but in 1871 the Communards burned it down. Nearby is the Jeu de Paume housing the greatest collection of French Impressionists.

The afternoon advances but Hélène insists we stop for a minute at the Place de la Concorde, one of the largest squares in the world. It was first known as Place Louis XIV but in 1792 it became the Place de la Révolution and witnessed the execution by guillotine of Louis XVI and Marie Antoinette. The square is surrounded by statues. In 1836 the Luxor Obelisk of Thebes, dating from the 13th century B.C. was erected here.

Having absorbed enough culture for one day we take the Metro back to St. Germain des Près. Emerging from the station Gabriel feels the insistent call of nature. Fortunately the pissoir is nearby.

-Ah but that was quick, Hèléne teases on his return.

-A study of the washrooms in the National Arts Centre in Ottawa revealed that a man spends about 41 seconds from start to finish. A woman however takes twice as long.

- Did you know that the penis of the great Napoleon was nothing much? It was removed after his death by the Emperor's confessor. I have read that it is lying around in some gallery in London, a dried-up object about one inch long, like a sea horse.

-Sic transit gloria mundi.

-I am hungry, where shall we eat?

-I have a desire for cous-cous, Hèléne says. You have never eaten cous-cous? On y va.

A short distance from La Fontaine St. Michel where the rue de l'Harpe meets the rue de la Huchette the aromas wafting out of the open doorways are pungent with spices. Hèléne proceeds to a tiny eating place full of young people. Magnes ton cul, she persuades them to make room and shouts to the cook at a steaming cauldron, Cous-cous for three. Hèléne explains that the Moroccan specialty is a ragout of mutton and vegetables on a bed of finely ground semolina sauteed with butter in a melange of onions, garlic, carrots, ground red pepper, crushed tomatoes, chick peas, celery, beans and courgettes. It is flavored with saffron, cinnamon, cloves and cumin. Appetizing, yes? After the first tentative mouthful we agree.

Hèléne takes us through alleys where snack bars offer North African delicacies. Eggs in puff pastry. Lozenges of sugar, pistachio nuts, almonds and lemon essence. Balls of paste, dried and coated with honey. Sponge cake in the shape of small hands. We continue down Boulevard St. Michel to St. Germain des Pres.

At the Cafe Flore, sipping Cointreau on the patio we watch

the throng passing by. The free theatre of Paris. A character out of the Toulouse-Lautrec demimonde comes into view. Flared pants, yellow and blue striped jersey, red beret and neckerchief, sideburns down to the jaw. Caressing the keys of his accordion, he romanticizes *La vie en rose*. The reaction is lukewarm and he follows with *The last time I saw Paris*, which is rewarded by a scattering of coins. Dispirited, he wanders away.

Hèléne's comments on the phoniness of la vie boheme are interrupted by the arrival of an anorexic woman in a blouse and skirt, auburn hair tumbling about her shoulders, a violin clutched in one hand, the bow in the other. Tuning the instrument she produces high pitched tones that run like squeaky mice up and down the scale.

At last she is ready and with the fiddle tucked under her chin she scratches out a gypsy air. Her efforts produce a few francs but undaunted she resumes playing. This time it is a virtuoso performance showing her mastery of glissando, pizzicato, sforzando, double stopping and sul pontecello. Now the violin is between her legs, now it is over her shoulder. She leaps about encouraged by the hand clapping and the shower of coins. As long as the francs are filling her purse she will continue to entertain. To frisk, frolic and flounce. To hop prance and bounce.

Monday June 26, 1967. Giselle Freund's atelier in Montparnasse is full of cameras and photographic equipment. Portraits crowd the walls. Books and magazines are stacked on the floor.

-I met James Joyce in the thirties when I was a student, Freund recalls as she pours coffee. Time Magazine had commissioned me to do a photographic essay on him but I was too timid. Sylvia Beach said to me: 'Since you have just married a young man whose name is Blum why don't you use this name when you contact Mr. Joyce? He is so superstitious that when he sees the name he will surely consent to sit for you.' So I wrote a letter to him and signed it Giselle Blum and I received a quick reply.

-When I arrived at his flat #7 rue Edmond Valentin, Mr.

Joyce himself opened the door. He was very tall and wore a red velvet jacket. His fingers were covered with rings. I showed him colour transparencies of photographs I had taken of famous people. He sat close to the screen and never said a word. When I finished he got up from his chair and struck his head against the lamp. 'You want to kill me,' he cried. I called to Nora his wife for a pair of scissors and placed it on his forehead so it would not swell. He did not protest. I think he liked the idea of a twenty-year-old girl taking care of him. Then I began to set up my lamps. The brightness must have been very disagreeable for him because he was suffering so much with the eyes but he sat in his chair with a book in one hand and a magnifying glass in front of his spectacles. I took a number of exposures, thanked him and left.

-On the way to the labouratory my taxi crashed into another car and the camera broke open and I was sure the film had been exposed. When I got home I phoned Mr. Joyce and told him about the accident. He sighed and asked me to come back tomorrow. I sent the film to be processed anyway. The next day when I returned Mr. Joyce was wearing a black jacket and different rings on his fingers. He looked very tired. I took another set of photographs and all of them including the ones in the first group came out very well.

-Did you include Nora? I ask.

-No. Nora said she wasn't important and would not allow herself to be photographed. Here is one of him in the garden with his grandson Stephen. He loved the boy. Stephen was the only person in the world who could bring him to smile. Here is a close-up of Mr. Joyce holding his cane. Notice how fine the hands are.

Giselle Freund has photographed many literary personalities including Alain Robbe-Grillet, Samuel Beckett and Thornton Wilder,. She recalls dinners with painters and writers at La Coupole and the hours spent at La Closerie des Lilas where Hemingway drank and Lenin and Trotsky played chess. She remembers the cocktail parties given by La Nouvelle Revue Francaise attended by many famous people including Vladimir Nabokov.

-Two minutes from here lived Jean Paul Sartre and Simone de Beauvoir. Across from the market in Montparnasse cemetery you can find the tombstone of Baudelaire. On Boulevard Raspail is Rodin's statue of Balzac. I would not live anywhere else.

Four o'clock. We scan the bookstalls along the Seine where before the war tourists searched for copies of *Tropic of Cancer* and *Lady Chatterley's Lover*. These days Maurice Girodias' Olympic Press has an agent in New York. Our search for Joycean references yields a copy of *La Fille Aux Trois Jupons* printed on coarse paper, the pages still uncut. Chapter X11 is titled: Amour! Amour! Quand nous tiens! As Molly Bloom said to Leopold: Get another book by Paul de Cock. Nice name he has.

Our final evening in Paris. Hèléne Joseph arrives at the Hotel Lenox with two bottles of Beaujolais, a package of Camembert and a baguette. Behind the locked door of our room with the music of Jacques Brel coming from the radio we break the rules of the establishment and enjoy an indoor picnic. Hèléne, in fine spirits, dancing about in bare feet, the caftan flying above her thighs, suddenly collapses on the bed. She summons Gabriel in a husky whisper.

-Je suis mourante. Do you know the last speech of *La Dame Aux Camélias*? Come, bend over me the better to hear my dying words. I shall say them in the manner of the great Sarah Bernhardt. Je suis mourante mais je suis heureuse aussi et mon bonheur cache ma morte. Parlez de moi quelquefois...je ne souffre plus...mais je vais vivre...ah--que--je--me--sens--bien.

Hélène is intoxicated. I cannot rouse her. We might as well retire. We wash in the basin, pee in the bidet and fall asleep beside the softly purring Dame aux Camelias.

9

Saturday July 1, 1967. The day local of the Sociètè Nationale de Chemin de Fer that leaves the Gare de l'Est is fuelled by bituminous coal. Since cinders from the chuffing engine shower into our compartment the portly woman in the seat opposite closes the window. In a couple of hours we shall enjoy the comfort of the Trans European Express. The retired school teacher from the Bronx has made this trip numerous times. Today she is travelling to her home in Basel. She keeps up with news about the U.S.A. in the pages of the International Herald Tribune. Have we heard about the purchase of the Da Vinci portrait, Ginevra dei Benci? The National Gallery of Art in Washington paid over five million dollars for it. Have we been to the new Metropolitan Opera House at Lincoln Centre? It is reported to be the world's largest, almost four thousand seats, and it cost $45 million. Her grandchildren adore the Beatles. John Lennon said that the Beatles were more popular than Jesus. Maybe not in Tulsa or Amarillo where the radio stations took the Beatles' songs off the air.

At the border town of Mulhouse we transfer to the T.E.E. operated by the Swiss Federal Railways. Our coach is an air-conditioned environment with reclining, airfoam chairs. A porter in a white uniform has just finished vacuuming the floor and emptying ash trays. The Trans European Express departs punctually, silently, powered by electric cables. The travellers with their briefcases and newspapers appear to lead productive, uncluttered lives. The Swiss penchant for cleanliness is evident in the sanitized washroom where a message in French, Italian and German begs the honoured passenger to rinse the basin after use and to deposit the soiled paper towels in the receptacle.

Switzerland is the roof of Europe. Jagged mountains soar to staggering heights, overshadowing much of the country. Below their wind-whipped, snow-covered peaks, pine forests shelter small mountain villages. The Swiss are famous for watchmaking, precision instruments and machine tools, jewelry cutting, graphic arts and music boxes. The Alps are Europe's winter paradise. St. Moritz, Zermatt and Davos attract skiers by the thousands. In ancient times Switzerland was called Helvetia after the Celtic tribe that inhabited the land. The country is known for its neutrality. One out of every three international organizations has its headquarters in Switzerland. The country's safe status and financial stability attract much foreign capital. A Swiss bank account is inviolate. There are three official languages. A variant of German called Schweitzer-deutsch is the most widely spoken, followed by French and Italian. A fourth language, Romansch, is spoken by about one per cent of the population who live in a mountainous area in the south-east. A fifth, understood by everyone, is Money.

The T.E.E. arrives punctually at Zurich's Haupt Bahnhof where Hans Schiefelbein, who has been anticipating our arrival since the Dublin Joyce Symposium, greets us with a hearty welcome. We follow him out to the Bahnhofstrasse, the tree-lined street of banks where James Joyce often strolled. Sailboats are bobbing on the placid surface of the Zurichsee. At the Parade Platz we get on the tram marked Uetli Hell which proceeds from the centre of the city along the quays of the Limmat River then ascends the Zurich Berg. Hans informs us that the patron saints of the city are Felix and Regula which may be translated as Prosperity and Order.

The Schiefelbein flat is in a small building on the third floor. The couch in the living room pulls out into a double bed and is quite comfortable, he assures us. His wife is out of the city but he hopes we'll be pleased with the light meal he has prepared.

Sunday July 2, 1967. The grave in the Fluntern cemetery is marked by Milton Hebald's sculpture of James Joyce sitting on a rock, ashplant at his side, book raised in front of thick eyeglasses. Nora Barnacle has been newly re-interred beside him. The groundskeeper tells us that many Americans visit the burial place of the Irish writer including Ezra Pound. The newspapers photographed the aged poet on the edge of lucidity, brooding beside the stone effigy of his protege. The lions in the Zoological Gardens nearby are roaring as we leave.

Hans suggests lunch at the Pfauen Restaurant, a favorite eating place of the Irish writer. We have Wienerschnitzel and Fendant Sion, the white wine christened by Joyce as having the delicacy of the urine of an Archduchess.

A walk about Zurich brings us to the Grossmunster and Fraumunster Churches, the historic Guildhouses, the Kunsthaus with its exhibition of Giacometti oils and drawings, the Centre le Corbusier, the Schauspielhaus, and the Opernhaus. Hans cites the number of renowned figures who have enjoyed the hospitality of Zurich including Goethe, Lenin, Wagner and Jung. Switzerland provided a haven for Albert Einstein. Hans does not mention that the foreign ministry in 1938 persuaded Germany to stamp a J on the passports of Jews seeking entry so the Swiss border guards could keep them out.

Monday July 3, 1967. We are in the parlor of the villa that Carola Giedion Welcker occupies with her husband Siegfried Giedion, the author of *Space, Time and Architecture*. The paintings of Arp, Leger and Archipenko endow the room with civility and grace.

-We had a great work to get Mr. Joyce into Switzerland, she recalls. The Swiss government insisted on a guarantee. After all it wasn't only James Joyce but the whole family. I was very angry. I went to see the official and told him that James Joyce was a great man like Goethe, but he was not impressed. Anyway we finally got the money together. At first the Germans didn't let him go, then the Vichy French wouldn't allow him through. There were so many technical matters to arrange. When I finally saw him I really got a shock. He looked so thin, so nervous. He and Nora together with the children and the grandchild spent Christmas with us in this house. He played the piano and said how happy he was to be in Zurich again where the earth was firm. In France with all those people wandering from one place to another it was like a trottoir roulant. But here everything was quiet. He liked the lake and the mountains, but not the people. The French were much nearer to him of course. He always said he'd go back to France, it was so beautifully dirty. He didn't like the Protestantism of cleanliness.

-While we were away skiing in the mountains he telephoned to wish us a Good New Year. He seemed to be quite happy. He said he wanted to write again, perhaps something more involved even than *Finnegans Wake*, and we were so pleased that he would have a quiet period of work. When we came home I telephoned to his Pension Delphine and the lady of the house told me that Mr. Joyce had been taken to the hospital, the Schwesterhaus zum Roten Kreuz. I sat with Giorgio in front of his door. Joyce had to receive a blood transfusion because he was very weak but they had trouble finding a vein. The doctor said that Joyce's skin was like broken paper. He should have had a long rest before the operation. To think he died of such a simple problem, a perforated stomach ulcer. He was only fifty-nine. The irony of it all was that he passed away on January 13th. He was always afraid of the 13th. He would never go out or do anything important on that date.

-The funeral was on January 15, 1941. It was sunny but cold and there were only a few people. The poet Max Geilinger. Professor Heinrich Straumann. Lord Derwent the British Minister made a little speech in English. The tenor Max Meili sang something from Monteverdi, I believe it was Addio terra addio cielo. There were no prayers. Nora said her husband wouldn't have liked to be prayed over. Nora was wonderful, so honest. She was a bit of Ireland that Joyce took around Europe with him. She provided the stability that he needed. She got wild when women admired her husband too much but she was au fond a very good-hearted creature. Nora came here one day after the funeral and told me: You know it's awful that Jim isn't around anymore. He would lie on the sofa when I was doing the housework. He was like a great cat all curled up. Now I am trying to read *Finnegans Wake* but it is a hard job.

Lotte Schiefelbein is preparing a Valais Fondue which originated in the French speaking canton. When the gruyere cheese sauce is ready Hans adds a dollop of kirsch. We sit around the table and dip squares of bread into the pot. When my piece drops off the fork I must kiss Hans. After supper Lotte has to see the mechanic about her car. Gabriel uncorks the Courvoisier and before long we are singing Lots of Fun at *Finnegans Wake*.

-How does it feel to be an internationally renowned authority on the works of James Joyce, asks Gabriel.

-Lonely, shrugs Hans. Joyce is not highly regarded among the burghers of this city. Hemingway is much more popular. The Swiss intellectuals have probably looked into *Ulysses* and would be able to tag a label to it like stream of consciousness but they don't appreciate him. When Joyce lived here from 1914 to 1918 he didn't have many connections with the Swiss. He associated chiefly with Frank Budgen who is English, with Greeks, with people from Trieste and with Jewish immigrants.

-Joyce would have been intrigued by your collection of Erotica, the volumes with German texts and photographs.

-It's a rather small collection I'm afraid. Much of the good stuff is so expensive, out of the reach of ordinary people who cannot afford to buy the books and aren't allowed to borrow them from institutions which have them locked away. I'd like to have access to the secret archives of the Vatican, the world's richest accumulation of original documents and records. The transcripts of the trials of Galileo, Pico della Mirandola and Savonarola. The laws of incest. The medieval church was absolutely fascinated by incest. I'd like to read about Beatrice Cenci's murder of her father. The Book of the Nativity of the Saviour and of Mary. The Book of the Obstetrician. Those treasures are wasted in the Vatican tombs.

-Many of the forbidden books go back to the Reformation, continues Hans. That's when it all began, the censoring of erotic material. Since that time of course the watch dogs have sprung up everywhere—even in Switzerland, where the guardians of morality censor everything, especially sex in films, because they believe it is harmful for innocent children to watch mommy and daddy making love. Christianity is obsessed with sex and sin.

-The Greeks had a more wholesome attitude. Their gods mated with the mortals and their offspring were kings and heroes, the god-born or god-nurtured ones. Aeneas was the son of Aphrodite and the Trojan prince Anchises. Achilles was born of the sea-goddess Thetis. But Zeus was the most active. As a swan he impregnated Leda who gave birth to Helen. He took on the appearance of Amphitryon the husband of Alcmena and sired Heracles. He visited Danae in the form of a shower of gold and she gave birth to Perseus.

-Jews don't regard sex as sinful, I venture.

-The God of Israel doesn't like his chosen people to screw around, counters Gabriel. The Old Testament is explicit in its proscriptions and the Shulchan Aruch is full of sexual taboos.

-At least Judaism doesn't expect one to accept the myth of the virgin birth and the divinity of Jesus.

-The Jews of the shtetl believed that Jesus was conceived by Mary in an adulterous relationship with a Roman centurion named Pandera. The account was first postulated by Celsus the Platonist who lived toward the end of the second century. The Toledoth Yeshu, the anti-gospel History of Jesus, records that a Joseph Pandera of the tribe of Judah who lived in Bethlehem lusted after Miriam who was betrothed to Johanan of the house of David. Pandera pretending to be Johanan called upon the chaste Miriam at the close of the Sabbath and forced her to submit to him. Some time after the event Miriam upbraided Johanan who expressed his innocence but there had been no witnesses so Pandera could not be punished.

-Since Miriam was with child Johanan was advised by Rabban Simeon ben Shetah to go to Babylon. On the way she gave birth to a son and named him Yehoshua after her brother and had him circumcized on the eighth day and when he was old enough she took him to the house of study to be instructed in the Jewish tradition. When the townspeople began to enquire about the boy's family background Miriam admitted that he was the son of Joseph Pandera and it became necessary for Jeshu to flee to the Upper Galilee.

-Of course Christians regard this as a libel against the doctrine of the incarnation. Origen refutes it in his Contra Celsus.

-The four gospellers invented a genesis to support their claims of Jesus as the Messiah whose coming was foretold by the prophet Isaiah.

-Matthew, Mark, Luke and John. The Mamalujo Propaganda Press.

Sunday July 9, 1967. The Trans European Express slides out of the Haupt Bahnhof. Gathering momentum it skirts the Zurichsee and the picture postcard view of Zurich recedes, giving way to pine forests, mountain villages and terraced farms with the white-faced Alps as backdrop. It speeds past Zug and

Andermatt with their chalets and ski trails. Up curving inclines and precipitous descents. Through stygian tunnels and out again into the brightness of snow and sky, hastening toward the Italian border.

At dusk we arrive in Milan's Stazione Centrale whose imposing mass, burdened with ornamentation, took 25 years to complete. Napoleon conquered the city. Mussolini was hanged upside down in one of its squares. The luxury hotels are air-conditioned but we have been directed to the second class Pensione Milano. The room is bare except for the bed. The air hangs hot, humid and motionless.

In search of a place to eat we discover the cruciform Galleria Vittorio Emanuele, the largest covered arcade in Europe. The central Octagon has a 50 metres high cupola whose four glass lunettes provide an immense skylight. A few tourists wander about, their footsteps echoing on the tessellated pavement. Since it opened in 1878 the Galleria has been the meeting place of Milan's statesmen and busines leaders, its artists, writers, opera singers and musicians. And its prostitutes, peddlers and pickpockets. Mark Twain came under its spell. The American artist Saul Steinberg who spent ten years of his youth in Milan recorded the grandiose environment of the Galleria including the crowds that gathered at the Biffi and Savini restaurants as well as the Campari and Motta bars, during an era when the music played and the gaslights bathed the popular forum in a mellow glow. This evening only the cafeteria on the second floor is open and we manage to get a plate of lasagna, a dish of spumoni and a cup of espresso.

A short distance from the Galleria's north door is La Scala. A poster announces the Fall Opening with Seiji Ozawa and the Toronto Symphony Orchestra. Il Teatro alla Scala replaced the church that stood for four hundred years on the site and was named after Regina della Scala, the 14th-century noblewoman who financed the construction of the church. When the opera house opened on August 3, 1778, a sixty piece orchestra was in the pit and the crowd of 3600 in the six-tiered auditorium heard Salieri's opera Europe Rioconsciuta. Arturo Toscanini, who played the cello in the orchestra as a lad, served on and off as La

Scala's conductor and artistic director until 1929, when he left for America. The theatre was partially destroyed by allied bombing raids but was rebuilt and on its opening May 11, 1946. Toscanini conducted. When he died in 1957 his funeral service was held here.

Exhausted by the oppressive heat Gabriel and I return to our spacious room in the Pensione.

Monday July 10, 1967. After a light breakfast we are eager to explore the city. The streets are busy with honking cars estimated at 500,000 a day in the vicinity of the Piazza della Repubblica where the Equestrian statue of Vittorio Emanuele recalls the glory of the monarchy. Buses and streetcars and the recently opened third line of the Metropolitan have not reduced the traffic congestion.

Our first stop is the Duomo. The white marble cathedral whose origin dates from 1386 is the most complex construction of Italian Gothic architecture, ranking with St. Peter's in Rome and the Cathedral at Seville as the largest in the world. It is built in the shape of a latin cross divided by soaring, fluted pillars into five naves. The Duomo has seen numerous revisions. Napoleon added his own ideas to the facade. The carvings in the great cinquecento portals with their bronze doors represent the creation of Eve, the Edict of Constantine, the life of the Virgin and the history of the Commune. Light enters into the vast reaches of the interior through the stained glass windows, some ancient, some recently installed, and falls onto the mosaic floors. The high altar is surmounted by a magnificent choir.

The roof seen from the ground is a lacy network of marble spires. Reached via flights of worn stone steps it presents a view of hundreds of turrets, columns, buttresses, arches and snow white saints, angels and cherubim. Set on the tallest pinnacle, reaching a height of 108 metres stands the golden Madonnina, the spiritual symbol of Milan. Its eminence has been reduced by the Velasca Tower a modern skyscraper intrusion. Another secular elevation counsels in bright neon: Bevete Coca Cola. We descend via the elevator.

Lunch at the Cafe Monferrato consists of sausage on a

roll with mustard and sauerkraut and double espresso coffee.

After relaxing in the Giardino Pubblico we visit the Church of Santa Maria delle Grazie to view the fresco by Leonardo da Vinci on the wall of the convent. Commissioned by Ludovico the Moor and finished in l497 the Last Supper is faded, only the outline clearly visible.

In the simmering evening we come by chance to the Trattoria Bagutta, a bustling establishment hidden away on a side street. Gabriel and I order veal scallopine and a bottle of chianti. The time passes pleasantly as we slip into a state of mild intoxication. Umbriago ma non troppo.

Tuesday July ll, 1967. The train out of Milan is stifling with travellers stacked in the corridors. It stops often along the Italian Riviera. At the border town of Ventimiglia we halt for the ritual of customs inspection and passport control. The aroma of salami invades our compartment. Eventually we are on the move again. Ventimiglia yields to Ventmille and the Côte d'Azur. Menton with its olive and lemon trees flashes past. The private estates of Cap Martin. The principality of Monaco. The yachts at Bealieu. The fishing port of Villefranche. The city of Nice.

At the Gare Centrale the Tourist Bureau arranges hotel accommodations. While we wait in one of the queues Gabriel rehearses his request. Une chambre pour deux a bon marché, s'il vous plait. The refrain develops in my head to the tune of Mademoiselle from Armentiéres, parlez-vous? As I am humming the World War One marching song a lean individual approaches. His business card reveals him to be Gaston Rochon, the manager of Hotel de l'Èmpereur. The rate for a suite with a magnificent view of the Mediterranean is a mere l5 francs per day. So, if we agree, he picks up our suitcases and advancing to the street stows the bags in the trunk of an old Renault.

The motor comes to life after some indecision and as we roll down the broad Avenue Jean Medecin our driver expatiates on the delights of the city. Nice is known for its night clubs, antique shops, boutiques and marché aux puces. Rochon indicates the Israelite Temple. The Casino Club. Place Massena with the fountain of Helios and his oxen in black marble.

We are in the old town now, the narrow streets clogged with horses and wagons. On Rue St. François de Paule, Rochon stops outside the flower market. Nearby is the old Opera. In that building Napoleon Bonaparte stayed. It says so on the wall. Carrying the luggage he bids us follow him through the lane into a courtyard to a stairway. Première étage. Hotel Joffre. Montez, he urges. Deuxième étage. Hotel V. Hugo. Montez. Montez. On the third floor the brass plaque reads: Hotel de L'Èmpereur.

-Nous voici. Rochon unlocks the door and switches on the light. We follow him along the hallway to one of the rooms that serves as office. We must register with Madame Rochon.

-Bienvenu. Madame's face is alabaster, the eyes dark holes. Your suite is numéro treize. Monsieur will show you. But first, your passports, which I shall return tomorrow.

The suite at the end of the hall is a single chamber furnished with table and chairs, a bed, wardrobe and chest of drawers, a wash basin and bidet. The walls are pastel blue. A screen encloses the kitchen.

The terrace looks out on the Baie des Anges with the sun setting crimson on the water. Palm trees, mimosa with spikes of white, pink and blue. And a six-lane road with surging sport cars. Rochon informs us that the city was founded by Greeks from Marseilles as a trading port called Nicaea. It was colonized by the Romans, subsequently owned by the Counts of Provence and Savoy, conquered by Napoleon, and became part of France in the 1860 plebiscite. Nice was a favored winter spa during the late 19th century when Queen Victoria and the Czarina of Russia headed the confluence of royalty and nobility from all over Europe. The Prince of Wales on his regular visits to Cannes, Monte Carlo, Menton and Antibes stopped in Nice, gracing the Promenade des Anglais with his suave boulevardier's presence.

-And now I must leave you. Au revoir, Madame, Monsieur.

How about going out to eat? I'm starved.

Madame Rochon intercepts our departure. She would like payment in advance for the accommodations.

-But Monsieur...

-You have not given him the money, she cries.

-He asked at the station for the first night's payment, says Gabriel.

-Nom de Dieu! So now if you will let me have the balance I shall give you a receipt for the full amount. I do not allow Monsieur Rochon to involve himself with the financial affairs because he is a gambler. He has lost thousands of francs on the horses.

Madame laughs harshly. Bony fingers stroke the pulse at her throat as Gabriel counts out the ninety francs.

-Merci beaucoup. If you are looking for a good place to eat, may I suggest the restaurant next to the wine cellar. It serves the regional specialities like pissaladière, the tarte d'ognon with anchovies and olives. I also recommend loup de mer, the bass fish that is cooked on a bed of fennel.

The stalls on the rue St. Francois de Paule have closed but the boulangerie and charcuterie are busy. An appetizing aroma of tomatoes flavored with garlic draws us to the modest outdoor restaurant. A young man welcomes us, whisks crumbs off the checkered table cloth and lights the candle. He leaves, returning momentarily with a basket of bread. Consulting the hand-written menu we settle for Salade Nicoise, soupe au pistou, loup de mer and a bottle of Pouilly Fuisse.

In the lamp-lighed dusk with fragments of music from the open windows we experience the delights of southern French gastronomy. Everything is to our satisfaction. We are enjoying the creamy Camembert and a second bottle of wine when the peace of the evening is fractured by a cry of distress. A woman in a summer frock darts in our direction. She carries a valise.

-Do you speak English? Thank God. The tour guide has given us an hour to see everything. It's been very frantic, 12 countries in 21 days. May I sit down? I'm exhausted.

-Certainly.

-Thank you. My name is Maisie Johnson. I'm from Cedar Rapids, Iowa.

-Have you eaten? I inquire.

-I wouldn't know what to order. It's all so foreign. I'm sure they would bring me rabbit, Maisie registers distaste. Maybe I'll have a green salad. We're all supposed to meet at the Casino on Place (she pronounces it Playce) Massena at nine o'clock.

Maisie's once-in-a-lifetime holiday abroad has been a disappointment. The hotels are old and the bathrooms primitive. Europe was supposed to be so romantic, that's why she signed up for the tour. Of course she has taken a lot of photographs to show the girls back in the office. But she will never leave America again.

Maisie nibbles at the vegetables. The coffee is too strong however. She must leave now to join the others. Delving into her bag she retrieves a handful of coins. Is that enough? French money is so foreign. She must go now, and dashes away, her heels clacking on the cobblestones.

Two cognacs later we are ready for a stroll. The shops on the Quai des Ètats Unis are filled with expensive jewelry as well as cheap trinkets like those offered on the Atlantic City boardwalk. Farther west the Promenade des Anglais is alive with Nannies wheeling babies in carriages, children licking ice cream cones, elegantly dressed demi-mondaines. The celebrated boulevard is endowed with villas and apartments once occupied by the grandes dames and messieurs of the 19th century who played baccarat in the Palais de la Mediterranée. The luxury hotels of that era, the Ruhl, the Royal and the Westminster are still thriving. The white-domed four star Negresco, monument to the son of a Romanian innkeeper, is the choice of Elizabeth Taylor and Princess Grace as well as the tourists who delight in the antique furniture, the opulent tapestries and paintings and the Louis XIV Restaurant with its ten ton fireplace, velvet walls and frescoed ceiling. The doorman is periwigged and costumed in the style of French classicism. While I admire the 18-foot crystal chandelier in the rotunda Gabriel discovers the men's washroom which is entered as if into a tent of the great Bonaparte himself. Upon his return he is pleased to report that he stood before the same urinal as Richard Burton, Haile Selassie, Pablo Picasso and various French heads of state.

Our travel book states that the four and a half mile Promenade des Anglais owes its existence to the asthmatic 18th century Scottish surgeon Tobias Smollett who gave up his

London practice at the age of thirty to write novels and satires on public affairs. The author of *The Adventures of Peregrine Pickle* came to Nice in December 1763 and wrote enthusiastic letters home. 'I must acknowledge that ever since my arrival I have breathed more freely than I have done for some years and my spirits have been more alert. Today, the first of May I splashed in the sea water to relieve the condition of my lungs and found the experience salutary.' Smollett's book *Travels in France and Italy* popularized Nice as a sunshine paradise. Behind the old port is his memorial Rue Smollett in the working class district.

After midnight we are again on the terrace of our apartment sipping Bisquit Dubouchet. The traffic below is a hum of rubber on macadam. The night sky is pierced by twin beams, the landing lights of the Air France flight from Paris. And so to bed.

Wednesday July 12, 1967. Breakfast of croissants and coffee. On St. François de Paule the housewives are making the circuit of baker, butcher and grocer. The flower market displays a profusion of blooms. The vegetable stalls are laden with white asparagus, artichokes, lettuce, tomatoes and cucumbers. A gamine clutching an empty bottle skips to the wine cellar for a litre of vin ordinaire. The air is mild, the sky azure. We walk as far as the fountain of Apollo and return by way of the bus station and the church of St. Francois de Paule.

-Vive l'Èmpereur, Gabriel gasps after the climb to the third floor. I must get to the toilet toute de suite.

-Bonjour Madame. Arms akimbo, Madame Rochon in a black robe smiles in greeting. Will you have a cup of coffee with me? Brushing strands of hair from the high cheekbones she inquires about my plans.

-We should like to make a few purchases.

-But of course, the magasins in the Arcade du Casino have much to offer. Ceramics, pottery, gifts made of olive wood, les Poupées Nicoises and of course perfumes.

-And how will you spend the day, Madame?

-Il faut faire des emplettes. Meat, vegetables, vichy water, a baguette. And a bouquet of carnations. I have already finished with the housekeeping. The rest of the day is for me to do as I please.

-Ah, you must have a lover, I tease.

-I do not deny it.

-Does Monsieur Rochon know?

-He is much too involved with La Vie Hippique. He is already on the road to the Hippodrome to wager on the horses. All he cares is that when he returns he will have his dinner on the table.

-Have a pleasant day Madame.

-That is my expectation.

The week passes in swimming, sunbathing and dining. In mid afternoon siestas and leisurely explorations. The Autobus takes us to the hill of Cimiez and the Matisse Museum on the second floor of the pink chateau where we view the exhibition of the artist's paintings and the illustrations for the limited edition of Homer's *Ulysses*. His palette, brushes and smock are also displayed. On the ground floor is the Archaeological Museum featuring Roman bric-a-brac.

Nearby are the ruins of the Roman walls, the baths and the 6,000 seat amphitheatre.

At the Musée Chagall we inspect the large Biblical canvases painted in the fifties and the engravings for a new Bible.

On the fourteenth of July we observe the military parade from the terrace. The tanks, the foot soldiers and the cavalry. The flags and banners. The tattoo of drums and the bugles' Marseillaise as the troops pass along the Quai des Etats Unis to the Monument aux Morts. Madame Rochon pours champagne. Vive la France. Vive le Canada.

In the morning Monsieur drives us to the Aeroport.

10

Sunday August 20, 1967. A visit to Montreal to attend Expo 67 and celebrate the one hundredth anniversary of Canadian Confederation. Located on two islands in the St. Lawrence River, the International World's Fair boasts ninety foreign, provincial, industrial and theme pavilions. Projected attendance of 50 million visitors during the one year run. Long queues for the movie presentations, displays of products, art and propaganda. The amusement park features rides and attractions including 'Le Monstre', an enormous roller coaster.

Paris, December 6, 1967

My dear Anna and Gabriel,

I can imagine what you must be thinking of me. But there are several good reasons for my silence. My father has been very sick since you left and has taken up a great deal of my time in spite of having a day nurse. I take over every evening at six and by the time I am through I am usually too tired to concentrate on much except maybe a page or two of a current book. Also I have had another fall.

If my father's health improves I hope to get to the U.S. for a short visit in April or May. I have been invited to Buffalo by Oscar Silverstein and I would very much like to see what they have done with the collection they purchased, most of which was saved by my husband, certainly all the Joyce books and papers. Maybe you will plan a visit to Buffalo while I am there. It would be lovely to have a little more time together.

I understand Mrs. Stanislaus Joyce has become a good friend of Miss Lidderdale. As you know she is the one who sold the famous letters and shocked most of Joyce's real friends. Miss Lidderdale (Miss Weaver's niece) seems to have taken over all of her aunt's responsibilities and is doing a wonderful, humane job as far as poor Lucie is concerned and in protecting the Joyce interests.

But it seems to me that from now on the effort we have always made to protect Joyce's integrity and name is no longer possible. It has become a Joyce and a family industry. And it is no use fighting windmills. I am not bitter about it, just rather saddened.

Warm regards to you both.

Lucie Leon.

11

March 13, 1968. Lyndon Johnson announces in a television address that he will not seek re-election as President of the United States.

April 4, 1968. Civil rights leader Martin Luther King is assassinated in Memphis.

April 23, 1968. The introduction of panty hose is welcomed by the women of America who express their relief at being able to abandon the thigh-high stockings with their garters and garter belts. The mini skirt is enjoying a great popularity.

Paris. Monday May 6, 1968.

The Vietnam Peace Talks are about to begin but there is rioting on the left bank. The labour unions have called a one day general strike in support of the students who have barricaded themselves in the Sorbonne.

The manager of the Hotel Lenox laments that this is a bad time for France, the fault of the communists and foreign elements like the scoundrel Danny the Red who should be deported to Germany.

Our unpacking is interrupted by shouts in the streets, the crashing of glass, the whoop-whoop-whoop of police sirens. From the window I can see people running down rue de l'Université. The rumble of vehicles. Rifle shots. Alert to a good news story Gabriel and I rush out to record the latest developments.

On Boulevard St. Germain the students are crouched behind over-turned automobiles. They have pried loose the cobblestones and ripped up the iron gratings around the trees as ammunition against the Compagnies Républicaines de Sécurité. Shouting insults: Sucez-moi le baton. Taunting them: Allez-vous faire enculer chez les Grecs. Steel-helmeted and masked the C.R.S advamce in a phalanx lobbing gas grenades. Eyes stinging, tears flowing, Gabriel and I retreat to the safety of the hotel.

Tuesday May 7. The newspapers carry front page photographs and stories of the carnage. The clashes are said to have been inspired by a small band of Maoist, Marxist, Trotskyite and Guevarist militants who streamed into the Sorbonne quadrangle and fought police attempts to eject them. Six hundred of the demonstrators have been arrested and the Sorbonne closed. At Nanterre, the suburban branch of the University of Paris, half the faculty have gone on strike in sympathy. De Gaulle warns that further violence will not be tolerated. An estimated 30,000 students singing the Internationale march along the Champs Elysees. Strikes and demonstrations have spread to provincial cities with high school students picketing to demand the release of l00 jailed rioters.

Wednesday May 8. The streets are calm but lingering traces of tear gas irritate our eyes. Lucie Leon has invited us to dinner, advising that we take the Metro since the police have thrown up barricades along Boulevard Saint Germain. Her other guests are David Davis, director of the American Centre and Maria Jolas who is working with Bertrand Russell to bring the United States to justice for crimes in Vietnam.

We offer our condolences on the death of Madame Leon's father, recalling our last meeting with the little old man in the stockinged cap and dressing gown, a Russian newspaper trembling in his hand.

During cocktails we review the events of the past three days, especially the brutality of the police and the intransigence of De Gaulle.

The manifestations are far removed from this pleasant apartment on the tranquil street named for Claude Casimir-Périer, President of France in the closing years of the nineteenth century whose duties were largely ceremonial like ribbon cutting and ship launching. His Jewish wife Pauline Benda, known professionally as Madame Simone, was an actress with an international reputation whose lover was her husband's secretary Alain-Fournier, the author of *Le Grand Maulne*.

In the twenties Paris was home for many American expatriates including Ernest Hemingway, F.Scott Fitzgerald, Frank Harris and Gertrude Stein. Emma Goldman—I do not believe in God because I do believe in Man—continued her struggle for a free society here in the freest of all cities.

During the dinner of filet mignon, white asparagus and strawberries, the conversation turns to the American presence in Paris. Davis mentions the cultural events sponsored by the American Centre on the rue de Dragon, poetry readings, concerts, art exhibitions and theatrical presentations. However, if the manifestations continue, much of the activity will have to be postponed.

-The seeds of student revolt in France were planted long ago, explains white-haired Maria Jolas. It's all because of the archaic system of higher education, supervised by a mediocre bureaucracy that resists all change. French Universities always overcrowded and short of professors fail about twenty per cent of the students every year and half give up and leave. As for the manifestations, well, the CRS have had virtually no education. They come from lower class backgrounds and take great pleasure in cracking the skulls of the smart-ass bourgeois kids. The CRS enjoy beating up and humiliating those whom they arrest. They are like wild animals suddenly let loose. Nobody has a good word for them. Not the press, not the public. Once the Algerian conflict ended work had to be found for them in France, so you see the result.

-Let us hope the situation will be resolved soon, says Lucie Leon pouring the coffee.

-Tell us about your friendship with James Joyce, urges Gabriel, and Madame Jolas is pleased to oblige.

-It started in 1927 when my husband Eugene Jolas began publishing instalments of *Finnegans Wake* in **transition**. It was a gradual sort of involvement. Joyce was in many ways an extremely helpless man. Nora, who was a charming woman, was not able to cope with the tragic events of their lives. She was absolutely— –the French have a word for it, ébranlée, overwhelmed— by the possibility that her daughter would never be able to lead a normal life. So Joyce needed somebody who was a bit outside and could do things such as accompanying Lucia to England. We got along well. I respected him as a writer. We both loved music and we had many informal evenings of singing. Joyce was a Dubliner and I came from Louisville, Kentucky, which had a large Irish population. The two cities had a surface similarity, the friendliness, the pleasure of getting together in the pubs. We were both provincials with a relaxed attitude towards life. It didn't have to dash ahead for us the way it did for Fitzgerald or Hemingway.

-There has been a tendency for people to think that Joyce exploited his brother and practically everybody he came into contact with. I don't agree. The James Joyce I knew was a much purified man to whom life had brought the most incredible suffering and who never stopped reaching toward perfection. What makes his writing so extraordinary is that we feel this sentient man behind the work, a human being with a mind that embraced the universe. He was the most loving father as well as a devoted husband. And a close, attentive friend. As for the hard-drinking, penniless, scrounging young man who appears from certain letters and from other accounts, well, they say that the human animal changes every seven years. Only a part of our original self is left. What did remain in Joyce was this constant refining of the inner instrument, what you might call the soul. You found it first in his idealism as a young man and it never really left him, reaching such a point of rarefaction at the end of his life that it was almost a flame.

It is midnight when we leave and Davis offers to drive us to the hotel. The gendarmes at the roadblocks ask to see our identification and want to know where we have been and where we are going before allowing us to proceed. St. Germain des Près is seething with demonstrators shouting De Gaulle Assassin, the tension building as we approach rue de l'Université. At the Lenox Hotel Madame unlocks the door, urging us to hurry in, and quickly secures it again. The rumble of CRS vans and the explosions continue all night.

Thursday May 9. The police have cordoned off the major bridges across the Seine. At noon Place St. Michel is jammed with students facing a battery of troops equipped with shields, clubs and gas grenades. No traffic moving. Not a sound. Only an eerie silence with each side alert to the expected confrontation. After a lengthy interval of mute antagonism the civilians disperse down Boulevard St. Michel. The police remain, stolid, invincible.

Friday May 10. The Battle of the Sorbonne. As the troops

charge into the quadrangle the students hurl stones, iron bars and Molotov cocktails, setting fire to automobiles. Retreating they denounce the CRS as S.S. bastards.

Saturday May 11. Premier Georges Pompidou promises to re-open the Sorbonne, proclaiming on radio and television that the reform of the University system is indispensable. He intimates that the appeal courts will deal lightly with the convicted student leaders. The latest tally shows 1158 have been hurt in the rioting, 596 of them police. Over 1,000 have been arrested. An illegal 24 hour general strike is being considered by the Communist, Socialist, Christian Socialist and Teachers labour unions.

Sunday May 12. Traffic moves normally with only the blare of car horns to disturb the gentle morning. Spring has repossessed the Left Bank, the birds are singing and the Bateaux Mouches are chugging along the Seine. The mood is optimistic among the espresso drinkers in the sidewalk cafes. De Gaulle will have to back down, even resign. Everyone hopes for an end to the official wiretaps, the news censorship, the arrest on sight and preventive detention, the keeping of dossiers on citizens and the secret house searches without warrants.

At Shakespeare and Company a few students are lying on pallets. George Whitman is sequestered upstairs in his Little Versailles, surrounded by autographed books including No. 515 of the one thousand numbered copies of *Ulysses* published in 1922 by Sylvia Beach. A young woman in denim shirt and skirt who has been meditating in the Lotus position smiles in recognition.

-So you have come back. Hèléne Joseph embraces us. Her jet-black hair is close-cropped, her figure leaner.

-We figured you'd be in Israel. Didn't you go?

-Oh yes. I went after the Six Day War. Do you wish to hear about my adventures? Very well, I will tell you everything. In Tel Aviv I was accepted into the Israeli Army.

-What was it like?

-We had many lectures, all in Hebrew, which I did not understand. A girl who could speak French tried to translate for me. In one of the classes we sat on logs en pleine aire no matter what kind of weather. They were narrow logs so we wouldn't fall asleep. After the lecture the officer asked questions.

When she came to me I just croaked that I did not understand
Hebrew and she yelled Mah? That means, What? So I repeated, I
cannot speak or understand Hebrew. Finally somebody told the
instructor about my problem and she did not know what to do
with me. For three months I just sat on the log and did not say a
word.

   -We did a lot of marching and drilling. We had to run five
kilometres with a pack and rifle. We learned to use submachine
guns and hand grenades. We had two sets of uniforms, fatigues
and dress, and they arranged the activities so we had to change all
the time. Two minutes to run to the tent and be out for inspection
and everything had to be perfect. Worst of all were the crowded
conditions with eleven of us in a tent for eight. Every morning we
had to get up at half past four. Imagine, 200 females waiting to
wash and brush their teeth and go to the toilet. Many mornings
there was no time even to faire pis-pis so during the day I would
try but there was always a queue and we had only two minutes
to get back so I would have the first chance to empty my bladder
only before the evening meal.

   -After basic training I was sent to a Nahal, a settlement
in the Sinai between El Arish and and the Gaza strip. At first
I was glad to be there. Everything was so exciting. We were
pioneers with no electricity, no plumbing, just one water pipe
where everybody ran in the morning to wash. Each day we
accomplished miracles, the progress was incredible. It was a
wonderful feeling, so different from my life in Paris.

   -There were sixty of us. I managed fine with the ones from
the United States and Canada, from Europe and South Africa,
but the Sabras considered us outsiders. It bothered me when I
heard them saying bad things about us, especially since we were
trying so hard to be accepted. I did not like the Sabras. They did
not read anything except cowboy novels. In Hebrew of course.
They liked pop music, very loud. The religious ones were more
conservative but basically they were all anti-intellectual. Bien
sur they were young, from 18 to 21 years. They asked why I read
such serious books in my free time and how could I listen to the
boring classical music. They preferred watching television.

   -Or discussing their sexual experiences, I suggest.

-It is not true what you may have heard about sexual freedom in Israel. Not for women anyway. The ones in the Nahal were puritanical, always thinking about getting married and having children. There is the double standard. The men are very macho, always trying to feel your tetons and get you into bed but most unmarried women want to remain vierges and those who do consent to faire l'amour would be very upset if their secret were discovered.

-How do they feel about Jews living in the Diaspora?

-They do not like that rich Jews from America send money to Israel and come to visit but do not make the commitment to stay while the Israelis sacrifice their lives in the wars against the Arabs. There is also a great deal of jealousy. Many of them dream of emigrating to America and making lots of money. They are very materialistic. And arrogant. To be courteous is considered like being slaves. That has been drummed into them, the suffering of the Jewish people in Europe even before the Holocaust when Jews walked with the heads down and didn't defend themselves. I suppose that is why many Israelis feel that to show courtesy is a mark of weakness. You go into a store and the person at the cash register ignores you while she talks to her friends and if you interrupt she will tell you to go to hell. Still, the Israelis have a wonderful capacity for reaching out to you. My real criticism is against the bureaucracy. That's what kills the spirit. You want to change foreign currency or cash a traveller's cheque so you go to the bank and wait a long time for the paper work to be finished.

-Is that why you left?

-There were other reasons. In the Nahal life became tedious. The same routine, working in the fields all day and on guard duty at night with shootings sometime. The tension from being isolated. We went on leave one weekend each month. The nearest city was Beer Sheva about 45 minutes drive. Jerusalem was four hours away. I met an army officer, a tank commander, so I moved in with him. It was O.K. for three months, making love was fine but we never became friends. Or equals. Whenever Moshe had anything to confide it was always to one of his copains. If something was bothering him he did not tell me. The

Israelis have been programmed to hold in everything, to be brave and strong. The Army stresses the need for survival instead of encouraging personal development.

-When did you return to Paris?

-Just three weeks ago. After the doctor told me I was enceinte. I have not yet decided about having the baby. In the meantime I am writing about my experiences. What do you plan for this evening?

-Madame Leon has given us tickets for the Bunraku Puppets at the Theatre des Nations.

-Ah yes, it is part of the Festival of International Theatre.

-Tomorrow we may go to a performance of Faust.

-I do not recommend it. L'Opéra does not have a good reputation. It is not like La Scala or the New York Metropolitan. Molière at the Comédie Francaise is magnificent but all the tickets have been sold. Maybe we can go out together tomorrow, yes?

Monday May 13. The placard above the head lamps of the green and white autobus displays a pair of female eyes and the slogan 'From the bus I can see Paris'. A fine morning for a ride along the quays, through the Bois de Boulogne, past Pere Lachaise Cemetery, the Place de la Bastille and the Place de la Concorde. The No. 24 continues along the Right Bank to the Louvre, crosses the Ile de la Cité over the old Pont Neuf beside Notre Dame and onto the left Bank. We get off at Quai St. Bernard and look for the apartment of Stuart and Moune Gilbert on the Ile St. Louis.

-You had no trouble finding the place? So, you took the bus. It is a cheap way to travel about the city and very instructive. It was Blaise Pascal who designed the first Paris omnibus service just before he died. That would be 300 years ago.

-Was he the one who invented the barometer? I remember something about Pascal's Principle from my high school physics.

-That is correct. He also invented the first mechanical calculator and I am told the ones in use today have cylinders and gears similar to those of Pascal's machine. He had a brilliant mind. Theologian, mathematician and philosopher. He was a

Jansenist and attacked the Jesuit theories of grace and moral theology. You are no doubt familiar with his aphorism: The heart has its reasons of which reason knows not.

-Of course, responds Gabriel. But I am more intrigued by the reference to Pascal in James Joyce's *A Portrait of the Artist as a Young Man* where Stephen says to Cranly, 'Pascal, if I remember rightly would not suffer his mother to kiss him as he feared the contact of her sex.'

-I recollect the passage, says Gilbert, eyes sparkling in the wise, old head.

-How can that be, Gabriel wonders, since Pascal was only four years old when his mother died? It presumes a precocity that strains credulity.

-Ah, you have just contributed a footnote to the Joyce canon, laughs Gilbert. He opens a humidor. Will you smoke? No? Quite right. Tobacco can shorten one's life. But I enjoy a cigar.

-You saw Maria Jolas? enquires Moune. I trust you found her in good health.

-She has inexhaustible energy, says Gilbert. When she isn't engaged in political or cultural activities she is busy with translations. Did she attend the Joyce Symposium in Dublin?

-No but there were other well-known personalities. We took photographs of the proceedings. Here is one of Padraic Colum.

-I am glad to see Padraic is looking very fit indeed.

-And this is Giorgio Joyce.

-He appears venerable and stately, like a Prime Minister, observes Moune.

-I thought he looked very much like his father.

-No, the father had a more pointed face, Moune studies the picture. I recall Monsieur Joyce used to sit on the couch where you are now and when I was playing the piano he got up and danced. But what was beautiful was when he sang. The Irish accent is so charming. It wins everybody's heart.

-Joyce learned a lot from the music halls. He especially liked the ones in Paris.

-Alas, many of them no longer exist, Moune laments.

Other well-known places have either disappeared or changed.
Fouquet's and Les Trianons where Joyce liked to meet.

-I would tempt him here with a bottle of Swiss Fendant
that he enjoyed very much. It is hard to get in Paris. Fendant
Sion tastes very innocent but it is rather intoxicating, a bit like
German Hock.

-How old was James Joyce when you first knew him?

-That was in 1927, about six years after he finished *Ulysses*.
He was forty-five. I met him through Sylvia Beach. Quite by
accident I dropped into her shop and learned that *Ulysses* was
to be published in French, and she asked if I would like to have
a look at some of the translation, a dozen pages, and I asked
if I could take them home because there seemed to be a few
words that weren't quite correct. When I returned with the items
underlined she said she would show my suggestions to the
writer. I offered to go through the whole text since I had nothing
to do at the time. You see, I had retired from my job as a judge
in Burma. It took me six and a half months of steady attention
and required great tact because the translator Auguste Morel
was a brilliant man but he had a tendency to make the novel
more Rabelaisian than was needed. Valery Larbaud, who had
the last word, was very sensible about it. He knew exactly what
was required and altered the tone when it was getting needlessly
vulgar.

-How did James Joyce get along with people?

-Quite well. He was always interested in their
backgrounds, their nationalities. He had no racial prejudice of
any kind. He had a number of Jewish friends, Paul Leon for one.
I once asked Sam Beckett why Joyce was able to make such great
friends with Jews throughout his career and Beckett replied, 'I
suppose it is because of their loyalty. Joyce said that a Jewish
person could be trusted to help you.'

-Why did Joyce choose a Jew, Leopold Bloom, to be the
protagonist in his novel?

-I think because he wanted to put himself in the skin of
somebody who could look at the Irish scene with detachment.
He had met some Jews in Dublin and liked them. He was also
inclined to go to the side of people who were suffering from

prejudice. The, Greeks too, had a fascination for him and there were many contacts between the Semites and Hellenes, in Crete for instance. And of course the Phoenicians were Semites. I quite like Leopold Bloom. I once told Joyce that Stephen was a bit too highbrow for my taste and that I preferred Bloom and Joyce said, 'I like Bloom too; he is a good man, kind-hearted.'

-Have you any idea whom Joyce used as the prototype for Bloom?

-I'm sure Bloom must be a composite character, part Italo Svevo, part Leopoldo Popper, totally humanitarian. Yes, James Joyce was on the side of Bloom. When I knew the author, he wasn't Stephen Dedalus by any means. I wouldn't have gotten on with him if he were. Joyce had mellowed. He was good-natured, in a cynical way, which I liked.

-Did the erotic passages offend you?

-They were not new to me, Gilbert shrugs.

-C'est la vie, adds Moune.

-Are you familiar with the writings of Jules Michelet the 19th century historian? He is known for his 23 volume history of France that spans 2,000 years and has been a great influence on De Gaulle. Michelet also kept diaries in which he detailed his sexual appetites including a lusty voyeurism of his wife.

Gabriel is reminded of the observation by Clémenceau: The most beautiful moment of a love affair is the one when you are climbing the stairs.

Hèléne Joseph is waiting at Shakespeare and Company to take us to Montmartre, named after Saint Denis, the third century martyr who was bishop of Paris and the patron saint of France.

Emerging from the Metro at Pigalle we discern the white dome and bell tower of the basilica of Sacre Coeur just as in the painting by Utrillo.

-Sacre Coeur was designed by the architect Paul Abadie in the Byzantine-Romanesque style and took 39 years to build. This I learned in school, Hèléne declares. It was supposed to commemorate the Franco-Prussian war but was not consecrated until 1919 so it has a great significance.

-Inspirational, Gabriel offers. Patriotism. Honour. Death in battle.

-As for me, Hèléne retorts, when I regard Sacre Coeur I remember the song of the poules of Pigalle.
Connaissez-vous l'histoire
D'un vieux curé de Paris
D'un vieux cu--d'un vieux cu--
D'un vieux curé de Paris?
Il amait la botanique
Il en cultivait les fleurs
Il en cul--il en cul--
Il en cultivait les fleurs.

-But you are interested in the night life, n'est-ce pas? It is a short walk from here.

-The Moulin Rouge promises the world famous French Can Can with the 40 Doriss girls, it says in *Paris by Night*.

-Ah, Hèléne explains, it is not the exciting dance that Toulouse-Lautrec witnessed. In his time the midinettes who came to the Moulin Rouge for recreation on a Saturday night did not wear culottes so they exposed their barbus, how do you say in English, their pussies, when they kicked the legs so high. Quelle spectacle!

-Here we are at Pigalle, the working man's strip tease place. The poules try to snatch the clients before the doorman gets to them.

-The Fifty-Fifty Club presents homosexual stage shows with half the performers dressed like women. Many fights and a murder every weekend. There is also the New Moon, for les gouines, the lesbians.

-The Folies Pigalle has an excellent stage show and is always crowded. The customers are obliged to drink champagne. A man without an escort receives the attention of an entraineuse, an underdressed beauty who encourages him to buy her many glasses of Mumm's.

-Sheherezade offers Russian Cuisine in the Grand Tradition and gypsy musicians. Very expensive.

-And of course the famous Folies Bergeres of Madame Martini, the Empress of Pigalle.

After the walk-about we stop for a Perrier-Menthe and observe the heavily made-up whores in deep decolletees, leather mini skirts, pink hose and high heels.

-The green neon lighting is supposed to make the chauffeculs look like corpses. But you cannot argue with a hard penis, hein?

Past midnight. The carnival that is Pigalle is just beginning but Hèléne admits to an unusual weariness so we agree to leave.

At the Metro Station Hèléne stumbles and falls down the stairs. Writhing in pain she is certain that her leg must be broken. Somebody in the crowd insists il fault appeler le SAMU. When the ambulance arrives Hèléne is taken to L'Hôpital Laennec on the Rue de Sèvres. As Gabriel and I wait in the emergency room for news about Hèléne's situation a woman arrives seeking information about her daughter and that is how we meet Ryvka Zylberstajn Joseph. During our lengthy wait we learn about the difficulties of her life during the war, her ill husband and the anxieties caused by a daughter who does not conform to the rules of society. Gabriel questions the mother about her Polish background expressing his own desire to return to the shtetl to rediscover his roots.

A doctor eventually appears with the information that Hèlène has suffered a sprained ankle and a tension bandage should suffice but there is another problem. The patient is experiencing cramps and is staining and he is afraid she may lose the child. He permits the distraught Madame Joseph to see her daughter. We send our wishes for Hèléne's recovery.

It is three o'clock in the morning. We take a taxi to the Lenox Hotel where we rouse the patron, who opens the door protesting about the lateness of the hour.

Gabriel falls asleep immediately. I am kept awake by the traffic noises and a replay of the day's events. In the apartment across the street a man and woman are clasped in a sexual embrace.

In Toronto at this hour it is family viewing time on television.

12

New York, June 17, 1968. The Gotham Book Mart. At the meeting of the James Joyce Society presided over by Padraic Colum we meet Charles Feinberg.

-I enjoyed your talk on Joyce, he compliments Gabriel during the social hour. Especially your comments on the profane in *Ulysses,* as embodied in the character of Buck Mulligan, that is to say Oliver St. John Gogarty. I knew Gogarty, had a lot of fun with him and some heartache. I met him in 1939 just before the war started. I had read Gogarty's autobiography, *As I Was Going Down Sackville Street,* and also his poetry. I knew of his times with the Black and Tans and how he had been imprisoned and that he had promised swans to the Liffey if he ever got out and when he did escape one of the first things he had Yeats do was to get a couple of swans and turn them loose in the river. Yeats had a high regard for Gogarty as one of the great lyric poets. The Oxford Book of Modern Verse contains 17 of his poems. Lord Asquith spoke of Gogarty as the wittiest man in London, a great conversationalist as well as an airman, playwright, senator and a noted surgeon.

-When I learned that he was to speak at Assumption College in Windsor just across the river from my home in Detroit I invited him to see my Joyce collection. I knew that he liked to drink and we started with scotch and soda. When we went in for dinner I had the maid bring Gogarty a bottle of Guinness. After he finished it he asked for another and he kept pouring Guinness through every course, getting up from the table only to relieve himself. By the end of the meal he had finished the case. Then he continued with the scotch and about two o'clock in the morning I took him to his hotel.

-I saw Gogarty again in the spring of 1941 in England where I was a house guest of Gerald Brockhurst, a member of the Royal Academy. I had met Brockhurst before the war when he came to New York to open the Exhibition of International Art presented by the Carnegie Institute and I had two of his paintings. He was famous at the time for his portrait of the Duchess of Windsor and Mrs. Paul Mellon and other society ladies. I arrived to find Gogarty who had come to spend a weekend with Brockhurst and six months later was still occupying the apartment in the studio about 100 yards from the main house. Brockhurst gave him spending money, enough I suppose so that Gogarty could walk to Ridgewood and drink at a pub called Towillingays. Gogarty would tell countless stories about the owner who not only ran the bar but was an undertaker as well. On the Saturday night that I was staying at Brockhurst's there were about 12 people altogether. Gogarty who had quite a bit to drink started to recite his antagonism of James Joyce. He said that *Ulysses* was the result of a disordered mind. He was very nasty about Nora, claiming that Joyce had picked her up and couldn't get rid of her and carried her along like baggage. Gogarty looked down on the class of people Joyce came from, referring to them as genteel peasants, whereas he himself had been born into a monied family with more social assurance. He said he didn't care to be immortalized as Buck Mulligan and how stupid people were to buy Joyce's letters and books. About ten o'clock I said goodnight and went up to bed, with Gogarty hollering that I was retreating from the battle.

-When I came down the next morning Brockhurst apologized for Gogarty's behavior. After breakfast we went out and Gogarty who was feeling remorseful joined us. We were walking along the country road when he asked if I would like to buy a Joyce letter addressed to Buck Mulligan. I said I'd love to buy it. It was historically important, how much did he want for it? He demanded $500 at a time when Joyce's letters were selling for about $75. I never bought the letter which is now in the Berg Collection at the New York Public Library. But I have all of Gogarty's correspondence.

-He certainly could be exasperating. He lived on other people, moving in with them, staying for months but he was a wonderful raconteur with countless stories about Dublin and the Irish and about his association with James Joyce. When he was on the lecture platform he would never fail to play up how he and Joyce were together in the Martello Tower and how he provided Joyce with so much material for the character of Buck Mulligan.

June 18, 1968. The auctioneer at the Parke Bernet Galleries consults his watch. Two o'clock. From the rostrum built like a pulpit with a back panel and a curved roof he surveys the audience, the bargain seekers and those who have come to be entertained and fixes his gaze on the professionals seated at his left in the pit.

-Ladies and Gentlemen, he speaks crisply into the microphone. We offer for your competition today a select group of items from the collection of Mr. Charles A. Feinberg as shown in the catalogue. Rare books and manuscripts of James Joyce and Walt Whitman.

He urges on the bidders with a rapid staccato, by repetition of phrases, by dexterous shifts and by repartee. His eyes dart about the room, calling out bids assisted by the bid spotters. The auctioneer understands the individual signals from the book dealers, the experienced private collectors and the representatives of the University libraries. A tug at an ear, the wink of an eye, a folding of arms, the removal of spectacles, the wiping of a brow, all signify a bid. Some of the items including *The Day of the Rabblement* do not meet the secret reserve figures and are not sold but today's highs will be noted in the records and their increased value will be validated.

Charles Feinberg is staying at The Plaza, the grande dame of New York Hotels, at Central Park South and Fifth Avenue. Since its opening in October 1907 it has been the address of the Vanderbilts and the Wannamakers. It still attracts American aristocrats as well as travelles from Europe and South America who pose for photographs before the Pulitzer Fountain. The salons of The Plaza cater to charity balls and coming-out parties, to weddings and bar mitzvahs. The oak walls in the wandering lobby feature portraits of Eloise, the irrepressible six-year-old Plaza resident in Kay Thompson's children's book. A queue waits outside the Palm Court Tea Room. The Edwardian Room, the Oyster Bar, the Oak Room and Trader Vic's are also busy.

From Feinberg's splendidly appointed suite on the 14th floor we can see the lights of Central Park and hear the faint hoof beats of carriage horses.

-Have some of the madeleine, he urges.. It is too rich for me but you are young enough to indulge without fear of gastric reprisal. Pour the hot fudge over it from the silver pitcher. It's a delightful gesture on the part of the Plaza management, a recall of the way New York used to be. Not that I was born into such a setting. My father was a shoemaker and my mother emigrated from London to Canada and I was born in Peterborough, a city of 50,000 about sixty miles east of Toronto. When I finished seventh grade I got a job. There was no night school but we did have a public library over a store thanks to the generosity of Andrew Carnegie. Did you know that Hugh Kenner's father was the principal of the high school?

-I remember a second hand shop on Charlotte Street that sold wash tubs and furniture. There was a bushel basket full of paperbacks for five cents each. You could read them, bring them back, get a 3-cent trade-in allowance and for 2 cents get another book. Frank Merriwell stories, Sexton Blake, all that sort of stuff. One day I fished out a hard bound book called American Poems, a selection by Wm. Michael Rosetti, which included Emerson and the American poets of the mid 19th century. The book was dedicated to Walt Whitman. In the Public Library I made another discovery. One of the literary executors of Whitman was a Canadian doctor, Richard Maurice Buck, who was head of the asylum in London, Ontario and who today is honoured as one of the medical pioneers in mental health. He is also remembered as a classmate of Sir Wm. Osler and as the author of a fascinating book that has gone through 30 editions and is still in print, called Cosmic Consciousness. In 1883 he had written a life of Walt Whitman and I suppose it didn't sell very well because every Canadian library had a copy which I assume had been presented by Dr. Buck. In any event, that too was a contributing factor to my interest in Whitman. I bought my first letter in a book shop, Tyrrell's, in Toronto while I was visiting my grandmother. It was a tremendous emotional experience because I had never seen a letter written by a famous author.

-When did your interest in James Joyce begin, asks Gabriel.

-In my twenties, about 1926. I was in Chicago and wandered into a bookstore run by Ben Abramson, who later opened the Argus Book Shop, and I bought a copy of *Ulysses*. It certainly was not a first edition Then I got hold of a volume of *Dubliners* and somewhere I discovered *Exiles*. They weren't very expensive in those days. My first real item came during the Depression when I bought a Joyce letter that was being sold at Macy's, part of the collection of Donald Freed, the publisher. Later I bought others through Kirshenbaum of the Carnegie Book Shop. He phoned me in Detroit to say that he had a package of 138 letters and postcards written by James Joyce to J.B. Pinker. Kirshenbaum had bought them from David Randall who at that time was in charge of the book department at Scribners. Randall obtained them from Frances Steloff of the Gotham.

-I offered the letters to Wayne State, which had just started a *Press*. I was close to a number of people at the University and particularly to Joseph Prescott, and I figured that any book we brought out would help the prestige of the new Press. We wrote to the Joyce estate in London for permission but they refused because they intended to publish letters of their own.

-When their book appeared we wrote again and were informed that they were contemplating a second volume. In the meantime Richard Ellmann, who had begun work on a biography of James Joyce, came to me about the letters and I photostatted them so he could use the information and be able to write about Joyce's life with more authority. After the biography was published Dick was invited to do the additional volumes of the letters and he asked if I would let him use those I had. By then I was depositing them at Southern Illinois University where they are now. In the meantime I had acquired additional letters and Joyce editions.

-Frank Budgen had written his own book about Joyce. I had a marvellous time with Budgen. As you know he is a Cornishman with an earthiness that must have appealed to the Irish writer. I bought his portrait of James Joyce and presented it to Southern Illinois. Budgen had a great interest in Whitman as well and we had an ongoing correspondence.

-I spent some time with Jacob Epstein whom I knew

through his Whitman interests. Epstein was anxious to get some of his sculpture into Westminster Abbey so I conceived the idea of his doing a head of Whitman for the Abbey and making two copies, one for the Library of Congress and one for myself. We would do this through the official channels of the American Embassy when I was next in London in 1953 to work on an exhibition of Walt Whitman and his British friends, Tennyson, Dowden, Havelock Ellis and others. About 95% of the material in it was mine but we borrowed a few things from the Morgan Library, the Library of Congress, Yale University and from a private collector, T.E. Manley, who was also a Joyce collector and whose collection is now at Texas. We issued a catalogue for distribution to English institutions. It was so fine that I ordered an extra thousand copies for the U.S.A. and abroad. The American Embassy then started to work on the Epstein project for Westminster Abbey.

-I remained in London at the request of the Embassy to help counteract the influence of Joseph McCarthy. You see, Cohn and Shine had come through England in 1954 like a dose of salts and frightened everybody. I would talk to groups about American literature of the mid 19th century or hold forth on Whitman and at the end of every lecture I was asked, what is Eisenhower going to do about Joe McCarthy? It made no difference where I spoke, whether at the Bibliographical Society of the American Embassy or at the Reform Club, the same question was always asked. So I developed a pat answer: We've had many peculiar people in American politics. Wm. Hale Thompson who fought George III one hundred years after the King was dead. Bilbo in Mississippi. The spectre of McCarthy would also pass. Mccarthy had been elected Senator from Wisconsin and the Senate would have to censure him.

-Towards the end of my stay I was giving a cocktail party in honour of John Hayward, a former room-mate of T.S. Eliot who had just recovered from an illness. It was a marvellous evening except that some woman asked me about McCarthy and I gave my usual reply. The next morning our cultural attaché Mr. Murphy phoned to ask if I had seen the newspapers. I was quoted in the Standard as having said that in time 'President Eisenhower would cut McCarthy down to the size of a louse.' Murphy said, 'I know you didn't say it. I was standing beside you all the time. I think you should come over to the Embassy as soon as you can.' I was about to go over to Paris to see Sylvia Beach but I was asked to meet with Winthrop Aldritch, the U.S. Ambassador (as frozen-faced a man as I have ever met in my life), who requested that I remain in England because as a private citizen I could say things that no one in the government could say. It wasn't often in his life that Aldritch gave his personal thanks to one of my faith.

13

27 rue Casimir-Périer,
Paris 7, August 29, 1968.
My dear Anna and Gabriel,
Frances Steloff of the Gotham Book Mart is currently in Paris. We shall have lunch tomorrow at the bistro downstairs. I have a lot to tell her and am sure she will be horrified when she hears what I have on my mind and she can relay it to the James Joyce Society of New York. And I hope Richard Ellmann gets to hear of it too.

The gist of the matter is this. While I was on vacation events took me to Zurich. My sister lives there and we had a morning so we went up to the Fluntern cemetery, such a beautifully kept and fabulously landscaped place. So Peaceful.

But that statue! It left us speechless. It is a disgrace. Peter Pan in Kensington Gardens is a work of genius in comparison. The sculptor has made Mr. Joyce look like a saltimbanque, almost a contortionist, straight from the circus. How could Giorgio have ever consented to this?

I was disappointed in the grave stones as well. Two small

granite slabs the size of your bath mat. It would have been so much more fitting if they had a headstone placed upright like the other graves, and if they had wanted some decor there are plenty of Celtic symbols in the Book of Kells. Or a menhir or dolmen suited to the timelessness and universality of Joyce's work. I feel very strongly about this. It is so darned dishonest, really part of the Joyce industry, the kind of thing Joyce himself would have shunned. As to the likeness, the facial expression is that of a provincial assistant teacher.

Enough of this. But you may say to anyone interested that his real friends are shocked and disgusted.

There isn't much else except what I read in the papers and hear over the radio and see on television. Somehow one's own problems evaporate before the catastrophe of Chechoslovakia. I was sure the talks with the Soviets would end up in a kind of Munich. But what a resistance the Chechs are putting up. It may well turn into a blood bath and the Russians will get very tough as time goes on. They have set the clock back right to Stalin.

The poor Chechs stand alone. No one is going to fight for them. No one went to war in 1939 for Poland. The radio played Chopin's funeral march and mazurkas for one whole week from dawn to dusk and that was it. This time they started playing Chech music and then by mistake ran into the Sibelius Valse Triste. Some French idealist had the bright notion of getting together one million signatures and postcards. What good will that do? Why not send packages to the starving children while they can still get them?

That's about all for tonight. The best to you both.

Affectionately, Lucie Leon.

14

January 22, 1969. Richard Milhous Nixon is sworn in as 37th President of the United States. The strike at San Francisco State College is in its third month.

Tulsa University appears tranquil. Students for a Democratic Society have established a base on campus and T-shirts worn by undergraduates in Afro hair styles proclaim 'black is beautiful' and other slogans of the insurgency. In the cafeteria the conversation is about the use of psychotropic drugs and the gurus Leary and Alpert.

-It was a real bummer. I had a helluva time coming down, recalls Laurelaine Baxter, hair like corn silk.

-I get stoned only on weekends, confesses a sallow young man in sun-glasses.

-What..is..it..like..for..you?

-It's like man, like nothing is real, things just start to happen. I dropped mescaline and what a trip that was. Like colour came out of the loud speakers and was kind of pulling me in like in a whirlpool. Did that ever happen to you?

-When I hallucinate everything becomes magnified. If you smiled it would be like a gush of pleasant warm air surging at me.

-I remember once after I dropped acid I went into a dark room and this chick thought I was a monster and she screamed and the scream came out like green cream and splattered all over me. Then there was this other chick, she wasn't enjoying herself and she had a frown and her face kind of caved in and all of a sudden she slumped over and I said, quick man, she's melting, pick her up and our guide said cool it man, she's not even here and I went into the other room and there she was with some other cats and she was crying. The tears were all over the floor and I must have stayed there for an hour and she was crying all the time and pretty soon the water was up to my belly button and I had to stand on a chair. Just like Alice in Wonderland.

-Yeah.

-That's the most psychedelic book I've ever read, says Laurelaine. Like the white rabbit and the caterpillar with the hookah. And the cheshire cat. And the other characters with their hangups.

-Well, I don't have any hangups. I feel like everyone is my friend. You can always tell if a person likes you if he'll dial a telephone number for you when you're high. I wanted to dial this cat and his name was Jesus but I kept getting the wrong number. Then I saw this dromedary walking past and like I said hey, could you dial a number and the old camel said okay and it was a real freak-out because someone answered, Jesus here.

At the end of the three day James Joyce conference the participants gather in the home of Tulsa University's Dean of Arts.

Fr. Desmond Fitzgerald, sipping Irish whisky, is expatiating on Molly Bloom as Gaea Tellus, the paper he delivered during the final session. The professor from Kent State University interposes a tangent proposition apropos of the rite of Onan mentioned on page 713 line 36 of *Ulysses* and the others in the academic circle offer their interpretations. During the discussion the priest is approached by the hostess who is intrigued by Molly's nocturnal erotic meanderings.

-Of course my dear I have no personal experience that would make me an expert in such matters but I have done considerable reading and have learned a great deal from knowledgeable lay people. So I drink to you and women everywhere. Molly Bloom. Penelope. Aphrodite. Here is to the ever-renewing flesh, to the celebration of life not enjoyed by the celibate.

Fr. Fitzgerald makes his way to the bar, where he is greeted by Laurelaine, Baxter who has just come in from the garden.

-Hi! she calls. The aroma of marijuana hangs about her blue denims.

-Hi! he responds. Both high. Their visions transmogrified by their chemical dependencies.

-I enjoyed your lecture, Father, particularly what you had to say about love as distinct from sex. I mean the involvement of the emotions.

-Oh, he knows a lot about sex too, the professor from Kent State intervenes.

-Please continue my dear.

-What I mean is if I were to express my emotions to a person, to say I love him, does sex have to enter into the situation?

-Beware, you are jousting with a Jesuit mind, warns Kent

State.

-If I say I love you, Laurelaine tries again, it means the way I love all people.

-Certainly, Fr. Fitzgerald takes her hand. And I love you.

-I don't believe there can be real love without the sexual fulfillment, the professor insists. Consider the case of Heloise and Abelard.

-Oh, but love doesn't have to be sexual.

-Are you denying sex?

-That's not love, that's desire.

-So desire is a pejorative emotion?

-No, it is a good thing, acknowledges Fr. Fitzgerald.

-Then why make a distinction?

-Because there is a difference between love and desire. You can have love without sex. You can suppress the libido.

-I think Laurelaine is right, the Jesuit affirms. If there weren't love how could people minister to others as they do, say in hospitals where nurses and doctors serve out of love for their patients.

-Do you know what has to happen before we can all love each other? The Ego has to die. What are you willing to do for me? How are you prepared to love me? Or anybody here?

-What about the physical act of love, pursues Kent State.

-Christ said, go thou and love others as I love you. In essence that's what Laurelaine has said.

-Wow! That's far out, Laurelaine hugs Fr. Fitzgerald. I really love you.

Fr. Fitzgerald excuses himself. His glass is empty.

15

Dublin. Monday June 9, 1969. The Montfort Hotel on Eccles Street is a renovated Georgian house. The parlor furnished with a sofa and chair, floor lamp and magazine rack serves as reception. Religious knick knacks adorn the mantel above the gas fireplace. A plump girl behind the counter takes our travel vouchers and consults the ledger, tracing each entry with her finger.

 -Here it is, she looks up triumphantly, Mr. and Mrs. Gabriel...what sort of name is that?

 -Gottesman. Man of God. Gabriel. After the Archangel who stands in radiant splendor on the right hand of the Lord.

 -Ah there's a lot of power in them two names. She sounds them slowly, respectfully. Are you Catholic?

 -Not everybody is an adherent of the Holy Roman Catholic and Apostolic Church. In the lands beyond the western sea are many heathens like ourselves.

 -Sure and you're codding me. Pale face, ingenuous, smiling.

 -You're not a Dublin girl are you?

 -I'm from the country, sir. Moyvalley on the road to Mullingar. I'm working here almost a fortnight. Mrs. Erskine is learning me the hotel business. Please write your name and address in the book. Ah that's grand. Now will I show you to your room. She trots up the stairs ahead of us.

 -Breakfast is from seven until ten. Will you be wanting me to knock yez up in the morning, sir?

 -No thanks. I have a built-in alarm system in my head.

 -Sure, you're codding me again.

 -The mind is a computer capable of solving all kinds of complicated problems. Don't you know that Man is the paragon of animals?

 -Father Doolan says to beware the sin of pride. It is God who makes all things possible. Her hand caresses the silver cross at her neck.

 -Do you go to confession regularly?

 -Oh yes, to St. Francis Xavier Church on Gardiner Street.

 -How old are you? I ask.

 -Sixteen. Me mother has passed on and I don't know where me Da is. Sister Mary Joseph asked would I like to learn a decent occupation and when I promised to mind my ways and work hard she brought me here.

 A splatter of rain against the window. Then sunshine again. The bell jangles and a voice calls up, Kathleen, attend to the door.

-If there's anything you're wanting be sure to say so. Kathleen runs down the stairs. In a few years, her youthful vitality expended, she will be Kathleen ni Houlihan, the poor old woman of Ireland.

Gabriel consults his appointment book while I unpack. It is clouding over, a silver streak lighting the dark sky, then the accompanying rumble folowed by a heavy downpour. Dublin weather is as uncertain as a child's bottom, Gabriel quotes Simon Daedalus.

The telephone is in an alcove off the parlour. As Gabriel inserts the pennies and waits for the connection I listen on the extension.

-Is that the Sineaid O'Callaghan Theatrical Agency? A very good day to you, ma'am. My wife and I are recently arrived visitors to your city and we bring greetings from Toronto. No, I am not joshing you. Who? I don't know anybody by the name of Liam. Tara asked me to get in touch.

O'Callaghan apologizes. She thought it was one of her clients who tries to fool her with bad imitations.

-Please forgive me. I'm anxious to hear about Tara.

-Why don't we have dinner?

-You'll not be holding my bad manners against me? Well then I accept. Where are you staying? Yes I know the place. I'll be there about eight.

While Gabriel goes upstairs for a nap I relax in the parlor with the Irish Times. Jack Lynch seeks re-election as Taoiseach. Constable Maeve Hamilton models the new uniform designed for policewomen in the Royal Ulster Constabulary. Hollywood screen star Robert Taylor dies of cancer. Yawn. On Eccles Street a lackey from the sanitation department shovels horse droppings into his cart. Yawn. Jet lag fatigue. I join Gabriel in bed, lulled by the roo-coo-cooing of the pigeons.

When we awake it is after seven, still daylight. Awaiting the arrival of O'Callaghan we chat with the proprietor of the Montfort. Joe Erskine is a friendly chap, grey-haired and well-built with an easy smile and a soft voice. A construction engineer, he is involved in urban development. The country has been benefitting from an influx of capital by West Germans but

Sinn Fein have been picketing the Embassy on Ailesbury Road in protest. Their manifesto: The land of Ireland is for the people of Ireland and we call for the restoration to the people of the land already held by foreign and native exploiters.

The Belfast clergyman is in the news again. The Rev. Ian Paisley was banned last week from entering Switzerland and detained at Geneva airport. He had gone to protest against Pope Paul's visit.

While we are discussing Neil Armstrong's flight to the moon a black Labrador retriever bounds in and stops before Erskine, its massive body quivering.

-Exercise time, Erskine explains. He runs five miles every day in Phoenix Park.

-What do you call him?

-MacCoul, after the legendary King of Ireland Finn MacCoul who is said to have engineered the Giant's Causeway in Antrim.

-I am intrigued by the Dermot and Grainne legend, says Gabriel.

-Ah yes, it ends so tragically, the son killed by his father and the girl having to marry the old King. It has its counterpart in the Tristram and Iseult story. Well I must be leaving. MacCoul is becoming impatient.

Leash in hand Erskine opens the door, the dog leaps out and a scream rends the air.

-Down boy. A hundred thousand pardons, miss. He is a friendly beast, full of energy, is all, I hope you're not hurt. Erskine's soothing Cork brogue.

-I guess not, just mussed up. A fine way to be making my entrance. The contralto voice is theatrical in its richness.

-Were you wanting to see someone in the house?

-Yes, the gentleman from Toronto.

-Ah, I believe they're expecting you. Go right in. Come on MacCoul, into the boot of the car.

Sineaid O'Callaghan, majestic in a cream linen pant suit, sails into view. Long titian hair billows about an angular face.

-Are you Gabriel?

-Hello. And this is Anna. I'm sorry about the slight

mishap.

-Here I am laid out like an altar because I want to make a fine impression and the beast knocks me down. Pardon the outburst. I'm usually quite refeened.

-Why don't we leave and find a place to eat. What do you say to the Shelbourne or Royal Hibernian?

-Ah, not the tourist places. There's a cozy restaurant nearby, highly regarded by the natives. Let's go.

The bells of St. George's Church are striking half past eight as we proceed along Eccles Street. A grey nun, her mien celestial, passes.

-They're the ones who own all this property. The Sisters of Mercy, they run the hospital.

-Mater Mary Mercerycordial of the Dripping Nipples. By the way, have you seen the *Ulyssses* film?

-The authorities wouldn't allow it to be shown here. There was however a private screening for members of the cast. I had a small part in it as a mad nun. We're all of us a bit mad, if you ask me.

Sineaid sets the pace up Berkeley Road. North Circular now. At Doyle's Corner she explains that J.C. Doyle the Irish baritone was considered the cream of Irish musicians, winner of the Feis Coeil of 1899. On Phibsboro Road she stops before a stained wood facade. We have arrived at Chez Gaston. The restaurant has two small rooms. Stucco ceiling and crystal chandelier, the walls decorated with Paris scenes. Monsieur Gaston in evening attire seats us at a table set with a silver service and porcelain bud vase containing a red rose. Only one other couple here.

-Muzak, she grimaces, just like in America. Sure and we're catching up with the rest of the civilized world. Well now, tell me about Tara.

-She is doing well, having appeared in several theatre productions in Toronto. At present she's in summer stock on the east coast. She hopes to be performing at Stratford next year.

-Ah that's grand. Is she still living with that actor she met on the film set in Kerry? I don't know what she sees in him. 'I'm weak for his bones' Tara mooned when she decided to run off with him.

Sineaid expands on Tara's free spirit and scandalous behavior. During the seafood salad she talks about the Dublin theatre community and her own career playing suffering Mother Macrees and prostitutes.

The Chateaubriand arrives grilled to just the right tenderness accompanied by home fried potatoes but the Bearnaise sauce has been sharpened with a little too much cayenne. The Chateauneuf du Pape lacks the bouquet of this famous vin rouge preferred since the time of Urban X. However after the second glass the wine has miraculously improved and Sineaid is telling us about the little people of Ireland and the Poulaphouca waterfall near the source of the Liffey. And have we heard about the Phoukah, the mischievous sprite trapped in a rock by St. Nessan. Over espresso followed by Courvoisier she recounts tales of the Sidhe, the gods of ancient Ireland who travel in great gusts of whirling wind and about Queen Maeve who is buried in a cairn of stones on the summit of Knocknarea in Sligo.

-Ah, here I am not knowing when to stop blathering. What must you be thinking?

-I'm thinking it has been very pleasant, I assure her.

It is eleven o'clock when we leave Gaston's. A luminous moon is sailing through the clouds and Gabriel conjectures that it must be the same lamp that 65 years ago looked down upon Leopold Bloom, a middle-aged Dublin Jew, and Stephen Daedalus, a young man afflicted with the cursed Jesuit strain. Arrived at the Montfort we indulge in pleasantries on the stoop until the chimes of St. George's Church toll midnight. At the taxi rank Sineaid rouses the driver of the solitary cab and instructs him as to the shortest route to Santry.

Eccles Street huddles in sleep. A single light flickers in the admitting room of the Mater Misericordiae. Gabriel is haunted by spectres. Near blind Sean O'Casey in cap and turtle neck sweater hunched over his writing in the cottage in nearby Dorset Lane. James Joyce, ashplant in hand, exploring the streets of the city, committing them to memory and posterity.

Tuesday June 10, 1969. Bright morning. Gulls screaming. Kathleen knocking on our door. Breakfast. Mrs. Erskine says to come down straightaway.

The dining room has been scooped out of a section of the basement. Sunlight streaming through the orange-hued plastic roof illuminates the panorama of Irish scenes on the wallpaper. Towers and castles, dolmens and celtic crosses, lakes and mountains. A scattering of guests including a couple with an infant in a backpack. Kathleen hurries past with an armful of crockery and returns to our table with platters of rashers and eggs and stewed tomatoes.

-Do you see those people with the child, Kathleen whispers. They're from California. They've been all over Europe with the little chiseller and he not yet two years old. They're roaming about the country in a caravan just like the travelling people. Aren't they the lucky ones.

-Would you like to see the world, I ask.

-Indeed I would but not on me own.

-Find yourself a young man, someone who will treat you decently.

-Ah, he wouldn't be an Irishman then, Kathleen pouts. I knowed a jackeen who was tackin' a girl so long he wore her into a cap and bonnet. If I met a real gentleman, from America say, I wouldn't mind doin' his washing. She allows herself an instant of reflection before hurrying away.

During the second cup of tea we scan the Irish Times. Item: The first transatlantic flight by Alcock and Brown fifty years ago is to be re-enacted next Saturday when a twin-engined plane will retrace the course from Newfoundland to Ireland. The venture announced by Premier Joey Smallwood will coincide with the celebrations in Clifden, Co. Galway. Item: Buildings on four big farms were set ablaze in the vicinity of Meath and Louth. Three Germans are victims. The Gardai believe the fires are the work of the IRA.

MacCoul is dozing near the front door as we leave. Children are playing hopscotch on the sidewalk. A chanting of nursery rhymes from the open windows of St. Brigid's orphanage.

On the other side of Eccles Street the house where number seven used to stand has been demolished.

On Dorset Street we pass the familiar names mentioned in the pages of *Ulysses*. The Dorset House Pub. Findlater and Company Grocery and Provision Merchant. C. Byrne Pork Butcher. At North Frederick Street we come to Findlater's Church.

In Parnell Square the Garden of Remembrance dedicated to those who gave their lives in the cause of Irish freedom is landscaped with ornamental shrubs and a variety of trees including the arbutus, beech and weeping silver birch. The raised reflecting pool is in the form of a latin cross, the floor a mosaic of blue-green waves superimposed by a design of weapons to commemorate the Celtic custom of placing arms in lakes and pools after the battles. In the smaller pond is Oisin Kelly's bronze sculpture representing the transformation of men into swans, based on the ancient Irish myth the Children of Lir.

At the bottom of the hill the Rotunda Rooms where Dubliners enjoyed concerts and circuses have been replaced by a dance hall, cinema and the Gate Theatre. The Rotunda Hospital, opened in 1757, still functions, world famous for obstetrics. Nearby, Charles Stewart Parnell the uncrowned King of Ireland stands on a pedestal, one arm outstretched (in the direction of Mooney's pub, the wags say). An Irish harp is etched on the base and below it the proposition: No Man Has The Right To Fix The Boundary To The March of A Nation.

O'Connell Street the heart of the Hibernian metropolis. The C.I.E. Information Kiosk is located on the pedestrian island where once arose the 134 foot Doric column to the memory of Herbert Horatio Nelson. It was blown up in the middle of the night three years ago.

Arnott's Department Store on Henry Street. The open air market on Moore Street.

The green, white and orange tricolour of the Irish Free State flutters above the General Post Office, its Corinthian columns scarred by shell fire during the Easter uprising. Within the portico on Easter Monday, April 24, 1916 Padraic Pearse read the Proclamation of the Republic: In the name of God and the dead generations from which she received her old tradition of nationhood Ireland summons her children to her flag and strikes for her freedom.

At Abbey Street stands the statue of Sir John Gray, owner of the Freeman Journal during the time of canvasser Leopold Bloom. By O'Connell Bridge the monument to the Liberator is attended by Courage, Fidelity, Eloquence and Patriotism, the buxom Victories blemished by bullets.

Eden Quay. Tugs and merchantmen are anchored in the Liffey, the river oozing out to Dublin Bay. On Marlborough Street the white brick and glass National Theatre of Ireland where Gabriel has an appointment with the artistic director.

Tonight's play is Shaw's St. Joan. After the performance Sineaid voices her disapproval. Uninspired, she laments, the Abbey isn't what it used to be. And she has had enough of the after-theatre carousing at the Plough Tavern. The Waldorf Astoria on Eden Quay is packed with tourists. All kinds of boozing sheds in this city of perpetual thirst. Would we come to her place?

On O'Connell Bridge a shawled figure cradling a baby extends a hand in supplication. Gabriel drops a coin into it and she mumbles God's blessings on you, sir. Poor gypsy woman. At Westmoreland Street Sineaid unable to restrain herself snorts, that was a tinker, the streets are full of them. Beggars in petticoats and sweaters, mothering dolls rolled up in blankets. Hands outstretched for alms.

By Trinity's iron railings the first drops splash warm on the face, fall hissing on the road. Heavier now, a summer downpour. As the cars slither by Sineaid whistles up a taxi. Lucky thing, getting the driver to stop in this weather. The cabby wipes the misted windshield with a rag as the rain beats a tattoo on the roof and the driver pilots the Ford Consul through the city out into the suburbs.

After a while we stop before a cottage with a tiny garden. The door is unlocked and the lights are on.

-Deirdre? Now where can she be? Excuse me, I'll be right down. Sineaid dodges past the loom in the hall and up the stairs.

A bridge lamp in the parlour reveals sofa and chair. An Irish harp and a stuffed kangaroo. A picture of Jesus with a bleeding heart hangs on the wall. An olive wood crucifix. A painting of the waterfall at Poulaphouca. Photographs of children dressed for first communion. Sineaid comes down highly agitated and peers out at the soggy street.

-Where can she be? It's too late for a fourteen-year-old to be running around. And after promising to stay home with the younger ones. Thank God they're asleep. At the sound of the door opening Sineaid hurries into the hall.

-Deirdre? Is that you?

-Yes, Ma.

-Where have you been at this hour of the night?

-Joseph and Emmett stopped by and we went for a walk and it started to rain and we waited in a shop for it to end.

-Well, off to bed. I'll talk to you in the morning. Sineaid returns, despair darkening her face.

-Ah, that one, Deirdre, she's too pretty for her own good. And too early developed. Her period first came on her when she was scarce eleven. Things would be easier if her father were here but he's away in London living with an actress young enough to be his daughter. He sends home a few pounds at irregular intervals and the toys you see lying about. That eases his conscience. He can always rely on me to see that the three girls are fed and dressed and packed off to school and taught their manners. It's enough to make Jesus weep. Oh but I'm forgetting the tea. Back in a jiffy. Will you try to get something decent on the wireless?

Radio Eireann is off the air. Radio Luxembourg presents Your Hit Parade. The British Broadcasting Corporation is offering Dvorak's New World Quartet.

Sineaid arrives with the tea and a box of Jacob's biscuits. She apologizes for not having any whisky. One of Deirdre's boyfriends brought six bottles of Guinness last week and when Sineaid got home from the theatre her daughter was playing Drink To Me Only With Thine Eyes on the harp and Emmett was lying stupefied on the floor.

-Drink. The traditional Irish malady. Only now there's

the other evil, drugs. The youth of Ireland high on cannabis and
L.S.D. You can find them stoned in Stephen's Green. To think of
it happening in this country.

-Insula Sanctorum et Doctorum, intones Gabriel. The Isle
of St.Patrick and St. Columba. And the blessed Oliver Plunkett.

-And the Maharaj Ji, adds Sineaid.

-The fat kid with the Rolls Royces?

-The same. I spoke with Father Dalton our parish priest
about Deirdre spending so much time at the Divine Light
Mission and he said not to worry so long as she attends Mass
every Sunday.

Saturday June 14, 1969. Lectures and seminars at Trinity
College. After five o'clock the participants at the Second
International James Joyce Symposium adjourn to the Bailey for
refreshments and the rhetoric continues.

-Paddy Kavanagh is not here tonight, observes Iseult
McNamara. I'm afraid he is not long for this world.

-And how is your husband, I ask.

-Judge McNamara died three months ago of a heart
attack.

-I'm so sorry. It must be a difficult time for you.

-Yes it is, especially tonight with all these bibulous
celebrants and me with a great thirst.

-Allow me to rectify the situation, offers Gabriel.

-The natives aren't impressed by all this activity. The
Irish have never been kind to their literary geniuses since every
Hibernian fancies he can do as well if he had a mind to. James
Joyce declared that no one with any self-respect stays in Ireland
but flees afar as though from a country that has undergone the
visitaion of an angered Jove.

-Here you are, Mrs. McNamara. Chivas Regal for you and
Vodka on the rocks for Anna.

-Thank you. The elixir of forgetfulness.

-How is your daughter, the lovely girl who played the
guitar so well at the Gresham two years ago?

-Sorcha ran off to Europe with a fellow and I have had
to take in boarders to help pay the expenses of the big house in

Dundrum. Some of the American professors have been urging me to sell Eamon's manuscripts to their Universities.

We are on the landing away from the chatter and clatter. The widow has fallen silent, eyes veiled, hair lank about the pinched visage. I admire the gold pin on her bosom.

-Easter Nineteen Sixteen. MacDonough and MacBride and Connolly and Pearse. I'm sure you know the poem by Yeats.

-Numbers are fascinating, says Gabriel. The Kabbalists use numerology, they call it Gematria, in a mystical interpretation of the scriptures.

-How does it work?

-Each character of the Hebrew alphabet possesses a numerical value so you add up the letters of a particular word to extract its hidden meaning. Let's take a simple example. The Hebrew word for Life is Chai. Numerical value Eighteen. Therefore an 18th birthday or anniversary is cause for special celebration.

-What can you do with nineteen sixteen?

-First we break it up into two numbers. A Hebrew word that adds up to 19 is Achi, my brother.

-And sixteen?

-Let me see, one of the letter combinations spells out B'yad, by the hand. So we may interpret 1916 as 'My brother, take my hand'.

-That is astonishing. Iseult McNamara presents the empty glass to Gabriel for replenishing.

Sunday June 15, 1969. The play at the Gas Company Theatre is a pastoral comedy about a native son who having emigrated to the New World returns to the old sod years later and rediscovers the homespun verities. Brigid O'Hearne is his brash American wife. The actors perform without restraint, eliciting from friends and relatives in the audience much laughter and curtain calls at the end. We wait for Brigid in the old auditorium with the wooden seats. She apologizes for having been so long, blaming the delay on her contact lenses. One fell out while she was removing her makeup and having searched in vain finally called upon Padre Pio because he helped her before when St. Anthony could not. And sure, she discovered the errant disc in her jar of cold cream. And isn't it time the Church declared Padre Pio to be a saint what with his powers of healing and prophecy and finding lost articles. And did we know about the stigmata? Padre Pio dripped blood for half a century until his death last year.

-Did you suffer much from watching the performance? 'Tis ruinous for a professional actress like meself to be appearing with amateurs. Well, let's get out of here. My chariot is at your disposal. Where to?

-We haven't been to Jury's since our last visit, I suggest.

-Climb aboard. The door on the driver's side is still banged up so I'll get in first. Anna can sit beside me.

The Citroen starts with a whimper and rolls away into the fog. The street lamps burn with an orange glow, out of focus as in a Fellini film, providing a translucent view of Dun Laoghaire. We glide past the police station, post office and town hall, past the cinema, the railway station and the Marine Parade. In the distance, solitary in Dublin Bay we can make out the Kish lighthouse.

Jury's of Dame Street is full of late diners. The bar with its mosaic floor and ceramic wall panels is frequented by the Dublin trendsetters. Over the noise and bustle the sounds of Jury's Irish Cabaret drift in from the dining room. Step dancers and fiddlers. Solor performances on the harp, accordion, mouth organ and tin whistle.

-Oh the tourists lap it up. They just adore the Irish stereotypes. And the sing-along of International Songs. Hava Nagila is a favorite over here.

-How are the kids? I ask.

-So far I've been able to keep them leashed.

-And Cornelius?

-The pater familias and I are separated. I caught him sneaking around with his lady love, an old sow, what he sees in her I don't know. I followed them all the way out to Ballsbridge disguised in the nun's habit me sister left behind when she was transferred to Africa. Oh I did look so pious, one of me better acting roles. I should have married a fine Jewish fellow like Gabriel. Well it's too late now.

-Why, you're not even forty.

-Over here that's an advanced state of decrepitude. Haven't you noticed how quickly Irish women age? Ah, it's a difficult existence. The poverty, the brood of children, the besotted husbands. Remember Olwen O'Sullivan?

-The goddess with the Kallypigian figure who played Molly Bloom at the Gresham two years ago?

-The same. Gone to seed. She left her husband and moved into a decaying Georgian house with a bunch of hippies to protest against its demolition. She gets the odd acting job but mostly she dosses around.

It is half past one in the morning and Jury's lounge is stifling. My eyes are smarting from the cigarette smoke. The comic is regaling the audience with Irish dialect jokes as we leave.

Brigid propels the Citroen through the foggy streets. Arrived at the Montfort, as Gabriel bangs the car door shut she hollers in her most outrageous brogue, the top of the morning to you, executes a U-turn and hurtles down Eccles Street.

Monday June 16, 1969. *Night Boat From Dublin* is a dramatization of the world of James Joyce familiar to those who are gathered this evening in the Abbey's Peacock Theatre.

When the play has run its course the Symposiasts gather in the Bailey. The talk turns to Molly Bloom's four cardinal points: Breasts, arse, womb and cunt. A discussion ensues as to the use of the word cunt in literature, its Anglo-Saxon directness, its abrasive quality, its nasty connotation. In the middle ages many a dark and disreputable passage was called cunt lane as witness Gropecontelane known to unsavory London characters. Its universality is vouched for by a European philologist who cites Kunte in middle low German, Kunta in old Norse and Kut in Dutch. By way of further explication he draws on a napkin the Egyptian hieroglyphs Ka-t which may be translated as vagina, vulva or mother.

-However, one can opt instead for twat which is much

used by stevedores and other labourers but can also be found in the Royalist Rhymes *Vanity of Vanities* of the mid 17th century:

They talk of his having
A Cardinal's Hat
They'd rather send him
As soon as an old Nun's Twat!

Someone asks for consideration of the slang expressions for the male member but this does not elicit the same curiosity until the philologist cites Schwanzparade, the term used for the German army's health inspection of naked soldiers with their drooping tails on view. James Joyce gets the final riposte: Phall if you will but rise you must.

Tuesday June 17, 1969. Lunch In the Unicorn Restaurant with Iseult McNamara who is wearing a black jersey dress that is sprinkled with cigaret ash. Her hand trembles as she lights a Number Five and erupts into a spasm of coughing.

Iseult recommends the Wienerschnitzel which will go nicely with a bottle of Liebfraumilch. She and her late husband used to come here regularly but these days it is popular with the American professors who are giving lectures at the Institute for Summer Studies. During lunch she smokes and drinks, eating little, and the intervals of silence grow longer. As the time moves on toward three o'clock the waiter enquires, will that be all sir, and Iseult requests a cognac as defense against the inclement weather. Half an hour later Gabriel helps her into a raincoat. On the street she suggests we find the nearest pub but Gabriel begs off because of another engagement. We'll surely get in touch with her on our next visit and trust that her situation will have improved. She replies flatly that within the year she hopes to be dead. She turns away toward Pembroke Street, a pathetic figure dissolving into the drizzle.

Merrion Row appears dismal. In Stephen's Green the memorial to Wolfe Tone is flanked by a screen of granite and behind it the metal sculpture of a stricken family of '98. The Shelbourne Hotel is a beacon of warmth in the soggy city. Kildare Street. The National Library and Museum. Grafton Street.

On Duke Street Davy Byrne's pub beckons. Behind the

bar a mural by Cecil Ffrench Salkeld depicts a picnic on the grass. Among the young men and women the artist has included Bernard Shaw and Davy Byrne reclining beside a tree. Pastoral innocence against a background of mountain, stream and forest. Genteel Breughel. The white-jacketed barman draws Guinness with dexterity, allowing the creamy froth to settle on the brim of the glass.

In the lounge Cornelius O'Hearne looks up from his pint, a flicker of recognition on the serious face. As he gestures for us to join him the door opens, bringing in a gust of rain and a trio who inquire if this is the Davy Byrne's mentioned in the book by James Joyce. Tourists, grunts Cornelius. Everything modernized to please the tourists. At the Bailey they tore out the insides, put in new fixtures and raised the prices. Only tourists and businessmen can afford to go there. It is no longer the Bailey that used to be frequented by Parnell and Griffith, by the Invincibles. By James Stephens and Oliver Gogarty. And a barrister known as Sodomy Cox who got the nickname because he supported Oscar Wilde during the trial. The wittiest assemblage in all of Dublin including O'Flaherty and Kavanagh. And Myles Na gCopaleen. Did we know that John Ryan sold the Bailey to a consortium headed by Garfield Weston the Canadian industrialist? Too many tourists in here, Cornelius repeats. Let us find another establishment.

Sunshine again. Cornelius points to the Bailey on the other side of the street, indicating where the exterior has been ruined by all the new brick and chrome, not to forget the railings and mirrors. We continue along Grafton beyond Trinity College into Townsend Street. Overhead the Tara Street station of the loop line railway. At Poolbeg Street we halt before John Mulligan Wines and Spirits, its aged front painted green and brown.

We are greeted by gas lamps, brass beer pumps, oak woodwork, wooden tables and chairs, everything the same since the day it opened 190 years ago, avers Cornelius. All the literary people came here, including James Joyce. This was one of the few places still open to Brendan Behan.

Over pints of ale and chasers of whisky Cornelius laments the state of Ireland. Not only because of the IRA and the bombings but also the uncompromising attitude of the Catholic Church in matters of divorce. He and Brigid are not living together and he has a female companion who expects him at her flat for supper, but not yet, plenty of time. Have another drink, he urges. We beg off, leaving him in contemplation of his glass, mumbling A land of youth, a land of rest, a land from sorrow free. It lies far off in the golden west on the verge of the azure sea.

Long day's journey, the sun still visible, the dome of the Customs House gleaming golden. The blue and cream Guinness barges ride at anchor in Dublin bay. The Lady Patricia with a crew of twelve and five thousand barrels of porter in the hold bound for Liverpool. The Lady Gwendolyn. The Lady Miranda. A dryness in my mouth.

At the Montfort Hotel Joe Erskine will not hear of us retiring so early. We must join him for a drink of Aquavit in the kitchen. I ask for orange juice. Erskine is saddened by the shooting of the four students from Kent State University. Slainte. Another glass. Joe recounts stories of his boyhood with songs of the sailors and have we heard the tale of the Runaway Cork Leg.

When the bottle is empty Gabriel rises unsteadily and I help him up the stairs to bed.

16
London, Thursday June 19, 1969. Afternoon tea in Frank Budgen's flat in Belsize Park .

-I didn't much like James Joyce when I met him in Zurich during the First World War. He put on a rather cold and distant air. He seemed to lack warmth until he got three or four glasses of white wine into him and then he began to thaw out. What I thought was going to be a pretty poor evening turned out to be an excellent one and as we walked down the hill together, the Zurichberg, down to where he lived in the Universitat Strasse, I asked why he was so stand-offish at first. He said he thought I was a spy from the consulate because at that time he was at war with the British Empire, a little personal war brought about because of the incident of the British Players in the Oscar Wilde play and a Henry Carr, a Consulate Official. Actually the man was a soldier invalided out of the German hospital on account of shell shock or something. There were a number of such exchanges. I knew three or four and they got minor jobs in the consulate and other services.

-Apropos of James Joyce, I regard myself as a synoptic in the same situation as the gospellers Mark, Matthew and Luke. They are known as the synoptics, the ones who were present at the time and recorded what they saw. The fourth book is the logos gospel according to St. John the theologian but the theologians can't do without the synoptics. That's why I call myself the writer of one of the synoptic gospels and leave the Joyce scholars, the theologians, to interpret and evaluate.

-When I first met him he was busy with the Lestrygonians, that is to say Mr. Bloom going to lunch. It took Joyce a hell of a time to write it. I remember a walk we took along the Zurichsee. I asked him what he had been doing all day and he said he had been busy with two sentences which didn't seem to matter very much because after all there are plenty of painters -- take Vermeer for instance -- who certainly spent as much time on two centimetres of canvas, so why not a writer?

-My painting of Joyce is in the possession of Jack Sweeney, the librarian at Harvard. There is another one somewhere in America. I painted three or four memory studies of him, evocations I call them.

-He was a very good companion. Oh he could be a bit of a mandarin at times but he never put on any side or pretended to be better. He obeyed the unwritten law that when you are sitting around a table everybody is equal.

-It has been said that he was irreligious. The interpretation of the word religion is difficult. If you are going to be very strict I suppose the word means to bind together, the bond between man and God. If a person regards religion as a net by which he has flown as did Stephen Daedalus then he must be reckoned as not belonging to that religion. But if despite that, it dominates his life, his mode of thinking, then he has never really escaped it.

-I alluded to Mr. Joyce's Catholic upbringing in my book and when Stuart Gilbert read the proofs to him Joyce insisted I should change that to Jesuit. He said it was the Jesuit Order that had stamped itself upon him, that the shape of his mind had been conditioned by the Jesuit scholasticism, the ratio studiorum of Clongowes and Belvedere.

-As far as I know interest in him has grown from the time he was first published. His life and works have become a mother lode for scholars, a kind of industry.

-The last time I saw him was Easter of 1939. After that we were cut off by the war and in 1941 he died.

London. Friday June 20, 1969. Our companion in the lounge of the Salisbury Pub is an agreeable but voluble young man in sweater and jeans. Facial stubble gives him a handsome ruggedness.

-Will ye no have another nip? We say in Glasgow that it is the cheapest lawyer's fee for settling a dispute with your neighbor.

-Do you miss Glasgow, I ask.

-Ah, no. It's hypocritical, it's unhappy, it's boorish, it's puritanical. You get drunk with the boys on a Friday and you remember some past glory. 'What dangers thou canst make us scorn! Wi' tipenny we fear nae evil! Wi' usquabae we'll face the devil!' Always ready for a fight.

-The thing with Scotland is it's rooted in the past. There are certain dates that every Scottish lad grows up with. Like the battle of Bannockburn in 1314 when Robert the Bruce defeated Edward the Second. And the Scots haven't won a single battle since.

-You've heard about Bonnie Prince Charlie, the Young Pretender Charles Edward Stuart, the grandson of James 11, a Catholic twit from France, hardly speaks a word of English, a big shmuck, right? And he's come to rally the boys in favor of his cause. So he gets together a ragged band of highlanders. The point about Scottish tradition is that it's feudal. The clan chief says, 'You fight for this guy or I'm going to kill you'. So that's how Bonnie Prince Charlie gained an extra ten thousand troops.

While we order another round of drinks he leaves for the loo. The Salisbury is the Actors Pub in the West End. Very

Victorian with frosted glass windows, etched mirrors, red plush seats. Lots of marble, brass and copper. When he returns he is ready to continue the condemnation.

-The saddest thing about Scotland is the self-imposed exile. Samuel Johnson said that the best road a Scotsman ever took is the road that led him to London. Yet the Scots are very proud. It doesn't matter that the English have more wealth and power.

-Then there is the attitude toward sex. The working class girls are totally unsophisticated. Direct. Open. Have you heard the Cod Liver Oil and Orange Juice song? 'From the east there came a hard man, ah ha ha. Glory Hallelujah. Cod Liver Oil and Orange Juice'. And it goes on and on about how a fellow comes up to a girl and says: 'Hey hen, are ye dancin?' and she says 'ah no, it's just the way I'm standin'. That's it. The image of the wench from the east end of Glasgow who comes in to the Locarno Dance Hall and all the men are standing around looking to get laid on a Friday night. And she winds up being fucked at the mouth of the Close or in the doorway of a tenement and somebody dumps a bucket of shit on them from a fifth floor window That's Glasgow for you. Ah, the shocking poverty. Robbie Burns sleeping with his cows in the barn.

-I belong to Glasgow, dear old Glasgow toon. There's nothing the matter with Glasgow for it's goin roon and roon. That's it! The drunkenness and the cursing. I'm mad as fuck! I'll claim ye! Yeah, I'm tough as fuck!

-We were frowned upon, me and my pals, because we used to get drunk at Jewish events. You don't do that if you are a nice Jewish boy. We went to the pub on Friday nights and you don't do that either. Scottish Jews don't drink much and that's the real reason why they are excluded from the golf clubs; they're not sociable enough. But there is a Jewish golf club. Poker and mixed drinks. Scotch and soda and the same again. Or they'll have a half pint of beer.

-I was ready to leave Glasgow at the age of five. Not many Jews make a full break. Most come here, particularly the Jewish girls. If they aren't married by age 21 they descend on London in droves and you find all the people you knew back home at a party in London. Then the years go by and they're still looking and hoping. The saddest ones are the 25-year-old girls who have been left on the shore by the sweep of social life and they end up in bed-sitters or sharing flats and pursuing careers. In Glasgow the worst thing a mother can admit about her daughter is that she's a school teacher, which means she is not married. The Jewish lads pursue the Jewish professions. Law, medicine, and dentistry. There are also a lot of salesmen in Ladies Fashions. After bumming around for a while like many of us who took Arts at the University, I wound up as an editor with London Penthouse Magazine.

-The Jews of Glasgow are third and fourth generation. They've got everything. Money, position, family, networks. And the Sabbath meal. That's universal isn't it? Gefilte fish and chicken soup on Friday night and for Saturday lunch it's always chicken and potato kugel of course.

-I've thrown off the institutional trappings of Judaism but I still retain the sense of Jewishness. I know what it is, two thousand years of suffering. When I was eleven I saw a book with pictures of the concentration camps. It was my brother's bar mitzvah present and I felt, hey, these people are mine and I thought of Rabbi Amnon of Mainz who composed the Insaneh Tokef, the Rabbi who was mutilated in the eleventh century and died saying the Martyr's Prayer that is still recited on Yom Kippur, 'Let us relate the awesomeness of this day'. That speaks to you, that kind of suffering. It links you with all the Jews of all times but I think you have to break out of the community before you can universalize that sensitivity. A few Jews like Heinrich Heine and Baruch Spinoza have done it.

-The Jews take great pride in Israel. I remember the outbreak of the six day war I was in the reference library, the day before my economics exam. There were a lot of Jewish students and someone brought in the evening paper and you've never seen anything like it, the feeling of community, the joy and the pride. Everybody contributed gold rings and other jewellery to raise money for Israel. We ran a charity shop for three weeks, selling stuff that the manufacturers had donated and all the money went to Israel.

-Will you have another glass?

-Ah, the gentle sweetness of Glen Fiddich.

-Here's to the land where the famous Scotch whisky is bred, blended and bottled. You can have it oily, fruity, peaty or clean. Great for the aches of colds and fevers. Hot toddies for the adults. A drop on a sugar cube for the bairns. And as a medicine for dabbing on the pustules of chicken pox or the eruptions of acne.

-Great Britain's biggest dollar earner.

Saturday June 21, 1969. Gabriel and I motor up to Birmingham to visit Hilary who is coping with an interfering mother-in-law and a husband who suffers from ill-fitting dentures and swollen hemhorroids. His sister Laura has left her spouse and is living with an electrician, a big, hairy chap who was almost electrocuted on the job. Badly burned about the arms and chest he spent weeks in the hospital with skin grafts. Laura's mother refers to him as the monster but Laura boasts that he is a demon in bed and very good to the children. Before our departure Hilary confides that she still feels the anguish of the weekend in Niagara Falls with a lover who will not answer her letters and is not aware that four-year-old Charlie is his son.

Bypassing Birmingham via the M6 we continue north past Stoke-on-Trent and Manchester to the Lake Country with its crags and tumbling streams and purple heather. At Langholm in the Scottish lowlands we spend the night in an old inn with a metered gas fireplace in our room. Up early to a breakfast of porridge and kippers, stewed tomatoes, toast and tea then en route again past golf courses and castles and towns with quaint names like Kirkstile and Galashiels. Towards evening we arrive in Edinburgh and check into the North British Hotel.

Our exploration of the city leads us to the Castle that towers over Princes Street and provides the same view that was seen by Washington Irving, who observed the contrast between the new town 'gay and glittering like a section of Paris seen from Notre Dame' and the old 'with shadows of a thousand memories, somber, sublime, silent in its age.' We traverse the streets of the Royal Mile with their alleys and museums, their shops and houses. Visits to the Scott Monument, St. Giles Cathedral, John Knox House and Holyrood House the official residence of the Queen. We dine on roast beef washed down with Younger's Ale.

On the third day we drive the 44 miles to Glasgow, hastening through the grimy Gorbals into the countryside to Prestwick. The VC10 jetliner is immoblized because of a malfunctioning compass and after waiting at the airport all day we are lodged at the Carlton Hotel where we pass the night in the lounge singing bawdy ballads with a group of Americans who call themselves the Burns Brotherhood. At four in the morning we are summoned for take-off.

17

July 18, 1969. Senator Edward Kennedy drives his car off a bridge on Chappaquiddick Island near Martha's Vineyard in Massachusetts. His companion Mary Jo Kopechne drowns.

July 20. Neil Armstrong is the first human to walk on the moon. To a waiting world he announces: 'That's one small step for man, one giant leap for mankind.'

August 16. Woodstock, N.Y. Half a million people from all over the USA gather on a 600 acre farm in the Catskills for four days of rock music.

October 15. Vietnam Moratorium Day. Vice President Spiro Agnew declares that the demonstration against the Vietnam War is 'encouraged by an effete corps of snobs who characterize themselves as intellectuals.'

November 15. A quarter of a million people assemble in Washington and march past the White House to protest the war in Vietnam.

November 16. Americans read the first reports of the My Lai massacre of March 16, 1968 when Vietnamese men, women and children were shot to death by US troops.

December 31. Gabriel sells his Advertising Agency to a group from Chicago. He has been offered a teaching position at York University in Toronto..

18

Belfast. May 1970. John Gamble is waiting outside Great Victoria Station to welcome us to Her Majesty's British Province of Ulster.

At the wheel of his Rover he has become expert at maneuvering past the barricades, the armored cars, the military trucks and the patrols of British soldiers with machine guns and rifles.

He is cautious about assigning blame for the troubles. Perhaps history is to blame. History, economics and religion.

The Europa Hotel was bombed again last week. Gamble's bookshop was strafed with bullets, so he has transferred the rare volumes to his home in the suburbs; but gunfire the other night forced him, with his wife and three children, to seek protection under the bed. He fears the situation can only worsen so he is pleased that Gabriel has agreed to purchase the collection of Irish, Scottish and English Ballads as well as the minutes of the meetings of the Loyal Orange Lodges of Great Britain, Ireland, Australia, the United States and Canada.

To satisfy the visitors' curiosity he drives into the centre of the disturbances. Corrugated iron fences divide the Shankhill and Falls Road neighborhoods. Graffiti scrawls are everywhere. Death to the Papists. No surrender. God Bless Paisley. The battle signs of the hard-line Protestants. Next year marks the 800th anniversary of the Norman Conquest of Ireland by Henry the Second and the beginning of the oppression.

North of Belfast we stop at Carrickfergus Castle, the stronghold begun about 1180 by the first Norman invader of Ulster, John de Courcy, and besieged by King John, Edward Bruce and others. Nineteenth century cannon line the outer wall. Nearby is the Antrim lookout which was used as a cache for treasure following the Viking invasions and beyond it the Giant's Causeway, the eighth wonder of the world. So quiet a beauty, the strand and the cliffs that reach out to the green waters of the Irish Sea.

On Saturday Gabriel and I visit Galway, the capital of the West of Ireland, an ancient city with a recorded history of a thousand years.

Originally part of the O'Halloran territories, the village and fort were seized by the De Burgos, who built a castle prior to 1240 and walled and fortified the area. Richard 11 of England granted the town a charter, making it independent of the De Burgos, and a brisk trade developed with Spain. The emerging city-state was ruled by the fourteen tribes, mainly Norman and Welsh merchant families.

Christopher Columbus before setting out across the western sea is said to have prayed at the Collegiate Church of St. Nicholas. While he knelt amidst the icons of Catholic Christianity, did he perhaps offer up secret praise to Jehovah the God of Abraham, Isaac and Jacob instead of to Father, Son and Holy Ghost? There is some evidence that he may have been Jewish. His last Will bequeathed half a mark in silver to a Jew who lived at the entrance to the ghetto in Lisbon. Speculation has been further increased by scholarly discoveries of his use of contemporary Jewish expressions and references that would indicate a first hand awareness of Jewish literature. There are reasons to believe that some of the crew and passengers of the Nina, Pinta and Santa Maria were Jews fleeing the Inquisition.

-Welcome to the city of the Tribes. Sean Kenny, amiable proprietor of Kenny's Art Gallery and Book Shop has been waiting for us all morning. We shall be dining on poached salmon caught only hours ago at the Salmon Weir. There is nothing as delicious as Irish salmon. Do you know the tale of Finn's tooth of knowledge?

-The story goes that Finn the son of Cumhal fled as a boy from his enemies the Clann Morna and took the name of Demna. At Linn Fec he became servant to a poet named Finn who having caught a great salmon gave it to the boy to broil but warned him not to taste of it. The heat from the fire raised a blister on the fish and the boy pressing with his thumb to keep it down scalded himself and put his thumb in his mouth because of the pain of it. And that's how he obtained the gift of divination for thereafter whenever he put his thumb under his tooth of knowledge the future was revealed to him.

At the table Kenny proposes a toast. *Slainte An Bradan Cugat*. Health of the Salmon to You. Or if you prefer: *Croide Folain Agus Fluic*. Heart Healthy and Beak Wet. The housekeeper serves plentiful portions of the fish with potatoes and vegetables.

-Galway has a great tradition of learning. The city's famous classical school founded in 1580 had an enrolment of twelve hundred when Alexander Lynch was headmaster. The Lynches, who were prominent in the affairs of Galway, were the most influential of The Tribes. Between 1484 and 1654 eighty-four different members held the office of mayor. You've no doubt heard of Judge Lynch the hanging judge. His son Walter murdered a young Spanish visitor and having confessed to the crime was condemned to death by his father but nobody could be found to carry out the sentence so Judge Lynch hanged him from a window to prevent his being rescued by other members of the family. Judge Lynch became Mayor of Galway in 1493 and was a stern chief magistrate. Lynch's Castle still stands. Galway fell to the forces of Oliver Cromwell and was besieged again at the end of the seventeenth century during the wars of William I, and then declined in importance. However, with the establishment of the Irish Republic the city began to prosper again.

Lunch finished, Kenny suggests we take a drive. Nora Barnacle was born here, attended the convent school of the Sisters of Mercy and worked at the Presentation Convent before leaving for Dublin and the chance meeting with James Joyce.

Galway is revealed before Kenny's enthusiastic oration. The merchant houses built of stone in the seventeenth and eighteenth centuries, many derelict but with doorways and windows intact. The Spanish Arch erected in 1594 to protect the Quay when Spanish ships unloaded their cargoes of wine and brandy. The Spanish Parade where Spanish merchants strolled in the evenings.

-There are a number of links between the Irish and the Spaniards, the Celtic similarities for one. The Book of Invasions mentions that the prehistoric inhabitants of the island migrated from Iberia. The Milesian invaders of Ireland came from the Spanish province of Galicia. Led by the three sons of King Mileadh they were the last of the legendary invaders of Ireland and thus are said to be the ancestors of the royal clans of Ireland.

-All Kings sons. Mentioned somewhere in *Portrait of the Artist As a Young Man,* Gabriel recalls.

-In the fifteenth and sixteenth centuries the Wild Geese, fleeing from British oppression went to Galicia. Some of the most illustrious personages in Spanish history bear Irish names. O'Donnell. O'Donoghue. At one time eight Irish military regiments were in the service of Spain.

-Here is the John Fitzgerald Kennedy Memorial Park where the late President received the Freedom of the City.

Kenny steers the car past the Library, the Gardai Barracks, the Galway Market, the Irish Theatre and the Customs House. The Passenger Terminal for the Aran Isles provides steamer service across the choppy waters or one can fly the short distance. The last outposts of Gaelic civilization, the unspoiled Gaeltacht with the remains of early Irish churches, the dwellings of the saints and the mighty forts of the pre-Christian Fir Bolg. The fishermen in their frail curraghs, the *Riders to the Sea* of John Millington Synge, still clinging to the old ways.

-While you are here you might like to visit Oughterrard. It is only seventeen miles north and contains the grave of Sonny Bodkin, the lover of Nora Barnacle. He is called Michael Furey in James Joyce's short story, 'The Dead'.

We are approaching the seaside suburb of Salthill, a proliferation of modest hotels, guest houses and cafes in a carnival setting of cotton candy, game stalls and a discotheque. Galway Leisureland offers concerts, movies and fashion shows. Weather permitting the promenade is a fine place for courting, says Kenny. To sit on a bench in the moonlight and look out at the waters of Galway Bay.

-Before you leave you will want to see what I have put aside for you. A rare collection of 153 hand-coloured Cuala Press Christmas Cards and a bundle of letters of Jack Yeats. When you come again I'll have more material. By all means let us keep in touch.

Cork is the city of marshes, the hills bathed in a blue haze.

The river Lee spanned by fourteen bridges is featured in the short stories of Frank O'Connor as are the Shandon Church, the four-faced liar's clock and the Coal Quay Flea Market. Foraging in the basement of Feehan's Book Store we come upon The National Music of Ireland, the Saorstate Eireann Handbook, Songs of the Gael and an eighteenth century Hebrew Grammar.

Dinner in Market Lane at the Oyster Tavern, elegantly Edwardian with dark wood trim, frosted globes of light and handsome wall mirrors. The salmon has a delicate texture and taste, the chilled Chablis is the perfect wine. We linger over coffee before returning via the Western Road to the Rosario Guest House on Mardyke Walk.

Sixteen miles from Cork is the coastal fishing village of Kinsale, the harbour gay with brightly coloured yachts. Narrow, winding streets with little shops and pubs.

The day is wet—Ireland's tears of angels—as we climb the slope of Compass Hill dotted with Georgian Houses. Kinsale received its royal charter in 1334 from Edward the Third. In 1602 the Spaniards who had sought to liberate all of Ireland from the British were defeated at the Battle of Kinsale and no Irish were allowed to settle within the walls for centuries afterward. The Lusitania, believed torpedoed by a German submarine, went down in these waters on May 7, 1915, about ten miles from the Old Head of Kinsale, with the loss of 1198 passengers.

We have been invited to tea by the Mother Superior, whom we met in Dublin. The Sisters at the Convent are entranced by Gabriel's stories of our travels, but after a time they become anxious about the absence of the priest who was to celebrate Mass with them. Mother Superior urges them to have faith, for the shepherd can be trusted to look after his flock.

They gather in the hall to bid us farewell. And will we come again? So, safe journey with God's blessing.

Dublin. Five of us attend a preview showing of *The Playboy of the Western World* at Telefis Eireann. After the film has run its course and Sineaid has commented upon its inadequacies, Father Desmond Fitzgerald invites us to his rented house in Rathgar for a late supper.

He bids us help ourselves to the Guinness and Irish Whisky as he leaves for the kitchen. He is adjusting to civilian life, teaching at a private school in Toronto and continuing with research on the Fitzgeralds during the summer holidays.

-The Catholic Church has lost a fine priest, laments Liam. The Pope should end the proscription against celibacy.

-And sanction the ordination of women priests, adds Sineaid. Consider the closeness Jesus had with women. He accepted them freely, journeyed with them from Galilee to Jerusalem. They remained faithful to Him while He lived and even proclaimed the news of His resurrection.

-And what about a woman Pope, asks Gabriel as Fr. Fitzgerald returns with the cold meats. Did you know that Pope Joan disguised as a man reigned for more than two years around 1100 A.D. Her secret was discovered when she was overcome with labour pains during a procession to the Lateran. It is said that she gave birth to a child and died thereafter. Isn't that so, Father Fitzgerald?

-There is no evidence to substantiate the story that was widely believed in the Middle Ages but has been rejected as an invention by serious scholars. The Bavarian Church historian Johann von Dollinger explained it in 1863 as a Roman folk-tale. The Church has appropriated much from pagan ritual like the idea of a sisterhood of women devoted to the religious life, who have taken vows of chastity, obedience and poverty. You'll find their precursors in the Vestal Virgins of ancient Rome, the priestesses of the goddess of the hearth and fire. Their hair shorn, dressed in white robes, they were under the control of the Pontifex. Any Vestal who violated her vow of chastity was beaten and immured alive.

-Don't you think that nuns choose lives of chastity because they have an unhealthy fear of sexuality which they transfer to their love of Jesus?

-Or they lavish their affection on animals. Veronica Giuliani who was beatified by Pius 11 took a lamb to bed with her in remembrance of the lamb of God. There must be a tremendous amount of sexual love sublimated in the worship of

Christ by the nuns.

   -Did you hear about the nun who was obsessed with what happened to the foreskin of Jesus after he was circumcised?

   -I am of the opinion that the religious life must appeal mainly to emotionally or mentally unstable women.

19

   Dublin. June 8, 1970. Fortified by a breakfast of rashers and eggs, toast and apple jelly, Gabriel and I pack for departure, with Kathleen promising to hold our room.

   On Eccles Street a gaggle of girls skipping rope is chanting.

> I'll tell my ma when I go home
> The boys won't leave the girls alone.
> They pull my hair, they steal my comb
> And that's all right till I go home.

The twine rotates faster and the lilt becomes a shout.

> She is handsome, she is pretty,
> She is the belle of Dublin city,
> She is courtin' one, two, three,
> Please won't you tell me who is she?

With Gabriel at the wheel of the Ford Consul from Ryan's Rent-A-Car we drive away from the Montfort and the children's voices fade into the clatter of the barrows on Dorset Street.

   At O'Connell Bridge we stop before a white-gloved policeman. As the backup grows longer the horns blare to a crescendo until the Gardai comes out of his reverie and signals for the traffic to resume.

   The Liffey embankment is swollen with lorries from Bachelor's Walk to the Michael Collins Barracks and the greenery of Phoenix Park with the commanding presence of the Wellington Monument.

   In Chapelizod we stop at the Caltex petrol station where a young woman displaying a gap-toothed smile enquires if she can hitch a ride. Upon hearing that we are bound for Sligo she whoops with delight and throws her knapsack into the back of the car. Her name is Mary Margaret Mulrooney and she is a student at the University of St. Louis. This is her first visit to Ireland for the Yeats conference.

Beyond Lucan we are in the country with its stone hedges, rock-strewn fields, grazing sheep and thatched cottages.

At Maynooth Gabriel draws our attention to the renowned College that dates from the thirteenth century and the remains of Maynooth Castle, the ancient seat of the Fitzgeralds. We pass through Kilcock and Enfield. Beyond Moyvalley a herd of cows brings the car to a stop. A collie barks at them while the farm boy observes us.

-Isn't the scenery just magnificent, Mary Margaret enthuses. I love to travel. Last summer, I hiked all over France, spent some time in the Burgundy area where the marvellous Chambertin wine comes from. Have you ever been to Macon? It's the birthplace of LaMartine, the French romantic poet.

Mulrooney entertains with travel anecdotes until we reach Longford, where we pull up at a public house. While she bounds away to the toilet Gabriel and I chat with the publican. Padraic Colum was born here, he says. And there's good fishing in the Camlin river.

After a lunch of soda bread, Irish cheddar, and Harp lager at an outdoor table we are on the road again. Carrick-on-Shannon. Ballinafad. Ballisodare. In the distance Knocknarea juts up and minutes later prow-shaped Ben Bulben comes into view. Sligo nestles in the valley.

The Eleventh Yeats International Summer School has attracted students from the United States, Canada, France, Italy and Poland. The first session deals with Yeats and Eliot. Still to come are papers on the Irish Literary Revival, Yeats, Joyce and Pound and The Allegory of the Wandering Oisin.

In the afternoon the participants are transported six miles to the village of Drumcliff. In the small church yard under bare Ben Bulben's head W.B. Yeats is laid to rest, his grave marked by a black headstone with the inscription 'Cast a cold Eye on Life, on Death, Horseman pass by.' On these grounds in 745 A.D. Saint Columba founded a monastic order, but all that remains

178 · Harry Pollock

is the lower portion of a round tower and a Celtic Cross with sculptured panels, one of which depicts Adam and Eve in Edenville.

The next stop is three and a half miles northwest. Lissadell House hidden within a forest of pine trees was the home of the Arctic explorer Sir Henry Gore-Booth and his daughters Eva and Constance. Their descendants the Misses Gabrielle and Aideen receive the visitors in the drawing room of the Georgian mansion where Yeats used to have tea. Here is the chair he sat on and his writing desk. Next comes an inspection of the furnishings.

Miss Gabrielle recounts how her aunt Constance married the Polish Count Casimir Markievicz in London, returned to Ireland and became active in the labour movement. She founded the Irish National Boy Scouts, aided the Dublin strikers in 1913, joined the Irish Citizen Army and during the Easter uprising commanded the Republican contingent in Stephen's Green, was sentenced to death and reprieved. In 1918 Constance was elected the first woman member of the British Parliament. She sat in the Dail Eireann as minister of labour in the insurgent Republican government and opposed the treaty of 1921.

When she has finished, the leader of our group thanks the sisters for their hospitality and hands Miss Gabrielle an envelope as we leave. A discreet financial transaction.

In Sligo the students disperse. Mulrooney has a date with an American professor. Father Desmond Fitzgerald is registered at the Imperial Hotel but he is not in his room.

The city offers a number of attractions. The Gaiety Cinema is showing *True Grit* with John Wayne. The Savoy displays a poster of *Oliver!* with Ron Moody as a leering Fagin. The Sligo Drama Circle presents Sean O'Casey's *Shadow of a Gunman*. The Museum exhibits a collection of historical and archaeological objects that date back to pre-Christian times. A special W.B. Yeats section features the manuscripts, first editions, photographs and paintings as well as the 1923 Medal of the Nobel Prize for literature.

In the Social Centre on Castle Street a rough-clad individual is reciting *Sailing to Byzantium*. Michael Maguire is a carpenter from Naas, a former navvy on the London docks, a self-educated scholar who enjoys surprising academics with his knowledge.

-What is your philosophy of life, a student asks.

-Ah, what is life? Maguire gropes for the answer, running fingers through a mass of hair. I often looked up at the sky and assed meself the question, what is the stars, what is the stars? And then I'd have another look and I'd ass meself, what is the moon?. Maguire accepts a pint of ale and asks would we like to hear his translation of *The Midnight Court* by Brian Merriman.

After the lecture on the Irish Literary Revival, Gabriel and I, accompanied by Mary Margaret Mulrooney, set out to explore the Yeats country. A short drive brings us to Carrowmore with its megalithic remains. Dolmens and stone circles, sepulchral monuments and carvings dating from the Bronze Age. Two miles away Knocknarea rises above the village of Strandhill to a height of a thousand feet. It is crowned by Misgaun Maedbh the immense cairn invested by tradition as the grave of Queen Maeve of Connacht who reigned in the first century A.D. We park the car by the side of the road and Mulrooney runs ahead. Rocks and prickly furze, tall grass and heather impede our ascent but Mulrooney scampers upward. The weather is changing. Dark, scudding clouds.

-Now for the very top. As she starts to climb the winds awaken, spinning the leaves around. The rain splashes angrily and we huddle in the underbrush until the storm ends and the sun comes out, the sky again serene. Mulrooney will not continue up to Queen Maeve's tomb lest she offend the ancient gods of Ireland.

A green and white sign points the way down to Primrose Grange via a stairway. A quick, easy descent.

Mulrooney is looking forward to the dance at the Social Centre.

Past ten o'clock in the evening and the sun still lingers in the west. The dining room of the Imperial Hotel commands a picturesque view of the Garavogue River rippling toward Sligo Bay. The swans are nesting in Doorly Park. Lough Gill and the surrounding hills provide a magnificent backdrop. We have enjoyed a dinner of steak and potatoes in the company of Desmond Fitzgerald, who is dressed in slacks and moccasins and a fisherman's knit bawneen sweater.

Father Fitzgerald has been researching his family history and as we relax over coffee and liqueur he shares the results of his investigations. The Fitzgeralds, also known as Geraldines, were a powerful Anglo-Irish family whose heritage goes back to the twelfth century. Maurice Fitzgerald the Earl of Kildare built Sligo Castle and founded Sligo Abbey for the Dominican Order.

-Gerald Fitzgerald, known as the Great Fitzgerald, was the mightiest of the Anglo-Irish lords. In 1495 during a conflict with Archbishop Creagh he set fire to Cashel Cathedral. Charged in council before Henry Vll he replied: 'By Jesus, I would never have done it had it not been told me that the Archbishop was within'.

-You've no doubt come across Silken Thomas in your reading. That was Thomas Fitzgerald who rebelled against Henry Vlll. He actually seized Howth to prevent the English from landing reinforcements but was captured along with five of his uncles and they were all hanged, drawn and quartered at a public execution in Tyburn.

-Lord Edward Fitzgerald was president of the military committee of the United Irishmen and the master-mind behind plans for the 1798 revolution. He was wounded and died in prison.

-And of course there was the poet Edward Fitzgerald, who translated *The Rubaiyat of Omar Khayyam*, I contribute.

-The Fitzgeralds were active in Sligo until the Great Famine of 1845 when several families left for America in the coffin ships. Those who didn't perish during the crossing wound up in Boston and New York.

-Impressive, says Gabriel. I have been able to trace my family tree a mere three generations to a village in Poland. I sometimes wonder what alien genes are lurking in my DNA as the result of the rape of my ancestors during successive European pogroms. Perhaps they account for my occasional Slavic melancholia.

-What about the black moods of the Irish? We have been ravaged and ravished since the ninth century by Vikings, Norsemen, Icelanders, Spaniards, Normans, French and English.

-But you assimilated all of them.

-Did you know that Ireland's patron saint was not Irish? His father who was a Roman official in Britain lived with the family in the vicinity of the Severn River. Patrick was captured by an Irish raiding party in 401 A.D. when he was sixteen. He worked as a swineherd in northern Ireland for about six years then escaped to France and wandered about Europe, returned to Britain and had a vision, voices calling him back to Ireland as a missionary. In 432 he landed near the Mourne Mountains and travelled all over the country routing the Druids and establishing churches. He spent some time in Sligo where it is said he lost a tooth at the entrance to a chapel. You can see it in the National Museum in Dublin.

-Wasn't it Saint Patrick who used the shamrock to illustrate the idea of the Trinity, I ask.

-Faith in St. Patrick and the Catholic Church is steadfast, marvels Gabriel.

-There was a time when I was strong in the faith, recalls Father Fitzgerald. The two years of my novitiate. Assembling at six in the morning for prayer and study. And the bells. Rise.. Go to chapel. Meditate. Bells for breakfast, make your bed, examine your conscience. Two years of monastic asceticism in order to become like Christ our Lord. As St. Ignatius Loyola has written: To choose poverty with Christ poor rather than riches. Serving at tables, washing dishes, scrubbing floors, cleaning latrines.

- We practised mortification of the body by the use of the Discipline a small whip of braided cords. Twenty-five strokes across the back to teach us to control our sexual desires. The chain too, with links of pointed wire worn around the thigh for penitence.

-Shortly after our arrival we entered into the Long Retreat. Thirty days of contemplation on the sin of Adam and Eve, the Fall of Lucifer, Hell, the Passion of our Lord, Death and Resurrection. How we prayed! With St. Anselm: Flee now for a little while thine accustomed occupations; hide thyself for a brief moment from thy tumultuous thoughts; devote thyself awhile to God.

-Sometimes during prayer I experienced instances of exaltation. I trembled with fear and anticipation of the Day of Judgment. Suffering periods of intense desolation I was sustained by the awareness that I was preparing to become a priest of the Holy Roman Catholic and Apostolic Church.

There is a great coming and going in the Lounge Bar. Gabriel observes that the Yeats scholars are helping sustain the economic well-being of the Sligo hotel keepers and publicans, good Catholics who are pleased to batten on the popularity of a family of disbelievers. John Butler Yeats, although an adherent of the Church of Ireland, was an acknowledged sceptic. His son Willie dallied with Theosophy and Rosicrucianism, embraced Blake and Blavatsky. He has also incurred the wrath of the Dublin-based Literature and Ideology Study Group which interrupted lectures at the Summer School by claiming that W.B. Yeats advocated the theories of Mussolini and showed contempt for the Irish people with his support of a decaying ruling class.

-*When you are old and grey and full of sleep and nodding by the fire*... Father Fitzgerald swirls the brandy in his glass.

-My favorite Yeats poem, I murmur.

-*How many loved your moments of glad grace*. Anna means Grace in Hebrew, does it not?

-Yes, from the word *khen*, I explain. May the Lord cause His countenance to shine upon you and be gracious unto you.

-I like the definition of Grace as the seemingly effortless charm of movement, the generous disposition. Of the three Graces in Greek mythology I see you, Anna ,as Euphrosyne, the daughter of Zeus and Eurynome. Joy.

-You are most generous in your praise.

-In Celtic legends Ana is the earth goddess of the Tuatha de Danaan, more often known as Dana, the goddess of fertility. Ana also signifies riches in Irish. It is fascinating to speculate on all the possible correspondences. For instance Ana-stasia in Greek translates as resurrection.

-I would rather be linked with the Biblical women of valour like Deborah, one of the Judges of Israel who helped her people free themselves from the Canaanites.

-What of the women in the New Testament, asks Father Fitzgerald.

-I think not. The females in Christian theology are regarded as inferior beings. I refer you to the dictum about women keeping quiet.

-Corinthians. Let your women keep silence in the churches for it is not permitted them to speak. Nevertheless they have had a great influence in the development of Christianity. The women prophets in Pauline times and in the Apocalypse. The church mothers, Paula and Mellania. Saints Teresa of Avila and Elizabeth of Hungary. Abbesses during the Middle Ages who were the Superiors of the Benedictine and Franciscan nuns. Powerful women in the secular life too like Mary Queen of Scots and Elizabeth the First of England.

-The Old Testament lauds the virtuous woman, sexually pure and passive. In ancient times the Rabbis pondered whether a woman was still a virgin if she had been accidentally deflowered by a stick. Or whether she committed adultery if she were impregnated while bathing in a public place where the sperm of a male bather unknown to her entered her body. The first chastity belt, the sinar, was prescribed by Ezra the Scribe after the return from Babylon.

-Of course, adds Gabriel, the old taboo menstruation sets her apart. As it is said, he who pursues a woman in this state even though it be his own wife has merited hellfire. Then there is Lilith, the long-haired demon of the night who seduces men and kills the children she bears them. Lilith in Midrash legend, the first wife of Adam who will not submit to him, forcing God to banish her and then He is obliged to create Eve out of Adam's rib. Lilith who roams the world with a host of evil spirits howling hatred of mankind and vowing vengeance.

-*The host is riding from Knocknarea.*

-In the room of a newborn Jewish babe , superstitious parents hang amulets bearing the injunction: Lilith Begone!

-The Catholic Church is in a bit of a ferment, asserts one

of the scholars. What is your position?

- As you know I have recently resigned from the active priesthood and have petitioned Pope Paul to free me from priestly obligations and the need to remain celibate. My struggle is against the conservatism of the hierarchy. After the upheaval brought about by the Ecumenical Council Vatican ll there were great hopes that John's successor would continue the process of Aggiornamento. There were several gestures. A woman was appointed subsecretary of the Council for the Laity and a few were brought into other offices but that's hardly worth mentioning. After all, of the 500 million Catholics in the world more than half are women and the activists among them are working for equality in the church.

-As for clerical celibacy, Peter, the first Pope, had a wife. The early church emphasized good morals with St. Paul admonishing the Bishops to be husband to only one wife. Pope Leo Vlll died of a stroke about the year 963 while committing adultery. Benedict Vlll reinforced the celibacy laws in 1018 by declaring children of the clergy to be serfs of the church and 31 years later Leo lX assigned the wives and concubines of priests to be maidservants at the Lateran Palace, the residence of the Popes.

-Homosexuality became so prevalent among the clergy that in 1102 the Church Council issued an edict that priests would be anathematized for obstinate sodomy. Pope Alexander VI, who lived until 1503, was an enthusiastic orgiast who once had fifty nude prostitutes servicing guests at a banquet where he offered prizes to the man who could copulate the most times. Thomas Aquinas trivialized women as just helpers in the work of generation. It wasn't until the sixteenth century at the Council of Trent convened as a counter move to the Reformation of Martin Luther that the practice of celibacy was spelled out in the most uncompromising manner.

-Eastern rite priests affiliated with Rome are married, I mention.

-The Dutch Pastoral Council has just made public its demand for the abolition of celibacy. Hans Kung the Swiss theologian is challenging the Vatican on the subject of equality for women, asserting that the Catholic Church has defamed them with the affirmation that through woman sin entered the world; that woman, unlike Adam, was not made in the image of God but created second; that menstruation makes woman impure. It will not be easy to change the historical animosity towards women on the part of the Church Fathers even though this attitude was alien to Jesus as witness his association with Mary Magdalene and Mary the sister of Martha.

-That brings us to the BVM. It is impossible for me as a Jew to accept the virgin birth let alone the concept of God having a mother.

-That's what you can expect in a Mariology formulated by celibate men, a Mary robbed of her sexuality who remains perpetually a virgin. Mary Immaculate, free from original sin who at her death is taken bodily up into heaven. Martin Luther criticized the excessive devotion to Mary as a false glorification by Rome. For a brief time after Vatican II the veneration of Mary declined, but there is now a resurgence with the Legion of Mary actively soliciting members again, dispensing Miraculous Medals during their door-to-door visits. May as the month of Mary. The Holy Hour. The Rosary.

-Isn't it paradoxical that the Roman Catholic Church, which accords the highest honour and love to one woman, denigrates and dehumanizes all women? Out of their unnatural celibate state the priests, having to fight the desires of the flesh and the resulting guilt, came to view woman as Eve the temptress.

-In the seminary we tried to banish the female sex organ from our thoughts, regarding it as a monstrous necessity for procreation.

-The vagina dentata.

-But I had no trouble relating to the Blessed Virgin Mary. When I was a youngster I loved to hear stories about Her gentleness and kindness. How St. Peter, who was chastised by our Lord for allowing sinners into Heaven, replied, 'I bar them at the Celestial Gates but your Mother lets them in by the side door.'

-I loved Mary with all my heart and soul. Holy Mary, her

smile beatific, her shrines welcoming the prayers of suffering humanity. The Cathedral of Chartres. Mother of God pray for us. Notre Dame de Grace in Paris. Our Lady most radiant. The Black Madonna of Czestochowa. Blessed art thou among women.

-But always there was the loneliness of the priesthood, the sexual desires and the guilt, the nocturnal emissions and the guilt, the masturbation and the guilt.

-The ministers of the other Christian denominations fared better. Martin Luther declared that God placed the creation of all men in women and therefore the state of marriage was the noblest way of life for both the laity and the clergy. But the Roman Catholic Church has remained immutable. Hans Kung asserts that Man has created God in Man's own image. As Man changes his perception, couldn't God the Father become God the Father-Mother with priests of both sexes joined connubially to worship the androgynous Godhead? Kung questions the central doctrines of the Catholic Faith. He contends that no church teaching can be infallible whether derived from popes, creeds, councils or the Bible itself. Nowhere is there evidence that Jesus believed he was the Son of God and Kung could not find in the teachings of Jesus any basis to found a new religion.

-The Jesuits have been criticized for causing confusion among Christians and anxieties to the Pope. Since its founding by Ignatius Loyola 430 years ago, the Society of Jesus has been active in the reinterpretation of church teaching on faith and morals. Jesuits were among the leading theologians at Vatican II. We are the largest religious order, an elite membership that vows special obedience to the Holy Father when we make our final profession seventeen years after we begin our training. So when a Jesuit confronts the Pope openly like advocating ordination of women he is quickly silenced by the Father General of the Order.

-Will you have another glass?

-Indeed, for in alcohol lies one avenue of escape. I know numerous priests who have taken that route. Yet there is grace for the drunkard. Matt Talbot was an alcoholic labourer for fifteen years before he underwent a conversion, took the pledge never to drink again, went to confession and began a life of prayer and penance. He worked in a lumberyard, slept only three-and-a-half hours a night on rough planks and a wooden pillow and wore chains that at his death were found imbedded in the flesh. Pope Paul declared that Talbot has become worthy of being proclaimed Blessed.

-Saints and martyrs. Embracing pain and torture, even death in the certainty of eternal bliss, says Gabriel. Eccentrics. Fanatically committed.

-A case could be made against our Lord, admits Father Fitzgerald. Mark recounts that Mary and her sons came to the synagogue to take Jesus home because He was rebuking the wind and ordering the sea to be still.

-I am inclined to agree with Havelock Ellis that the whole religious complexion of the modern world is due to the absence in Jerusalem of a Lunatic Asylum.

Today we go up to Rosses Point with Mary Margaret Mulrooney. From Memory Harbor we can look out on Sligo Bay where a swimmer hurls himself against the surf and children build castles in the sand. Yeats walked here, observed the Metal Man in the river and experienced metaphysical manifestations which he set down in his poems. Brother Jack with canvas and brush limned the special beauty of this place where today sail boats bob at anchor in the Yacht Club. The Yeats Country Ryan Hotel and the bed and breakfast houses are filled with summer vacationers.

We visit the rugged charm of Lough Gill, stopping at Dooney Rock and the woodland trail. Nearby at Holy Well where fugitive priests celebrated mass during the penal days only the stone altar remains. Seated beside a clump of trees we can discern the Lake Isle of Innisfree. There is peace in the lapping of the water. Mulrooney confides that she has found love at the Summer School, a professor of Anglo-Irish literature. She is having dinner with him at the Baymount Hotel in Strandhill.

This evening we drive into the country to meet a 93-year-old Shanachie, one of the last guardians of the oral tradition that extends back to the prehistoric past. Songs and legends that used to be told at wakes and weddings and around the fire on a cold night, those that travelling beggars would relate along with news from the other parishes.

Bertie Anderson lives in a clearing in the woods. The cottage illuminated by an electric light hanging from a cord is furnished with a rocking chair, a couch, a table with books and newspapers, a buffet and a television set. After the greetings we uncork the bottles of ale with a goblet of wine for Anderson. In turtle neck sweater and corduroy trousers the venerable story teller presides over the gathering.

Did he know Peig Sayers? asks a young woman. Indeed he knew her. She was the queen of the Gaelic storytellers, a native of Dingle who died twelve years ago. She had a repertory of 375 narratives including forty long wonder tales.

Would he recite something? Of course. Perhaps we would like to hear the *Tain Bo Cualigne* and answered with applause he narrates a lengthy passage from the *Cattle Raid of Coolley*, investing the phrases with measured cadences. A musical offering follows. Down by the salley gardens my love and I did meet.

Anderson is persuaded to talk about the Druids, who could read omens and foretell the future and who imparted learning by having their pupils repeat the words in chorus. How the students had to compose their own poems while lying on their beds in a pitch-black cabin and when they emerged were expected to declaim their verses. The Bards of Ireland knew by rote the Epic works, the Sagas of great daring recounted in the presence of the ancient kings and nobles. Anderson relates the one about Finn in search of his youth.

An interlude of Schubert Lieder is rendered by an American student with a pleasing tenor voice.

-Would you like to hear something by the blind Irish minstrel Raftery? He spent most of his life in County Galway singing and playing the fiddle. He was fond of such songs as *The Drunkard's Dispute with the Whisky*. Raftery composed ballads for people who helped him. He made up political stanzas in aid of Dan O'Connell, songs against the English, love lyrics and occasionally a religious piece.

- Well, now I come to the *Drowning of Annach Doon*. In the year 1828 there happened a great misfortune upon Loch Corrib. Thirty-one people went aboard an old boat together with ten sheep for to go to the fair at Galway, a distance of about eight miles, but when they had come close to the town a sheep put its foot through the bottom of the boat. One of the men when he saw the water coming in laid his overcoat on the hole and bruised his foot down on it but he did it too strongly and drove the plank out of the boat entirely. The boat filled with water and went down with nineteen young persons drowned. It was in the beginning of September on a fine, calm, sunny morning.

Bertie Anderson sings the lyrics in Gaelic in a quavering voice. When he is finished it is past midnight. One by one we offer our thanks and go out into a night sky that coruscates with myriad stars.

Engines sputter and headlights switch on. The cavalcade moves off to the beat of rock music pounding from the car radios.

The bus scheduled to depart after breakfast waits for the stragglers. Mulrooney is the last to arrive.

The lush fields of Erin spread before us, small parcels of verdure enclosed within stone boundaries. One of the students begins to sing and the others pick up the melody. *Suil, suil, suil go cuin.*

My thoughts turn to Yeats and Maud Gonne. He was twenty-three when he fell in love with the tall English woman of the weak chest and sunken eyes but she turned him down and went off to France to become the mistress of Lucien Millevoy, the anti-semitic, right-wing Deputy. After thirteen years she left him to marry John McBride but soon parted from him. When McBride was executed after the Easter uprising Yeats now fifty proposed to the widow but Maud refused him again whereupon he offered himself to her daughter but Iseult Gonne rejected him. In October 1917 he married Georgie Hyde-Lees who was young and very much in love with Willie.

Another song. *Am I a slave they say, Soggarth aroon? Since you did show the way, Soggarth aroon?*

After two hours, past Tobercurry, Ballyhaunis, Tuam and Clarinbridge the main road flows into a secondary artery thence to a country lane with signs pointing the way to Coole Park. The driver labours over the steering wheel as the bus strains amid ruts and overhanging branches and there untenanted among the wild grasses is the Big House of Lady Gregory. Visitors to Coole Park included W.B. Yeats, Douglas Hyde, John Synge and Bernard Shaw. Faintly visible on the autograph tree are the initials GBS/WBY. The graceful water birds with plumage white and soft are gone from the place where once upon the brimming water the poet counted nine and fifty swans. Now nettles wave upon a shapeless mound and saplings root among the broken stone.

En route again to Thor Ballylee, a seventy foot high square Norman tower designated as a tourist attraction with parking lot and tea shop. While Gabriel joins the queue at the toilets Father Desmond Fitzgerald and I walk to the bridge that spans the river Cloone. Nature sounds are amplified here in the plash of water, the chatter of birds and the drone of bees. Yeats purchased the tower, the cottages and an acre of stony ground in 1917 for 35 pounds. A plaque affirms:

I the poet William Yeats
With old mill boards and sea-green slates
And smithy work from the Gort forge
Restored this tower for my wife George.

Beyond the wooden door is the dining room with a trestle table and two chairs. Up 'a winding stair, a chamber arched with stone, a grey stone fireplace with an open hearth, a candle and a written page'. This was the bedroom and later the study. Georgina covered the walls with hand-woven tweeds and painted the ceiling in brilliant colours. A cage of canaries hung in one of the windows. Empty now. Damp and chill. A climb to a white-washed room with an arched stone ceiling, wooden floor, three open windows and a view of the river, the garden and the meadow. The guest chamber is on the third floor. Then up the narrow stairs to the battlements. Desmond Fitzgerald in measure recitation:

-To the north Tulira Castle. To the east Dublin. To the south the Clare Hills and the Shannon River. To the west Connemara and its lakes, mountains and moors and black-faced sheep and the ould ones in their white bainins and red petticoats and the ancient customs and traditions.

Mary Margaret has been silent since we left Sligo. Now as we continue to Dublin she finally confides that she is suffering from a discharge, a yeasty thing with itching and burning. I advise her to see a doctor.

We stop at Mullingar. The pub displays the seal of the corporation, a mill wheel within an archway, a tower and a demi-griffin. The women here are unkindly referred to by outsiders as Mullingar heifers. They are said to have a dispensation from the Pope to wear the thick ends of their legs downwards. After a ploughman's lunch and a pint Gabriel finds a copy of the Irish Times at the news agent's. A brief paragraph on the front page draws his attention: 'Member Of Prominent Irish Family. Iseult McNamara, wife of the late Judge McNamara, choked to death last night on a chicken bone during dinner.' A short obituary follows.

Dublin. Mary Margaret has been to the Mater hospital where a young doctor after a brief examination advised her that she had contracted a case of Gonorrhea. He prescribed Tetracycline and cautioned her against sexual intercourse and alcohol. She figures she must have gotten the infection from the Anglo-Irish specialist. My God, she wails, if you can't trust a professor, who can you trust?

This evening the program at the Peacock Theatre consists of *The Rising of the Moon* by Lady Gregory, *Purgatory* by W.B. Yeats, *Krapp's Last Tape* by Samuel Beckett and *In the Train* an adaptation by Hugh Hunt of the short story by Frank O'Connor. Afterward we sample the night life at P.J. O'Molloy's under the railroad bridge on Talbot Street.

No sign of Mary Margaret at breakfast. In the afternoon when we return from shopping at Switzer's on Grafton Street, Kathleen informs us that Miss Mulrooney has departed. She came down with her suitcase, paid for her lodgings and left in a hurry. She said something about going to the airport to fly home.

20

Friday February 19, 1971. Laurelaine Baxter is waiting in the Arrivals Concourse. After enthusiastic hugs we follow her to the cream-coloured convertible in the parking lot. The Buick Wildcat motor revs up with a roar and Laurelaine pilots the car out of the Tulsa International Airport.

-Welcome back. The actors are eager for their first rehearsal with you this evening.

Sequoyah Loop coming up. General Hospital. Onto the Crosstown Expressway with the city before us nestling in the Osage Hills. The speedometer moves up to 76 miles per hour as we speed by the Methodist, Baptist, Presbyterian and Episcopal Churches. Past J.C. Penny, Oklahoma Natural Gas and Rose Hill Cemetery. Laurelaine enumerates other landmarks.

-Tulsa is the home of Oral Roberts, president of the 500 acre Oral Roberts University, the Healing Waters Corporation and the Oral Roberts Evangelistic Association with headquarters in the Abundant Life Building. Another of this town's illustrious sons is Billy James Hargis the crusader against long hair, rock and roll, modern art, sex education, Playboy Magazine and the United Nations, all deemed to be instruments of world communism. Billy James operates out of the million dollar Christian Crusade Cathedral complete with publishing and broadcasting facilities, library, auditorium and Museum of Christian Art.

At Yorktown with its white ranch homes Laurelaine steers the Buick onto a black-topped driveway and hurries to the house. As she unlocks the kitchen door three Afghan hounds rush to her, whining softly. She nuzzles them, mommy will have din-din ready in a couple of minutes. Selecting filet steaks from the refrigerator she puts them through the meat grinder as the dogs press about her. There. A full bowl for each of mommy's darlings. She sits on the floor stroking their long heads as they slurp hungrily. When they have licked the bowls clean she takes the canines out to the enclosure, returning with a parade of Siamese cats. For the felines Laurelaine has gefilte fish.

While we are sipping Jack Daniels and branch water in the living room the nursery school van delivers a boy and girl. The children run to the television to watch the Road Runner and mommy brings them milk and cookies. Then she puts the Swanson frozen chicken dinners into the microwave. The kids aren't hungry so Laurelaine sends them bawling to their rooms. When they have quietened down they are allowed to join us at the table where they sit picking at the food.

After the last gulp of coffee Laurelaine leaves for the bedroom emerging some time later outfitted in a black jersey pantsuit. When the high school student arrives Laurelaine tells her to make sure the kids are in bed by nine.

The actors assembled in the Central Library theatre are discussing motivation when we arrive.

-It's such a demanding role, I hope I can do justice to it. Dark, nervous Melody Lee who is to play Nora Barnacle the wife of James Joyce says she will need lots of coaching from Gabriel.

-I'll coach you. A shaggy-haired midget scrambles onto the stage declaiming: That's all you're good for, Jim, going out and getting drunk. Cosgrave told me you were mad. Faith, I tell you I'll have the children baptized tomorrow.

-That is Temple Lee, whispers Laurelaine. The only begotten son of your leading lady.

-Hey Temple, get off the stage, shouts Lu-Ellen, the assistant director, but Temple ignores her and continues to emote: Go to bed now and let us have a little peace or by Christ I'll knock some sense into you.

The ten-year old is persuaded to leave the stage so the rehearsal can begin. Lu-Ellen hopes that Gabriel will be pleased with the way she has cast the play. After an hour Gabriel calls for a break and makes a few general comments, commending the actors on their diligence.

-Can I be stage manager, asks Temple Lee.
-How would you like to be a go-fer?
-What's that?
-First thing tomorrow, pick up a dozen sky hooks at the

hardware store. While you're there see if they have any shore line, about thirty feet.

After the run-through the cast agrees to relax at a roadhouse off Broken Arrow. Gabriel has to confer with Lu-Ellen, so we are the last to leave the Civic Centre parking lot. Soon we are in the country overtaking trees and bushes, the headlights picking out the road signs. From the car radio comes the plaintive song of a cowboy, *I'm so lonesome I could cry*.

The sign spells BAR in blue neon. Waves of smoky air greet our entrance and a child's voice is piping, *There's no business like show business*.

-Temple Lee. He has to be on stage all the time otherwise he throws a tantrum, says Laurelaine.

-Why doesn't Melody leave him at home, I ask.

-Daddy split last year so mommy takes him everywhere.

Temple stands on a chair gesturing as he sings, *And on your dressing room they've placed a star*. Melody pulls him down as the waitress arrives with a Shirley Temple cocktail for the cute little kid. The juke box blares, *Your cheatin' heart*.

The members of the Oklahoma Repertory Company engage in theatre talk. A graduate from Lee Strasberg's school in New York has been teaching them the Stanislavski method. Look what it did for Marlon Brando. The electricity that first night on Broadway when he made his entrance as Stanley Kowalski in A Streetcar Named Desire. The Oklahoma Rep will be tackling Hamlet in the spring.

-To be or not to be, declaims one of the actors. Less precisely in contemporary idiom to put the question thus: Do we at this moment in time have an ongoing eco-situation? Or do we call time out, existence-wise? That is to say, does the cat who really has his head together stay loose and hang in there when the fickle finger of fate lays a bad trip on him?

-You still want some shore line? Temple asks innocently.

-Sure thing, says Gabriel.

-You're putting me on. Melody says it's a trick.

-She's right. Just wanted to see how much you know.

-I know plenty. Temple pushes Gabriel's glass off the table. Melody hollers, time to pack it in, school tomorrow. Temple protests it's only half past twelve and anyway he can play sick.

-Up yours, she retorts. I have to study my script. Night everybody. She pulls the reluctant youngster with her. Okay, I'll let you cue me. The others decide to leave as well.

As we enter the Baxter bungalow, the cats bound towards us and Laurelaine, scratching their heads, shoos them back to their basket beds. The children and their guardian are asleep.

-G'night, Laurelaine yawns. The two of you are in the guest room. Bed is all made up. I sleep in the arms of Jesus.

Saturday February 20, 1971. Waiting for the actors to arrive for afternoon rehearsal Gabriel and I inspect the newly-built Tulsa Library. Posters proclaim Pride in Heritage Month with lectures on the customs and traditions of the Southern Plains Indians. Ceremonies, dances and dress of the Creeks. Authentic American Indian foods. Greek folk dancing. Judaic art. Kosher refreshments.

In the downstairs theatre Lu-Ellen has set up the Kodak projectors with their carousels of three hundred slides. Temple Lee is whining because he isn't allowed to climb the ladder to focus the spotlights. The actors stand about reading their lines. Lu-Ellen calls, Places please.

Six o'clock. Laurelaine has been at the stable grooming her horse. Home again she puts the roast in the oven and attends to the pets and the children. A relaxing bath before dinner is what she needs. While Gabriel, exhausted from the rehearsal, settles for a siesta, I scan the books in the den. It appears that Laurelaine's literary interests revolve around horses. *The Indian and the Horse, The American Quarter Horse, Stallion Management.*

I am reading *Practical Horse Psychology* when Laurelaine returns in a gown, her hair tied in a pony tail. She smells of lavender.

-That's an excellent book. I never would have been able to handle my mare Pegasus without it.

-Pegasus was the winged stallion, the son of Medusa and Poseidon. He was tamed by Bellerophon with the help of Athena and the golden bridle but when Bellerophon tried to fly to heaven Pegasus threw him off and he fell to earth maimed and ended his life begging for alms.

    -I told Dad we were having dinner at half past seven, Laurelaine muses. I wonder what's keeping him and Violet.

    -Your mother?

    -No, his girl friend. Mom is in a private hospital. I visit once a month but Dad hasn't seen her since he had her committed a year ago.

    They arrive after nine. Florid, white-haired Cyrus J. Comerford and his plump inamorata. He demands to see his grandchildren but they are in bed and he should have come earlier. Violet apologizes for being late but she wouldn't give him the keys to the car until he was sober enough to drive.

    -I leave everything in the hands of the Senior Partner in life's enterprise, the Lord God Almighty who leads me in the paths of righteousness.

    Comerford, an oil company executive, belongs to Businessmen for Christ, a fellowship that meets every Tuesday morning in the Oklahoma Oil Centre for a Prayer Breakfast. After orange juice, rolls and coffee the men take Bibles out of their briefcases and read a verse from John or the Psalms. Then they consider such questions as: Is it Christian to make a profit? Well of course it is. Remember the parable of the talents in Matthew. In Proverbs we find that the poor man is hated even of his own neighbor but the rich man hath many friends. The meetings help to relieve the pressures of the corporate world and Jesus brings serenity and self-confidence into their lives. Before departing they kneel in prayer for those who are afflicted. It could be a relative with cancer, a wife who has diabetes, a friend recovering from a heart attack. Comerford has been organizing prayer meetings all over Oklahoma and out of state at petroleum conventions. He got the idea from the weekly Senate and House prayer breakfasts. Yes sir, he found the real manual of operations for the marketplace right in the scriptures.

    -You are not a Christian, Comerford studies Gabriel from behind bifocals. The long hair and high cheekbones tell me that you're an Indian. I should know. Hell, I've seen enough of them.

-Dinner is ready, Laurelaine calls.

-What tribe? asks Comerford when we are seated.

-I could claim to be a Mohawk from the shining big sea water of Lake Superior or an Onancock whose ancestors lived on the Chesapeake shore of Accoma County, Virginia but I admit to being a Cherokee.

-Hah, I thought so. He waves the wine glass in triumph. I wouldn't trust an Indian.

-I haven't scalped anybody but I've been reading up on the technique brought here by the white man along with whisky, firearms and syphilis.

-Primitive savages.

-You're so wrong, Dad, protests Laurelaine. The Cherokees had their own culture. Sequoyah, the Cherokee Chief devised an alphabet and taught his people to read and write. They published books and newspapers. The Cherokees had free elections and law courts by the late nineteenth century. They became Christians and built churches. But the U.S. government rounded them up and put them into concentration camps. We took away their lands in Tennesse, Alabama and Georgia and drove them into exile. Over 4,000 perished from disease and starvation and the heartbreak of separation from their families by the time they reached the Oklahoma territory. The Trail of Tears.

-Your mind is full of Communist propaganda. Goddamit I'm a one hundred percent American. I'm descended from President Andrew Jackson.

-Now there's a real American hero, Laurelaine smirks. Chicken Snake Jackson who stole the Cherokee property and divided it among his friends and made a fortune. The Georgia legislature gave the Cherokee lands to the white settlers through a state lottery.

-Hell, I've heard enough. Vi, pour me another drink.

-Did you know the U.S. Army dragged the Cherokees from their homes and penned them into stockades? That's how Jackson repaid them for saving his life and helping him win the battles that made him the frontier hero.

Comerford consumes a lot alcohol during dinner and

leaves soon after coffee, his companion urging him to let her drive.

-I shouldn't have lectured him on Andrew Jackson and the Georgia Guards, says Laurelaine.

-Maybe you should have mentioned Oklahoma's favorite son, Will Rogers, who began his career as a Wild West Show roper known as the Cherokee Kid then went into vaudeville and became a star of the Ziegfeld Follies, says Gabriel.

-And a movie actor, I add.

-Will Rogers, the homespun humourist and philosopher who never met a person he didn't like. He was the most popular man in America until his death in a plane crash.

-We could have talked about Jim Thorpe the All-American Football player who won both Pentathlon and Decathlon events at the 1912 Olympics. He was a Sac and Fox Indian, voted the greatest athlete in the first half of the twentieth century.

-I should have asked Dad what he thought of Major General Clarence Tinker an Osage who died in combat at the Battle of Midway. But we don't communicate very well.

-Does he know about your Timothy Leary phase? The tune in, turn on, drop out days?

-Haven't dropped acid recently but the rushes still come. I've nibbled at the magic mushroom and a bit of mescaline. Today is the first day of the rest of your life. The slogan no longer has any meaning. Carl Alpert aka Baba Ram Dass in beads and sandals is giving classes in Hindu mysticism. Practise Yoga, gain serenity. A couple of the University students hiked up to his Ashram in New Hampshire, lived in tents, worked on their consciousness. Take your dreams as reality! My reality consists of the children, the dogs and cats and of course Pegasus.

-How did you get involved with horses?

-Summers on the farm. I was fourteen, not a sociable young lady, didn't go to school dances, didn't have a boyfriend. Dad sent me to riding academy. When you are having difficulties growing up, a horse is like a Teddy Bear.

-Or a substitute for sex, suggests Gabriel.

-Well of course there is the erotic feeling in the physical contact. You hold on so strongly, the horse's muscles quivering under you, the coarse hair between your legs. And the gamey odor. There is nothing like the thrill of riding naked in the moonlight, the wind in your face. I love to go swimming in the Arkansas river with Pegasus, to hug her tightly around the neck so as not to slip off because she moves in such great leaps. I enjoy giving her a bath, washing off the sweat with buckets of water and rubbing her down with liniment.

-What happens when she's in heat?

-Oh, she just goes a little nuts. Rubs up against the wall of the stall and paces about, acts difficult when I come near her. Most of the time she is a wonderful companion.

-Your husband...

-He took off and I haven't heard from him in two years. Gotta get my mind off that subject. Let's just relax. Enjoy some Acapulco Gold.

We share the cannabis, inhaling deeply, the glow of the cigarette hypnotic in the dark. Bursts of laughter. Then silence. The clock chimes two. Laurelaine and Gabriel have fallen asleep on the couch. As I begin to doze, the drug-induced fantasy comes into focus.

Around the campfire sit the Cherokee braves beating on tom-toms. In a feathered head dress Henry Wadsworth Longfellow is reciting the Kalevala of the American Indian. 'By the shores of Gitchee Gummee, by the shining big sea waters.' Three maidens at the flap of a wigwam reply: 'On the cobbles of the alleys, leading off from Mabbott entrance, Leopoldy Bloom the Mighty, known to all as Blumiguchy.' The voices fade, the human shapes disappear. The Great Seal of the Sovereign State of Oklahoma brightens the night sky. *Labor Omnia Vincit.*

A lone cowboy, heavily spectacled, a black patch covering one eye, sits tall in the saddle on a golden palomino. On his head is a silver stetson, the band ornamented with a circle of stars. He wears a chamois shirt and a red neckerchief. From the pockets of his buckskin vest he brings pouch and paper and rolls a cigarette, striking a match against the chaps. Tied down behind him are saddle blanket, oiled canvas raincoat, lasso and quirt. A Colt revolver is in each holster.

The sound of hooves in the distance grows louder and

the Cherokee Chief on an Indian pony reins in alongside. He wears a gold turban and a grey robe. A medallion the gift of King George III hangs from his neck. A cane stalk blowgun is slung across his back, wood darts feathered with thistle-down lie in a quiver. The horses whinny and paw the ground. Sequoyah points toward the rainy horizon.

-Soft morning, he observes. Are you native to these parts?

-No. I have escaped from the old sow that eats her farrow and have come to America to witness the academic activity arising out of the books I have written. The dissertations, the seminars and the advancement of careers. This spot has the same flat-topped appearance as the Hill of Allen where Finn the son of Cumhal, the commander of the Fianna of Erin had his palace.

-I have read about him. Sequoyah takes a puff from his long-stemmed pipe. Now I shall show you the local mythological giant. Behold the Golden Driller, 76 feet tall, constructed of metal with a skin of cement and plaster. His hat size is ll2, shoes 333 DDD with a 48 foot belt. He is anathema to my people. Let us attack.

They advance, whooping about the massive statue. The Dubliner twirls the lariat above his head and as it encircles the Golden Driller's neck, James Joyce pulls on the rope; but the 45,000 pound figure stands immovable, its right arm secure against an oil derrick. Sequoyah blows darts into the chest but they ricochet.

Onto the scene gallops a band of hard-riding movie cowboys. Roy Rogers, Jack Hoxie, Hoot Gibson, Gene Autry and William Boyd.

As they attempt to topple the Golden Driller, lightning rends the sky, followed by a crack of thunder. The face of Cyrus J. Comerford appears in the Great Seal. Cease, disperse, he commands. The cowboys retreat in clouds of dust. Joyce and Sequoyah vanish into the recesses of memory.

The Golden Driller stands intact on the grounds of the Tulsa State Fair. A steam calliope fractures the silence with the State Anthem OKLAHOMA!

21

Washington. April 30, 1971. Two thousand Vietnam veterans protest against the war. Many throw their combat medals on the steps of the Capitol.

Washington. May 3. Anti-war demonstrators engage in civil disobedience. Police arrest 12,000 people at random.

New York. June 13. The Times begins publication of the Pentagon Papers, a government history of the Vietnam War which reveals that the U.S. has consistently lied about many aspects of its involvement in Vietnam.

Trieste. June 14, 1971.

The Third International James Joyce Symposium is being held at the Circolo della Cultura e delle Arti under the High Patronage of the Regione Autonome Friuli-Venezia Giulia and the Auspices of the Commune di Trieste. The participants from America and Europe are staying in the first class hotels of the city but Gabriel and I together with our performers have been booked into the Pensione Stella, a boarding house of the third class located on the Via Bonafata in the seaside suburb of Barcola. The padrone is a friendly little man with a nervous wife and an imperious mother-in-law. After a supper of veal and eggplant enjoyed under a bower of grape leaves he produces a bottle of homemade grappa, and we linger, conversing in Italian and English. The padrone is not fond of his wife or her mother. He would like to leave them and live with his rich uncle in Syracuse New York.

The theatre is in the Questura building, the police headquarters. Across from it is the ancient Roman amphitheatre constructed between the first and second centuries A.D. and given to the city by Quintus Patronius Modestus, a Roman noble whose name is etched in the stones. The Italian actors Fulvia Gasser and Paolo Cociani, who are already familiar with the script, are pleased to be working with the Irish members of the cast, Claire Mullen, David Byrne, and Joe Dowling, who are on leave from the Abbey Theatre.

The play is well received by a sympathetic audience familiar with the life of the exile from Dublin. After the performance, Letizia Fonda-Savio, the daughter of Italo Svevo comes backstage to congratulate Gabriel.

-I must say that I was very enthusiastic about your play, *Jacomo Joyce*, since you put together all the most pregnant things about the Joyce family and about Italo Svevo my father. Listening to them brought back many memories. You see, Mr. Joyce was the teacher of my father in Trieste and mine too in Zurich during the First World War. The sympathy began immediately between the young teacher and his older pupil. He gave Mr. Joyce the two books he had written--*Una Vita* and *Senilita*--and the praise gave my father the strength to continue writing, because his first books had no acclaim.

-When Mr. Joyce was in Paris after the war Svevo sent him his third novel *Zeno*. Joyce was so enthusiastic that he gave the book to Valery Larbaud and Benjamin Crêmieux, and these critics found a translator, Henri Michaux. As a result my father received a number of letters from unknown people and the sudden fame brightened the last years of his life. He said that Joyce renewed for him the belief in the resurrection of Lazarus. In every country they wish to do translations, to make films. Did you know that *Zeno* was done at Il Piccolo Teatro de Milano?

-Was Svevo as humorous as his hero in *Zeno*? asks Gabriel.

-Oh he was always making jokes. Of course he was serious too about death and to be old and sick but mostly he joked.

-About his smoking?

-Yes, I remember we were in the garden and father came from town and said, 'I am another man today because I have not smoked since three days and this other man wishes a cigarette.' He was always joking about L'Ultima Sigaretta. When he was dying after the motor accident he said, 'Don't cry Letizia, it is nothing to die, it is very easy.' Then he asked me for a cigarette and the doctor said absolutely no and my father said, 'This will be my last one.'

-Whom did your father marry?

-Livia Veneziani. She was his second cousin, very

beautiful.

-*Anna Livia Plurabelle.*

-He was very much in love with my mother but he was upset at the idea of growing old like in *Senilita*. It is his only autobiographical book.

-*Zeno* has something of his life, the cigarette business, the funeral. You know the story about how my father went to a funeral of a friend? He brought flowers, he was so sad, and then he saw the funeral was moving into the Protestant cemetery and he said to his companion, 'Was our departed friend not a Catholic?' You see, they had gotten mixed up with another funeral. So they got out of the carriage and went home. He put that into *La Coscienza de Zeno*. But *Senilita* is about my father's life, really. He had great sorrows. His father lost everything in commercial enterprises and his beloved brother and young sister died but my mother provided him with serenity. She put order in his life and gave him confidence.

-That episode about the funeral and your father's cynicism about life remind me of the dark humour of Leopold Bloom at the burial of Paddy Dignam, says Gabriel. Was your father the prototype for the hero of *Ulysses?*

-Joyce was very interested in my father's personality and perhaps he found in him a model for Bloom, but also in Teodoro Mayer of Il Piccolo and Leopoldo Popper, who was the father of Joyce's pupil Amalia.

-How did the Triestines regard Joyce?

-At first they did not understand that he was a great writer. He was always without money, he was drinking very much, he went in all hours to the osteria, but when they read *Ulysses* there was an enthusiasm for Joyce's work.

22

January 14, 1972. Gabriel presents 'Thuartpeatrick', a view of James Joyce and the Catholic Church. Central Library Theatre, Toronto.

March 17, 1972. 'Vice Verses'. Poems and snatches, lyrical, doggerel and scatalogical in the works of James Joyce. York

University, Toronto.

May 8, 1972. 'The U.S.A vs. Ulysses'. A lecture on the *Ulysses* trial by Morris Ernst, who defended the James Joyce novel in the U.S. Federal Court and obtained its acquittal on the charge of obscenity. Central Library Theatre, Toronto.

We have been invited by the Committee for Canadian-Polish University Co-operation to participate in a five-week course organized by the Institute for the Theory of Literature, Theatre and Film at the University of Lodz and the Catholic University of Lublin.

Sunday July 9, 1972. London. At Victoria Station we take the train to Dover and the ferry across the English Channel to Oostend, where we board the Berlin Express, sharing a compartment with two other couples. I have prepared sardine and egg sandwiches for lunch with beer purchased from the porter.

An uneventful afternoon spent dozing and reading as the train speeds through the German countryside. Frankfurters and tea for supper. At eleven the six couchettes are made up, each with a sheet, pillow, and blanket. It is hot in the compartment and the other passengers make frequent trips to the toilet.

In the middle of the night, wakened by shouts of Passport Control we present our documents to the youthful West German official. When we have crossed into East Germany the agent of the German Democratic Republic appears demanding to see our transit visas, which we do not have but which he supplies for two dollars American.

Three hours later we arrive in West Berlin with its lighted thoroughfares and rainbows of neon. After the ritual of Passport Control we are on the move again, climbing the ramp toward Checkpoint Charlie and the opening in the Berlin Wall.

At Friedrichstrasse in the eastern section of the divided city we stop. The station is gloomy and drab, the streets below dark with little traffic. Blocks of monolithic apartment buildings are etched against the grey dawn.

After a period of shunting we transfer to the Moscow

Express. Our coach is old and dirty. The luxurious railway car next to ours identified by the gleaming seal of the USSR is for Soviet travellers. A peek through the curtained windows ,before the uniformed guard orders us away, reveals de-luxe seats with antimacassars and luxuriously-carpeted floor.

We share our proletarian space with a teenage boy and his mother. As the train chugs past farms and villages we converse in German answering the lad's questions. How big is our country? Do we have many lakes and rivers? Are there schools of science in Canada? He lives in Torun, the birthplace of Copernicus, and hopes to study astronomy. A taciturn porter arrives with breakfast of cheese on melba toast and coffee in glass tumblers.

At the Polish border the man from Orbis comes aboard to sell Zlotys at the official rate of 33.20 American . We buy ten-dollars-worth, standing fast against his insistence that we would need more. A woman in black dress and babushka appears silently and silently empties the ashtray into a pail, sweeps the floor with a whisk, and departs.

I must go to the toilet but the cubicle does not invite a lengthy stay. The wash basin is streaked with, grime, the water is cold, the soap dispenser empty. Used paper towels overflow the wire receptacle.

The train is slowing down. Gdansk Station. We have arrived in Warsaw.

No sign of our host, but a taxi takes us to the Metropol Hotel for one American dollar. Our reservations have been switched to the Polonia, the sister establishment around the corner on Jerosolimskie Street. While I unpack, Gabriel searches for listening devices that may have been planted behind the pictures on the wall or inside the lighting fixture. He unscrews the telephone receiver but finds no bugs. Nevertheless he cannot avoid the feeling that we are under surveillance in the People's Republic of Poland.

After the thirty hour train ride subsisting on snack food, we are ready for a full-course dinner. The Metropol boasts a Category S (for Superior) restaurant, but the doorman insists the establishment is fully booked. We search without success for another eating place, passing by liquor stores and taverns, so we return to the hotel, where Gabriel confronts the manager, showing him the official letter of invitation and threatening to report the hotel to the Polish Ministry of Education. Deferentially he escorts us to a table.

The dining room, newly decorated with pastel walls and indirect lighting, boasts linen table cloths and elegant place settings. Most of the patrons are dressed casually, although I notice several business suits and gowns. A quartet is playing *By Mir Bist Du Shayne*, the violin backed up by drums, guitar and accordion. Two women are dancing cheek to cheek.

The waiter presents the menu, printed in Polish, German, and English. We initiate the evening with a half bottle of vodka. For dinner we choose beet borscht followed by Kotelet à la Volaille.

-O sweet and lovely, lady be good! The quartet renders the song in a jazz version that elicits polite applause from the diners. The next number is a treacly interpretation of Fascination, and the dance floor fills with couples, arms extended, gliding in long sweeps.

During our dessert of ice cream tortes, the fiddler is soloing with *I Can't Give You Anything But Love*, and the dancers are more exuberant. Gabriel and I refill our vodka glasses. As the musicians segue into *Ochy Chornya*, the fatigue sets in and we get up to leave, with the manager escorting us to the door, bowing, inviting our return visit.

The street is incandescent with lamps, thronged with pedestrians. A few vintage cars roll by. The thirty-storey Palace of Culture and Science, the gift of Josef Stalin as a symbol of Polish-Soviet friendship, looms over the city.

In our hotel room nothing seems to have been disturbed.

Tuesday July 11. Messrs. Stefan and Roman from the Film Institute in Lodz assemble the group for a morning tour of Warsaw, but their lack of organization results in delays, so Gabriel and I wander off on our own to inspect the shops on Marszalkowska Street.

We rendezvous for lunch at the Bristol Hotel with Virginia

Rock, a colleague of Gabriel's from York University. With its salons and appointments, the former meeting place of the Polish aristocracy caters to bureaucrats and wealthy foreign visitors. We dine on smoked salmon, cream of mushroom soup and roast duck, our appetites fuelled by Wyborowa Wodka. Late in the afternoon after cheesecake and coffee, we part. Virginia has been invited to a reception at the American Embassy. Gabriel and I attend a performance at the National Theatre, where we try to follow the intricacies of a classic Polish play.

In the lobby of the Polonia Hotel the ladies of the night are available for Dollars, Deutschmarks or Francs. Exquisitely dressed and coiffured, they respond to male salutations with a smile and a wink. Assignations are discreetly arranged.

Wednesday July 12. We are taken to Wilanow, the enormous summer palace built by King Jan Sobieski for his wife, where our guide expatiates proudly on Poland's sovereigns. The Communist state is fascinated by its royal history.

Thursday July 13. After the noon meal at the University of Warsaw, the group leaves by bus for Lodz. It is a sunny afternoon and we are full of expectation. As we reach the outskirts of the city, black smoke blots out the sun and we breathe in the acrid stench of sulphur.

At the University of Lodz, which occupies a block on Patrice Lumumba street, we check into the student residence. Our quarters are on the fifth floor, a squalid room with a table and two chairs, frame beds with straw pallets, a chipped sink with neither soap nor towels. Unswept floor, unwashed curtains. We have time for a visit to the community toilet before hurrying down for a supper of fried eggs, rye bread and tea.

Since there are no recreational facilities we return to our room. Radio programming is controlled from a central source and we are entertained by Shirley Temple rendering *On the Good Ship Lollipop* and other songs from her movies. It is raining and the drops filtering through the industrial pollution splatter like ink on the windows. The pallets seem comfortable and I look forward to a good night's sleep. About four o'clock in the morning

Gabriel is jolted by the first tram of the day clattering past the residence. The cattle cars, he screams. Jews being transported to Auschwitz. I soothe him awake.

Friday July 14. We wash in cold water and descend to breakfast. Noodles in warm milk, a gelatinous dessert and excessively sweetened tea. Rumblings of displeasure erupt from our Canadian colleagues.

The initial session is at the University library (a mere hundred metres distant we are assured) so we start off with Rek and Gazda setting the pace. The sky turns cloudy , then the rain starts but we keep walking and twenty minutes later we are welcomed by Professor Stephania Skwarczynska, a once beautiful woman with a throaty voice and the presence of a diva.

- Mes chers amis, she launches into a protracted welcome. When she is informed that many of the students do not understand French, a bilingual member of our group translates her remarks. Seated on wooden chairs in a dimly lit room we listen to presentations by earnest academics.

Today we set out on a tour of Lodz. This is a grim industrial city with cobble stone streets in need of repair. Propaganda posters on empty lots display heroic workers building a utopian Socialist State.

The bus slows down at the Museum of Textile Industry. Before the First World War, 150 mills produced cotton, wool and linen, with the Jews of Lodz supplying much of the raw material. Gazda says they also owned many of the factories. We pass the Academy of Art and the Artur Rubinstein Gallery of Music. Lodz is one of the biggest cultural centres in Poland, with thousands of people employed in the arts. Gazda cites the contributions of its Jewish citizens to the Academy of Fine Art, the Academy of Music and of course the State Academy of Film, Television and Theatre. Since 1945, Lodz has been the capital of the Polish film industry with at least a dozen feature films every year directed by such well-known graduates as Roman Polanski and Andrzej Wajda. Lodz has the only Museum of Cinematography in Europe.

We stop at the Children's Memorial, a huge heart with a gaping hole. Etched in the stone one can see the emaciated youngsters, six thousand of whom were slaughtered by German soldiers. Two thousand more died from dysentery in the death camps.

On to the factory where prisoners were caged before being shipped to Auschwitz. In 1944, with the advance of the Russians, the Germans machine-gunned and burned 2500 of the inmates, leaving behind charred timber and gouged stone.

Saturday July 15. A few of us show up for the seminar on the music of Krzystof Penderecki.

Sunday afternoon we drive out to Zelazowa Wola, the birthplace of Frederic Chopin. Visitors throng the spacious grounds. In Chopin's cottage a guide talks about the life and works of Poland's greatest composer. The Steinway grand piano and elabourate candelabra are gifts of the Polish-American Chopin Society. Relaxed on the grass we listen to a sonata, the music issuing tinnily from the loudspeakers in the trees. Upon our departure we purchase souvenir photos of ourselves taken two hours earlier.

Monday July 17. Visit to a department store where we buy one and a half meters of 54 inch material, enough for two body towels.

Wednesday July 19. Rain all day. It is warm in our room but we hesitate to open a window because of the smoke that spews from the textile factory. Flies are buzzing on the stained formica table top. After a radio program devoted to the Beatles an analysis of the news. For the noon meal we had potato soup, mashed potatoes, a small cut of veal, slices of cucumber and a cherry drink. Suppers are light, sometimes scrambled eggs. Sunday morning we have cream cheese and onions. The campus grocery store sells canned grapefruit juice, mineral water, beer and wine. We buy a package of Pickwick Tea Bags.

Gabriel and I sleep for two hours this afternoon, then head for the showers. One of the students came down with a case of crabs and had to walk a thousand meters for a doctor who prescribed an alcohol splash.

We are no longer surprised to hear the North Vietnamese, Sudanese and Indian students conversing in Polish after the year of indoctrination. Gabriel is beginning to speak it as well, a subconscious retrieval of the tongue he knew as a child in Opatow. French is the second language. The Francophones from Canada are loath to communicate with us in English. The other night at the Halka Restaurant, in honour of Rosemary's twenty-first birthday, they shouted Vive le Québec Libre.

Stefan presented us with a copy of the Polish edition of Joyce's *Ulysses* translated by Maciej Slomczinsky. From it we discover the Polish word for shit is gowno. Gabriel's favorite phrase however is psiakrew cholera, an expletive universally used under duress.

Natalia, willowy in a silk dress, arrives at the seminars with a tape recorder in search of material for a radio documentary. She has already interviewed important theatre people in Warsaw. Pale of face, eyes outlined with shadow and liner, she glides about like Theda Bara.

The Canadians are coming down with diarrhea and stomach cramps. The vegetarian couple swallow vitamin pills but the malaise does not spare them.

This evening we are at the Teatr Wielki, the newly completed Grand Opera House located in a spacious square with fountains splashing at the entrance. In the lobby , cylindrical chandeliers hang from the ceiling. Checking of coats and bulky articles is mandatory. The seats in the vast auditorium are deeply cushioned. Full house tonight with many neatly dressed youngsters. The toilets are presided over by a woman who charges 2 zlotys for service.

As the lights dim and the proscenium curtain is illuminated the conductor appears in the orchestra pit to sustained applause. Tonight's presentation is Poland's national opera Halka by Stanislaus Moniuszko, a contemporary of

Chopin. It premiered in 1858 in Warsaw. The plot revolves around a peasant girl who is seduced by the lord of the estate and the revenge exacted by her family. The stage is populated with splendidly costumed soloists and chorus who chant prayers and raise the cross. While the voices are adequate the music never soars but the work is enthusiastically applauded. The season's repertory includes Cosi Fan Tutte, Lohengrin and the ballets les Sylphides and Daphnis and Chloe.

Thursday July 20. After a visit to the Museum of Fine Arts to view the collection of twentieth century paintings, Dr. Krawiec of the Film Institute invites us to lunch at the Grand Hotel. He recommends Chlodnik, a cold soup of beets, cucumbers, chives, sour cream, eggs and prawns. Refreshing on a hot summer day. For the main course Dr. Krawiec and I choose steamed trout. Gabriel selects Steak Tartare, a half pound filet of chopped beef with onions, capers and a dash of brandy topped by a raw egg. Conversing in a mixture of English, French and German we discuss the current Polish cinema including adaptations from the novels of Henryk Sienkiewicz and Bruno Schultz. We learn about Andrzey Wajda's recently completed *Ashes and Diamonds* and Roman Polonski's *Knife in the Water*. The *Bolek and Lolek* animations popular on children's television.

Our lunch has been delicious and the Vodka plentiful. During coffee Gabriel expresses his interest in the Jews of Lodz. What has been their fate?.

-At the outbreak of the war, responds Dr.Krawiec, we had about 200,00 Jews, about one-third of the total population. Before the Greman army arrived on September 8,1939, many of the Jewish social and cultural elite left the city to find refuge in Warsaw. Some fled to the territories occupied by the Soviet Union. Those who remained were evicted from the centre of Lodz to make room for Volksdeutsche and segregated in the old town. In March of 1940, Bloody Thursday, the Germans organized a pogrom and many Jews were murdered. A hundred thousand were driven into a ghetto of less than four square kilometers.

-When the Red Army liberated Lodz there were about 900 Jewish survivors but within two years the number had risen

212 · Harry Pollock

to 50,000, at that time the biggest Jewish community in Poland. Newspapers were published in Yiddish and Hebrew. Repertory theatre and revues appeared. Jewish social institutions flourished. However, during the Sovietization of the country half the Jews emigrated to Israel or America. Today there are virtually none left in Poland.

Friday July 21. Having slept this morning until eleven we improvise a breakfast of bread and cheese from our personal cache and boil water in a pot for tea. There is time for a few postcards to family and friends and at half past one we descend to the mess hall. The blonde serving woman in the white uniform doles out bowls of barley soup and plates of pork patties with mashed potatoes and grated carrots.

Lunch completed, I ask the porter for the key to the laundry room, which is in the basement of the residence. We discover four tubs with wash-board sides and an antique machine with manually operated wringers. I hang our clothes to dry on lines strung wall to wall.

Saturday July 22, 1972. We rise at six, eager to get away for the weekend. As the bus heads north the students sing and joke. The greyness of Lodz yields to the countryside lush with grassy tracts and fields of grain. Two hours later the welcome sign proclaims our arrival at the Soczewka summer camp. Gabriel and I are assigned a cabin with two beds, a table and chair. After the sheets and blankets have been distributed we are summoned for a breakfast of cottage cheese, chives, bread and tea. The camp is operated by the Socialist Students League for the relaxation of those who by their service to the State are deserving of a holiday. We meet doctors, engineers, factory workers as well as students. We spend the afternoon swimming and kayaking. Some play volleyball.

After the study session (obligatory for the Polish campers) extolling the virtues of Socialism we troop into the dining hall where tables have been arranged in a U shape for tonight's banquet. The chairman welcomes the Canadian guests, then it is time for the presentation of medals and diplomas. The egalitarian nature of the occasion is manifest when the camp cleaning women, humble of mien and dress, are honoured. Now we drink to the undying friendship between Canada and Poland and are urged to help ourselves to the potato salad and processed meats. A bottle of Vodka is passed mouth to mouth and soon the hall resounds with folk songs and patriotic melodies ending around midnight with the national anthems of our two countries.

Before retiring we find our way to the Sanitary Pavilion. In the women's washroom I am assaulted by the reek of soiled menstrual pads deposited in an open garbage can.

Sunday. We are awakened at dawn by the crowing of a rooster over the loudspeaker. After breakfast we spend the day sunbathing or competing in kayak races. We are to have a camp fire this evening but it starts to rain so we enjoy Kielbasa and tea indoors.

At nine o'clock we are set for departure but the bus is locked and a search ensues for the driver. Some time later he emerges from the Skoda in the company of a dishevelled female and enquires with a grin if we are ready to leave. To shouts of do vidzenia , the staff and campers wave goodbye as we move beyond the gates, past a gang of drunken bikers demanding entry.

After an hour the driver announces that his fuel gauge is showing empty. In search of petrol, he passes two State stations that are dark before he comes upon one that is open. While the tank is being filled and the oil checked we get out to relieve ourselves behind the bushes.

We arrive without misadventure. After the spartan camping experience our University dormitory appears luxurious.

23

Tuesday July 25, 1972. At four in the morning the Lodz railway station is crowded. Gabriel and I have decided to absent ourselves from several sessions at the Film Institute to visit the city of Krakow. During the six hour ride I doze while Gabriel with the help of his Polish phrase book converses with the other passengers.

Our first view of Krakow is a pleasant surprise. On this sunny summer day the city with its medieval Barbican has an old world charm. Here is the University where Copernicus studied. We have reserved a room in an old house on Ulica Venezia with bed and breakfast 100 Zloty per day. The landlady insists that we must visit Wawel Castle and the salt mines. Aber sicher.

The elegance of Krakow shows in the shops, in the book stores, in the horse-drawn droshkis for the tourists. We have lunch on the patio of a downtown restaurant and realize that this is a part of Poland that was alien to most Jews of the shtetl.

After a relaxing afternoon we enjoy dinner at the Krakovia Hotel. Vodka for starters followed by vegetable soup, chicken cutlets, ice cream and coffee. We spend a couple of hours in a jazz cellar frequented by students and artists.

A night club is presenting an American style entertainment, the strip tease. Entrance fee 200 zlotys. We forego this capitalist diversion and get to bed after midnight.

Wednesday July 26. Our destination is an hour's drive from Krakow. We pass farms and hamlets, stopping along the route to discharge a trickle of passengers until we reach the village of Oswiecim. The driver indicates we are to stay on the bus until it reaches the State Museum, known by the rest of the world as the extermination camp of Auschwitz. A hotel outside the entrance accommodates survivors and their families who come to remember the millions who perished.

In the exhibition hall pictures and maps document the Nazi crimes against humanity. We are in time for the next showing of the liberation of Auschwitz. As the film flickers onto the screen, the narration in Polish, the tour guides provide translations to their groups in a variety of languages, including German. After a panoramic view of the block houses, the camera cuts to the gas chamber, the piles of corpses, the ovens. The arrival of Soviet troops, the liberation of the camp. The gratitude of the skeletal survivors. We have seen these scenes in the cinemas back home and on television but here, where the atrocities occurred their suffering is palpable.

A hundred meters ahead is the entrance to the camp. Above the iron gate *Arbeit Macht Frei* still proclaims the obscenity. The guard house is empty, the double metal fencing capped with barbed wire is no longer charged with electricity. The grounds have been swept clean. As if Auschwitz had not been the largest death factory in history, as if the gas chambers had never asphyxiated 60,000 adults and children a day from all over Europe. As if the smoke of burning flesh had never risen from the crematoria chimneys.

Sixteen of the block huts are closed. The other twelve contain enlarged photographs and charts detailing Hitler's master plan for the extermination of Jews, Poles, Gypsies, Homosexuals and other inferior groups. Every country in Europe with its quota and network of Concentration Camps.

A plaque outside Block 27 reads: Zydow. The Pavilion of Martyrology of the Jews. The interior is filled with phylacteries, pages from torah scrolls, jewellery, clothing, and children's shoes.

One of the barracks has been reconstructed with triple decker bunks, each of which accommodated six prisoners. A coal burning stove. A desk. The sleeping quarters of the Kapos.

We walk by the Commandant's House and the SS Hospital. The Storehouse of the Property seized from the Victims. The row of gallows in the execution yard. The Gas Chamber with the hole in the ceiling through which issued the Zyklon B. The conveyor belt that carried the corpses into the crematorium. Did Gabriel's grandparents, uncles and aunts perish here? We stand for awhile before the rusting ovens then leave like sleep walkers. Beyond the open gates the sun shines in the blue sky and the birds sing.

Tadeusz and his sister occupy a studio apartment on the top floor of a building in the Nova Huta suburbs of Krakow. In his seventies he still designs stained glass windows for the cathedrals of the People's Republic of Poland. We must have a glass of Bulgarian wine, insists Tad's sister as she shoos the tabby off the coffee table. Paintings and sculptures scattered about the room remind me of Fleur's atelier in New York with the old sofa and easy chairs. In this bohemian menage we learn about the relative freedom of the Polish artist from the constraints of social realism demanded in the Soviet Union.

At ten o'clock Mary Filippi arrives to take us to meet Dr. Rieger the Music Director of Krakow University and his daughter who teaches English. They share a tiny flat dominated by a grand piano. A curtain divides the bedroom into two sleeping areas. During wine and cheese we discuss music and art, books and world affairs. Dr. Rieger who listens to the Voice of America is intrigued by the Watergate affair.

Thursday July 27. Lunch in a Category One Restaurant where we share a table with an actress from Warsaw who has just returned from a tour of eastern Europe. Before leaving she gives me her address and I promise to call her.

Gabriel and I stroll through the Market Square and the Cloth Hall. Mid-afternoon coffee in Mariacki Square, part of the old University quarter. In front of Mary's Church a blue Oldsmobile 99 bearing Michigan licence plates has attracted an admiring throng. The windshield sticker warns that the vehicle and its contents are protected by Barnes Security.

Back at our lodgings the landlady says she will give us a discount if we settle our bill in dollars. We tell her our Travellers Cheques are locked in a vault at the University of Lodz and we carry only Polish Zlotys. Schade, she laments. It is a pity.

The train leaves the station at dusk. Halting briefly at Katowice it continues north, the lights in the carriage dimmed, the passengers asleep in their seats.

Dawn presents a skyline of factory chimneys. We are back in Lodz.

Friday July 28. I scratch myself awake. The weals on my body are from the ticks that have been lurking in our straw pallets. Gabriel rubs me down with Vodka.

We have returned to attend the screening of Andrzej Wajda's latest film *The Wedding* scheduled for tonight at the Film School, but it had been shown while we were away. Gabriel is furious. The entire Lodz enterprise has been a disaster. No wonder half the original group has departed. I suggest an evening of dining and dancing as an escape from our situation.

The Halka Restaurant is full of cheerful patrons, the orchestra is playing *Stardust*. After a glass of vodka we are able to relax and order dinner, agreeing on beer soup and lamb chops. During the meal a heavy-set individual comes over to our table and, bowing, kisses my hand. Sympatichny, he murmurs, gold teeth gleaming. Pointing to the dance floor he repeats Sympatichny. Reluctantly, at Gabriel's encouragement, I agree.

He holds me in a tight embrace, cooing Sympatichny, propelling me about the floor as the orchestra plays *Dancing in the Dark*. At the end he bows and leads me back to Gabriel. During the chocolate tort dessert he returns with a bottle. Na Zdrowie. He would like to drink to my health but first he must have a kiss. As I resist and he persists and Gabriel is looking about for the manager, a woman advances towards us shouting in Polish, a torrent of abuse directed at the amorous citizen who slinks away muttering Sympatichny.

Gabriel invites my rescuer to join us. A brunette in her late twenties, she pronounces her name Bar-ba-ra. When I thank her for rescuing me she laughs. The restaurant is full of men like him. And women of questionable character. She indicates the table where a heavily made-up female dressed in a sailor suit sits smoking, surveying the customers. Kurwah, she explains. Prostitute.

Bar-ba-ra is a chanteuse. She knows all about the entertainment industry in America. Sold out concerts. Platinum records. Big bucks. She prefers the intimacy of cabaret, her specialty being impersonations of Marlene Dietrich. *Falling in Love Again* is one of her favorite pieces.. She regales us with her musical experiences until we are ready to leave and escorts us outside to a taxi.

Saturday July 29. At 9.30 Stephania Skwarczynska holds forth on the Polish Theatre before the war, the last lecture of our course. When she has finished the Dean presents books to the students, ours being Le Cinèma Polonais Contemporain by Stanislaw Kuszewski. We have lunch as guests of Rek and Gazda at the Grand Hotel with much drinking and vows of friendship.

This evening we meet Bar-ba-ra at the Europa Restaurant across from the headquarters of the Polish Socialist Party. A wedding banquet is in progress with repeated toasts to the newly married couple. Sto lat. May you live to enjoy a hundred years. The band plays waltzes and polkas. Bar-ba-ra recognizes an acquaintance and the four of us dance and drink until midnight.

Sunday July 30. The fleas are still feasting on my body. Rek says we should have left the key with the porter when we departed for Krakow. While we were away all the rooms except ours were fumigated and naturally the insects migrated to our dormitory.

After breakfast we are taken to the town of Lowicz whose Museum reveals the life of the peasantry in the eighteenth century including a cottage with thatched roof, courtyard, stable and tools. The visitors include a group of downy-cheeked Soviet soldiers in dress uniform. Gabriel asks Rek if the troops are encamped nearby and he retorts that they are permanently settled in Poland, their presence established by the Warsaw Pact.

While we are relaxing in the adjacent park a woman in flowing skirt and peasant blouse approaches with the help of a cane. A kerchief covers her head. She wears pendant earrings. Rings sparkle on her fingers. She addresses us in Polish then asks if we speak German and when Gabriel answers she requests a cigarette . After a few puffs she asks for 10 Zlotys and she will read my fortune. She promises a long life with much happiness. Re-union with distant relatives. The others wish to have their palms read as well. With her flashing eyes and animated face she reminds me of Gabriel's mother. I wonder how many of the Roma's kin have been incinerated by the Nazis?

After lunch in the village of Tum we inspect a stone church built in 950 A.D. The sun shining through the opening in one wall reveals an empty sanctuary with a few chairs. Not much to see, somebody observes, but I feel a communion with the human beings who worshiped here over a thousand years ago. And who carved the inscription on the bench? Non Sedeo Sed Eo. Gabriel translates the Latin: I do not sit but I go.

Monday July 31. At the farewell reception Gabriel consents to be interviewed by the Polish Broadcasting Service. Have we enjoyed our stay in Lodz? Most assuredly, he replies. The people at the Film Institute have provided us with an experience we shall never forget. We hope to reciprocate their many kindnesses.

Gabriel and I are invited to lunch at the Grand Hotel by the Rector, Madame Skwarczynska and two members of the faculty. Plentiful food and drink. Earnest Discussion on art and life and the situation of the Academic in Canadian universities. After three hours we part with handshakes and embraces.

Piotrkowska Street viewed through a benign alcoholic haze does not appear so grim. On the tram back to the residence on Ulica Patrice Lumumba the faces smile back at us.

In the evening the students gather in the Grand Hotel around a table decorated with miniature Canadian and Polish flags. Long live the People's Republic of Poland, they salute. Vive le Canada.

24

Tuesday August 1. We leave for Lublin at eight in the morning accompanied by Stefan and Roman, who helped us survive the Lodz ordeal. Stefan with his humorous disposition and eyes for the women. Mild of manner Roman communicating in French but seemingly able to understand English. Gabriel thinks they may be government agents. And what about the young man who came over to our table at the Grand and said he was an American studying in Poland? He was friendly but asked too many questions. And Bar-ba-ra who had been so helpful? What was her secret agenda? And were the high priced prostitutes also instruments of the People's Republic?

The bus stops outside the Unitas Hotel where Father Taras welcomes us in the name of the Rector of the Catholic University of Lublin and directs the driver to the Poczekajka, the retreat of the Ursuline Sisters.

The main road veers off to a country lane that leads into private grounds where the Sisters are waiting to assign our rooms, the students in the three-storey residence, Gabriel and I in the guest house. Our apartment is furnished with a wardrobe, four beds, a writing desk and chair.

Lunch is ready. A savory aroma greets us as we take our seats at tables set with dishes and cutlery and fresh-cut flowers. After a welcome by smiling Sister Irena the kitchen staff brings in tureens of soup, bowls of potatoes, platters of meat and dill pickles. Several students from the Catholic University are present to make us feel at ease. The meal is the best we have had and we are pleased with our new situation. Our quarters are conducive to relaxation. The curtained windows look out on a grassy field. The wash basin yields hot water. The beds have springs and mattresses. We are free for the rest of the afternoon.

Supper is a collation of bread, ham, cheese and jam, tea with lemon. When we are finished Gabriel and I take a bus into the city accompanied by Jolanta, a graduate student. In the lounge of the Hotel Unitas we talk theatre and drink Krupnik, the Polish barley liqueur. I have taken a liking to the friendly Montagnard with the freckled face and braided titian hair.

Wednesday August 2. After breakfast we meet the urbane Rector of the only Catholic University in the Socialist block. He is circumspect in his references to State and Church relations. His fundraising activities in the United States and Canada have earned much-needed hard currency. The academic program offers courses in Theology, Philosophy, Civil and Canon Law, the Humanities and Social Sciences. He talks about the devotion of faculty and students to their alma mater, whose motto is Deo et Patriae.

During lunch the Sisters beam because of our enthusiasm for the quality of the cuisine and the sing-alongs led by the effervescent Jolanta.

Our four o'clock lecture is Living Folk Traditions in the Polish Theatre, presented by Dr. Irena Slawinska.

Tonight in the lounge the students are hosting a party with rock music and jazz. They enjoy Louis Armstrong and Dave Brubeck. Monique Leyrac is popular. They want to know about Glenn Gould. When Jolanta has finished dispensing the fruit juice she asks my permission to dance with Gabriel, who is flattered by the attention and does his best to keep up with her.

A quiz follows to test our knowledge of Poland. What is Torun noted for? Answer: The birthplace of Copernicus. Name the three Baltic cities. Gdansk, Gdynia and Sopot. Polish composers. Chopin, Paderewski, Penderecki. Polish actresses. Helen Modjeska and Pola Negri.

When the dancing resumes I go outside. The full moon reveals Professor Jan Kowalski seated on a bench, smoking. Darkly handsome, he speaks English like Charles Boyer. We make small talk. The weather is just fine. Yes we are enjoying our stay. What about his situation, I ask, and he pauses before responding. 'To live one has to adjust to circumstances, to accept those conditions one cannot alter.' I mention that our visas must be renewed and he volunteers to accompany us to the Milicja but quickly reverses himself. Maybe he should not go. It is best to remain unknown to the police. He suggests we ask one of the students to take us.

Thursday August 3. On our way to the Milicja I ask Jolanta about the Jews of Lublin. I had read that before the war the city boasted a world renowned Talmudic School and that in the Jewish cemetery are buried rabbis from the sixteenth century. Jolanta recalls that a monument to the memory of the 300,000 Jews in the province was unveiled several years ago. They were murdered in their homes by the Germans or transported to the death camp of Majdanek three kilometres away. There are no Jews here now.

On the main street we pass small shops. Grocery. Delicatessen. Bakery. The book store has a display of works by Farley Mowat.

The security police are located in a three-storey building with marble floors and a sweeping staircase. Jolanta asks us to wait in the lobby while she investigates. The walls are decorated with tourist posters advertising the charms of Russia and the other Soviet Republics. A sign reading Socialists indicates the bureau that handles the affairs of travellers from the eastern bloc. A department designated Capitalists is for visitors like us from the West. Employees carrying documents appear from one office and vanish into another. Eventually Jolanta returns with the information that an official will see us.

Behind a mahogany desk , soberly attired in a dark three-piece suit befitting a senior bureaucrat of the Polish Peoples Republic, he appraises us. How long have we been in the country, he asks. Why do we require an extension of stay? Turning the pages of our Passports he makes notes on a sheet of paper then engages in a dialogue in Polish with Jolanta, glancing occasionally in our direction. When he is finished Jolanta turns to us.

-I'm afraid you'll have to sit outside while he reviews your dossier and substantiates what I have told him. Don't worry. Just a formality.

In the waiting room those who have been summoned speak in whispers. Among the notices on the walls we recognize the injunctions Uwaga-Attention and Zabronione-Forbidden. We have seen them posted on fences and street corners but in this place they appear ominous. Gabriel's paranoia surfaces again. Why the delay? What is Jolanta saying about us? Could our dear friend be a secret agent? Have Rek and Gazda before returning to Lodz revealed incriminating information about us? Since Gabriel was born in Poland, would he still be considered a Polish National despite his Canadian citizenship?

I recall the visit to the Canadian Embassy upon our arrival in Warsaw. After a courteous reception the Ambassador warned that we should not expect any assistance from his office if we got into trouble. He cited the case of a Canadian who had been arrested for taking photographs at a railway station and spent three months in jail. The Embassy was powerless to help.

When Jolanta returns we inquire how things stand. Is

everything okay? Yes and no, she replies.

Out on the street she explains what detained her. The official asked if we had made any derogatory remarks about conditions in Poland. Could she vouch for our integrity and moral behavior? Would she agree to keep us under surveillance and report anything suspicious? In that case all he required was a letter from the University attesting to our attendance. Jolanta telephones for the confirmation to be delivered to her in the nearby coffee shop.

-When the letter gets here I'll take it to the Milicja. You might as well go back to the residence.

Before supper Jolanta returns with our Passports. Any trouble? No, she replies, with a grimace. Just the waiting. And the questioning. Always the waiting and the questioning.

Tonight the theatre department is presenting two pieces. A sound and light extravaganza titled Fibres uses music, mirrors and rotating spotlights. Next comes the story of Kain and Abel, a morality play. A discussion follows with the students eager to hear the criticism of the Canadians.

25

Friday August 4. Sister Irena has prepared a picnic basket for our excursion to the town where Gabriel was born.

The Lublin Bus Station is adjacent to the market, the stalls filled with flowers, fruit, pots and pans and clothing. Women bargain in loud voices. Old men rummage through bushels of hardware. Jolanta in lederhosen and jersey bounds ahead of us, hair in braids down to her waist. She is coming along as our interpreter.

The bus, a Skoda with extra seats that swing out into the aisles, fills with passengers carrying valises and parcels. Jolanta erupts into song once we are out in the country, encouraging the travellers to join in. They get off at dusty villages and two hours later we are approaching Opatow, where a Jewish settlement has existed since the sixteenth century.

Our research has revealed details of the liquidation of the

Jews of Opatow accomplished from October 20--22 in 1942. The German police set fire to the area around the market place where many Jews lived and rounded up the men. Some escaped to Soviet-occupied territory. A number of youths planned resistance, buying arms from the Polish underground and storing them in the attic of the synagogue. When the Germans were informed they shot a group of girls who were found there. With the help of a Ukrainian detachment they surrounded the ghetto. The President of the Judenrat, having tried to alleviate the suffering through diplomacy and bribery, was ordered to prepare lists for the labour camps, and the Selektion was carried out in the town square. Six thousand Jews were marched to the railway station near Ostrow, loaded onto wagons and transported to Treblinka. Others were taken to a camp in Sandomierz. Several hundred were killed in the fighting. A few were left to sort Jewish property and then were assembled in the cemetery and shot. Thus one of the most energetic Jewish communities had been effaced.

Gabriel was five when he left Poland with his parents. By train to the Baltic port of Gdansk thence by steamer (third class) across the Atlantic, arriving in Halifax at the beginning of the great depression. Contact with relatives in Opatow continued until the outbreak of the Second World War.

The official guide book describes Opatow as a county town thirty-five miles ESE of Kielce, recognized from the year 1040 as a settlement on the trade route from Russia. Known among foreign merchants as the Magna Civitas Opatow, it flourished at the end of the fourteenth century trading with Greece, Persia, Armenia and Holland but was destroyed by the Tartars in 1512 and subsequently rebuilt. The defense walls of the Warsaw Gate still stand. The Romanesque collegiate church constructed of rough stone dates back to the second half of the twelfth century. On the opposite bank of the river stands baroque Bernardine church and monastery.

Opatow devoid of Jews has a current population of six thousand. The chief industries are chemicals, cement products and brushes.

-We have arrived, announces the driver as the bus pulls into the parking lot in front of the terminal, a faded green wooden structure. Loungers lean against the railing. A woman seated on a crate is selling fruit and vegetables which she weighs in a hand-held scale. A tired horse pulls a wagon, the milk cans rattling as it crosses the bridge on the road to Ozorow.

Gabriel, feeling the call of nature, inquires at the restaurant if he may use the Toaleta. The woman at the counter points to the location. Upon his return he advises us to choose the field in preference to the fly-specked hole-in-the-ground.

A cursory inspection of the town reveals a few cottages and apartments with peeling stucco built since the establishment of the People's Republic of Poland. In the Market Square, comprising several small shops including a pharmacy and watch repair, a memorial has been raised to the partisans who died in battle and the civilians murdered by the Germans. A monument surmounted by the Polish Eagle outlines the history of Opatow. The Jewish cemetery behind the square has been obliterated. The synagogue demolished.

Gabriel conjures up childhood memories of the market square with Jews buying and selling chickens and fish, produce, even a new-born calf. Jews celebrating the sabbath. Klezmorim with clarinet, violin, trumpet and drums playing at Jewish weddings.

We locate his grandfather's cottage, two small rooms and a kitchen that once housed a family of seven. The present occupant, a grizzled peasant, moved in after the war. Jolanta asks if he knew the Jewish cattle dealer who used to live here. No, but there were many Jews in Opatow, and they were taken away by the Germans. Not one Jew returned.

On the street where Gabriel lived there is no sign of the house. Only empty lots.

At the top of the hill we come to a dwelling ascertained by the Registry of Deeds in Kielce to be the address of Gabriel's uncle, but no one answers our repeated knocking.

We walk by the post office and the cinema. The hospital. The school. The jail where Gabriel's grandfather served a month in a communal cell for default of taxes and to which the family came every day with his meals.

In the apple orchard the trees are burgeoning with fruit.

The stream purls nearby. We spread the blanket on the grass.

-What a lovely little town this is, declares Jolanta as we have our picnic lunch. I am experiencing a sense of loss.

At the bus Station we purchase postcards for mailing to Gabriel's family. They will have to wait until our return to learn that everything Jewish has been erased. What remains of Opatow is the lethargy of its Christian inhabitants.

26

Saturday August 5. Our bus arrives at the convent of the Ursuline Sisters in Czestochowa in time for a substantial noon meal then we are off again with Father Taras to the Jasna Gora Monastery and its basilica of the Virgin Mary, one of the most important Catholic shrines in Europe.

We move slowly among a throng of pilgrims, past souvenir stalls that offer statues, candles, medallions, rosaries and crucifixes. Our driver finds a space in the crowded parking lot.

We pass through halls and balconies, into chapels and ante rooms admiring the crowns, sceptres, jewels and paintings. Priests and acolytes are everywhere.

In the sanctuary a Mass in French is ending. The worshipers genuflect and leave, the sound of myriad feet echoing in the vaulted vastness. Newcomers fill their places, kneeling on the marble floor, counting their beads. Father Rudy, a Canadian, is to be celebrant at the next Mass with Father Taras as his assistant. Jolanta will be reading from the prayer book. Gabriel and I stand to one side with the non-believers in our group, bemused by the spectacle.

The altar dazzles in gold and precious stones. From behind the drawn curtain appears the Black Madonna and Child, the icon said to have been painted by St.Luke the Evangelist on a piece of cypress wood from the table used by Mary in Nazareth. It was brought from Jerusalem around 1386 and installed here. Matka Boska. Mother of God.

Father Rudy, resplendent in his vestments, recites the

liturgy in English, and the congregation responds in a variety of tongues. Gabriel whispers that he prefers the majesty of the Latin text.

The sun's oblique rays are illuminating the buttresses and alcoves as we leave, choosing to walk back to the Ursulines. Stopping before one of the stet stalls I inspect a Black Madonna and Child under glass. When I shake the globe, imitation snow swirls around the tiny figures.

Before the war Jewish merchants owned many of these booths. When the Germans marched in they were dispatched to labour camps. Or deported. Or herded into gas chambers.

After a light supper we proceed to Krakow, arriving about midnight at the International Students Hotel, a complex of high rise buildings. Ours is called Babylon and over the entrance is the sign Cs'esc, which Jolanta translates as This Is It. Flags of the socialist countries as well as those from the United States, Britain, France, Germany, Italy and Sweden flutter in the breeze.

Young people are milling about the lobby, scanning the bulletin board, crowding into the bar. After a couple of drinks Gabriel and I leave and take the elevator to the top floor. Our room has two beds, a desk and wardrobe. Lamp lights twinkle in the square below.

I rise early and head for the community showers where I shiver under an icy spray, but the Russian student in the next stall laughs at my complaint. We capitalists have been spoiled with too many luxuries, she says.

The dining room resounds with a Babel of voices and the clatter of dishes. A female server brings our breakfast of bacon and eggs, toast and coffee.

We have time to look around before the morning excursion. The campus contains shops, recreational facilities and lecture halls. It is good to be in Krakow again, the former capital of Poland, the city of princes since the twelfth century, the centre of culture and learning. Father Taras informs us that Karol Wojtyla enrolled in Krakow University in 1938 and eight years later was ordained as a priest. He made a pilgrimage to

Auschwitz and returned with a container of ashes for burial in Krakow's Rokawicki Catholic Cemetery. I wonder how he could differentiate between the Jewish and Christian remains.

Marek takes us to the old Jewish quarter of Kazimierz. Once a separate town, it was settled by Jews in 1495 and saw a huge influx in the 1630's from Germany and Ukraine. They were shopkeepers and innkeepers, restaurateurs and grain merchants, goldsmiths, barbers and furriers. And one Jewish surgeon. From 1867, the 11,000 Jews enjoyed unrestricted right of settlement and Jewish students were allowed into the faculties of law and medicine at the University and into technical colleges. Between the two world wars the city became an important hub of Jewish life.

-In 1938 there were 60,000 Jews in Krakow, twenty-five percent of the total population. In advance of the German, two thirds fled the city. In 1941 those who had remained, about 20,000, were shut up in the ghetto. The following year about 5,000 were sent to the Belzec death camp and several hundred were murdered in the ghetto itself. The balance died in Auschwitz. Jewish fighting organizations harassed the Germans and maintained contact with Jewish partisan groups in Kielce and Warsaw.

-After the war the Jewish quarter was not re-established. The few who returned, about 4,000, numbered only one percent of the population.

An encompassing stillness here as if the pulse of the city had slowed to a faint beat.

There are two Jewish burial grounds in Kazimierz, the Remu'h and the Zydowski. The Remu'h is identified by the Star of David. A sign in yiddish requests that visitors be suitably attired, especially head covering for the men. An old caretaker stands quietly observing.

-This is one of the oldest Jewish cemeteries in Europe. The Germans desecrated it, smashing and overturning the tombstones, pouring excrement on the graves. After the war the Polish government with the assistance of American Jews cleaned the ground, re-set the monuments that remained intact and cemented the broken ones into the wall.

Gabriel reads aloud the Hebrew inscriptions on a few of the stones. Name, occupation, birth, death and next of kin.

-The synagogue is closed because there are no services today, explains Marek, but beyond the open window you can see the benches where the men sat separated from the women. Also the holy ark where the torahs are kept. The synagogue seats a thousand but there are hardly any Jews left in Krakow. Seven hundred or so, mostly elderly. In 1969 Cardinal Wojtyla and a parish priest came here at the invitation of the chairman of the Jewish community. He chatted with the leaders and with head covered, stood at the back of the sanctuary listening to the service.

Our next point of interest is a centuries-old Sephardi synagogue which is maintained by the State as a Museum. Inside the domed edifice the walls are a celestial blue. The bimah in the centre is surrounded by a wrought iron enclosure and wooden benches. A red plush curtain with the ten commandments in gold letters framed by two lions conceals the Ark in which the scrolls of the Torah are kept. A smaller chamber in the rear is for the women. Marek directs us to the religious items arranged behind a grillwork and explains the significance of the Torah crown and pointer, the prayer shawl and the phylacteries. It is an academic lecture about an alien culture.

-Many Jews lived in our country before the war. They did not mix with the rest of the population.

We visit Wawel Castle with its sumptuous drawing rooms, its paintings, treasures, and tombs including the remains of Queen Elzbieta, the wife of King Kazimierz the Great.

Tired and thirsty we relax in the square with bottles of Piwo Ococim, the best beer in Poland. Later, browsing in a book shop, Gabriel finds *Selections from James Joyce*, a handsome volume in Polish and English with fine illustrations.

After supper we spend the evening in a Jazz Cellar where the air is blue with cigarette smoke. We sample Russian Champagne and switch to Egri Bikaver. When the brass and percussion overwhelm us Gabriel and I join Father Taras in the upstairs lounge. We get back to the Babylon Hotel at two in the morning.

Monday August 7. We drive out to Tarnow to view the only new church built in Poland since the end of the war. Perched on a hill, it is a concrete and glass structure with straight lines that reach toward the sky. Sunlight pouring through the stained glass windows bathes the sanctuary in a rainbow of hues. The chapel in the basement is dedicated to the memory of the three million Poles who died in the concentration camps. The representations of Jesus and Mary are familiar, but a third figure wearing the striped uniform of a concentration camp inmate is Maximilian Kolbe, the priest who died in Auschwitz in 1942 after volunteering to take the place of another prisoner. Father Taras recounts that in 1971 the Cardinal of Krakow went to Auschwitz for the beatification of Father Kolbe. My thoughts go to Janusz Korczak, the Jewish doctor who insisted on accompanying a group of children to the gas chamber in the same camp.

27

Tuesday August 8. In the library of the Catholic University of Lublin Dr. Ireneusz Pawlak lectures on religious music and the few of us who attend listen to magnificats and motets by Polish composers of the baroque school who wrote in the style of Bach and Vivaldi. The next session will deal with the romantics and lastly the modernists, including Krzystof Penderecki.

After lunch we view a movie, *The Passion of our Lord*, during which Jesus staggering under a heavy cross is whipped by Roman centurions. Peasants carrying boulders climb up toward Calvary. Close-ups of bleeding bodies, faces charged with agony in emulation of the Saviour. All too realistic. In the darkness of the auditorium I seize Gabriel's hand, distressed by the animosity toward Jews that the film must arouse. At the end the students voice their enthusiasm for this cinema verite masterpiece.

I have read about the attacks on Lublin Jews in the nineteen-thirties led by students of this same Catholic University, whose rector was the author of anti-semitic pamphlets. In

1936, August Cardinal Hlond the Primate of Poland declared in a Pastoral Letter, 'It is a fact that Jews are fighting against the Catholic Church, persisting in free thinking and are the vanguard of godlessness, bolshevism and subversion. It is a fact that Jews deceive, levy interest and are pimps. It is a fact that the religious and ethical influence of the Jewish young people on Polish young people is a negative one.' With the arrival of the Germans, the Cardinal fled the country.

Between the two world wars the Jews of Lublin enjoyed a lively social and cultural life with dramatic societies, libraries and orchestras. Jewish trade unions flourished. Zionist organizations were active. Parochial schools provided the Heder for boys and the Beth Jacob School for Girls. The Lubliner Togblat printed in Yiddish appeared daily.

After the city was overrun by the Germans in September 1939 Lublin became one of the centres for mass extermination. The ghetto established in 1941 had a population of 34,000, but by the time the Red Army arrived in July of 1944, more than 30,000 Jews had been sent to the death camps of Majdanek and Belzec.

Such a long history dating from 1316, when King Kazimierz the Third permitted Jews to settle in lands adjacent to Lublin. Three centuries later 2000 lived in the city, occupying houses that belonged to the clergy and feudal lords who were beyond the jurisdiction of the city council. Jews participated in the Lublin fairs. They were tailors, brush manufacturers, brewers, bakers and tanners. Expelled, they were later re-instated. In the 16th to 18th centuries the Polish High Court was convened to hear blood libel cases against them. When a Jew was found guilty his execution was carried out on a Saturday in front of the synagogue with the elders forced to attend. Attacks on the Jewish quarter included the Chmielnicki pogroms. Nevertheless by the end of the nineteenth century the eight thousand Jews of Lublin formed over fifty percent of the population.

After the war some Jews, former guerillas and soldiers in the Polish Army, returned to the city, but most of them left within five years because of the prevailing anti-semitism. By 1968 the Jews of Lublin had disappeared.

Wednesday August 9. This afternoon we make the short trip to Majdanek. The visitors move silently about the camp inspecting the wooden barracks with their piles of shirts, socks and underwear. Dresses and trousers. Shoes and caps. The barbed wire perimeter is punctuated by sentry towers. A memorial in the shape of a huge concrete urn contains the ashes of those who were gassed and incinerated in November 1943 during Sukkoth, the Jewish Festival of Thanksgiving.

At the farewell gathering in his study the Rector produces a bottle of George V Scotch in addition to the vodka and wine. We nibble on cakes and sandwiches, drink tea brewed in a brass samovar. After toasts to the friendship between our countries he presents the Canadians with books on Poland's history and culture. Gabriel voices his appreciation of the kindness shown the Canadians this past week by the students and faculty and by the Ursulines who have been so solicitous of our well-being.

28

Warsaw. Thursday August 10, 1972. Slawek, a graduate student of English, is waiting for us in the lobby of the Metropol Hotel. After we have said goodbye to the remnants of our group he carries the luggage to the street car. He has arranged for us to stay at the home of Dr. Elzbieta Urbanska and hopes our stay will be enjoyable.

Dr. Urbanska, a gynecologist, occupies an apartment in a block of twelve-storey buildings with shops and services on the ground level. Children are riding tricycles on the walkways. Mothers with baby carriages congregate in the parkette. I notice one of the street names. Mordecai Anielewicz. Slawek says this used to be the Warsaw Ghetto. Members of various professions and Communist Party functionaries live here.

Blonde, slender Dr. Urbanska welcomes us. Her husband, a physicist, is on a seaside holiday in Gdansk with their two girls and she hopes we will be comfortable in the children's room. The kitchen is for our use. The television also. We may come and go as we please.

After unpacking we walk with Slawek through the streets where thirty years ago half a million Jews were confined, enduring hunger and disease before the mass deportations to the death camp of Treblinka. Slawek has studied the history of that period. He knows that armed resistance begun in January 1943 by the 60,000 who still remained in the ghetto climaxed in the uprising on the eve of Passover. Over 2,000 troops of the Wehrmacht and SS attacked the Jews who fought until mid May from fortified bunkers and from roof tops, windows and sewers.

We have arrived at the site of the bunker where the chief of staff of the Jewish Combat Organization along with Mordechai Anielewicz committed suicide. A stone slab marks the spot at 18 Mila Street. Slawek says that the Polish Underground supported the Ghetto Uprising with arms and military actions. The German General Stroop reported over 5,000 ghetto fighters killed and the capture of 56,000, of whom 7,000 were executed. The Polish underground press estimated German losses at 400 killed and 1,000 wounded.

-After the uprising the Germans blew up the Great Synagogue on Tlomackie Street and devastated the beautiful round one in the Prague district, says Slawek. The Nozyk synagogue has been renovated with services held on the Sabbath and Jewish holidays.

The Memorial to the Heroes of the Warsaw Ghetto is located in the square that was the main bunker of the Jewish Combat Organization. With inscriptions in Polish and Hebrew it was dedicated on April 19, 1948, the fifth anniversary of the Warsaw Ghetto Uprising. It is fashioned of bronze and granite from Sweden ordered by Hitler in 1942 for a monument that was to celebrate the total victory of Germany.

Slawek's cramped apartment is in the west end of the city. The walls are decorated with gatefold spreads of nudes from Playboy. A mobile hangs from the ceiling. Sitting on cushions, munching cheese and crackers, drinking wine, we listen to jazz from his sizable collection. He is planning a holiday in London when he has accumulated sufficient hard currency. I remember

234 · Harry Pollock

that we need more Zlotys and a hundred American dollars change hands.

Elzbieta greets us on our return. When I ask about a bath she is ready to oblige but it is necessary to heat the water on the stove. The boiler stopped functioning three months ago and she is waiting for the ministry to send a repair man.

Friday August 11, 1972. Gabriel and I visit the Okopowa Street cemetery that dates from the nineteenth century. On the tomb stones are etched lions and deer. Those of the Kohanim show hands bestowing a blessing; the Levites by a jug of water. A philanthropist is depicted by a coin inserted into an alms box. A hand holding a book signifies the grave of a scholar. We note the names. Ludwig Zamenhof, the inventor of Esperanto, which was to have been the universal language leading to peace among all people. Mayer Balaban, Director of the Warsaw Rabbinical College in the nineteenth century. The writers I.L. Perets and S. Ansky. The president of the Jewish Community, Adam Czerniakow and his wife. A section for Jewish officers and soldiers of the Polish Army who lost their lives in the 1939 defense of Warsaw. The common graves of those who succumbed to starvation and disease or were murdered by the Germans.

Warsaw, known as the Paris of eastern Europe, was the home of 400,000 Jews, one third of the population with its own schools, theatres, hospitals, orphanages and homes for the aged. The city was the hub of Jewish political, social, cultural, professional and commercial life. Today the government boasts about the Esther Rachel Kaminska State Theatre with head sets for translation of the Yiddish dialogue. The Social and Cultural Society of Jews in Poland publishes a weekly in Yiddish and Polish. The Jewish Historical Institute is funded by the State.

Gabriel and I have encountered no Jews. Most left in 1968 after the outbreak of anti-semitism.

Slawek meets us in the Stare Miastow, the medieval old town that was destroyed along with the Royal Castle by German bombers and artillery but reconstructed after the war from the original architectural renderings. We stroll through the square, admiring the facades on the buildings until we come to a restaurant with a patio where, seated beneath an old chestnut tree, we have dinner and recall the experiences of the past five weeks.

We continue our walk to the column of Zigmund 111 and the Krakowskie Przedmiescie, the handsome Avenue of cinemas and book stores, government offices, the Parliament and the University of Warsaw.

At the tomb of the unknown soldier, two honour guards stand at attention. Gabriel's thoughts go to the 100,000 Jewish soldiers in the Polish Army in September 1939, many of whom were killed and wounded. To the Jews in the Polish Armed Forces in the West, in the Polish People's Army created in the Soviet Union, in the civilian resistance movements and guerilla detachments.

To the Jews who were active in earlier national uprisings, including Colonel Berek Joselewicz, who formed a Jewish cavalry regiment in 1794 that took part in the Kosciuszko Insurrection and who was killed in battle.

Saturday August 12, 1972. Slawek accompanies us to the Warsaw International Airport and waits until we have completed the exit formalities. We promise to keep in touch. He and Gabriel shake hands. For me, a kiss on both cheeks. At the departure gate we wave goodbye.

29

Toronto, September 1972. Gabriel has been experiencing headaches and blurred vision. I think he may be suffering from migraine.

When the vomiting begins we visit our family doctor Leon Mosshammer and chat briefly about our Polish experience before he turns to Gabriel's problems. After a thorough examination he arranges an appointment with a neurologist. Dr. Lewis Levitt orders a brain scan that reveals a tumor in the left temporal lobe. Our next consultation is with Dr. Harold Lurie, the eminent neurosurgeon, who prescribes drugs to reduce the swelling and when the pain subsides Gabriel is admitted to hospital for a series of tests.

Dr. Lurie schedules surgery.

I wait in the lounge, downing cups of weak coffee, turning the pages of old magazines. Toward noon Dr. Lurie appears with the comforting news that the operation has gone smoothly and Gabriel is in recovery.

Mid afternoon a nurse takes me to the intensive care ward where Gabriel lies bandaged and sedated. I sit by the bed until Des Fitzgerald arrives from the Jewish High School, where he has been teaching since he left the priesthood. Standing over Gabriel his lips move in a silent prayer.

When we get home Des pours the drinks. The chamber music program on Radio Canada includes Schubert's *Death and the Maiden*. After the ten o'clock news Des retires downstairs to his apartment, leaving me alone, sobbing in the king size bed.

I have been with Gabriel from early morning until five o'clock when Des appears and sits by the bed for awhile before we leave. After supper we watch television. One night we saw *Death of a Salesman* and I remembered how deeply the Broadway production had affected Gabriel, who identified with Willy Loman, the salesman with a smile and a shoe shine. I thought of other plays we enjoyed during the fifties and sixties on our frequent visits to New York: *The Iceman Cometh*. Gabriel was fond of the *Three Penny Opera*. The cultural ferment of the Weimar Republic fascinated him. The jazz, the cabarets, the works of Brecht and Weill, the theatrical experiments of Max Rheinhardt.

Day number three. Dr. Lurie is hopeful that radiation and chemotherapy will arrest the spread of the cancer. Des says that medical science has been making good progress in the treatment of glioma and urges me to look on the bright side.

We go to George's Spaghetti House for supper and listen to the Moe Koffman Jazz Quintet. And finish a liter of Chianti.

At home we have a nightcap.

I awake feeling sick and find my way to the bathroom where I kneel over the bowl, retching. Des comes up and applies compresses to my head and sits with me until the throbbing subsides and I assure him that I should be able to sleep now. He bends down to kiss me and I put my arms about him and ask him to stay and I find comfort in his presence and out of the depths of our grief we make love.

November 1972. Gabriel is discharged from the hospital. The anti-convulsant steroids and other drugs have weakened him but his headaches are gone. After two weeks I drive him to the Princess Margaret Hospital. The radiation fatigues him, the chemotherapy makes him nauseous. He has lost his appetite and his food has a metallic taste.

Gabriel's father comes in the afternoon and sits by the bed, murmuring the Psalms of David.

January 1973. Gabriel has become obsessed with the rituals of death, the embalming and cosmetics, the plush lined oak casket within a bronze outer sarcophagus. He declares his preference for the simplest funeral, like the cash and carry cremation service for $137.50, complete with a quart-sized cardboard box for the ashes. On the other hand, the Rocky Mountain Casket Company of Seattle is offering a container for only $125 (plus shipping) for advance use as a pool cue rack, gun cabinet, silver storage or hope chest. But what intrigues Gabriel is a graveside memorial for $6,000 which will show a ten minute videotaped obituary. The stainless steel box with a television screen covered by bullet proof glass is guaranteed to last for 500 years. The unit, 2 feet long, 22 inches wide and 20 inches deep is powered by rechargeable batteries.

Gabriel and Des talk about the research of Elizabeth Kübler-Ross on the dying and their sensations on the verge of the beyond, the soul floating out of the body, the feeling of peace and wholeness, the meeting with someone who previously passed on. Who will be waiting for Gabriel? Samantha Lawrence, murdered by her Black Muslim lover? Raphael Beckerman, dead of osteosarcoma? Hilary Bennett, killed in a crash on the M4?

I join in the discussion about funeral rites of antiquity. The ancient Greeks put a coin in the mouth of the deceased to pay for the soul's ferry ride across the Styx to gloomy Tartarus or to Elysium, the abode of the happy spirits. Tutankhamen's tomb was plentifully stocked and furnished for the afterlife. Why is it that we all feel the need for personal continuity? I have immortal longings in me, cried Cleopatra. John Donne declared that one short sleep past we wake eternally and death shall be no more. But Arnold Toynbee observed that death is the un-American affront to our inalienable right to life, liberty and the pursuit of happiness.

Des brings home issues of the Foundation of Thanatology in New York and the Journal of the Ars Moriendi Society. The articles deal with the breaking down of the barriers that isolate the dying from the rest of society and the growing awareness that mortality is a natural and inevitable part of living.

April 1973. Gabriel's speech has become slurred. His right arm and leg are weak. He requires increased doses of pain killers and sleeps more during the day. When he awakes it is time for his pills and juice. He likes to sit in the wheel chair by the window, looking out at the trees and flowers.

May 1973. The disease has reached the optic nerve and Gabriel can no longer see. Des Fitzgerald, who is spending all his available time with us, helps him to the toilet. Dr. Lurie recommends that his patient be transferred to the Palliative Care Unit at Baycrest Hospital, but I refuse. I want to be with Gabriel at the end, not summoned by a telephone call from the duty nurse. Since I cannot banish death I will make his dying a social event with friends calling. Benny Kirsch arrives with the medication. Max Rubinstein, functioning again with the aid of Chlropromazine and living with his mother in an apartment on College Street, visits regularly..

The cancer has spread through Gabriel's nervous system. With the increased intra-cranial pressure he lapses into a coma and his breathing is irregular.

Thursday June 21, 1973. Gabriel's heart stops beating at 1:33 this afternoon. I sit by the bed memorizing the sunken cheeks, the cartilaginous nose, the eyes closed in the final sleep.

The undertaker's men arrive and when they have left I remove the bed sheet with Gabriel's last outpouring of vitality, fold it and put it away.

Friday June 22,1973. During the service in the chapel the rabbi speaks about Gabriel's return to the people of Israel and recites the El Mole Rachamim asking the Lord to grant perfect peace to the soul of the deceased.

Desmond Fitzgerald helps me into the limousine with Gabriel's parents. As the driver eases behind the hearse and the cortege winds through the streets, Gabriel's mother begins to weep.

At the cemetery, the familiar words of the Kaddish: 'Exalted and hallowed be the name of the Lord'. I hear the caw caw of a crow flying overhead and in the distance an automobile horn tootling Show me the way to go home. The service is ended. And Gabriel is lying under a mound of clay.

We drive back to the house where Haim Holtzman's wife has set out the hard boiled eggs, herring, smoked salmon and bagels. Des pours the drinks and the guests drink *lechayim*. To life. It is like old times but without Gabriel, the renaissance man who participated con brio at life's feast until Death came knocking, mocking, demanding payment.

Saturday June 23,1973
Morning. I put away the Journal that has been my companion this memory-filled night and prepare to meet the reality of the new day.